BOGUS U.

BOGUS U.

PAUL M. LEVITT

TAYLOR TRADE PUBLISHING
Lanham • Boulder • New York • London

Published by Taylor Trade Publishing
An imprint of The Rowman & Littlefield Publishing Group, Inc.
4501 Forbes Boulevard, Suite 200, Lanham, Maryland 20706
www.rowman.com

Unit A, Whitacre Mews, 26–34 Stannary Street, London SE11 4AB

Distributed by NATIONAL BOOK NETWORK

British Library Cataloguing in Publication Information Available

Library of Congress Cataloging-in-Publication Data

Levitt, Paul M.
  Bogus U. / Paul M. Levitt.
    pages ; cm
  ISBN 978-1-63076-064-9 (softcover) — ISBN 978-1-63076-065-6 (electronic)
1. College stories. I. Title.
  PS3612.E935B64 2015
  813'.6--dc23

                                                              2015002455

Printed in the United States of America

DEDICATION

To the advancement of education in America

CONTENTS

DISCLAIMER

This book is a work of fiction. Any similarities between persons or events, past or present, are purely coincidental.

A NOTE ABOUT THE AUTHOR

Born in Pégairolles de l'Escalette, near Montpellier, Romain A. Cleft came from a distinguished family of furriers who emigrated from northern Greece. When unrest in Albania spilled across the border, the Cleft family settled in the south of France. Madame Cleft, a student of continental letters, remained a lifelong devotée of Romain Rolland, after whom she named her son, schooling him in literature with the hope that he might someday attain the stature of the French master. Romain proved a precocious student and won a place at the Sorbonne, where he took a double degree in Comparative Literature and Philosophy. Offered a graduate teaching assistantship in the American West, he came to the United States to pursue a Ph.D. In the third year of his studies, to the surprise of professors and friends, Interpol arrested him. Currently under house arrest, he awaits his impending trial on charges not yet disclosed to the public.

ACKNOWLEDGMENT

I owe university life a debt for its infinite comedy.

HOW PHINEAS ORT
MISSED HIS PLANE

On a raw March day in 1998, Phineas Ort's taxi left the Empire Hotel and drove through Central Park. A black Mercedes, with tinted windows, followed close behind. The taxi's passenger, Professor Phineas Ort, had achieved academic prominence through his discovery that in ancient Greece the letter X when reversed is still X, and therefore has equal linguistic stature with the Roman alphabetic letters A, H, I, M, O, T, and U. Having spent the previous day at the N.Y. Public Library, contentedly poring over a papyrus of pornographic lyrics, he was in an expansive mood when he directed the cab driver to take him to La Guardia, where he intended to catch a plane for Rodeo International Airport. A university car would then take him to his destination. But not far from the Metropolitan Museum of Art, the Mercedes overtook the taxi, forcing it onto a wooded service road.

"You off your rocker?" the furious cab driver yelled, stepping out of his cab, which screeched to a halt amid the sound of gravel and the smell of brakes. As the doors of the Mercedes opened, he bellowed:

"If I call the cops, they'll kick your ass out your throat." He would have used some truly pungent expletives had not two men, wearing ski masks, emerged from the Mercedes with long-barreled pistols in hand. Raising his arms, in anticipation of a stickup, he explained docilely, "I ain't got much dough."

One of the masked men told him to get back in the cab and pop the trunk. As his companion removed Phineas's luggage, the masked leader slid into the back seat next to Professor Ort, who was so absorbed in Sophocles's *Antigone* in Greek that he failed to notice the cab had been run off the road. Only now did he look up.

"Yes, may I help you?" he said in a voice that bore an uncanny resemblance to the timbre and tone of a bass fiddle. It resonated, even in the cab,

1

like sound in a well-designed concert hall. "Outta the car!" said the intruder, a stocky fellow wearing a blue nylon parka with a New York Giants logo.

"There must be some mistake. I specifically requested the driver to take me to La Guardia, not to the ski slopes."

The man took Phineas Ort by the arm. "I don't want you gettin' hurt," he said, as he drew Phineas from the car. "This ain't personal."

"My briefcase!" he complained. "It has my disquisition on the relationship of universities to the Greek city brothels. I am to read it tomorrow at Bogus U."

The second man, the taller of the two, reached into the cab and removed Phineas Ort's briefcase, running his hand over the hide. Made from an albino rhinoceros skin, it had come to Phineas from a woman in Tanzania, who had admired his book on Athenian bird watching. Giving Phineas the briefcase and leading him to the Mercedes, the taller man slipped the cabby three c-notes and told him to "take a long silent beer at his favorite bar and forget what just happened." Torn between conscience and kale, the cabby, taking for his moral compass Wall Street, pocketed the hush money and never said anything to the police, lest he have to return the dough.

In the car, the two men removed their ski masks and introduced themselves to Phineas Ort, who sat by himself behind a glass partition, with speakers in the side panels of the back doors that transmitted the voices of his captors, as well as his own. "He's Eddie Doyle," said the stocky man in the passenger seat, referring to the driver, "and I'm Jackie Brown. Yous is the guest of Brooklyn Benny Bronzino, a guy dat I'm sure you ain't heard of, given your line of work, but one that yous will soon meet."

Eddie, a fastidious dresser, who fancied expensive dark silk suits and white shirts, complemented with Italian shoes and ties, regarded himself as high class, a conviction that induced him to frequent the New York musical theater. He had seen several shows, including *Evita* and *Cats*, and had taken his aged mother to see *Phantom of the Opera*, which they both loved. His desire to be regarded as cultured had even driven him to buy an original painting from Scot Marco, the famous California art dealer. Jackie, on the other hand, liked beers, bourbon, babes, and bebop. His idea of fashion rose no higher than his shoes. He wore Florsheims with jeans and a blue sweatshirt sporting the inscription: Lawrence Taylor, Linebacker. The two men also differed in other ways. Eddie, a thin balding man just under six feet, watched his weight. Except for Eskimo pies, he ate no junk food. He had a pale face with hollow cheeks and dull eyes. A reader of the tabloids and *People* magazine, Eddie took pride in knowing the names of the governor of New York and the mayor of the city. He took long walks in Central Park to admire the girls in their pink summer dresses, and he made it a point never to drop his g's—as in comin', goin', seein'—because someone had told him that the retention or omission of a "g" divided the gents from the jerks.

Jackie, short and muscular, spent all his free time lifting weights. When a patron of Curly's gym said that the mind was greater than the muscle, he knocked the guy flat on his ass, thus proving him wrong. Jackie's nose had been redirected in a fight, a mark, he thought, of his manhood. As if pointing out this sign of his masculinity, he often ran his right index finger along the fracture line, a habit that had become as automatic to him as feeling his right biceps with his left hand. He also bore a scar over one eyebrow and a missing front tooth. His speech, unlike Eddie's, barely rose to the common. But then he had come from a home distrustful of learning and offended by eloquence. Secretly, such was his view of professors that had it been up to him, he would have plugged Phineas Ort, who represented a culture that Eddie could not understand and therefore could not countenance.

Phineas, still weighing the rights and wrongs between Antigone and Creon, convinced himself that he had been transferred from one cab to another because Bogus U. had decided to guarantee his safety on the way to the airport. New York City, after all, can sometimes be violent. The thought of a special armed guard pleased him, reinforcing his belief that Bogus U. would go to any lengths to recruit him as its new president or, in the lingo of the Ottoman Empire, upon which Bogus U. had fashioned itself, its Sultan Caliph. (Footnote: in keeping with the administrative hierarchy of Bogus, the familiar titles such as chancellor, provost, and dean, had been replaced with the nomenclature of the Turks: Grand Vizier, Vizier, Pasha, and Bey. The last two presidents, to their credit, had found the title Sultan Caliph slightly too exalted for their modest talents and therefore chose to forgo the honor, causing their spouses no little displeasure.) Although the titles Pasha and Bey were designed for deans, they took for themselves the title Vizier. Anything less, they regarded as demeaning. Given the bizarrerie of Bogus, it certainly had need of Phineas's good sense and probity. Unlike Jimbo Brummagem, the recently cashiered Bogus U. president, Phineas had no ties to the Free Love Party, took no bribes, kept his mistress off the payroll, eschewed drunkenness, and made no under-the-table payments to cronies, whether Mormon or moron.

Professor Ort's only glaring defect was his quaint belief that a football coach, even at an institution as prestigious as Bogus U., should not earn ten times as much as a professor of chemistry. Let us amend that last sentence. He also suffered from another defect: a surfeit of literacy. He could, to the chagrin of the alumni and trustees, make a subject and verb agree, though neither group regarded this trait as fatal. His public speeches were neither plagiarized nor prosaic. He quoted Euripides and not Henry Ford, Cicero and not Ronald Reagan. When he spoke, people had a glimmering of the heights to which the fine art of oratory could take one, and therein lies the reason why Phineas's detractors called him an elitist.

The black Mercedes drove east to FDR Drive and then north, two turns that convinced Phineas Ort that he was headed in the right direction. He therefore returned to his reading. Passing over the Willis Avenue Bridge (Eddie Doyle knew how to save on tolls), the car continued on to the Major Deegan Parkway, which eventually became the New York Thruway and then the Adirondack Northway (Interstate 87). During the journey, Jackie Brown and Eddie Doyle sat utterly absorbed in CDs of Johnny Cash and Patsy Cline. Except for an occasional "that's tight" or "really dope," they said little, even when Phineas Ort eventually tried to discover why he'd been shanghaied.

Four hours into the trip, a sleeting snow began pelting the car, and the road conditions worsened. But Eddie Doyle never slowed down until Exit 27, north of Pottersville, where the car left the main highway and drove a few miles along Route 9 to the hamlet of Adirondack, huddled next to Schroon Lake, at which point the car turned into a dirt road, coming to a stop at a yellow log cabin that looked large enough to sleep dozens. From the sweeping porches that provided an incomparable view of the lake to the double-glazed picture windows and the four chimneys, the hideaway screamed wealth. Ushered inside, Phineas saw an enormous open-timbered room, with a yawning fireplace six feet high and eight feet across glowing warmly and smelling sweetly from several hefty apple wood logs. When the fire sparked, the andirons, shaped like owls with transparent red eyes, emitted a devilish light. Although deeply impressed by his surroundings, Phineas, a punctilious man, still had in mind his flight reservation.

"I have missed my plane," Phineas said, deducing correctly that his seven o'clock arrival at the cabin had left him no time to catch a plane scheduled to depart at five that same afternoon. Ignoring Phineas's perspicacious comment, Eddie explained that he would be held only until Bogus U. had selected a new president.

"But I am he . . . the principal finalist!" Phineas exclaimed.

"He what?" said Jackie Brown, not comprehending.

"The new president, or putatively so."

"Huh?"

Eddie Doyle cut through the fat. "Mr. Ort, or should I say Professor . . . ?"

"Doctor will do."

"You're a doctor," Jackie Brown interrupted delightedly. "Well, why didn't you say so? A professor ain't worth shit, but a doctor—now that's something else. I got a real problem with hemorrhoids. Whaddya recommend?"

"Ah, yes," Phineas knowingly replied, "from the Greek *haimorrhoïdes*, which means flowing with or discharging blood, as in veins."

"I said, whaddya recommend?"

"A great many Greek plays run with blood. But I would suggest you start with something less gory, for example, *Antigone*."

"Can you get it over the counter?"

"I have it with me here."

"Doc, you're a real pal."

"No trouble, really. We can look at it together."

"Both of us?" Jackie Brown gulped.

"Why not?"

"Well, you're the doc. You know best."

Phineas, always pleased to induce a listener to consider the merits of Greek literature, now returned to the subject. "You were remarking, Mr. Doyle, about my stay here."

"You're our guest, until Bogus U. picks a new prez."

"But what about my own candidacy?"

"Forget it, doc. We're here to protect you from those con men and thieves. They don't need you; they need someone just like themselves. You know the old line: it takes a thief to catch one. Well, in this case they need a mobster to manage the mugs. Trust us, doc, we're doing you a big favor."

As Phineas considered Eddie's argument, a beautiful woman exited one room, glided through the hall, and disappeared, short-circuiting his line of reasoning. Eddie, oblivious to Phineas's panting, expatiated on the merits of cabin life at Schroon Lake. "A gorgeous area, with forests and lakes. Breathtaking walks. And what about this place? Fit for a prince. Brooklyn Benny's no piker. It's got all the booze you could drink, a chef, a housekeeper who's a real looker, color TV, a video and blue movies, a complete set of *National Geographic* magazines, and a freezer full of Eskimo pies. What else could a guy want?"

As if some supernal deity heard Eddie's question, the young woman returned, flashing a come-hither smile and lustrous eyes looking out from under long dark lashes.

"This," said Eddie Doyle, "is DeeDee Lite, the housekeeper." The celestial vision, marred only by her chewing and cracking of gum, lost its Botticellian luster when she spoke:

"Me and the boys are really glad you came here."

Eddie added, "You'll also want to meet the chef. I'll call him." But before Eddie could summon him, Jackie Brown put two fingers in his mouth and let out a piercing whistle, which brought into the room a man holding a spatula and dressed in a white bib apron, with a white stove-pipe hat. "Dis," said Jackie Brown, "is Reynald Eclaire. Reynald, dis is duh doc."

Phineas intended to shake Reynald's hand but instead found himself holding DeeDee's, and for some inexplicable reason could not let it go. As he locked eyes with hers, he felt himself being drawn into a vulvar vortex. Unable to move, he stood, his hand in hers, anticipating multiple orgasmic pleasures.

"Monsieur, permit me to introduce myself. I am zee chef, Reynald. Meester, you hear me? I said I wuz zee chef. Meester?"

But Phineas heard nothing until the spell passed. By this time, Reynald had decided that Phineas suffered from an otological disorder, and muttered, as he decamped for the kitchen waving his spatula, "*Merde*! Zee man is either deaf or dumb. Maybe, I think, both."

Reynald normally cooked for Brooklyn Benny, but as Benny wanted only the best for Phineas Ort, whom he sought to keep out of sight until he put into effect his perfidious plan, he had sent his chef ahead to Schroon Lake. Reynald, a wiry fellow with curly dark hair and droopy eyes, had worked for many years at a famous restaurant on the upper West Side, but had deliberately retained his French accent, which served him well among the limo crowd. Reynald's pinched Gallic face included a thin upper lip and a pencil mustache that twitched when he grew agitated, a state that also elicited wild hand movements and utterances that should not be repeated in polite circles.

Eddie, no fool, had noticed Phineas's trance and smiled, convinced that his charge would give him no trouble, as long as DeeDee had him in hand.

DeeDee Lite, the housekeeper, had previously resided in Albany, where she had grown up poor but comely, also curvy and wanton, qualities that satisfied the lust of at least one legislator, perhaps more. Her father had worked a lifetime in a low-ceilinged shop on a side street of the capital sharpening knives and scissors. She had met Brooklyn Benny during one of his frequent trips to Albany to grease the palms of legislators on the payroll of the Robaccia Mafia family, for whom Brooklyn Benny had initially worked, and from whom he had received his own territory, which included the Rocky Mountain region. DeeDee had originally been supported by the generosity of Antonio Penile, whom she kept in tip-top condition with her gymnastic skills. Antonio, a tough customer, had made sure that all the cement contracts went to the Robaccia family. But whether owing to loss of nerve or old age, Antonio got soft, and nothing DeeDee or the Mafia brotherhood did could bring him back to his old hardness. As luck would have it, Brooklyn Benny met her at this juncture. He had put her to work on small jobs, knowing that the big one would soon come along. Phineas Ort fit the bill.

"You're a tall fellow," said DeeDee admiringly to Phineas, who stood well over six feet. "Guys your size usually come with big equipment."

"Well, to tell you the truth," replied Phineas, "I have a Dell 733 Mega-hertz, which comes with a GX 110 mini tower and a sizable optiplex monitor. My printer's older, but it's one of those huge Hewlett-Packard war horses."

"Sounds good to me," said DeeDee, who had schooled herself in eu-phemisms to improve her *CV*. "Whenever you want to go on line, just say the word."

A shapely, pulchritudinous redhead, with the lissome legs of a dancer and the dimpled cheeks of a child actress, DeeDee had literary ambitions. She wanted to write romance novels that would instruct and delight. Given her belief that most romance stories needed more juice, and her conviction that the best writing comes from experience, she was always open to new endeavors, but the thought of wooing a professor had never before crossed her mind. Adding this string to her bow, she figured, would deepen the thrust of her novels, enabling her to include in her plots intellectuals as well as stockbrokers, lawyers, and dentists. The drillers and fillers, in particular, she knew would provide rich material. But a professor! If Phineas were truly imbued with the spirit of research, he could plumb new depths, and she could climb new heights. So DeeDee, in the interests of art, offered to show him all the comforts of the cabin, "especially the master bedroom with its new extra-firm mattress."

Over dinner, a steaming ratatouille, Phineas began to perspire. The combination of the food, DeeDee's knee rubbing up against his, and the realization that he would not be offered a job at Bogus U. caused him con-siderable palpitation. The first two sources of his unease he knew could be cured with a sedative and a snuggle. But without an offer from Bogus, he couldn't wave it under the noses of the trustees at his own institution, the University of Three Falls. He knew that market, not merit, counted. And Phineas's worth on the open market had shot up considerably since he had raised millions at his own institution.

"Do you think," he asked Eddie and Jackie, "that your friend Brooklyn Benny could be persuaded to pay a penalty for keeping me from improving my salary? Bogus U., you see, would probably give me more money than

I'm now receiving. I would guess the difference to be $20,000. Over a period of ten years—I would never stay longer—that comes to $200,000. If he'll top that figure, I'll gladly write Bogus to tell them I wish to withdraw my application for the position."

The cabin windows began fogging up, as if a respirating universe took note of DeeDee now running her hand up Phineas's leg. Ignorant of objective correlatives, Eddie picked his teeth behind his linen napkin and nodded in the affirmative. After his dental dig, he replied:

"Brooklyn Benny's a man who understands money, and what it can buy."

"You ain't kidding," said Jackie Brown. "He's got a dozen Albany scumbags in his pocket right now. Money! Boy, does Brooklyn Benny know greenbacks. He ain't no cheapskate or four-flusher. If he owes you, he pays. If you got it comin', he deals. You can say what you want about Brooklyn Benny, but unlike some cheap S.O.B.'s, he don't intend to die wid his dough."

BROOKLYN BENNY EXPLAINS
HIS PHILOSOPHY OF MONEY

"Think of money as manure," said Brooklyn Benny to his boys, who had been summoned to the abandoned firehouse below Brooklyn Bridge from which Benny ran his small but efficient Mafia operation. "You gotta spread it to make things grow." A rubicund and corpulent creature, unnaturally hirsute (he regularly shaved his chest and, with difficulty, his back), he appealed to some women in a prognathous, simian way. He paused and looked around.

"How come, I don't see Christy the Chump? Where the hell is he? I thought I said all of yous had to come to this meeting!"

"The last time I seen him," volunteered Izzy the Gimp Shapiro, "he was playin' the slots down on Surf Avenue and, as usual, losin'."

"I give him a master key for all the parkin' meters in Manhattan, and what do I get in return? Excuses! He claims business ain't good. How in the world can the street-parkin' business in Manhattan be bad? If that little prick is usin' my change on the one-armed bandits—"But here Brooklyn Benny broke off, realizing that he had lost the thread of his thesis. He cleared his throat and began again. "Money don't smell like manure, but it does the same thing. And all the better it shouldn't stink, because then it's harder to trace. The more of it you spread, the greater your return. Better you help many down on their luck than just one. Even when guys can't pay back, they owe you. It don't make no difference if they settle their debts in cash or in favors. Sometimes, in fact, favors will do you more good. You gotta be generous. That's the important thing. In the *Talmud*—you know that book, don't you, Izzy?"

"Yeah, I heard of it."

"For Chrissake, what are you, a moron? The *Talmud* is the holy book of the Jews."

Izzy the Gimp Shapiro looked crestfallen. "Sorry, Benny, I thought it was duh Old Testament."

"According to my bookie, Irving Aaronson, it's the *Talmud*. He says that's where you find all the tough questions. Anyone can make up fairy tales, but it takes a holy book to answer the ball breakers, if you see what I mean."

The boys nodded their heads in agreement, though not a one of them had caught Benny's drift.

"Well, this book, the one I've been talkin' about, the one with the tough questions and the smart answers, well, it says that generosity is an act of piety. Now I want you dunces to think about that. Some of the best thinkers in the world say that money and religion go together. A magnificent idea! Hell, even the Baptists believe it. I suppose that's why rich people leave their dough to the church, so the priests will say daily prayers in their memory. According to this sacred book, when I give money I am bein' pious. Of course, the book don't mention me by name, just principles. A guy's gotta believe in somethin'. Right?"

The boys all agreed, nodding their heads in appreciation of this penetrating logic.

"Now I don't want you to get me wrong. Piety ain't the only reason I'm generous. The other reason is the one I was talkin' about. Generosity makes things happen and, if you think about it, makin' things happen is pious. Don't the Bible say we should be fertile and fuck, or somethin' like that? The one thing I don't want to see is my money bein' used to shaft me. That's why I want to get my hands on Christy the Chump. Anyone who don't come clean with me is screwin' me over. But to get back to the point . . . money ain't no good sittin' in a bank rottin'. Only a sucker settles for five percent. Just look at the big boys. They get back fifty times what they invest. But in our business to get that kinda percentage you gotta be generous. If you are, you walk off with a hefty sum *and* you go to heaven. You can't beat that combination, can you?"

The boys all agreed it was unbeatable. "So," asked Danny Darter, an accomplished second-story man, "what's your idea?"

"I've already begun to dish out what for a long time was cookin' in my noggin. Jackie and Eddie have kidnapped some sap, and in his place we're goin' to put one of our boys."

"I don't follow," said Blowtorch Maxie, one of the best enforcers on the east coast.

Brooklyn Benny produced a box of Habana cigars and passed them around. "Light up, boys, 'cause I want you to appreciate your boss's brains."

He paused for effect. "We're gonna invest a bundle in a new enterprise I've spent some time checkin' out—a university."

Several men dropped their cigars. Others, stupefied, burned their fingers, forgetting to extinguish their matches. "You lost your marbles, Benny?" one-eyed Won Hong Low exclaimed courageously. "My kid goes to a university. They're always begging for money 'cause they're broke."

"They're broke because there are more skims in universities than in the Mafia."

Won, who came from a culture that valued education, and who had in fact frequently given generously to his son's institution, seemed unpersuaded. "Professors are always pleading poverty."

"Great, all the easier to bribe them."

"To do what?" Danny asked.

"State universities are the biggest con in America," said Brooklyn Benny, warming to his subject. "They receive millions from taxpayers and donors, money that the big boys use for cars, boats, planes, parties, booze, football games, airplane tickets, hotels, and, best of all, for their cronies. Hell, one broad out west, president of some cow college, just hired a friend for a cool half a mil. That's why we're hornin' in on higher education. When one of our boys gets appointed president"—and here Brooklyn Benny decided to employ a new phrase he had recently learned—"to the winner goes the spoils."

"What's that mean?" asked Three-fingered Tony Pazzia.

"It means, you stupe, that if we have our guy in the president's office, we control the dough."

"Why didn't you say so?" replied Tony.

"I just did, a second ago."

Brooklyn Benny's understanding of the relationship of memory and time left his interlocutor speechless.

Using the example of his son, Won again tried to make the point that universities had little to offer in the way of easy pickings. But Benny had anticipated this argument, and now played his ace.

"Teresa's kid, Laura, works out west, at Bogus U. Maybe you heard of it. She works in the president's office and tells me that they spend money like it was free. Which it is, 'cause the people in the state are payin'. Shit, they think nothin' of forkin' out a grand just for flowers. And the kids . . . they're all lookin' for a high. The stories she tells me would make you want to invest in poppy fields and greenhouses."

Paddy I.R.A. Murphy, having worked for some of the best criminal minds in Belfast, immediately apprehended where the bomb had to be placed. "To get our boy in as president, we'll have to make sure the guy we grabbed never shows his puss."

"Precisely!" said Brooklyn Benny, silently congratulating himself on having recruited Paddy. "But in this case, instead of nitro we're gonna use greenbacks."

"Why spend good money? A car bomb is cheaper. Besides, ain't knockin' off a president in the great American tradition?"

"Remember what I said about generosity. Just look at our boys in Albany. The folding stuff is better than force."

"How much will it cost us?" asked Bobby Solomon, puffing worriedly on his cigar.

"Bogus U. is run by some fatheads called trustees. There's nine of 'em. What a deal! They let others do the heavy liftin' and weed out the duds, then they put their official stamp on the last guy standin'. Slick, huh? Even slicker, just to make sure they get the stiff they want, they put three of their own mugs on the recruitin' committee." Brooklyn Benny paused. In light of what he had learned about the trustees, Brooklyn Benny pondered whether he should tell his boys how the world ran: others do the work for you to produce the results that you want. Were he to let them in on the secret, they might question his authority. They might, in fact, understand the real meaning of the golden rule: he who has the gold rules.

"You didn't answer my question," Bobby prompted. "How much dough do we have to come up with?"

Benny, still debating whether to share his coruscating knowledge with the boys or just return to business, decided that his lads were not up to such exalted ideas. "My hunch is that fifty thousand for each of the three trustees would get the job done."

"What makes you think so?" said Paddy.

"Laura tells me those guys scheme just to get free eats at the school cafeteria."

"And the guys on the committee who ain't trustees, what about them?" asked Tony.

"They're even more desperate. They'd kill for a grand."

"That's 250,000 ducats," said Solomon, who had won an award in his elementary school for being the first kid in his class to learn addition and multiplication, though someone else won the prize for subtraction, a subject he was constitutionally unfit to absorb.

"Bobby, you're forgettin' what I said. It takes money to hit the jackpot. *And* . . . you get a bonus. People regard you as pious."

"Tell me more," said Izzy, still trying to recover from his not having known that the *Talmud* trumped the Old Testament.

"I've already worked things out. Laura, she's on the recruitin' committee, and also my brother-in-law, Harry Hasty-Pasty."

"How dya manage that?" Bobby asked.

"The bum who runs the committee, he's a trustee hisself and likes to paint. Mind you, his canvases ain't worth a fart, but I'm his best customer. Everything I buy I give to the institute for the blind. I tell him I got some important friends, all in the market for his kind of art. He drools. What I want in return, I says, is for him to let Teresa's kid and Hasty-Pasty in on the search, and to follow their lead. He agrees, which is lucky for us, because without them in charge, the other stiffs might get confused and pick some gassy professor, like the sap they wanted to hire, the one we nabbed."

"Geez, we could get life for snatching the guy," said Blowtorch. "I wish you had told us your plans in advance."

"Nothin' to worry about. It went off smooth as silk. I want you boys to know what a good job Jackie Brown and Eddie Doyle done. No rough stuff. No problems. From what Eddie tells me, the guy has already fallen for DeeDee and is happy as a maggot in manure. In fact, he has our guys studyin' somethin' together."

"Huh?" Tony grunted.

"Beats me," said Brooklyn Benny. "I think they're studyin' some ass hole."

But Blowtorch's concern had filled the others with apprehension. Body snatching comes at a high price: life in prison, and, in some states, the chair. The Robaccia family had no scruples about dealing in dope, no reservations about running a numbers racket, no misgivings about murdering the occasional mobster, but they had qualms about abducting a person whom they had no plans to kill. The dead don't talk, witnesses do.

"How can we be sure," Paddy inquired, "that this bozo won't finger us after we let him go?"

"When Eddie called, he said our pigeon wanted penalty pay for bein' snatched. The moment I heard that, I knew he cared more about his bankroll than Bogus. So we'll pay him his price, and use him for our own purposes. Like I said, we're pious."

"I'm worried we're moving too fast," said Blowtorch. "Maybe we oughta think this plan over some more."

Brooklyn Benny heard a car outside, on the road that ran past the firehouse to the river. It came to a stop. "Could be Christy the Chump." Looking out the window, he saw two teenagers undressing in the back of a

1956 Oldsmobile. He watched as the boy mounted the girl and, in under a minute, pulled up his pants.

"This," replied Brooklyn Benny, who put great stock in the importance of imagery, "is not a screw and bolt job. I have been plannin' Operation Bogus for almost a year, ever since Laura first started workin' in the president's office. Trust me, Blowtorch."

"Okay, Benny, but I think we oughta ice the guy Eddie and Jackie are holdin'."

"First, let's see if we can use him. If we can't, we can whack him then."

"Tell us," said Won, "who you got in mind to pull it off?"

"Now this other guy is outta the picture, the trustee who thinks he's Michelangelo agreed to let three of our boys make the final list for the job of Bogus U. president."

"Will his pals go along?" asked Izzy.

"Leave that to me."

"Which three?" asked Danny Darter.

Benny paused for effect. The only sound, a faint sibilance, came from the cigar smokers exhaling smoke.

"Bobby Solomon, Tony, and Paddy."

Not surprisingly, the three men objected, essentially for the same reasons: their lack of education and knowledge about universities, which would quickly expose them during their interviews; their wish to remain in New York; and their belief that professors were an exotic, incomprehensible breed.

Brooklyn Benny shook his head emphatically no. "You are one hundred percent wrong. According to Laura, profs are so blind to what goes on around them that they need seein'-eye dogs. She says the trustees and stiffs who run the place are imbeciles. So you'll fit right in. As for leavin' the Big Apple, I hear the Rocky Mountains are a great place to party. Harry Hasty-Pasty will fix you up with some good pals and some hot chicks. He promised."

The boys still balked.

"For Chrissake, one of yous is going to be runnin' that joint and sendin' the skim back to Brooklyn. The more you take, the richer we are. Squeeze 'em dry and you'll get handshakes from all the padrones, and maybe a nice summer house at Bradley Beach."

Not until Brooklyn Benny pointed out that the new prez would get to see all the football games, home and away, did the three men reluctantly agree, though each hoped that one of the others would be appointed.

"All right, you bums," declared Brooklyn Benny, "this here meetin' of the Robaccia family is over. Go home to your wife and kids—and don't stop on the way for a piece. It gives the Brooklyn firehouse faction a bad name."

Once the men left, Brooklyn Benny retreated to his office at the back of the building, where he sat behind a large oak desk toting up proceeds from betting, loansharking, dope, hijacking, money laundering, and numbers, but nothing from parking meters. Where was that thieving Christy the Chump? He knew that Christy had a way with numbers; he could juggle figures almost as well as Abbadabba Berman and could be as slippery as a fish. A certain slant of light that comes on cold March afternoons made Benny shiver. Feeling the chill of the dying day, he reached for a cardigan his mother had knit, as a door slammed at the front of the building. He knew from the sound of the steps the name of the person.

"Listen to me, you bag of shit!" Brooklyn Benny rudely said to Christy the Chump, who stood accused in front of Brooklyn Benny's desk. "When your grandfather was stealin' from collection plates, mine worked for Legs Diamond. When your old man was rollin' drunks, mine worked for Bugsy Siegel. You'd still be a small-time punk, if not for me."

"B-B-Brooklyn Benny, you c-c-can call me wh-whatever words you like, b-b-but when you s-s-speak of my f-f-family you m-m-must be respectful, es-s-s-pecially of my d-d-dear, d-departed grandfather."

Benny spat into an antique brass spittoon. "Your grandfather—that chiseler, that suede-shoe operator—just to undermine the competition, he used to do jobs for less than the goin' price!"

"My g-g-grandfather had his p-principles. He did not b-b-b-believe in overtaxing the p-people."

"You stinkin' puddle of piss, your grandpa was a double-dealin' fink. When everyone else demanded five dollars for punchin' a guy, he accepted two. Both eyes blackened, he took four bucks when the goin' price was ten. A leg or arm broken, he took nineteen when he shoulda taken forty. Shootin' a guy in the leg, twenty-five instead of fifty. Doin' the big job, a hundred instead of three hundred. It's 'cause of guys like him—and you!—that people say there's no honor among thieves. You, Christy the Chump, are a crook! I give you a key that will open all the parking meters in Manhattan, and what do you bring me back, a few hundred measly bucks. You little crock of crap, Izzy seen you losin' on Louie the Louse's slot machines down at Surf Avenue. In case you need remindin', you was losin' *my* money! You never had a pot to piss in till I taught you the ropes. Is this the way you treat your benefactory, your sea daddy, your real father?"

"B-B-Brooklyn Benny, if my l-l-lemons had l-l-lined up in a row, if my apples had f-formed a s-straight line, I would have hit the j-jackpot. With all that money, I was p-plannin' to d-double the amount that I owed you."

"You lyin' lump of dog shit, do you know what I plan to do to you? I plan to have the boys pour you a pair of concrete shoes and dump you overboard ten miles offshore."

Brooklyn Benny turned his back to unlock the floor-to-ceiling wooden cabinet behind him that housed the gang's sawed-off shotguns and pistols with silencers. Envisioning being shot and having his body stuffed into a barrel topped off with cement, Christy the Chump grabbed Brooklyn Benny's paperweight, depicting Big Ben and the Houses of Parliament, and hit Brooklyn Benny on the crown of his head. The sound, like the crackle of chicken bones, and the stream of blood from Brooklyn Benny's head convinced Christy the Chump that the inert body lying on the floor belonged to a dead man. Rather than risk the chance of running into any of the Robaccia gang, Christy climbed out the rear window of the firehouse, scampered down the alley, hailed a cab, and headed straight for Penn Station in Newark—to take a train for Chicago and points west. At the station, he ran into a neighbor, an elderly woman, Henrietta Fine, who had worked for the mobster Hank Rodman. Thinking nothing of disclosing his plans to a friend, especially one famous for her underworld exploits, he told her why he intended to hide out at Bogus U. But unbeknownst to Christy the Chump, she and Brooklyn Benny's mother belonged to the same bingo club. And therein lies the explanation of how Brooklyn Benny came to know the whereabouts of Christy the Chump.

HOW CHRISTY THE CHUMP
HEARD ABOUT BOGUS U.

A digression is in order here, lest the veracity of this tale invite skepticism. On Beeker Street in lower Manhattan, the Antonella Barber Shop, which to this day enjoys the patronage of the city's patricians, saw Christy the Chump show up like clockwork every other Thursday. Having been directed to this hairdresser by the famous physical trainer Stanley Guralnick, Christy the Chump did not fail to notice the first time he ever arrived at the shop—no wider than a coffin, with only five chairs—that Antonella, the owner, stood at the ready with scissors in hand. Ignorant that she'd been called by the chief of police on his private car phone, Christy the Chump vaulted into the empty chair, only to be told that he would have to wait till she had applied her tonsorial skills to a much bigger head than his own. While reading a girlie magazine, Christy the Chump saw Antonella repeatedly dust off the first chair, an action that she conspicuously performed as the dignitary arrived at her front door in a limo. He wore a dark suit and a white shirt with a red tie. Two bodyguards stood sentinel on the street. Their presence made Christy the Chump most uneasy, and had he not feared attracting attention, he would have vacated his seat and made for the boulevard.

"How's the action?" the chief asked Rocky, the former owner, who stood behind the second chair and sported a brass name plaque over his mirror.

Rocky, an inveterate sports fan, said, "Depends on which game?"

The chief laughed.

Was it a coincidence or serendipity (perhaps they're the same) that the phone rang at that precise moment—but only once—and that a small red light, attached to the phone, lit up? Rocky and also the chief knew that the call was being redirected to the back room, approached not from Beeker Street but from a side alley.

"That game!" the chief said, referring to the light. Christy the Chump could see that Rocky understood, and so too did Antonella. What Christy the Chump could not see was that in return for free haircuts, the chief turned a blind eye to the action in the back room: numbers and book-making. Whether the chief received a cut from these activities, only his hairdresser knows. A moment later, a squat, swarthy fellow, with a head that looked more like a bowling ball than one in need of a haircut, peered out of the backroom and called:

"Chief, it's for you. Your kid."

The bowling ball, Joey Avocado, a member of the Nocciola Mafia family, immediately disappeared into the back room as the chief of police took his call right where he sat. After a number of nods and "uhuhs," the chief hung up and remarked:

"That son of mine . . . what a piss cutter. He goes to Bogus U. and says the place is run by poltroons." The police chief hesitated, hoping that his audience would appreciate his diction. But seeing only blank stares, he jettisoned generalities and grew particular.

"I work hard for my dough and others steal it."

Antonella, an immigrant from Rumania, remarked, "What do you mean steal? In a university . . . steal? No! This is America not Bucharest."

"I hate to say it, but from what I hear the president's on the take from all the companies and concessionaires doin' business with the U. The Grand Vizier puts his putz in every aperture on campus. The football coach makes almost a million bucks a year and whines that he's underpaid. The professors spend more time in planes than in class. My kid says that everyone's got a shtick . . . that the number of angles in the university make those in a geometry class look paltry. It's a thieves' paradise."

Christy the Chump remembered that comment as the cabby passed through the Holland Tunnel heading for Newark. When his train arrived in Chicago, he changed for one going west. At Horsehead Station, he asked a porter how to get to Bogus U. The porter, an elderly man with gray hair, chuckled and murmured skeptically, "You mean where they have faculty who form the future?" Christy looked blank. "That's what they say," remarked the porter, "but I don't believe it, unless they mean sci-fi." Christy asked for directions. "It's about an hour from here. You can take the bus."

A DAY IN THE LIFE OF BOGUS U.

The Tuesday that Christy arrived at Bogus U., the sun rose as usual, at least half the student bodies raised themselves from their torpor to trudge off to class, and a few professors put aside their research and travels long enough to confuse the students with their abstruse learning. Let us, exercising the privileges of omniscience, look at a typical Bogus U. day.

8:00 A.M. "FINE ARTS"

In a red-brick building, the hallway branches off into a small cul-de-sac that displays a prize-winning art work: a canvas with rows of symmetrically placed, upside-down, transparent plastic cups glued to the surface. Under each cup can be seen a word, painted on the canvas. A small wall card next to the canvas says: "The cups represent the suppression of free speech in China; or, looked at in a different way, the words, selected willy-nilly, express the randomness of the world."

Over the frame appears the word "Honors." If the truth be told— and why shouldn't we tell it—the canvas had created quite a ruckus. One judge wanted to fail it, but the student's advisor, absent during the discussion and voting, went to the Honors Committee on the Q.T. and convinced the committee that the student, having recently lost her mother, deserved honors.

In the many art studios similar projects are under way, virtually all of them devoid of talent, but esteemed by professors lacking the courage to call dreck by its right name.

9:00 A.M. CHEMISTRY

Further along the walk we come to the chemistry building, and discover numerous students beavering away in labs but nary a prof, owing to a scheme whereby professors originate the experiments and the students run them. For those uninitiated in the ways of university life, let us add that since most scientists devoutly believe that thinking and teaching, like oil and water, don't mix, classes are more often than not taught by part-timers and graduate students.

Given the university's lucrative policy of selling intellectual properties, that is, cashing in on the fruits of the professors' experiments, we should not be surprised to learn that the research has a decidedly commercial flavor. In the first lab a graduate student is leaning over a pot that contains an awful-smelling solution for restoring hair and curing baldness. On the lab bench rests a book, *Medieval Medicus*, the source of the formula. If it proves successful, the chemist will add a few new ingredients and the university will patent it.

In a second lab, the pots cooking over an open flame smell even worse. The student monitoring the temperature has been told by his professor that this experiment will lead to a penile hardener with a "firmer feel than the others and the absence of nasty side effects." This work too could eventuate in a patent, unless the U.S. Marines, who have sponsored the research, declare it a state secret.

In the third lab a recognizable aroma rises from a slowly hardening paste: coca. A real, live professor, heavy-set and dark-haired, has made his reputation testifying as an expert witness at drug trials. To check the testimony of those charged with crimes, he reproduces their methods. He hopes to expand his activities and sell the cocaine as a relaxant, reasoning that if labs can extract digitalis from foxglove, why shouldn't he extract cocaine from coca leaves? He already grows and sells marijuana for medicinal purposes.

We would move on but for a suspicious-looking fellow lurking in the hall, hovering around a particular lab. He looks like a tough from the hood; he needs a shave and wears an overcoat with the collar pulled up and a hat tipped down to conceal his face. Inside, a coed bends over some beakers that contain Dr. Kronkheit's surefire cure for bunions. The man suddenly darts into the lab and asks how he can reach the professor. Disappearing into a back office, the young woman returns almost immediately followed by a bespectacled septuagenarian, stooped and dwarfish, who extends a palsied hand.

The strange relationship between the two men began several years before, when the shady-looking bloke came into the lab and inquired, "Can you make an ink which will last for only two or three hours and then disappear?" Dr. Kronkheit assured him he could. In fact, he could make an ink that would last a week before fading away. In a few days, the man returned, the good doctor gave him a sample of the two-hour solution, and charged him only for the labor. "If the ink works," he said, "we can discuss money later." The man came back pleased as a pig in slops and told the doctor that the ink worked like magic and that he needed twenty more samples. He offered ten thousand bucks. Dr. Kronkheit, lacking money for his research on dissolving bunions, took it without asking why his customer wanted the ink. Only later did he discover that the man ran a sports-betting establishment. When one of his customers made a wager likely to cost him money, he wrote out a chit with the disappearing ink. The fact that the chits vanished after two hours allowed him to escape paying off a number of bettors.

This ink will play an important part in our plot.

10:00 A.M. FRENCH LITERARY CRITICISM (IN TRANSLATION)

From the chemistry labs, we wend our way toward the Humanities building, where a few laggards sit in the lounge knocking back lagers. The bell for the start of class rings. In a large lecture hall, the first few rows are crowded by a number of students aspiring to reach the intellectual zenith of unintelligibility. The professor has a head of wild hair and a red nose, inflamed from inhaling glue. Mentioning Virgil and Dante and Petrarch, he moves to Foucault and Derrida and Lacan and to what he calls the philosophy of language.

"It was the subject of my thesis from the Sorbonne," he proudly explains. "It is a vitally important subject, one that enables us to deconstruct a sentence before we even attempt to construct its meaning. However, once the deconstruction takes place, we then realize that there can be no one meaning. Rather, we are faced with several meanings, most of which are contradictory. Just look at the simplest unit of written expression: the word. Take, for example, the word flammable, which means easily set on fire. Now the word inflammable should mean the opposite, not easily set on fire, because the prefix 'in' normally means not or no. Hospitable, inhospitable. Sufficient, insufficient. The first is yes, the second no. There, you see! I just created an interpretative problem by the statement, 'the first is yes, the second no.' Did I mean by 'the second no,' the second of the two pairs is no: inhospitable and insufficient; or did I mean the second example, sufficient-insufficient is no; or did I mean that I had now said no twice? In which case, there's a further problem. I said no only once, not twice. So there is no antecedent for 'the second no' and it therefore can't refer to a prior no. Consequently that example is void. But I digress. As I was saying: the word flammable means easily ignited, but so too does its opposite, inflammable. Now if the negative in this case means the positive, how do we know that it doesn't mean the positive for other words and phrases and sentences? Well, in fact it does. The negative is often used to indicate the positive. For example, my wife says, 'You don't call your lectures enlightening?' by which she means, you do call them enlightening—and because you do, you're out of your mind. Hence, when we say no, or when someone else tells us no, the meaning is very likely to be yes. The linguistic subtlety, though lost on politicians, is well known to men and women who are courting. Now do you see why deconstruction precedes the construction of meaning?"

11:00 A.M. ENGLISH

A few doors away, we find a young woman who keeps tossing her head and running a hand through her hair. Lecturing about "menstruation in the flow of English letters," she explains that Jane Austen's novel *Emma* is "informed" by her menses. "You see," says the woman, "whenever Emma becomes unruly and feverish with matchmaking, we know it is her time of month. Not that Austen would ever breathe a word on such a subject, but we can tell from Emma's behavior that she suffers intensely painful periods. We must therefore reconsider the novel in light of Austen's biology if we are to understand the true actions and nature of Emma. Let me add that it is only because of all the new research into the body as text, as both book and person, that we can now discover the underlying organismus of fictive motivations."

The remainder of the lecture, a series of examples in defense of her thesis, we leave for the students to endure, as we proceed to the College of Propaedeutics, where a professor of educational psychology is lecturing on the subject of grades.

12:00 P.M. PEDAGOGY

The students sit in a circle because in this college proactive learning, that is, chatting, has supplanted lecturing, the latter deemed elitist and patriarchal. Asking the class what they would like to discuss, the professor, Benedict Dooley, is greeted with shrugs. In the absence of a subject, he manfully asks a question, "Given the gelatinous state of the human brain and the prevalence of student discouragement, should professors grade honestly?" Having introduced the one subject that unfailingly engages students' attention, he plays the devil's advocate and posits that grading has a moral dimension: that professors who fail to tell their students the truth about their work are like physicians who fail to tell patients about the nature of their ills. This analogy is greeted with unanimous complaint. One objection after another tumbles forth.

"The process should count as much—or more—than the product. Trying is what counts."

"It's all subjective anyway."

"Where's the positive reinforcement in bad grades? They discourage students."

"Bad grades are a sign that the professor failed as a teacher."

"Low grades are like a stick. They inspire fear, not pride."

"What about self-esteem?"

Professor Dooley, a short, swarthy fellow, whose underdeveloped nose gives him a porcine quality, has graduated from the ranks of Peace-Corps teaching in Somalia to the level of university professor. His students know that his questions are no more than a form of catechism designed to prepare them as pedagogues who may have to justify the inflated grades they will shortly be giving. In this spirit he points out that some patients want their doctors to tell them the truth and others do not. The same division occurs among students. Some want an honest evaluation of their work and others merely want to hear cheering words.

The class quickly comes to a consensus: when honesty proves hurtful, it is better to dissemble. A pretty coed, hugging herself to keep warm—having left her digs scantily dressed—replies that her methodology professor begins each semester by informing his students that everyone will receive an A and certainly no less than a B. She likes his reasoning: that once the fear of a poor grade is removed, students prove receptive to learning.

"What is education, anyway?" asks a student rhetorically. "How we feel about ourselves matters more than what a person learns. An ego lasts a lifetime, a paper vanishes by the end of the term."

This comment opens the door to a number of anecdotes, in which students recount how a high grade made them want to teach so that they could do the same for others. Without actually saying so, they suggest that high marks save souls.

Since Professor Dooley himself believes that grades are merely a convention and therefore arbitrary, he sees no difference between an A or a C. Why not make the kids feel good about themselves and, at the same time, keep whiners from your office and invite good evaluations from the students? Knowing that the College of Propaedeutics has enshrined praise as an inviolable principle, he insincerely says that the class has made compelling arguments that will stand them in good stead when they enter the K–12 system.

1:00 P.M. JOURNALISM / HISTORY / SEMAPHORICS

Professor Nett, having failed as a newspaper reporter, has found a home at Bogus U. A woman in her late forties, with short straight flaxen hair and teeth like kernels of dried corn, she too believes in proactive learning, which explains why she is holding a large red beach ball. To enliven the class, she will ask a question and then toss the ball to the person she wants to answer it. If the student responds incorrectly, she predictably says, "You dropped the ball." She thinks of her approach as a reified metaphor; but since the person hardly ever actually drops the ball, the metaphor becomes not only mixed but addled.

"Josh," she calls and throws him the ball, "what's the rule about words all set in caps?"

He zips it back to her and replies, "Leave extra spaces between words."

Again the sphere takes flight. "Justine, what can you tell me about headlines?"

Justine pauses briefly before returning it with a flick of the wrist. "They should never be wider than the body copy directly below."

"Anything else?"

The ball is again in Justine's grasp. She laughs and wings it back to the prof.

"Headlines look best when they fill up as much of the available space as possible."

The prof arches the ball to Jody, who is a double major in Business and Journalism.

"What are the no-no's about ads?"

Jody, who regards this class as cool and the professor as cool and the beach ball as cool, gushes:

"Don't float ads as islands in the middle of reading matter. Don't fill up a column by piling up small ads. Don't. . . ."

Her list goes on, but we shall make a graceful exit to attend the class next door, where the history professor can be found standing on his desk, wildly gesticulating.

Whenever Professor Tyler wishes to make a point he vaults onto the desk and towers above his audience, his arms a windmill of whirls. The students anxiously wait for these moments, which make it, if we can trust their course evaluations, a fun class, taught by a fun professor, who makes fun assignments, like cutouts for bulletin boards. To give the students a sense— somehow—of the American Depression, he has them putting together a display of 1930s cars. An automobile buff, he too finds the assignment fun.

Two doors away, a semaphorics professor, Mr. Gustatory, still recovering from last night's repast, burps. A student aide shows a slide depicting some cartoon figures. In fact, the course, "The Semaphorics of Cereal Boxes," which the professor justifies on the grounds that cereal boxes are read by more people in America than any other text, has been nothing but a succession of slides because the prof, whose own graduate dissertation treated "the function of the pause in communication," finds ideas taxing and cereal a subject to which he can relate, food. In addition, he can give his students true-and-false exams or short answer tests which spare him from reading their execrable writing. Professor Gustatory can't wait for the bell to sound so that he can retire to a two-hour lunch at a European-style restaurant downtown that cooks every dish in copious amounts of butter. His mind drifts toward the menu as he debates which of several dishes he should select. Finally, he decides that he will be guided by the sauce of the day.

"Day."

"What's that?" Professor Gustatory says.

"Do you think this cartoon," asks a student, "on this cereal box is a caricature of Doris Day?"

"Hollandaise."

"What?"

"It's my favorite."

Fortunately, the bell releases both the students and Professor Gustatory, who makes immediately for the restaurant.

2:00 P.M. BUSINESS: MARKETING

In the hope of inspiring young women to follow a career in commerce, the College of Business has their marketing course, a student favorite, team taught by a man, Professor Bingo Donnie, and a woman, Professor Ingrid

Hohenstaufen. Dressed for success in an Italian silk suit with matching shirt and tie, Bingo Donnie is lecturing the class on how to succeed in the commercial world.

"You have to be result-driven. Proactive. Think outside the box. But always keep a sharp eye on the bottom line. Keep expenses in the ballpark and yet strive for total quality. That's the right mindset: win-win. You have to appreciate the synergy and strategic fit between buyer and seller, at the same time remaining client focused. Never be found outside the loop. My own benchmark is empowerment through gap analysis and best practice fast track."

A student asks, "How do you feel about gambling?"

"Having the name Bingo, I know a lot about games." The student looks nonplussed, having meant gambling as in risk taking.

"I ran the state lottery at Calvary, Idaho for years before coming here as a professor."

An enterprising student, who chairs the Republican Club, inquires, "Like, what if we sponsored a lottery, maybe a lot of them, and like in return the winners got a like tuition-free education for four years at Bogus? The cost for a ticket like wouldn't be much, but like the prize would be: a college education. We could make millions."

"You, William Bushie, belong in marketing. With your knowledge base and aptitude for leveraging money, you could swell the bottom line."

Professor Donnie continues. "Although Bushie here has suggested a way to lay claim to a value-added education, let me remind you that business, not education, drives America. We have empowered the country by revisiting the principles of win-win, fast track, and strategic fit."

On that stirring note, Bingo turns over the class to his colleague Professor Ingrid Hohenstaufen, a tall, thin woman, with dark hair, who holds degrees in global gouging and market forces. Her shiny gray suit looks as if it just arrived from Paris, as in fact it has. Prof. Hohenstaufen had originally gone into business to pay for her millinery and dressmaking bills, but having grown bored with the boardroom, she is now willing to slum for a mere 250k.

"When employees complain," she says, drawing on her expertise in personnel, "you can be sure the cause is money. Pay people a market wage and you'll have no trouble with them."

"But what about inequities," asks a socially-minded student. "Teachers make very little and business people make a lot."

"Market forces."

"Even so," the student replies, "there's a question of equity."

"The problem is that there are too many teachers. Cut their numbers, create a shortage, and then teachers will make as much as business people."

"You seem to be saying that fairness doesn't matter."

"The market can't be governed by morality. It has to respond to supply and demand. The market is our lifeblood, the compass for all our decisions."

3:00 P.M. SOCIOLOGY

Professor Guevara is talking about life in the barrios where, he repeatedly makes the point, the predominant color is brown. In fact, the course, "The Sociology of Poverty," has been nothing but a succession of riffs on the color brown because the prof, intoxicated by the imaginative book *Brown*, cannot bring himself to prepare a lecture, which would require him to discuss events that did not touch upon his personal life, events that for him to know about would require sustained scholarship. But since he prefers the personal mode of teaching—talking about himself and his own experiences as a means of elucidating barrio life—he frequently lapses into confessionalism and self-absorption, which he justifies on the grounds of its therapeutic value. For himself or his students, he doesn't say. Using self as his text frees him from having to prepare for class and invites the students to write personal narratives about their lives. Professor Guevara prefers this genre of writing because it eschews ideas and minimizes sociological jargon, leaving him free to grade the students for style. When he feels especially moved by a student's confession of pain, he raises the grade. But of late many such confessions have surfaced. Having deduced that tales of travail improve their grades, the kids are laying on their woes with a trowel.

Ms. Fanny Hill, a pretty lass from England, is reading the conclusion of her paper.

"Hence, my parents marginalized me through their social construction of a deviant home in which praxis *qua* sexual correlated with their authoritative status. In short, at least twice a week, my father climbed into my bed and fondled me, with the result that not a day passed in which my mother didn't beat me for alienating my father's attentions. But the significance of these events cannot be compared to the relevance of the psychological deprivation that I suffered from having my space violated and therefore reconfigured, forcing me to re-theorize my place in the familial context."

Professor Guevara praises the paper excessively. He knows that he has only himself to blame for this madness and looks forward to mid-semester, when he will dismiss the class for the rest of the term to engage in community service. The kids will receive academic credit and be graded not by Professor Guevara but by the department secretary, freeing him and numerous other colleagues who likewise have fobbed off their students on the secretary to pursue their discussions into the causes of failed academic communities.

4:00 P.M. FOOTBALL PRACTICE

Before Coach Caiaphas permits the players to shower, he has them assemble in the training building at the end of the stadium and grills them on their Bible reading. A handsome well-built man with a grainy face, a full head of pepper-and-gray hair, and stores of energy, Boaz Caiaphas grew up in Nanking, China, where his missionary parents had assisted the local population during the rape of that city by the Japanese in World War II.

Perhaps owing to the Asian influence on his life, he practices a form of Pentecostal Confucianism. The Grand Panjandrum of a religio-fraternal organization devoted to promoting male authority, he is by no means a tyrant, believing that such worship obliges him to care for his family's financial and spiritual well-being. Of his own pharisaical behavior, we shall speak shortly.

Pacing the room in a T shirt and shorts, he frequently pokes the vacant air to make a point. "Before we get started, let me remind you of what I've been saying since the day you arrived. Just as there is one God in heaven, there is one father over the family. Just as there is one head coach, there is one starter for each position. God, father, and coach—the holy Trinity—all look after their flocks. We are responsible for the women and the children and, most important of all, for winning. Now, let me assure you that no one wins without Jesus, father, and coach caring for you. To successfully run and pass, block and tackle, you gotta have the Lord on your side. He's comin' to town one of these days, and He knows who's been bad and who's been good, who's been naughty and who's been nice. That's why I've been giving you Bible lessons. So when He arrives, you'll be ready. So when you take the field, you'll be prepared for the battle. With Jesus Christ leading the way, you can't fail to win. If you've studied your Bible and said your prayers, He'll run interference for you. He'll smite the opponent."

A player holds up his hand.

"What is it, Mandelbaum?"

"What if the other team has also been calling on Jesus?"

Coach Caiaphas knows that Manny Mandelbaum is Jewish, and assumes that Manny's vexatious questions have their source in some mysterious inchoate faith.

"He'll listen to us and not them, and I'll tell you why. Because he knows that your head coach—me—is not only a believer in the book, but also a teacher of what's in it." He looks around and says, "Now let's see how well you have translated my lessons into good behavior. Brawley! You got an A on my last quiz. What does the first book of the Old Testament say about drunkenness?"

"The book of Guinness . . . it says the grape brings pleasure."

"Close enough. Ross! Although we don't know the name of Noah's wife—"

Ross interrupts. "I know it coach: Joan of Ark."

"Nice, Ross, really nice. Lynnford! What do you know about Lot's wife?"

"By day she was a pillar of salt, and by night a ball of fire."

"Not a bad way of saying it, Lynnford. Denny! Where did Moses go to get the Ten Commandments?"

"Easy, coach. Mount Cyanide."

"Spear! Did Moses lead his people to the promised land?"

"No, coach. He died before he ever reached Canada. Then Joshua led the Hebrews in the battle of Geritol."

"I gotta admit, we have some pretty clever guys on the team. Snell, why don't you share with the others the speech you delivered to the Rotary Club."

Snell, glowing with pride, repeats it. "Samson was a strongman led astray by a Jezebel called Delilah. Our team shall never let the weaker sex detour us from a winning season. We shall live by the commandments. And the first one orders us to win, also the second, and the third, and everyone but the seventh, which commands us not to admit adultery. Some people think that for us to have a winning season would take a miracle. But miracles do happen. The greatest one occurred in the Bible, when Joshua told his son to stand still and his son obeyed him. Coach often says we have to play as a team and look after each other. He says we're one big family, and preaches holy acrimony, which is another name for marriage. Our team, the Wildebeests, has only one goal: to marry victory, just like Christians who have only one spouse because they believe in monotony."

The players applaud Snell for a "great speech." Coach Caiaphas slaps him on the back. "I'm proud of Snell and all you boys. How many football teams in this great nation of ours can say that the players know their Bible and have dedicated their lives to winning for Jesus? Not many, I can tell you. So, remember, lads, put your trust in Jesus and all will be well. Any questions? Yes, Mandelbaum?"

"What if you're Jewish?"

"So was Jesus. And don't you forget it."

BENNY'S PLAN TAKES SHAPE

Even though Benny had disappeared, the Robaccia gang faithfully agreed to see his plan through to the end. As Benny had advised, the gang contacted the boys in Schroon Lake and directed them to have Phineas write a letter of withdrawal to the Bogus U. trustees. Phineas, on hearing that his request for penalty pay had been granted, gladly complied. The effect of the letter cannot be overstated. It resonated throughout higher education.

> Dear Board of Trustees and Members of the Search Committee, I no longer wish to be considered a candidate for president of Bogus U. My reasons follow. The educational resources that nourish my work are in the east. The west has many attractions but too few first-rate libraries. And the one at Bogus will take several lifetimes to become a major repository. I have always enjoyed teaching and tried to keep my research current. But the work that will be required to improve Bogus will leave me no time for study and the classroom.
>
> Having made three site visits to Bogus in which I had the opportunity to meet faculty, staff, and students, I have come to the conclusion that what Bogus needs in the office of president is a mobster. The school's chronically sick budget will not improve until you have an accomplished extortionist negotiating with the legislature and running the campus. Scholar-administrators are a thing of the past, or should be at schools like Bogus. Strong ills require strong medicine. Bogus is seriously ailing. Without an injection of millions, it will atrophy and die. Those millions can be raised only by a gangster president, a new breed of university administrator. I have, during my many travels, come across several such people. All of them have brought financial health and order to their campuses. Admittedly, their methods may be unorthodox, but they are effective. The legislature and faculty will listen when they speak—and results will follow.

Lest you worry that Bogus's reputation will suffer with a hoodlum president, let me assure you that both the country and innumerable other institutions are currently thriving under piratical presidents. Just think of the university as a microcosm of the United States and ask yourselves this question: given the political sophistication of the electorate, who is more likely to succeed, a Greek scholar or a hit man? Trust me, go with the gun.

Wishing you every success with your search and thanking you for the many courtesies extended to me, I am

Yours sincerely,

Phineas O. Ort

Every evening after supper, Phineas and the others spent an hour or two discussing the Greek way of life. At bedtime, Phineas, who had a history of unsuccessful affairs, found unbounded sex. Gloriously, DeeDee had reignited his interest in bedroom gymnastics, a sport that he had given up when his previous lover lay munching an apple and reading *People* magazine as he humped and sweated. A further sign of his good luck was that his own university, Three Falls, had reluctantly agreed to give him a leave without pay until the fall. Although the governors found his secretiveness uncharacteristic, they decided that Phineas must be experiencing either a difficult medical problem or a thoughtful reevaluation of his life. One of the governors even hazarded that the two might be related, but another pointed out that a midlife crisis usually involved a woman.

On the first day, Phineas had suggested to his captors that they convene as a seminar, but had been initially thwarted when Jackie Brown, upon discovering that a doctor of philosophy lacks the qualifications to treat hemorrhoids, told him to "piss off." It had taken a while to earn everyone's respect. At this moment, they were seated at the dining room table, noshing on brioches and pralines.

"Now that I have finished telling you about Cicero and Plato, we can return to *Antigone*." In fact, Phineas had spent a great deal of time schooling his companions in Greek philosophy and culture, and had even spent many hours describing the war between Greece and Troy, though in a fashion suitable for gangsters. "By reading Sophocles out loud," explained Phineas, "we can embody the cut and thrust of the debate. DeeDee can play the part of Antigone; Jackie, Creon; Eddie, Haemon and Teiresias; Reynald, the

Guard and the two Messengers; and I will assume the female roles of Ismene and Eurydice, as well as that of the Theban chorus."

"What are you, queer?" said Jackie Brown indignantly. "Why would a guy wanna play a dame? Two dames, in fact. I thought you was funny from the moment we picked you up."

Phineas correctly surmised that Jackie resented some people playing multiple roles, while he had only one.

"Although the play is called *Antigone*, the largest part goes to Creon. He holds center stage. The great moral struggle revolves around him. I would even go so far as to say that he is the play." Jackie needed only a second to reflect.

"No shit! Well, then, let's get started. And all of yous just remember, I'm what it's all about. The doc just said so."

"Permit me," said Phineas, "to summarize the story, so that when we read it, you will understand the action and the nature of the struggle."

Everyone agreed to this idea, though Reynald grumbled that if they each had their own copy of the play, they wouldn't have to pass the book around.

As Phineas began, the phone rang. It was the Brooklyn office of the Robaccia gang. For economy and safety's sake, the boys wanted Phineas iced. Jackie, who took the call, led Eddie aside. The news put both kidnappers into a funk. They liked the earnestness of the big fellow, his love of learning, his quaint belief that ideas mattered more than possessions. They had never met anyone like him and frankly found the novelty amusing. Although the order perplexed both men, Jackie insisted that "an order's an order."

Eddie, however, balked. He argued that the good of the gang would suffer if he and Jackie didn't follow the study schedule that Phineas had outlined for *Antigone*. "The gang's only thinking of saving money," said Eddie, "but we got higher things to think about."

Jackie touched his nose and tried to imagine what could be more important than greenbacks.

"How often," continued Eddie, "does a chance like this come along? You never made it past the sixth grade, and I dropped out of high school. We got an opportunity to learn stuff that we'd never know except for him. It'd be a shame not to use what we got here." Running his left hand over his right biceps, Jackie said, "Whadda ya suggest? We can't cross the boys."

"The greater good," said Eddie, employing one of Phineas's favorite phrases, "tells me we ought to talk to the pigeon himself. Maybe he'd be willing to disappear on his own and forget the dough."

"Yeah, but can you trust him?"

"Can you trust anyone?" replied Eddie, trying his hand at being philosophical.

Jackie looked hurt. "You'd say that to your own best buddy, me? I'm worried that this Phineas is gettin' to your head."

Eddie, absorbed in his own thoughts, merely mumbled that if Phineas didn't keep his word they could always ice him. When they returned to the table, Phineas was introducing Reynald and DeeDee to a Greek dramatic term.

"*Peripeteia* . . . reversal . . . from *peripetis* . . . falling in with, changing suddenly."

Jackie plopped down in the chair next to Phineas. Eddie paced. It took a moment before Phineas looked up.

"I think maybe you oughta wrap it up," Jackie said.

"Any change of heart or mind has to be logical . . . in a play, that is. Life's vicissitudes are something else."

"Right," said Jackie, uncomprehending.

Phineas removed his reading glasses. "Is there something you want to tell me?"

Jackie, a man known for his directness, said bluntly, "Eddie and me got to talk to you alone. So Reynald, yous and DeeDee scram." As soon as they had left, Jackie explained the situation. "That's why you gotta vanish. If you vanish, you live."

Phineas looked perplexed. "I don't understand. Haven't I been cooperative?"

"It's like this," said Eddie, "since you can identify us, you've gotta disappear."

"Disappear?"

"You know, assume a new identity, like the canaries in the witness protection plan."

"I see . . . change my life . . . reverse directions, so to speak."

"Exactly."

Phineas's mind raced. He had always wanted to spend his life reading and writing free of the distractions of teaching and administration. Perhaps that was now possible. "Could I remain in hiding here, in Schroon Lake, on a small salary?" he asked timidly. "I'd accept far less than the gang originally agreed to give me."

Jackie rubbed his misdirected nose. "The Robaccia gang's always open to deals, whadda they get in return?"

Phineas needed only a moment's reflection to reply. "Most of the great classical and renaissance authors had patrons. I will dedicate all my books and articles to the gang."

"They wouldn't understand things like *Antigone*," said Jackie.

"They ain't like us," said Eddie.

"Never fear," replied Phineas, "I have long wanted to write a novel for the general public. Crime fiction sells better than biography. This is my chance. In return for your teaching me the tricks of the trade, I'll tell the gang about university scams. Such knowledge will assist whomever you put in my place at Bogus U. You can also tell the gang that if they buy my idea, I will make them a major player in the book. And once it's published, they'll be as famous as the gangs run by Arnold Rothstein and Dutch Schultz. The gang name will become synonymous with daring and imagination."

Jackie flexed his right arm and hazarded that the gang would like the notoriety. "Them guys all wear flashy clothes and diamond rings and drive big cars. So it's my guess they'd like to have people readin' about 'em. What do you think, Eddie?"

"There's one way to find out," said Eddie, heading for the phone in the other room.

Jackie and Phineas sat wordlessly, neither looking at the other, waiting for Eddie to return. They could hear what he said but couldn't tell from the protracted silences whether the gang was buying. While Phineas contemplated his own death, Jackie worried that he might have to pull the trigger. They could hear Eddie return the receiver to its cradle and then his footsteps. A second later, he stood in the doorway, expressionless. Suddenly a great smile animated his face.

"Start writing!" he said.

That evening, Phineas, who composed all his first drafts in longhand, wrote: "On a raw March day in 1998, Phineas Ort's taxi left the Empire Hotel and drove through Central Park."

CHRISTY FINDS A JOB

Looking somewhat bedraggled by the time he arrived at the university, Christy the Chump went directly to the personnel office to find temporary employment. He sat down next to a swarthy lad who looked no older than fifteen. The boy had a small hand-sized chessboard with differently shaped black and white pegs that he moved rapidly as he played against himself. Striking up a conversation, Christy gathered from the young man's accent that he had been born elsewhere.

"Cambodia," the boy replied when Christy asked him.

"W-what are you doing here?"

"My father suggested I come. He works here . . . cleaning the geography building."

"H-how old are you?"

"Seventeen."

The boy struck Christy as the clever sort of kid who would be running errands for Brooklyn Benny if he lived in New York. Not tall, but robust, he had a round face enhanced by a set of teeth that could be featured in an advertisement, and a head of thick black hair, parted down the middle.

"You in school?"

"Yes."

"B-but Bogus ain't started yet . . . not for two weeks."

"No, it start already, the special classes for at-risk students."

"Then what are you doing here?"

"I go till noon and afternoons bust tires. My family needs money. But I think I can make more working as a janitor."

Christy detected the smell of food on the boy's breath, as if he had just come from a meal. The odor was exotic and pleasant.

"Where'd you learn English?"

"In a refugee camp . . . from a nun. I'm not so good at it. My name's Sophanna Houth."

"M-mine's Christy, Christopher Mahon."

Sophanna, having arrived in the office before Christy, interviewed first. When he came out, he smiled brightly. "I got a job . . . cleaning in the president's building, Tinnitus House. America's a lucky place. Here you can make money and go to school." He buttoned his patched parka, waved, and went out the door, leaving behind the strange scent.

Given Christy's appearance, the woman behind the desk wondered if he could hold a job. "Have you any references?" she asked.

"I've just c-come off a job w-workin' for a guy in B-Brooklyn so important I can't give you his n-name."

Correctly surmising that his unprepossessing appearance could cost him a position, he added, "You know, s-secret stuff. That's w-why I'm d-dressed this w-way. I'm t-travelin' in-a-cog-nito, you know, hush-hush."

Not knowing whether to laugh or send for the campus police, the woman, a good-hearted soul and the proud descendant of Irish grandparents, said:

"Mahon, I knew people by that name, from County Clare."

Noticing the nameplate on her desk—"Moira Mulhern"—he knew immediately how to proceed. "H-Hooly m-mother of Jasus," he said, affecting an accent, "tuh s-second I w-walked in 'ere I knew tat I was s-smellin' tuh s-sanctity of Irish g-goodness."

A delighted Moira Mulhern said, "You haven't, by any chance, seen the Rock of Cashel?"

"N-No, but I've heard m-me ould Irish m-mother s-speak of its r-rarity."

"Last June, my mother and me flew to Shannon and rented a car . . ."

Moira then proceeded to narrate a holiday that took her to all the holy sites. On finishing, she offered Christy the choice of three areas to which he could apply his custodial mop: the alumni center, the men's gym, or the administrative building, Puppet Hall. Christy had no idea what the word alumni meant, but did know the smell of men's sweat, so he selected the last.

Fortuitously, he began pushing a broom the very week that the presidential search committee began meeting in Puppet Hall. Accustomed to eavesdropping, and many things worse, Christy was living proof that chance favors the prepared mind.

HOW CHRISTY
CAME TO EAVESDROP

The patient reader, we trust, will suffer us to pause long enough to say that a doorway connected the Puppet Hall meeting room and the Grand Vizier's office, which had its own bathroom. Late in the afternoon, when Christy the Chump thought the Grand Vizier, Daily Cummings, had left for a meeting across campus, he entered this office to dust. But hearing love moans issuing from the bathroom, he peeked in and saw a young lady with her derrière perched in the sink and her legs spread.

Christy the Chump, bred on the Bible and schooled as an altar boy, knew only one kind of sex, the missionary position, and therefore found himself shocked to see the Grand Vizier pearl diving. Equally disconcerting were the disembodied voices issuing from a heating vent near the top of the bathroom wall. At first, he believed that the Lord had chosen a strange conduit to convey His celestial displeasure. But realizing that the voices came from the meeting room, he concluded one could comfortably sit in this room and eavesdrop. Shortly thereafter, Christy the Chump arrived at a third conclusion: that Daily Cummings spent most afternoons not in his office, but in the condo he kept off campus for trysts. Christy the Chump, therefore, took those occasions to spend a few hours each week listening to the revealing discussions of the committee next door while admiring himself in the bathroom mirror. A quick study, Christy quickly realized how the presidential search could be turned to his own advantage: privileged information always has a buyer.

OF THINGS PAST AND PRESENT

Named after the illustrious Dutch philanthropist Hieronymous Bogus, who had uncovered a fabulous vein of silver in the Rocky Mountains, Bogus University had for years entertained alumni and trustees with lawn parties and lavish boxes at football games, with a Sun Valley chalet and skiing retreats, until one day the exchequer announced that the university had squandered the Bogus Endowment. In short, self-interest had run rampant and the institution needed to find new sources of money. Now dependent on the largesse of the legislature—for the most part a collection of right-wing realtors and ranchers and religious fanatics—the U. ranked 48th in the nation for the amount of public support it received. The wealthy, as we've long known, do not abhor learning; after all, they send their children to private and parochial schools. What they can't abide is public education. It smacks of socialism.

Once Bogus fell upon hard times, its presidents fell too, like ten pins. Either the legislature fired them for being too liberal or the trustees sacked them for being too intelligent or willful (no man ever lost his office for being too stupid). Those few who survived used the position as a springboard to land something more prestigious or lucrative. Faced with Jimbo Brummagem's resignation effective July 31, the trustees had appointed D.U.M. Bakeless to find a replacement. His choice, Phineas Ort, had the respect of all the trustees. But when he withdrew, Bakeless, for reasons of self-interest, formed a search committee that included Mr. Harry Hasty-Pasty and Laura Favoloso.

Agreeing to meet twice weekly in their current digs—a rather tasteless room, long and narrow with white walls and two walnut tables shoved end to end—they waited for Bakeless to return from the men's room, to which he had repaired because of a chronic case of flatulence. The windows, providing the only real amenity, a view of the mountains, attracted several of the search committee members, who perspicaciously observed that if the draught continued, the grass would turn brown.

Gertrude Steif, secretary of the Board of Trustees, a woman admirably schooled in Teutonic promptness by a German father stationed with NATO in Malta as an expert in ordnance, simpered appreciatively when D.U.M. Bakeless returned from the loo just as the clock—and the campus bells—struck three. Dressed in a tasteless see-through blouse that revealed less than the eye might desire, and a skirt that made no ripple as it passed over her butt, she nearly choked when Mr. Hasty-Pasty, a pipefitter, proposed that the committee act on Phineas Ort's suggestion. He observed that in light of Bogus U.'s self-serving faculty and their elephantine egos, its riotous students barely able to read and write, and its administrators regularly bellying up to the table of privilege, the new president should be a person with experience not only in theft, but also in mayhem and murder. Mr. Hasty-Pasty put his novel idea in the form of a motion, and Laura Favoloso seconded it. A brief discussion was followed by a positive vote.

How, though, does a university advertise for a hoodlum? The first people who came to mind were ex-military types, because their battlefield experiences seemed to qualify them for the job. And indeed, a number of colonels and generals received serious consideration. But the committee decided that military strategy and discipline could not command the faith of the faculty. A number of professor/administrators who had long ago abandoned scholarship for swindling also sounded promising. But on closer inspection, their thefts were deemed inconsequential. Given the state legislature's policy of calculated starvation, the search committee knew the next president would have to be a consummate thief. The trustees had had their fill of pickpockets and purse snatchers.

At an impasse, the committee decided to turn to its own members for personal recommendations. The alums, one a realtor, the other a stockbroker, submitted a list of thieves whom they knew from their own lines of work—people engaged in land swindles, price gouging, shoddy workmanship, kickbacks, insider trading, and dishonest accounting procedures. The faculty governance representative demurred, volunteering that since professors had a long history of soul murder, the committee should pick a particularly flagrant violator and promote that person from killing the spirit to killing the body. This recommendation might well have carried the day—it had a religious ring to it—had not D.U.M. Bakeless objected, reminding the members that any candidate the committee selected would have to receive a majority vote from the full Board of Trustees, a group famously suspicious of profs, but not of administrators who had happily left the classroom.

With the members at an impasse, Bakeless adjourned the committee for a week to mull over the alternatives. During the recess, a courier delivered sealed envelopes to the three trustees on the search committee. Each envelope contained $50,000 in cash and a succinct note instructing them to "do what Mr. Hasty-Pasty says." The courier gave lesser sums to the other members of the search committee with the same instructions. For reasons known only to Brooklyn Benny and a higher intelligence, when the group reconvened, it urged Mr. Hasty-Pasty to suggest a slate of finalists. The three trustees, in particular, went out of their way to applaud his selections, a state of affairs that all but Mr. Hasty-Pasty found surprising. Alas, Dame Fortune's wheel turns in inscrutable ways.

MR. HASTY-PASTY RECEIVES A
DISQUIETING TELEPHONE CALL

In the manner of many plots, our story depends on a conjunction of events. To say that it truly began when a flunky interrupted the search committee to say that Mr. Hasty-Pasty had an urgent call would allow that beginnings are knowable. But since even Aristotle and Plato disagree on this point, we will simply say that during the sequence of events, which to some might appear concatenated, Mr. Hasty-Pasty took a call in the outer office from his brother-in-law, Brooklyn Benny. Harry knew of the attempted rub out of Benny but not the details. Well aware of the lack of privacy, Mr. Hasty-Pasty artfully disguised the identity of the caller and the nature of the message.

"Harry," moaned Benny, "I got a job for you."

"You don't sound so good."

"It took twenty-five stitches to sew me up."

"Who done it?"

"A snivelin', no good runty rat: Christy the Chump. Remember him?"

"Sort of," Mr. Hasty-Pasty said without conviction.

"He's a little bag of shit who's scared of his own shadow. I'm told he lammed it to the Rockies."

"It's a big area."

"My contacts say he's hidin' out at your joint, Bogus U."

"Benny, although I am now in the pipefitting business, I don't mess with heaters."

"I am not askin' you to do any rough stuff. No rearrangin' of noses or breakin' of kneecaps. You did your time, and your sister made me promise that I would not lead you into temptation."

"I'm still waiting to hear why you called."

41

"If you can locate the quiverin' coward and set him up, I'll do the rest. You must remember him. He's tongue-tied and, unlike me, ain't got no talent for words. And he can't pass a mirror without stoppin' to look at his-self." In his two years at the university, Mr. Hasty-Pasty had learned enough university lingo to ask, "What is the honorarium?"

"Huh?!"

"The remuneration."

"What's that?"

Smiling at one of the secretaries, who seemed unduly attentive, Mr. Hasty-Pasty decided that culinary code words would be safer than academic ones. "You know, the gravy, the bread, the juice."

"Well, why didn't you say so! Cash on the barrelhead!"

"No small potatoes. For the good of the U., of course."

"Five g's."

"I'll call you back as soon as I find the recipe."

Mr. Hasty-Pasty hung up and smiled at the secretary. "My sister, Dolores. She never did learn to cook. You wouldn't have a free night next week?"

Blushing, the secretary held up her hand to show him a marriage band.

"Lucky guy," said Mr. Hasty-Pasty, "if I'd got there first you'd be married to me. You're Anita, right?" Her appreciative smile told him that he could call her any time in the future for a favor.

MR. HASTY-PASTY EXPLAINS

"You came up with this list on your own?" asked one of the three trustees.

Mr. Hasty-Pasty detected a faint trace of alarm in the question. But with his usual deftness, he dispelled the cloud of unknowing. "If you are wondering how such people would come to my attention, the answer is easy. If you look on the internet under criminology, dot prisons, dot parole, you will find the three most dangerous men paroled in the last several years. They are Three-fingered Tony Pazzia, Paddy I.R.A. Murphy, and Bobby Solomon."

Awed by Mr. Hasty-Pasty's knowledge of crime and computers, which often go hand in hand, the committee members asked how they could contact these men. Laura Favoloso knew them all well, because her mother, Teresa, was Brooklyn Benny's favorite girlfriend. In Laura's youth, when Brooklyn Benny had called on her mother, he often had one of his mugs in tow, to occupy Laura while he bedded the mama. Tony usually took her for ice cream, Paddy for pizzas, and Bobby for lessons at the shooting range. But of course, she could not blow her cover. Instead, she volunteered that if Mr. Hasty-Pasty wanted to put those three names forward as the finalists, she would second the motion.

"Moved and seconded," ruled D.U.M. Bakeless. "Ready for the vote? Those in favor? Those opposed? The motion carries unanimously."

"I move the nominations be closed," said Laura.

D.U.M. Bakeless, delighted by their progress, moved straight ahead. "Those in favor of closing the nominations? Those opposed? Unanimous." He sighed deeply. "We have our three finalists. I will forward their names to the other trustees. If they agree, the search committee can begin the interviews as soon as possible, perhaps as early as next week."

43

It must be admitted that a few of the trustees, normally shameless, openly worried that their endorsement of these finalists might cause among the faint of heart some angina pains. But D.U.M. Bakeless persuaded his colleagues that they should make a virtue of necessity by declaring themselves in favor of giving ex-cons a second chance, in the interests of fair play. The public, gullible enough to have elected a number of outstanding ignoramuses to the Board of Trustees, fell for this explanation when one of the born-again trustees gave it a biblical twist: "Blessed is he whose transgression is forgiven, whose sin is covered" (Psalms 32:1). This trustee, in the manner of a great many scoundrels, twisted the original meaning to suit the group's purposes, and proclaimed that by their forgiving the transgressions and sins of the ex-cons, they were behaving in a blessed manner. Such is the world of biblical exegesis that scholars can always discover in the text what they want to find.

WHAT CHRISTY LEARNED
FROM EAVESDROPPING

By listening assiduously to the confidential discussions, Christy learned when the finalist thugs would be brought to campus to appear before the search committee for their interviews. At one time or another, Christy had worked with all three and could therefore appreciate their records, inside and outside prison. Three-fingered Tony Pazzia specialized in chainsaw assaults, which explained the loss of two fingers. Paddy I.R.A. Murphy preferred bombs and always had about him a slight whiff of cordite. Bobby Solomon, the son of Bobby Solomon, Sr., who had worked for Hank Rodman, liked the quiet efficiency of a baseball bat. All three had in common an imperfect command of the English language and a predilection for shiny silk suits. Christy the Chump hoped to use to his advantage this knowledge and his unerring impressions of faculty behavior.

The schedule called for the committee to interview Pazzia on Monday, Murphy on Wednesday, and Solomon on Friday. The Grand Vizier had flown to Stockholm to make arrangements for his impending retirement in January, at which time he and a blonde Swedish bombshell would take up residence on a small island off the coast, where he planned to sculpt sea birds and lose himself in the realm of the senses. In fact, the trustees had forcefully suggested that he take early retirement owing to the trustees' knowledge of his priapic pursuits. In the Grand Vizier's absence, Christy the Chump had the executive bathroom to himself. From this vantage point he could follow the interviews and, better yet, take note of the post-interview comments.

On Monday, Tony Pazzia showed up smoking a cigar. Christy, listening next door, heard the trustees tell him that the university had a no-smoking policy and he would have to extinguish the stogie. "When I'm prez, first thing, the smokin' rules change." The interview seemed to go swimmingly until Tony made the mistake of asking how much the president earned.

D.U.M. Bakeless proudly declared, "Two hundred and fifty thousand dollars."

"A month or a week?" asked Tony.

At the conclusion of Tony's interview, and with him well out of ear-shot, the committee agreed that no college president should earn more than the football coach, traditionally the highest paid employee in the state. Christy the Chump dutifully noted this fact.

On Wednesday, Paddy I.R.A. Murphy presented himself to the group and immediately announced, "I want yous to know from the start that I don't like killin' dames and kids. But if it's necessary, I get paid double."

After Paddy's interview, the committee members agreed that though he could probably terrorize the faculty, and though he exhibited an admi-rable flexibility, they couldn't abide doubling the pay.

Unfortunately, on Thursday evening, Mr. Hasty-Pasty came down with a virulent flu and hadn't the strength to tell D.U.M. Bakeless that the search committee had now left itself no choice but to take Bobby Solomon.

On Friday, Mr. Robert Joshua Solomon guaranteed the committee that he always wrapped his baseball bat in velvet and never left any marks on his victims.

"There is one thing. I never work on Rosh Hashana or Yom Kippur."

D.U.M. Bakeless, always concerned about saving the taxpayers money, asked, "What do you expect in the way of salary?"

"The right price or no dice," replied Bobby, figuring that his ability to make a rhyme would qualify him for an academic career.

Once Bobby had left, the committee members found themselves split. Half liked the idea of Bobby's velvet touch and his religious scruples, while the other half objected to a president expressing sectarian views. Bakeless broke the tie, voting against Bobby on the grounds that "the right price or no dice" left too much to the imagination, and might lead the university to offer more for his services than was actually necessary.

With the rejection of Bobby Solomon, the bribe-takers now felt ab-solved. Hadn't they held up their end of the bargain? That the candidates fell short was not their doing. In Mr. Hasty-Pasty's absence, the alumni and trustees on the search committee resolved to repair their public im-age, which had suffered when they announced their intention to give ex-cons a second chance. Having paid lip service to a liberal opinion, they retreated to tradition, again nominating chums for the job. The alums, in particular, hoped to see one of their own installed as president, and to that end asked the committee to bring to campus some accomplished land swindlers. The trustees, however, overruled them, proposing that they return to their own vizier, Sejanus Pinchbeck, who had been receiving nibbles from other schools.

"Which proves," said Bakeless triumphantly, "that he must be first-rate."

"Which universities?" one of two profs on the committee asked.

"Latvia Lutheran, Bolivia Baptist, Pomerania Presbyterian, to name just a few," said Bakeless proudly. "Our administrators impress!"

"He's as cold as any fish," remarked a staffer.

D.U.M. Bakeless wisely countered, "Not according to his second wife."

"He's a cheap S.O.B. and a pusillanimous, burned-out scholar," said another prof. "He'd dock the pay of a woman in childbirth. And any decision he arrives at he attributes to a committee."

"Well!" Bakeless huffed, "if she's in labor, she's not in the classroom. I'd call that an admirable economy. As for his being a coward, he walks the campus without an armed guard, even though he's disliked by virtually all the faculty and staff. That shows you he's gutsy. And as for his being burned out, he recently made a major discovery that he published in the *Encyclopedia of Phrenology*: that the skull, if struck hard enough, will swell, sometimes with injurious results." This disclosure might have carried the day had not Laura Favoloso objected.

"But he never broke a kneecap in his life, just the spirit of his faculty. I work in the president's office. Everyone knows that Sejanus Pinchbeck has as much spine as a slug."

The committee, at odds, fell silent. Christy the Chump, hearing the noise of that silence, knew it was now or never.

HOW CHRISTY BECAME
PRESIDENT OF BOGUS U.

Christy cautiously opened the door and entered the meeting room through the Grand Vizier's private entrance. A stunned search committee stared at this man attired in soiled custodial overalls.

"We're not through," said Bakeless, assuming that the intruder had arrived to clean the room.

Had Mr. Hasty-Pasty been present, he would in all likelihood have recognized Christy, especially given Brooklyn Benny's telephone call. Laura Favoloso thought that she had seen this fellow before, but since Christy the Chump did not hold a high position in the Robaccia family, she couldn't be sure. "I think we may have met," she said; "aren't you—"

But her sentence went unfinished, because Christy the Chump, taking Laura's surprised look for approval, blurted out the name he had long wished to have. "Christy the Ch-Chop!"

"Oh, for a moment, I thought you might be someone else," said Laura. "You reminded me of . . ." she mumbled, trailing off.

One of the alums, long an admirer of television cop shows, volunteered an explanation of the word chop. "You know, like you give someone the chop. Kill him. Hit him. Whack him."

Except for Laura, the other members of the committee smiled in appreciation for the translation and looked at Christy in awe. Sensing the pulse of the crowd and knowing what they wanted to hear, he said, "Yeah, I'm c-called Christy the Ch-Chop b-b-because I d-done in s-s-some guys. N-Nothing p-p-personal, you understand. F-For the g-g-good of the m-m-mob."

"You're not on our interview list," said Bakeless, rapidly turning pages to determine if somehow he had failed to notice one of the résumés Mr. Hasty-Pasty had given him.

Laura, fastidious about her English grammar, asked, "For example, whom did you whack?"

Glancing around the room to be sure that uninvited ears weren't listening, he answered in a stage whisper, "B-B-Brooklyn B-B-Benny Bronzino."

WHY LAURA FAVOLOSO
ADMIRED CHRISTY THE CHOP

Married as teenagers in Sicily, Santino and Teresa Favoloso came to the United States and had one child, Laura. They lived in Queens, Long Island, on Jewel Avenue. Santino, a lone operator, rifled cars parked at Kennedy Airport and then fenced the goods. He and his wife raised their daughter to be a straight shooter, literally and figuratively. She attended the exclusive Spence School in Manhattan, graduating at seventeen and winning a scholarship to spend a post-graduation year in Rome, where she perfected her language skills and met a brilliant young lawyer who schooled her in the labyrinthine politics and personal rivalries of the papal court, as well as in the pleasures of sex. Her school record got her admitted to several Ivy League colleges, but she chose to attend Stanford because of its reputation and its distance from Queens. In five years, she had earned a B.A. and an M.A. in English, but decided that in light of the poor academic job market, she would not complete her Ph.D. dissertation on the Irish playwright J. M. Synge. Instead, she took a position at Bogus U. as Brummagem's presidential aide, assisting him with reports and memos and speeches, and making herself indispensable as a sounding board for his ideas and complaints. Before long, as is often the case among presidential staff, she had acquired an inordinate amount of influence.

In her teens, she had lost her father to larceny. One of the cars that he pilfered belonged to the Nocciola family. The fence tipped off the Don, and Santino fled to Patagonia to save his life. When last seen, he was living with a Welsh matron and her three children on a hacienda. Brooklyn Benny, a longtime admirer of Teresa's, cultivated her goodwill by paying off the mortgage on her house. In no time, Brooklyn Benny and Teresa had become lovers. Gabriella Bronzino, Benny's wife, having lost interest in sex after the birth of their eighth child, didn't mind. A good daughter of the Church, she decided that abstinence transcended birth control. Benny never uttered a single complaint. He dutifully and manfully found other women. But his favorite remained the Sicilian beauty Teresa Favoloso.

Laura had inherited her mother's dark radiance. Olive skinned, she had heavy black silky hair and lustrous green eyes. Her small rounded mouth, distinguished by the sensuous curve of her puffed upper lip, and her tall thin figure and ample Latin bosom, which she unabashedly displayed by wearing dresses and blouses that elderly Jewish women call "deep plungers," made men think of greater pleasures to come. A spirited young woman, she usually got her way. Even Brooklyn Benny had noticed her ravishing looks, pinching her butt on several occasions. That behavior had earned him Laura's displeasure, since she had been schooled to believe that women should be neither preyed upon nor pawed. Brooklyn Benny also provoked Laura's ire by urging his two elder sons to court her, though not at the same time. The boys, finding themselves outclassed by her intelligence and wit, wisely decamped, else she might have shot off their testicles. Resignedly, Brooklyn Benny had to admit that his sons lacked the brains and the brass to keep up with La madonna favolosa.

When Laura heard Christy the Chop say that he had killed Brooklyn Benny, she concluded that only a brave man would throttle the head of the Robaccia family. Her mother, she knew, would not want for men. In fact, Teresa had been seeing one of the mugs in the Nocciola family on Sundays, when Brooklyn Benny and his family attended Mass. Although unprepossessing, Christy proved immediately attractive to Laura, who liked ballsy men.

"Did you kill him with a loy?" she asked Christy.

"W-What's that?"

"A farm implement."

"Until n-now, I n-never l-l-left the c-city."

"Did you kill him with a long knife? In the underworld they often use bloody knives."

A scandalized Christy replied, "D-D-Do you take m-me for a b-b-butcher?"

"Was it then a shot in the back of the head with a pistol?"

"I've n-no l-l-license to use a w-weapon. B-B-Besides, I'm a l-law-fearing man."

"Why, I don't believe you killed him at all."

"I c-c-certainly did. He t-turned to his s-s-safe to g-get a g-gun, and I p-p-picked up a p-p-paperweight and c-conked him one on the c-crown. His head b-b-bloomed like a p-p-poppy, and he w-went d-down like a s-s-sack of p-p-potatoes."

Laura smiled wondrously and exclaimed, "Wow!" which led Christy to believe that she admired what he'd done.

"There's a daring fellow," said one of the trustees.

"Oh, glory be to God!" cried one of the staff members.

Understandably, Christy took these expressions as signs of praise and encouragement. Christy the Chump's or Chop's real name was Christopher Mahon. His grandparents and mother had emigrated from County Mayo to New York. So perhaps it was right and proper that the Irish proverb, "Praise a lad and he'll prosper," aptly fit him. The fine words spoken in support of his murderous act miraculously transformed his speech, though not his grammar. For the first time in his adult life, he began to talk without stuttering.

"If anyone crosses me, it's curtains! These overalls, in fact, they're working clothes. I just mopped up." He paused, indescribably glad that he had spoken without stuttering. "Did you hear?" he cried, alluding to his fluent speech. But the others thought he meant: did you hear what I just said about what I do to two-timers?

To a man they all breathlessly said they quite understood. Laura, now fully absorbed in the unfolding scene, earnestly remarked, "It must have been a terrible provocation."

"There was more than one. We go back a long ways. He tried to get me to marry his cross-eyed daughter Maria, who weighs two hundred pounds. He's been raggin' me for years. Just recently, he had me stealin' from parkin' meters in the worst part of town, where the drivers don't put any money in, and the cops turn a blind eye. When I told him that business was bad, he accused me of cheatin' him, and reached for a rod. So I grabbed the paperweight and let him have it."

"You tell a marvelous story," said Laura. "Tell it again."

The other committee members concurred.

"Well, here's how it happened. I pull up at the firehouse knowin' that Brooklyn Benny's inside and the gang has gone. How do I suss this out? I see that only one car is parked outside, a red Cadillac. And that is the color and make of Brooklyn Benny's car. So I figure he is inside. I no sooner enter the door than he begins to yell at me, insultin' my family and callin' me names. Now it is one thing to poor-mouth me, and quite another to pick on my family. Any good son would defend the reputation of his father and grandfather. So I complained and told him that he could not disrespect my ancestors. He sneered and swiveled in his chair to open the safe that holds guns and ammo. I knew I had to act. My eyes scanned the desk. His letter opener was layin' there but, like I said, I'm no butcher. So I snatched the paperweight—the very one that he likes so much because his name is

Benny and the scene encased in the glass is of Big Ben—and I brought it down on the top of his head with a whack. His chair slowly revolved bringing Benny face to face with me. Before he fell, I could see his eyes closed, his mouth open, and his head a geyser of red. Washin' off the paperweight, I put it back on the desk and eased out the window. No one was around."

"Courage takes practice, and as anyone can see, you've had a lot of it," Laura said for the benefit of the others, convinced that she would propose Christy the Chop for president of Bogus U., and function as his indispensable tutor and guide.

"That's a grand story," said one alum. "You tell it lovely."

Overcome with wonder and satisfaction, Christy volunteered to tell it a third time. But D.U.M. Bakeless said that he had a clear picture of Christy's accomplishments.

"But I didn't describe what poetic thoughts crossed my mind while gazin' at the bridge, its glorious span, its lyrical loops of cable, its majestic towers and brilliant stonework—"

Bakeless interrupted. "I must rule any aesthetic discussions out of order. Although I myself admire painting and the plastic arts, we never allow beauty to influence our decisions."

"At last," declared Laura, "we have our president! I so move."

"Maybe now," said one of the staff members, "we can disband the committee and go home."

"First, we vote," said Bakeless. "Do I hear a second?"

The same staff member, keen to retreat to the recreation center, where he made it a point at the end of each day to stand under a hot shower for thirty minutes, seconded the motion.

"Any further discussion?"

The rigid Myrtle Steif, whose abhorrence of indiscipline Christy exacerbated and whose disdain for this unlettered fellow in overalls she could barely hide, said tartly, "Mr. Mahon, you understand, don't you, that Bogus U. expects the new president—whoever he is!—to speak and comport himself like a gentleman and to start work August 1, because President Brummagem goes to trial that month for conspiracy to defraud."

Christy the Chop assured her that his work came before his personal life. He could start today if they wished.

Bakeless then requested Christy to step outside. Of course, Christy merely repaired to the Grand Vizier's office and took up his post at the bathroom vent.

"All in favor?" asked Bakeless. "All opposed? It's unanimous, except for Allan."

"I'm abstaining," said Allan, one of the alums, "because I still think a realtor would have been the man for the job. The U. will need to expand. To destroy old homes and neighborhoods, to steal properties, and to deface the land will require experience. Who better than a realtor?"

Laura, fearful that Allan's comments might cause the others to reconsider their vote, observed, "Bogus U. has a long and proud history of violating the trust of the community. I can't imagine that Christy the Chop would dishonor that tradition. He will fit right in with the fools and the feckless, the liars and the louts. You can hear it in his storytelling. He's not the least bit interested in an idea, just in the story. Doesn't that characterize Bogus U.?"

THE FULL BOARD
OF TRUSTEES VOTES

To assuage any lingering doubts, the trustees decided that a private meeting with Christy would enable them to raise the kinds of questions they dared not ask with alumni, faculty, and staff present. When Christy arrived, he looked around and happily noted the absence of Ms. Steif, who had assumed her new duties as executive secretary for the viziers. Wearing a double-breasted black suit, a silver shirt and matching tie, and wing-tip shoes, he displayed in his vest coat pocket a red handkerchief. A toothpick, which he had forgotten to toss aside, lodged in the corner of his mouth. The effect of his dress and the lumber merely reinforced Bakeless's report and persuaded the trustees that here stood the hit man that could lead them to the Promised Land.

"What did it feel like?" asked one of the trustees.

"I ain't followin'."

"To kill someone."

"Hell, there've been so many I don't feel nothin' no more. You know, like it's second nature."

Admiringly, one of the trustees remarked, "Nerves of steel . . . no conscience . . . I like that."

Trustee Bakeless said, "You never use a gun or a knife. What do you use?"

Christy, trapped by his own bragging, hemmed and hawed. "Uh, I've got my ways."

A flurry of excited questions followed.

"You must know a lot about poisons—"

"Or blunt instruments—"

"Maybe it's choking you prefer—"

"I read about a fellow who always resorted to a rope—"

"Did you ever drown a man?"

Christy affected a sneer. "You all heard of *omertá*? The oath of silence. I can't say nothin'. That way no one gets hurt. *Capish?*"

To a man, they said they did.

Trustee Woodrow Hardwood suddenly insisted on a point of order. "How can we offer the presidency to Mr. Mahon," he said, "unless we're sure he will agree on our terms?"

"Shoot!" said Christy, a word that elicited nervous laughter.

Each trustee set forth his expectations.

D.U.M. Bakeless apologized that the job paid only $250,000 a year— and no more—and hoped that Christy wouldn't mind.

Lowering his eyes in the best manner of a choir boy, Christy said, "I live a simple life and can therefore live on less. Now if that ain't puttin' the U. before the Y-O-U, then correct me."

Trustee Frank Edsel, a successful used-car dealer, reminded Christy that the president had to elevate the football team above other interests and agree to pay the coach a million dollars.

"Is that all you pay him?" Christy said. "Hell, that's peanuts. In the south, where they know what a university is for, they cough up twice that amount. It's the pigskin that matters, not the sheepskin."

Trustee Marvin Pismo, a weight lifter and health-food addict, inquired about his willingness to recruit ex-cons to play football.

"I believe in diversity."

"Even," said Pismo, "if they don't have the academic record?"

"Hell," said Christy, "they got something better, a criminal record!"

Trustee Norman Digital, a proctologist, who usually buried himself in his work and said little, wanted assurances that he could reverse the red ink.

"Hey, this is America. There ain't no free lunches. My policy won't be pay as you go, but cough up first or don't show."

Trustee Herman Lewdoff, a retired general who wished that respect for authority could be instilled in the civilian population, emphasized the importance of Christy maintaining a tight grip on the campus.

"Ach, from vat I see the faculty vaste endless time in meetings, and nothing around here, even at the top, ever gets accomplished. Vere is the steel, the iron discipline?"

"Under this roof we'll have rules and results. Any lip from some gasser and I'll blow him away."

Trustee Peter Feather worried about all the pending sexual harassment cases, particularly the one against Grand Vizier Cummings. "How will you deal with them?"

Unaccustomed as he was to acknowledging women's rights, Christy pondered the question. When he answered, he felt as if he were standing outside the person who spoke, as if observing himself. "Hey, this is the twenty-first century. America ain't what it used to be."

Feather smiled and added, "Sometimes settling is cheaper than going to court."

"Thanks, I'll remember that," said Christy.

Trustee Theodore Boodle, a timorous fellow, afraid to be direct, observed that a president had to be a skilled fundraiser.

"Before Brooklyn Benny and me parted ways, I helped him raise tons of dough for his church. All it took was one pipe bomb goin' off at the country club and all the members signed on as donors. I learned from the best: fundraisin' through gun raisin'."

Trustee Gerald Jackson, who had a passing interest in education, hazarded the opinion that it would be an improvement if the students could read and write when they graduated, and that far too many undeserving students graduated with honors and A's.

"My motto will be: either read or bleed; learn to write or else goodnight. As for all them high grades, I'll put the faculty on a quota system."

Trustee Hardwood, never one to mince words, admitted that he was squeamish about Christy's criminal background and patois, and boldly asserted that although he could overlook Christy's felonious past, he had reservations about Christy's ungrammatical street talk. Given that the president would have to speak to fraternal organizations, church groups, alumni, and parents, Christy would have to amend his language. "After all," said Hardwood, drawing on his readings in American criminal history, "Willie Sutton spoke like a gentleman—and he succeeded as a thief."

Christy had actually heard of Willie "the actor," the slick dandy who frequented parties with actors and celebrities. In fact, more than once, Christy had wished that he himself could speak elegantly and move in the company of spiffy women. He therefore replied, "No sweat, just give me a month's time and I'll be spoutin' English like the Queen."

Trustee Hardwood said that Christy's candor had put to rest his concerns. Trustee Digital, however, held up his middle finger, his professional one. "Gentlemen, you seem to have forgotten," he said to his colleagues, "the tenure case of Professor Monroe Larson."

The trustees apologetically acknowledged their oversight with comments such as "Norman is right," "How could we?" "How silly of us," "The fate of the football team rests on it."

D.U.M. Bakeless suppressed a burp by clearing his throat and assumed a magisterial posture in preparation to lie.

"The Board of Trustees is often called upon to micromanage the campus. Every day we receive calls of complaint from faculty and administrators, from students and staff. But we studiously avoid getting involved. Micromanagement is tantamount to," and here he paused, wanting to relish the right word, when Hardwood interjected.

"Meddling."

"Interfering," said Jackson.

"Intruding," said Pismo.

"Tampering," said Boodle.

"Butting in," said Feather.

"The campus should be run by the president, not the trustees," said Lewdoff.

Recovering from his lost moment, Bakeless said, "We of course are the body that grants tenure, but our governance laws require the president's signature, lest we undermine the due process of the campus."

"At the very least," added Edsel, "there has to be the appearance of democratic procedures. We are not tyrants."

"Far from it," said Hardwood.

"Therefore," continued Bakeless, "we would like you to make the recommendation, sign it, and forward it to us. That way, we stay within our own laws, as well as preserve the authority of your office. The last thing we want to hear is the faculty saying that the decision came from us."

"Precisely!" said a satisfied Digital. "My thoughts exactly. Trustee Bakeless, you have a way of hitting the hole on the head."

Bakeless beamed, oblivious of the mixed metaphor.

Christy could understand the requests for a disciplined campus, a winning football team, money-making operations, an end to sexual-harassment suits, even a well-educated student body. But he found the tenure request perplexing. "First of all, what's with this tenure business? Second, why the fuss?"

Bakeless patiently explained the meaning of academic tenure and its importance, concluding with the observation that the Larson case was to some people, though not the trustees, a vexed case.

"You're the Dons. You call the shots. Do what you want. Otherwise, what's the good of bein' the boss of the bosses?"

"Perhaps you misunderstood. The procedure requires your signature. We can express our feelings from behind the scenes, but you have to be the actor on stage. Appearances count."

Christy studied his cuticles and decided he needed a manicure. "Appearances, you say. Then I'm nothing but a puppet."

"This is Puppet Hall," said Pismo facetiously; "just joking."

Trustee Edsel said impatiently, "We've spent enough time on this matter. There's really nothing to it. All you have to do is sign a contract recommending tenure for Professor Monroe Larson. We'll approve it, the young man will have the lifetime job that he wants, and the Wildebeests will be well on the road to a bowl game. Bakeless, as far as I'm concerned, it's time to announce that Christy Mahon will be installed as the sixteenth president of Bogus U."

Though still not clear about the meaning of tenure, Christy thanked the trustees, all of whom concurred with Edsel.

CHRISTY MEETS
THE GRAND VIZIER

Paying due deference to rank and acknowledging that Grand Vizier Cummings Dailey would soon be leaving the university, Christy invited him to his office.

A fair-haired fellow with a degree in wood turning, Cummings Dailey specialized in gully yodeling and fancied himself a Lothario. The faculty familiarly called him "Tuna Taco." His legendary sexual appetite led some of his detractors to say that he could not pass an aperture, even a keyhole, without trying to insert his pecker. Other detractors, nastier ones, said that given the size of his putz, the keyhole story was by no means apocryphal. Married to a long-suffering woman of admirable restraint, he made it a point to get her out of town as often as possible. On those occasions, his neighbors would make book on the time it would take from the moment his wife left until one of his girlfriends drove up to the house (Dailey liked his women to come to him). The longest wait ran to 93 minutes; the shortest, five minutes 46 seconds. Watching from their living room windows, his neighbors knew that as soon as the electric garage door rose, an automobile would soon be arriving. Inevitably the car would pull into the garage and the door would close behind it.

A second pool concerned how long the woman would remain in the house, for Dailey sometimes had two and three ladies visit him in a day, and a third pool the length of time it would take for the next car to pull up. If none appeared, the money remained in the pool until the next day, when the game would ineluctably continue.

That he managed to complete any work at the office was owing to the fact that he surrounded himself with competent staff. As a lowly professor he had learned that first-rate teaching and scholarship require painstaking labors; he therefore eased himself into administration at the first opportu-

60

nity. Eventually the trustees, who had known for years about his behavior, were called on the carpet by some state reps who espoused "family values"; the trustees therefore offered him a retirement package he couldn't resist. It came at an ideal time for Cummings; his wife had decided to leave him, and he had taken up with a Nordic naiad whom he had met the previous June in Sweden, where he was ostensibly conducting riparian research but really sporting through the long days of summer light.

The night before his meeting with the new president, Dailey retired late. He dreamed, not surprisingly, about buttocks, bosoms, and buttons. Finding himself in an old three-story Victorian house that bore a strange resemblance to the one in which his first sexual conquest had lived, he thrust open the front door and entered. On every floor he was greeted by a naked woman, on the first by a Miss Juicy Dally, who cupped one pendulous breast in her hand and invited him to have "a suck" and "to show me your manhood." He fondled her breasts but, thinking her looks rather ordinary, refused her offer of lovemaking and proceeded to the second floor, where he encountered another naked woman, a Miss Bubbles Berband, lovely in every regard. He wanted to ravish her, especially when she held out her arms and asked him to enter her before she died of desire. But his organ suddenly deserted him; it just wouldn't respond. He reproached himself for not taking two Viagras before leaving home. His only recourse was to promise her that he would shortly return to ride his cock horse to her Banbury Cross. Ascending to the third floor, he saw yet another naked, succulent woman, Fluffy Richards. Without so much as a word, they devoured each other's lips and ran their hands over and into every erogenous zone. This time his steed rose and stood on its hind legs. Praising it, she guided the swollen member through her lubriciously wet gates of paradise. In the satyr's Eden he sported like a porpoise, playing sucky-fucky and restraining himself in order to sustain the immeasurable pleasure she gave him. Withdrawing without losing his precious white fluid, he promised Fluffy that he would always be there to comfort her muff and help her career. When the blood returned to his throbbing joy stick, he repeated his licorice labors—until he came in his pajamas, awoke, and remembered that he and Christy Mahon had an appointment, one that would preclude his leaving the office early for a much-anticipated assignation.

Christy politely asked him how he wished to be addressed.

"Tuna," replied Dailey amiably, as they shook hands.

"Make yourself comfortable," said Christy.

Tuna sat down and stretched his legs. He figured from what he had heard that Christy would wink at his indiscretions.

Seeing no need to bluff, Christy put his cards on the table. "Bogus is broke. Any ideas for raising money?"

"No doubt about it. We need to raise the level of giving . . . erect it to a point of prominence . . . and plunge in. Unless we score, you know, go over the mountain, we'll never satisfy the itch. We could offer an escort service for visiting alumni. That would jack off, I mean, jack up donations. Then when they come, they'll want to keep coming—and remember who pumped them up. And if they can't get a stander, we can always ask the medical school to specialize in meat injections. Given the number of men in America who have such problems, we could clean up, even open a women's clinic."

"That doesn't sound kosher to me," said Christy, who knew a few Yiddish words, though he had never tasted kosher food in his life.

"Hell, it's the oldest profession in the world. Ever been to Amsterdam? Now that's how to merchandise it . . . women sitting in store windows giving everyone a gold-plated gander. We have some coeds and secretaries—whew, I could tell you a few things about the latter that would make you drool. Justine Dallas, WOW!" He pumped a clenched fist in the air. "Hell, some of those secretaries could make us a fortune. I've just been waiting for the right kind of president to come along. Brummagem thought nothing of knocking it off on the side, but he refused to capitalize on all our natural resources. I figure you for a different sort of guy."

In truth, Christy liked women and had known women (in the biblical sense) from his teenage years, but his strict Catholic upbringing militated against pimping. Besides, he knew that Tuna, at the request of the trustees, would be leaving the university in January, and Christy, still unfamiliar with the U., didn't know anyone else who could run a stable. So he thanked Tuna for his help and moved on to the pressing matter of his sexual indiscretions.

"Three dames," he said, eyeing a report from the legal office, "claim that you—"

"Only three?" Dailey interrupted incredulously. "There must be some mistake."

"Then you don't deny. . . ?"

"That there were dozens? Not at all. Petty crooks go to jail; big crooks run the country. I have always lived by the precept that one should sin with amplitude and panache. It shows regard for the American dream."

On that declarative note, Dailey took his leave.

THE PLOTTERS

In a fashionable hillside house tastelessly but expensively furnished, the three viziers sipped martinis and discussed how they could rid the university of Christy Mahon. Having met him the day before, they all agreed he was a cancer in the academic body, needing to be removed either by poison, or bullet, or knife.

Each of the viziers, of course, was convinced that he would be the one to replace the deposed thug.

Vizier Brigham Pyrosis, a cadaverous fellow whose capillary system showed through his skin, making his face look like a hematological map, had left the lecture room for the boardrooms of administration because three hundred minutes a week did not offer him enough scope for speechifying. A student of coprolite—the fossilized excrement of animals—he never failed to tell a crowd that you can learn a great deal from the ancient droppings: for example, animal diets, diseases, digestive systems, and the plant life of the period. Handpicked by Brummagem to be his future replacement, Pyrosis had been biding his time, waiting for the call that had not yet come. In the position of Brummagem's right-hand man, he had served uncomplainingly as a hewer of wood and a drawer of water, driving him to meetings and, when the president had drunk too much—alas, a rather frequent occurrence—sitting in for him and assuming his duties. When reporters asked why Brummagem's car was parked overnight outside a particular woman's house, Pyrosis fielded the questions and garrulously bored the newspeople into silence. Sadly, Brummagem's derailment sidetracked Pyrosis's chances. Well aware of Sejanus Pinchbeck's vaulting ambitions, Pyrosis had watched gleefully as Sejanus failed to make the short list, trusting piously that by keeping a low profile and faithfully carrying out the tasks asked of him, he would eventually displace the Irish street punk, and move from Puppet Hall into Tinnitus House.

Vizier Bill A. Stine had learned from his barber that the way to make people like you is to make them feel good about themselves; and from observing American universities he had discovered that an absence of thought was no obstacle to a learned position, with a modest salary and a modicum of prestige. Years before, he'd figured out that elementary-school teaching would never exhaust his few resources; even if he showed up unprepared, he could always make it through each day's classes, since the canned lesson plans included questions and a list of assignments at the end of every chapter. As a result, he entered the school system and devoted his free time to microbrewing. The grading of papers, which devoured the lives of most teachers, Bill fobbed off on a succession of student teachers, all of whom shortly left the profession.

A product of public education, he chose to give back to the taxpayers what they had given him: a free ride. This beneficence took the form of a lavish distribution of "A" grades, which produced such glowing performance reports that he decided to attend graduate school, where owing to the grace of God and the absence of a foreign language requirement he received his degree.

The first few years, Bill wallowed in a welter of witless schools—the names are too many to reproduce here—until he wrote his magnum opus, a brief but stunning article that took the world of pedagogy by storm and earned him a position at Bogus U. It read:

How To Improve Student Learning
by
Bill A. Stine

1. Make students feel good about their writing, no matter how poor it is.
2. Make students feel good about their reading, no matter how halting it is.
3. Make students feel good about themselves, no matter how uncivilly they behave.
4. Advise students to praise others so that they may be praised in return.
5. Think positively and never criticize; all criticism is negative.

This article caught the eye of Bogus U.'s School of Propaedeutics, which promptly offered Bill a job in the hope that he could help the school improve its woeful academic ratings.

Bill did not disappoint. Shortly after arriving on campus, he published a second important article, this one entitled: "How Do You Know When a Child Is Ready to Read?" Although most scholars had heretofore thought that reading readiness was related to a knowledge of the alphabet or inquisitiveness about words, like those that appear on billboards and road signs, Bill proved them all wrong. Instead, he contended that children were ready to read when they could identify the following elements of a book: the cover; the title; the beginning; the words; the direction to read lines and turn a page. These discoveries left the educational establishment breathless.

But it was when he applied for an administrative position that good fortune struck. As the *Evening Lens*, the local paper, reported: "Yesterday afternoon, in executive session, the Board of Trustees selected Bill A. Stine to fill the vacant post of Vizier to the Faculty. The trustees cited as the principal reason for their selection his adaptability and also his ability to negotiate treacherous terrain without causing harm. Readers of this paper may remember that just a few weeks ago, as theater-goers and diners were crowding the Main Street sidewalk one evening, Stine drove his SUV around the tables and through the throngs without hitting a single person, or tipping over a single glass, or spilling a single drop from his own bottle, lodged between his thighs."

Once in Puppet Hall, Stine surrounded himself with staff who could add, subtract, and write his memoranda. Exuding a disarming compassion, he nodded appreciatively when others brought their problems to him, promised that he would make every effort to help, and moved on to the next problem.

Vizier Sejanus Pinchbeck had been told at three years old that he was the most gifted child on the block, and that someday he would make his mark in the world. Never one to doubt the wisdom of his parents, he had earned his degree at an Ivy League school and counted on finding a job at one of the premiere institutions. When nothing materialized except a small college in Missouri, his preening self-regard suffered immeasurably. He expressed his indignation by refusing to be wrong—for surely, in a minor league outfit like Bogus, there could be no one likelier than himself to be right.

The upcoming meeting with the president had put him in a state of high excitement. During such times he discharged his nervous energy through tonsorial attentions to his thinning hair and his dearly beloved mustache—leonine, lustrous, ludicrous—which hid a meandering nose. Applying a Venetian formula, he had painted the soup strainer until the last gray hair disappeared. A head with strands of silver hair he thought gave him a continental look, but his mustache had to be jet. He reached for a tweezers to pluck an offending hair that refused to darken to his taste, but thought better of such rashness and merely cut it back to the skin.

Returning the tweezers to the drawer, he noticed the letter that Margaret, his first wife, had sent him after she walked out. It lay underneath the manicure set she'd given him, the one in a handsome leather case. She had borne his coldness in the hope that she could melt his self-worship and make him look outward, at others, at her. But she soon realized that his aloofness, which had initially seemed so sophisticated, was nothing but the absence of feeling. He had never really learned how to express warmth with a touch or a gesture and, as a result, he either refrained from any physical contact or awkwardly groped. The first time she recoiled from him, he knew the marriage would fail. As he gazed at the envelope, unopened for years, his thoughts migrated to her. She had a way with words—and with other women. He had always prided himself on being a lady's man, but she proved more successful than he with her numerous female companions, some of whom he secretly wished to bed. Reaching for the letter, he paused. Did he really want to read her hurtful words again? It had taken him a long time to convince himself that her bill of particulars had no merit. But even so, he had kept her letter, a sign that he recognized as telling. With Caroline, his current wife, out of town, he had the house to himself. Thinking about Caroline, he smiled at his good luck; she brought to the union not only wealth from her successful business enterprises but also mental compatibility. She agreed with him, for example, that Bogus U. was merely a temporary stop on his way to bigger and better pickings. Caroline would never have written a letter to correct his behavior. On those occasions when she disagreed with him—he took great pains to stay on her sunny side—she merely arched her eyebrows, twisted her wrist in a gesture of dismissal, and turned away. He knew not to question those semaphores.

Sucking a stuffed olive—all that remained of this third martini—Bill A. Stine confessed that although a gentle man by nature, he had, on occasion, both killed and imbibed a few spirits. Sejanus, unamused by Bill's wit and unaccustomed to strong drink, opined in slurred speech that the time was ripe for deposing Christy. "I'm all ears," declared Pyrosis. "I'll pay for dirty tricks, but I want no part in them." When Sejanus scoffed that a payoff was the same as pulling the trigger, Pyrosis said, "Then our taxes make us culpable for murder, whether on a battlefield or in an electric chair." This statement, the most perspicacious that Pyrosis ever uttered, left his two colleagues speechless.

A clock ticked. A dog barked. Recovering their senses, the men engaged in some shallow moralizing about Judeo-Christian ethics and agreed that each of them would put up ten thousand dollars to pay for a hit man. But how would they find such a person? Pyrosis suggested an ad in *Soldier of Fortune* magazine. Stine proposed university custodians, who were always poor and mostly foreign, and ventured that if Christy crossed the Athletic Director, they had their man.

"Ee-she," said Pinchbeck, struggling to regain control of his tongue. "Jush look at the shape of . . . um . . . someone's head."

The skepticism that greeted Pinchbeck's suggestion led him once again to defend his doctorate in phrenology and to promote the virtues of "bumpology." He explained that what people call the mind was an unscientific term for the brain, an organ that directs all our faculties, like speech and movement. Each faculty resides in a particular part of the brain. As our faculties develop, they affect brain size and shape. For example, on autopsy, London taxi drivers, who have phenomenal spatial memories, exhibit a highly developed right hippocampus. The larger the brain part, the more effective it is. And because brain size determines the contours of the cranium, the surface of the skull can be read as an accurate map of the person's psychological propensities and attributes.

He hiccupped and injudiciously concluded, "Perhaps I shouldn't say so, but, um, the shape of my own head indicates, um, I have a genius for leadership, a finding that, um, led me to leave the classroom for administration."

Alas, the other viziers were too brain numb to tell Sejanus that days are like scrolls, and that one should engrave on them only what you want remembered.

THE VIZIERS EXPRESS
AN OPINION

Christy, for politic reasons, had decided to consult with the viziers about the Monroe Larson case.

"Where do you stand, Bill?"

Bill felt faint. His hands shook. He motioned toward the bar.

"At this hour? You must be kidding. Try a glass of water and two Alkies instead. I've got a pocketful."

Bill broke into a sweat, thumped his chest, sighed, and pleaded, "I'm only a cog, nothing more. A gear. A—"

"Just give me a yes or a no."

"Whatever you want done, President Mahon, just ask," said Bill, his mouth smiling but not the rest of his face. "I specialize in carrying out orders."

"No ideas of your own?"

"I never go there. It's too dangerous. Besides, my mind doesn't work that way."

"Bill, I can see you're on to somethin'. I think we can work together."

"Like I said: whatever you want done, I'm your man."

To test Bill's mettle further, Christy asked, "From your point of view, how come we got a problem on our hands?"

"Tenure decisions are always the most difficult, because there are good arguments on both sides. I can give you the reasons for saying yes and for saying no."

"Which side do you lean to?"

Bill could see that he would have to answer the president's question. "As painful as this decision has been . . . and Lord knows I have prayed and looked into my heart and studied the record . . . but since the trustees want it, I would have to say that . . ."

"You want it."

"I suppose so, but I could be convinced otherwise."

Christy grudgingly admired Bill A. Stine for having at least one virtue: he knew himself. He knew his own weightlessness.

While Christy shuffled papers, Sejanus, seeing Bill's discomfort, tried to apply the coup de grâce. "Did you, um, know, Bill, that President Mahon's family comes from, um, County Mayo?"

"Really?"

Without looking up, Christy mumbled, "Yeah, that's right."

"I've, um, visited," said Sejanus. "Lovely, um, area. Ever been, Bill?"

Stine thought hard. "Is that where Virginia Mayo comes from?"

Christy said, "Come on, you musta heard of the potato blight?"

"Really," Bill exclaimed, "here in the west? When did it start?"

"Never mind," said Christy, making a mental note that putty has its purposes.

Sejanus smiled at the thought of how deftly he had caught Bill in his snare.

"Brigham, what's your opinion about this guy Larson?"

Pyrosis, convinced that analogical arguments are the most persuasive, said, "To get to the nub of this disagreement is like getting to the kernel of coprolite. You have to chip away the exterior, but once you do, you find the layers of petrified excrement. Little details, from specks to granules, will provide you with a world of information. For example, on one dig that I participated in—"

Christy cut him off, wondering how this guy ever accomplished anything. But maybe that was the point—he didn't, and no one cared.

"What's the cost, one way or the other?" Christy asked.

"Tenure is a million dollar investment," explained Pyrosis, glad to be lecturing again. "Our actuarial tables show that over a lifetime a professor can expect to earn at least a million dollars. Of course, recently we have been cutting down on that expense by hiring part-timers and instructors who give us a ready labor supply without the worry of tenure. In the Larson case, the special interests are so many and so influential that I would advise," and here he drew himself up and straightened his tie, prepared to play the role of valued presidential counselor, "a yes vote—depending, of course, on what university counsel has to say."

"The hell with the lawyers. Just tell me: does Larson deserve it?"

"Competence is not a consideration at this level. That's for the department to decide."

"The department said no."

"That's why the case has landed on your desk. It's on appeal. Now there are three types of appeal: procedural error, for example, not everyone qualified to vote got a ballot, discrimination, such as blackballing Uzbeks, and substance, which means an issue of great magnitude, like a person owning history-making letters that will shortly be published. Now, as to those letters Monroe found . . . we cannot overestimate the importance of letters in providing a window on history. I learned that in college. Letters enable the dead to speak, the past to come alive, the private thoughts of people to be known, the secrets of governments to come to light, the epistolary adornments of the age to shine through, and the handwriting to provide a wealth of material to graphologists. Letters, letters, you have no idea how important letters are to the world because without them . . ."

Bill suppressed a yawn and Sejanus recalled parts of Margaret's letter:

Insensitivity to the powerless earns only their silent disdain. The university janitors, the freshman composition teachers, the dishwashers, the secretaries and clerks keep you from the muck of this world. Treat them well. If you go out of your way to be generous, they will repay you with faithful service. To this moment, I can hear you bragging—in front of people who could barely pay the rent—that you had the means to retire at any time, that you could just retreat to your boat and put your feet on the gunwales. Know your audience, and even if your listeners do not earn much, respect them.

It is quite apparent that you like your female colleagues to be simpering and simple. Those with gem-like intelligence put you off your game. Many women are smarter than you. Use their talents. You have the brains to appreciate high culture. Yet how many times have I teased you about your lack of history and philosophy and literature? Try moving up from The Lion King. Attend classical music concerts and serious plays. Visit museums and galleries. Know the difference between Caravaggio and Chianti.

The written language is not your strong suit, nor is oratory; but you can improve your speech by simply removing all the "ums." I used to sit at faculty parties and count them. They ran into the hundreds. Since you have designs on higher office, you will want to upgrade your public speaking. Watch for the bored looks, and learn from them. You will undoubtedly meet another woman, someone who has more patience than I do. Show her that you are educable, that you can become something better than you are. Don't disappoint me. One day, I want to be able to look back and say, "Behold the man; change is possible."

Honestly yours,

Margaret Kaplan Pinchbeck

"Sejanus, do you think any change on my part is called for?" Pause. "Sejanus!"

Pinchbeck snapped out of his reflection. "What's that?"

"Any change in the Monroe Larson recommendation."

Ignorant of the context, Sejanus fell back on his usual pose of intellectual superiority. "I, um, feel confident that Monroe Larson's, um, scholarly discovery—a project, um, I'm proud to have sponsored—will shortly put Bogus on the scholarly map."

"The record looks pretty thin."

Pinchbeck slapped his forehead as if beseeching the president to tell him that he had misunderstood what he'd heard. "Surely you can't, um, be speaking of Professor Larson!"

"The guy with the so-called letters."

"Do you realize, um, what you're saying!"

"I know a million-dollar scam when I see one."

"Sir, you are, um, making a mistake that will go down, um, as one of the great blunders of the century."

"I haven't decided anything yet. I just want to see the goods before I buy."

Had Pinchbeck been a man of biblical bent, he might have said, "Oh, ye of little faith." But being a phrenologist, he cried, "Monroe's cephalic index, um, indicates brilliance, genius, success. How can you say—!"

"That some guy may be tryin' to sell a pig in a poke? Easy. I worked with con men who depend on suckers like you and your pals."

While Pinchbeck angrily scribbled notes on his writing pad, Christy tossed aside the Monroe Larson file and opened another. "I'm told that the president has at his disposal a million smackers that he gives each year to the football team. True?"

Bill A. Stine and Sejanus Pinchbeck gladly remained silent. They knew that Brigham took for his province athletics, and that Christy was likely to put him on the griddle.

Vizier Pyrosis answered with one syllable, "Yes," a feat of language that he never again repeated for the rest of his life.

"I heard you was lookin' after the green till a new prez got picked."

"My reputation for probity is well known. Frankly, it goes back to my childhood, when I found a nickel in the hall and gave it to my teacher. Then there was the time a clerk gave me too much change—"

Christy again interrupted. "Cut to the chase!"

Vizier Pyrosis blanched. Even though such a phenomenon seems impossible, his colorless skin became even paler. Christy poured a glass of water from the carafe and dropped in two Alka-Seltzers.

"Although last year, we hit bottom—you know, bankrupt!—we were able," he explained with a smile meant to ingratiate, "to put aside, for the special needs of the athletic department and, in particular, the football team, a certain sum of money."

"How much?"

"One million dollars, which we deposited in the president's discretionary fund, with the understanding that the money would go only to the gridiron."

"And if I don't?"

"Don't what, President Mahon?"

"Use it for football."

A hush fell over the room that resembled the one visited upon the Garden of Eden when the Lord first learned of man's disobedience.

"You're not serious!" Pyrosis exclaimed, mopping his brow and popping a glycerin pill for his heart.

"'Fraid I am. I got other plans for the dough. So make sure it ain't spent on petrified shit. I'll hold you personally responsible if it is. I don't like anyone crookin' me, *capish?* You guys can take off."

With Stine's and Pinchbeck's help, Pyrosis staggered out of the meeting and collapsed in a chair outside. A secretary asked him if he required medical attention, and he said yes. In fact, that night the university hospital installed a pacemaker in Brigham Pyrosis's chest.

CHRISTY AND MR. HASTY-PASTY
COME FACE TO FACE

They gassed over lunch a few days after Christy's selection as the new playboy, that is, president of Bogus U. Since Brooklyn Benny had agreed to lie low until Mr. Hasty-Pasty could entice Christy to Sun Valley, Mr. Hasty-Pasty omitted telling Christy that Benny was alive and kicking. No need to make the mark anxious.

"Christy, who could have imagined! You, the chief honcho," said Mr. Hasty-Pasty, warmly extending his hand. "You, the new king of the hill."

Christy failed to return the greeting.

"What's that you got in your paw?"

Sheepishly, Christy pocketed a small mirror. "Just countin' the gray hairs."

"You've changed. I would hardly have recognized you."

"So you noticed."

"How could I miss it? You don't stutter no more."

"What can I do for you?"

"Terrible, ain't it, about Brooklyn Benny?"

"My condolences to your old lady, Harry. I'm sure he was a good brother to her."

"None better. But she'll get over it. After all, he left her sitting pretty."

"Really?"

"Yeah, the guy who beaned him neglected to look in the safe. Benny had millions stored there."

Of course this statement had no basis in truth, but it had the desired result. Christy Mahon's lower jaw went slack (upper jaws can't move); he broke out in a sweat; and his skin turned a jaundiced yellow. "You gotta," he gulped, "be kiddin'. Just my luck . . ."

"Forget it," said Harry, interrupting Christy's train of thought. "Let me show you around. There's the campus above ground and the steam room below, with all its tunnels and levels and plumbing and pipes. If you need to hide, it's a hell of a place."

Although initially skeptical, Christy decided that maybe Harry had a point. A good hiding place was indispensable.

"Do you mind if I pick up my aide?"

"Go right ahead," said Harry.

They walked across the lawn to the president's offices, and Christy asked Laura to join them.

Harry led them to the power plant, five minutes away. Inside, a tracery of pipes ran overhead, and enormous conduits disappeared through the floor. The vast generators that power a university labored in oil and steam and thunderous noise. Clapping his hands to his ears, Harry shouted: "Follow me!"

He led them to a metal staircase that descended for three floors to a steel door that opened into a tunnel with track lighting overhead. They followed it downward, past connecting tunnels, one level, then another, their constant companion the sound of steam and water gurgling through enormous pipes running along the walls. Finally they reached the basement floor, a large open space, and here, to Christy's and Laura's amazement, a river of water ran through an open viaduct that fed an enormous walk-in refrigeration unit. Unlike the floors above, the basement registered nearly freezing, and inside the unit, the temperature stood at ten degrees Fahrenheit.

"It does a good job powering the university's air conditioning," said Mr. Hasty-Pasty, "but unfortunately requires constant monitoring. Right now there are probably four or five people, wearing Arctic gear, inside servicing it. The turnover's terrible. We can't get people to work year round in such cold conditions."

"A number of tunnels feed into this place," observed Laura. "Where do they lead?"

"To every building on campus."

Instead of taking them back the way they had come, Harry guided them down a passage that eventually branched in two directions: one leading to the basement of the president's building and the other to a steel ladder that rose several stories to a light, yes, at the end of the tunnel. With Laura and Christy at his heels, he climbed the rungs until he reached a grate that he lifted with his shoulder. As they emerged, they found themselves a few steps away from Puppet Hall, in the parking lot behind Tinnitus House.

"Who would have ever thought . . ." Christy mused. "I bet the power plant's a great place to do the dirty."

"Too bad Brooklyn Benny couldn't have lived to see you as president of Bogus U.," said Harry. "He would have been impressed. What I admired about Brooklyn Benny was that he always looked out for the gang. The boys came first. He came second. They say there ain't no honor among thieves. My advice to you, kid, is remember the family, and you'll be all right."

For the rest of that day, Christy entertained a riot of thoughts. The Robaccia gang was one family, the university another. And what about him? Didn't he deserve a fair portion for the risks he would run? He fully intended to make the school financially successful. No bogus YOU, him. When he had more time, he'd have to think about Harry's remarks. Maybe even talk them over with Laura.

IN THE BEGINNING WAS THE WORD

Needing digs of his own until he could move into the presidential manse, Christy rented a modest suite at the Florisette Hotel. His bedroom and balcony faced the mountains, a majestic view of stone plinths set against a cerulean sky that moved him to reflection. Historians would one day cite this hotel as the beginning of the Bogus revolution. Each morning for two hours Laura, who had readily agreed to stay on as his presidential aide, met Christy in a private meeting room on the first floor of the Florisette. Arriving with an armful of folders, she would brief him about university life: administrators—from viziers to beys, and their peccadilloes—students' habits and tastes, dormitory living, classes, college requirements, athletics, the abysmal state of the library, and the feckless faculty.

Christy never failed to notice Laura's radiant Latin looks and to remember her admiring comments during his interview. The first time they huddled for a briefing session, he had sprung to his feet, offered her a chair, and, in the true administrative manner, sat practically on top of her. His propinquity, however, discomfited her and she repositioned herself a few feet away, causing Christy to apologize for his forwardness.

"Between you and I, I ain't used to the job, if you know what I mean . . . or nice dames like you."

"Between you and me."

"So, what about us?

"Nothing, I was just correcting your grammar."

"Whadda I say wrong?"

"Some other time, not now."

"You promise to teach me?"

Laura nodded. She would be an ideal tutor because she could draw on not only the experience of the president's office, but also her boyfriend

Shawn Keogh, a graduate student in Semaphorics, who worked in the Athletic Department, one of the major centers of graft.

"I met the viziers. What's up with those oddballs?"

"They're factotums."

"Never heard of the word."

"Caretakers. Water carriers. Errand boys."

"Who, then, are the guys with ideas?"

"No such person. Bogus U. is a business run not by brains but by buffoons, and therefore badly. For example, you'll see in Sejanus Pinchbeck's file a self-evaluation that says he's perfect. These guys have no shame."

"Perfect? What the hell does that mean?"

"He's never done anything right. He unfailingly fails. No exceptions. His staff spend most of their time cleaning up his messes."

Christy wouldn't be able to use any of the administrators for his purposes; they were petty thieves with no real talent for large-scale larceny. His years in the rackets had taught him this much: imagination is even more important than smarts. He knew a lot of brainy guys who never had an original idea. But the mugs with the creative minds were the ones who made the most dough. He began to realize that if the Bogus bosses had no more initiative than merely to keep their jobs, he would have to devise a few schemes of his own.

Laura then repeated the information that Shawn had gathered on the football coach and his operation: his prayer sessions, the slush fund controlled by the fund-raising arm of the university and channeled through the president's office for the use of the team, the under-the-table payments to players, the do-nothings on the payroll, and the fatuous alums all too willing to part with their bankrolls in order to sit on the fifty-yard line and dine with the coach. "For a lousy lunch with Caiaphas, they're willing to plunk down thousands."

She also filled him in about the area: its ranchers who defiled the land, its farmers who exhausted and polluted the rivers, the gun nuts who took the phrase "a well-regulated militia" to mean well-armed, and the housing developers who hoped to destroy the mountains as thoroughly as they had the plains. She explained that the legislature preferred imprisoning people to educating them, preferred cutting down forests to preserving them, preferred reducing taxes to supporting hospitals.

Each day brought new problems. "Here," said Laura, "is an unanswered letter from last year. 'Dear President Brummagem, I am owed an apology AND an A. I slept with Professor Pokus regularly for three months and he gave me a B in his course. Now he's fooling around with my roommate. What goes on? If you don't look into it, I'll get a lawyer.'"

"Why are these dames givin' it away for free?"

"That's a sexist comment. Women behave no better or worse than men."

Frankly, Christy did not take kindly to moral instruction, particularly from women. Had she been just any dame. . . !

"I have a letter here from Professor Slimchik, a Polish expert, who compares his salary to the dark days of communism in Warsaw. 'Do I have to get another offer to make you look my way? I dislike the deceit.'"

Laura explained that a great many profs tried to get offers from other schools just to jack up their salaries at Bogus. "Some of them are so poorly paid, they can't even afford the price of a joint. They grow their own poppies and pot."

Christy immediately smelled a money-making operation. "Those greenhouses I seen on the campus . . . what's in them?"

"The Biology Department uses them for plant studies. They also have some off-campus greenhouses."

"Keep talkin'."

"Talking," Laura corrected. "Hit the 'g.'"

What he wanted to hit was Laura.

"We received a letter from a student who wants her money back because she never learned anything in her English class."

"What's the story?"

"The truth is that Bogus's educational standards leave much to be desired. I went to a private school in New York City. My teachers were more demanding than the profs here. Except for the sciences, the courses at Bogus are mostly a laugh. Right now, for example, I'm auditing a graduate course in Semaphorics—my boyfriend Shawn suggested it. The class is studying the backs of cereal boxes."

"How come?"

"The prof says that cereal boxes are America's favorite reading. I think," Laura opined, "he means for kids. And you'd have to agree, millions of kids read them."

Christy could already envision himself approaching General Mills and asking for big bucks to sponsor cereal-box studies. "Keep going."

"At least this prof's around. Most of the others can hardly be found."

As Laura got ready to leave, he remembered a subject that they had failed to cover: Monroe Larson. Was he at the center of some unfolding story?

"You'll get to meet him at the start of the semester. He spends his summers in Vermont."

Afternoons Christy spent in the accounting department scrutinizing Bogus U.'s books. Keen on numbers since grade school, he perused not only the financial records but also graphs of student grades and reports that faculty turned in every year indicating the division of their labors: what percentage of time they devoted to teaching, to preparing for class, to doing research, to attending meetings, to holding office hours, to consulting, and to other activities.

"I want ya to write some words from me to the faculty," said Christy at their next meeting.

She immediately opened her laptop computer. "I'm listening."

Lest she think him a loose cannon, he explained, "The trustees . . . they want certain things done. If I take care of it now, when August rolls around everyone knows what's expected."

Laura brushed a speck from the screen, rested her fingers on the keyboard, and waited. She did not realize that Christy had no idea how to start.

"Where I grew up," he said vacantly, "a fountain pen was a luxury."

Laura, surmising that for some reason he was reluctant to dictate, tried to draw him out. "Shall we begin 'Dear Faculty' or 'To Whom It May Concern?'"

"Yeah, I like the second. It sounds high class."

"What's the subject?"

"Rules. The first one's about meetin's and the second's to do with gettin' things done."

"Yes?"

"What I say goes. I expect the faculty to fall into line."

Laura smiled and said, "Pay them and compliment them and they'll roll over and lick your hand."

"That comes later. For now, no more meetin's. They're wastin' entirely too much time chewin' the fat. Unless it's a matter of life and death, no meetin's."

She typed.

"Second, all administrative decisions have to be made within ten days. I don't want no stallin'. Foot-draggers will see their salaries cut. Delays cost money."

The third rule enjoined faculty to use a grading curve: no more than ten percent A's, twenty percent B's, fifty percent C's, fifteen percent D's, and five percent F's.

Laura shook her head skeptically.

"Hey," he said, "I seen the figures. They're outrageous."

"Do you own a flak jacket?"

"No, why?"

"You may need one."

"Crap, what's in a grade?"

Christy's comment took her breath away. "What's in a grade?" she gasped. "Self-regard, expectations, honors, admission to graduate school, parental approval or disapproval . . . and that's just on the students' side. The faculty could give you a dozen more reasons for their inflating the grades."

"A new boss means change. It's not a bad thing when the employees find the ground underfoot a little slippy."

After Laura had finished the *diktats*, she packed up her laptop and left. Christy returned to his room to prepare for a meeting with "Noodles" Moran, a freelance enforcer who did jobs for a number of families and gangs. Noodles had grown up on the same Brooklyn street as Christy. Shaped like a fireplug, he had dropped out of school in the sixth grade and celebrated his liberation with his first tattoo, a blue and pink angel playing a golden harp with one word written underneath: Mother. He called Las Vegas home and spent most of each day at Caesar's Hotel playing video poker and betting on sporting matches. His thick arms rippled with muscles and bore numerous scars from knife fights. A nose mauled by a baseball bat, not from skirmishing but from catching without a mask behind home plate, resembled a squashed sausage. By no means a dolt, despite his name, Noodles had earned his moniker because his hands were always idly, lazily noodling about, touching any object within reach. Christy had paid for his plane fare and had booked him a room in the Florisette Hotel. The two men had enjoyed a steak dinner in the hotel dining room and had returned to Christy's suite.

"I couldn't give no specifics over the phone or in the restaurant, but here's the deal. I want you to work for Bogus as a fundraiser."

Noodles fingered the arm of his chair. "When you called and said you was the new prez, you could have knocked me over with a nylon stocking. And when you told me you had a job for me, I jumped. But what the hell do I know about fundraising, except maybe with a gun?"

"Precisely! That's why you're my man. You got experience. Now you see this list?" Christy removed a folder from the coffee table. "There's dozens of names here, all big rollers, guys who can give millions to Bogus. I want you to call on each one. My secretary will make all your travel arrangements and Bogus will pick up the tab. You get a ten percent cut on what you raise."

Noodles ran a hand over his mouth and looked doubtful. Then he pulled at his left ear. "I never dealt with college types before. What do I say?"

Christy had asked Laura the same question and merely repeated her answer, adding a fillip of his own. "Here's the price list printed on the inside of the folder. They can have a seat in the theater with their name on a plate; they can have a classroom named after them or a lab or one of the campus restaurants. But the top drawer is naming rights. For any old building, thirty million, for the basketball arena, forty million, for the football stadium, fifty million."

"I thought the taxpayers owned them?"

"So what's new about screwin' the taxpayers?"

"Next question: what if these guys ain't buying?"

At this point Christy added his own inimitable touch. "Then just take out your rod and spin the chamber a few times. But under no circumstances let him say he wants to think it over. Tell him that you don't leave without the check in hand, and warn him what happens to guys who stop payment on their paper."

"A ten percent cut . . ."

"Yeah. On a million that's a hundred grand."

"You were always quick with the numbers."

Noodles opened the folder and looked at the names. "No Rockefellers or Fords."

"Not in this part of the country."

"Okay, I'm your man. Anything else? I see you got another folder on the table."

"Football."

"What about it?"

"Bogus U.'s team ain't worth shit. They'll be lucky to win three games out of twelve. I want you to fix it with the other coaches that when they play Bogus, they lose—or else! Our first game is with the Texas Little Horns."

Fidgeting with his silver belt buckle, embossed with a turquoise Navaho symbol, Noodles immediately calculated that if he had advance notice of fixed games, he could clean up at Caesar's, maybe even make enough to retire to Palm Beach and buy a palatial white house next door to some CEO who'd bankrupted his company and received five hundred million to retire.

"Some of those coaches are thugs themselves," said Noodles, having second thoughts. "And they got some players who would make Dutch

Schultz look like a boy scout. Every day I read in the papers about another one of those guys arrested for assault. What do you suggest I do about protecting myself?"

"Tell 'em if they don't play ball, we'll rig their locker room with nitro and they'll never get out of the stadium alive."

Noodles shook his head skeptically. "That's all right for games at Bogus, but what about the times they play in their own backyard?"

Christy pondered Noodles's problem and then replied, "Give 'em some cock-and-bull story that you learned your trade in Iraq and blowin' up cars is your specialty. From what I hear they all drive BMWs or Audis or Saabs and care more about them than their families."

Noodles looked perplexed. "I don't even know where Iraq is."

"What are you, a dumb mutt? Anyone knows it's next to India."

"Which side?"

At least twice a week Christy heard from Noodles, whose fundraising earned rave reviews from the Development Foundation. The requests for renaming classrooms and labs and theater seats came in by the dozens. Renaming buildings proved a harder sell, but Noodles did persuade two families to put up the requisite amounts. Then suddenly Noodles stopped calling. Christy knew that he had flown to Texas to speak to the Little-Horns' coach.

Several days later, as he passed through the hotel lobby, Christy stopped dead in his tracks, shocked by the headline.

FIXER DISEMBOWELED

He found the story even worse. The local newspaper had picked up an article from the *Texas Garrote*, one of the most widely read tabloids in the Lone Star state. According to the *Garrote*, a man by the name of Myron Moran, also known as "Noodles" Moran, had tried to bribe Coach Ransom Wall. And here we quote.

> The meeting between the two men took place in the Spare Ribs Restaurant in the Dallas suburb of Holy Ghost. Moran allegedly threatened the coach's life if the Little Horns did not throw their opening game against the Wildebeests. Billy Joe Bestiary, the Little Horns middle-

linebacker, sitting in an adjoining booth, overheard Moran, slipped into the lobby, and used his cell phone to call three other players, Bill Bob Bucksaw, Lance Halberd, and Rocky Strappado. "Waiting in the parking lot, the four men grabbed Mr. Moran as he approached his car. Driving him to Rattlesnake Reservoir, they tied his hands and feet to stakes and started a fire to heat a branding iron. While they waited, they sang the Little Horns fight song.

> *In Jesus we trust*
> *And therefore we must*
> *Win, win, win, win, win!*

When the iron glowed red hot, they branded Mr. Moran's forehead with the words "Little Horns."

Billy Bob Bucksaw then left and returned with a case of beer and several bottles of whiskey. In testimony given to Sheriff Hapless, Lance Halberd admitted that the men got 'knee-walking drunk.' In this state, they took turns using Billy Joe Bestiary's Bowie hunting knife to disembowel the victim. Other indignities, not suited for print in a family newspaper, were also visited upon Mr. Moran.

Sheriff Hapless said that although the murder was a particularly heinous one, and although the local citizens devoutly believed in capital punishment for wrongdoers of any age or mental condition, he doubted that a jury in Holy Ghost would find the defendants guilty because "these boys were just upholding the honor of Texas and our punishing them would only serve to undermine the team's chances of success."

Coach Wall said that he had left Mr. Moran in the parking lot and knew nothing of what followed.

The investigation continues.

BROOKLYN BENNY PUTS OUT
A CONTRACT ON CHRISTY

Reading his own obituary galvanized Benny. Although he was lying low and couldn't yet surface, he could start to put into operation his nefarious plan. It began with a telephone call to his "hit person" and ended with Mr. Hasty-Pasty arranging for the killer to join the Bogus U. faculty. (Note: Benny's diction reflected the changing world of crime, in which the daughters of Mafia bosses are no longer married off to seal alliances, but rather sent to Ivy League colleges. Hence it should come as no surprise that these young women, including Brooklyn Benny's oldest daughter, persuade their fathers to avoid gendered language.) With his hit person sitting across from him, Benny spelled out the assignment.

"I gotcha a job teachin', in fact, you'll be actin' head of the department, which oughta be right up your alley since you got a fancy degree in that stuff anyway."

"It's called a Doctor of Philosophy," the hit person explained, "or Ph.D. for short."

Brooklyn Benny poked the air with his cigar. "From what I hear, you can say anything, so long as you say it with a little pizzazz, and the kids will think you're a genius."

"I hope you're in no hurry for me to punch his ticket."

Brooklyn Benny, who much preferred competence to haste, shrugged and held up the palm of one hand. "Take your time. First, you gotta get close to him. Win him over. Then you can let him have it. Harry Hasty-Pasty will help you."

"I prefer working alone, but I have no objections to his serving as a backup, just in case."

"Harry's gettin' a place where you can safely clip the runt."

"You mind if I have a cigarette?"

"No. I see you're still smokin' those foreign weeds."

"Kreteks. They're Indonesian."

The hit person lit up.

Benny waved his copy of the *New York Post* to clear the air.

"Do you prefer arsenic or arms? I can use either."

"Your choice. The important thing is a clean job. No slip-ups."

"I assume that's why you called me."

"Only the best."

The killer inhaled deeply and exhaled slowly. "You got it."

"I only wish I could see you pop him," said Benny, gingerly touching his head wound, which had required twenty-five stitches to close.

"It may take a while to learn the lay of the land."

Benny relit his cigar. "I prefer my tobacco to yours. Like I said, no rush. The murder counts more than the money. I want the double-crosser iced!" For a minute or two he greedily puffed on his cigar, as he thought about Christy lying in his grave.

"How can you get me hired as acting chair when school's already begun?"

"You're a replacement. The head man came down sick—by special arrangement."

"I intend to remain inconspicuous."

"Fat chance. Just look in the mirror."

"Appearances are deceptive, a fact that every assassin counts on." The hit person again inhaled deeply and reflected. "I once killed a man with a poisoned dart . . . in Sumatra."

"Where's that?"

"South of the Malay peninsula. A large island. It was my first job. Then I moved on to Singapore, Kuala Lumpur, Hong Kong, Seattle, Chicago, and now New York."

"You really got balls. How old were you when you first made your bones?"

"Fifteen. The guy never expected to get hit by a kid. I made an appointment with the guy down at the docks, by the bales of copra. I stole up behind him and, with a blow gun that my father had taught me to use, I hit him in the back of the neck. He slapped the spot, as if an insect had bitten him. But he found a dart instead. Wheeling around, he stared at me, tried to point a finger, froze, and fell over dead. I was paid ten dollars and thought it a fortune."

"To look at ya now, who would believe it? Why dya do it?"

"For the money."

"Nothin' personal?"

"I never let my feelings affect my work. Can't. A clean hit requires one to be bloodless."

Brooklyn Benny held up his cigar, admiring the length of the ash, just as a great many Dons liked to do to show nonchalance. "When he dropped," said Benny, "he musta been thinkin' how could I get chopped by a kid."

"I'll tell you something, Benny, most thugs know why they get hit. They know they're living on borrowed time. It's all part of the game. They say, if you're not in, you can't win. But if you're in, you know where you've been."

Brooklyn Benny, like a great many people who think in sound bites and bumper stickers, fancied epigrams because they made no demands on his mind. "I can see you weren't born yesterday. Where were you born?"

"In Malaya, but after my mother died I moved with my father to Sumatra."

"You and your old man musta been close."

"He indentured me to a copra plantation owner, Mr. Chee, a Chinese emigré. A year later, I ran away and took refuge in a Catholic orphanage. The nuns treated me well and in two years gave me the equivalent of a high-school education. An English charity raised the money for me to attend the University of London. Later I went to Yale." The hit person walked to the window and impassively stared at the Brooklyn Bridge, the maze of cable and the glistening cars. "America's a prosperous country, unlike Malaya. How much do I get for the job?"

"All expenses and fifty K for clippin' the mug."

"What about my lecture fees?"

"You gotta be kiddin'!"

"I can't run the department and go into class unprepared. They both take time. I'll probably have to grade papers as well, and we all know about that. Forty thousand extra for each class I teach."

Benny, ignorant of international politics, except for the usual clichés, remarked, "This ain't Russia. No teacher in America makes that kind of dough. Ten thousand."

The hit person smiled, recognizing in Benny the typical American, who says he wants good schools; he just doesn't want to pay for them. "That's why none of the kids can read and write. If you want a professional job, you'll have to pay for it."

"Tell you what. A hundred K, and that includes everything: expenses, the hit, the department business, and the teachin'. Fair enough? I don't want it ever said that Brooklyn Benny's a piker."

"Cash, in small bills."

"There is one thing."

"Yes?"

"If you run into a good-lookin' chick called Laura Favoloso, remember that me and her mom are pals. You know what I mean."

"I take it she's a student."

"No, she works as some kind of aide to the pigeon, helpin' him write speeches and makin' sure he don't screw up his grammar. She's damn smart, so watch your step."

PHINEAS ORT
EXPLICATES ANTIGONE

Never before had Phineas enjoyed such an engaged audience as he explained, "The play is a tragedy, written about 441 B.C."

"Shit, that's more than 2000 years ago," exclaimed Jackie. "I didn't know people way back then could read and write." He lit a cigar and leaned back in his chair.

"The city of Thebes has just conquered the city of Argos. Among the dead are the Theban king and his two sons, Eteocles, who fought on the side of the Thebans, and Polyneices, who led the Argive army. The two brothers killed each other during the struggle."

"How come?" asked DeeDee, miraculously chewing gum and munching pralines at the same time.

"Polyneices married the king of Argos's daughter. When Argos tried to conquer Thebes, Polyneices fought on the side of his wife's family, while his brother remained loyal to Thebes."

"Dames!" Eddie Doyle exclaimed, reaching for a brioche, "they never fail to put you in the dip."

Phineas continued. "With the king and his two sons dead, the throne passed to the king's brother, Creon."

"Sounds like the rackets," Jackie Brown observed. "Big Mo gets whacked, and Little Mo takes over."

"Creon's first order as king is that anyone who buries the body of Polyneices will be sentenced to death. The order has scarcely been made public when word comes that Antigone, Creon's niece, has attempted to bury the corpse."

"My seester," remarked Reynald, "she would do zee same for me, were it not for zat dreadfeel husband of hers. He is, how you say, tractor trash."

Phineas let Reynald's comment sink in, because he believed that plays have the most effect when audiences internalize them.

"Antigone makes no attempt to hide her deed, and even goes so far as to challenge Creon's right to issue an order that the gods clearly oppose."

Eddie, preparing to light a cigarette, blew out the match. "Whoa! What's with the gods business? First of all, we got only one. Second, I went to Sunday school and the teacher never said anything about putting a mug underground. So what are you talkin' about?"

Phineas decided that rather than lecture the group on Greek burial rites and the world of the gods, he would answer Eddie's question in modern terms. "The gods are like the Dons. You know, the godfathers. What they say matters. They want someone underground, you bury him. If you cross them, you pay the price."

"That makes more sense," said Eddie, lighting his cigarette and voraciously inhaling the smoke.

"To proceed. Antigone, honoring the word of the higher-ups, tries to bury her brother. But Creon says that as the new king, he has the right to call the shots."

"Well, if the old Don ain't around, and he's number one, he's got a point," observed Jackie Brown.

Phineas smiled. "You're beginning to see Creon's difficulty." He reached for a brioche. "Furious at Antigone for crossing him, he sentences her to be sealed up alive in a cave."

"Sounds like what we did to wee Charlie Langdon. 'Cept in his case, we put him in cement. Right, Eddie?"

"Yeah, right up to his neck."

Phineas began playing footsie with DeeDee. Although keen to hear more, she immediately responded to his pedal dalliance by running her foot up his leg.

"Creon has a problem, though. His son Haemon is engaged to marry Antigone."

"Whew!" said Eddie Doyle. "This thing's really getting complicated."

"Let me mention still another difficulty. Antigone's sister, Ismene, sides with Creon."

DeeDee, now fully absorbed, said, "Geez, it's better than the soaps. I can't wait till we start reading."

So great in fact was DeeDee's absorption that she had removed her gum from her mouth and her foot from Phineas's crotch.

"But the townspeople—think of them as the gang members—they and this wise old blind guy, called the prophet, they take Antigone's side. Now the prophet is like the Don of Dons, the godfather of godfathers. He warns the king that if he doesn't let Antigone go, terrible things will happen."

"I was hoping it would end happy," said DeeDee.

"But it doesn't. By the time Creon reaches Antigone, she has hanged herself, with a noose of linen soft as silk."

"No!" gasped DeeDee, horrified.

"And Creon's son, weeping over her, draws his sword and tries to kill his father. But Creon evades the sword thrust. Haemon, out of sorrow for his bride and contempt for his father, falls on his sword and kills himself."

"Sheesh, does he die?" asked Reynald. "A brave boy, he should live to eat escargots."

"Sadly, he perishes."

Eddie Doyle admired his cigarette ash and then gently let it fall into the tray at his elbow. "Sounds like the Valentine Day's Massacre."

"Worse," said Phineas. "Virtually an entire royal family . . . wiped out. You see, Creon's first son, Megareus, also killed himself. And when Creon returns to the palace with Haemon's body, he learns that Eurydice, his wife, while standing at the altar, thrust a knife into her heart."

Eddie Doyle shook his head. "My guess is the family had bad genes, what with everyone running around killing themselves."

"I was gonna get a beer," said Jackie Brown. "But after hearin' this, I need a swig of Scotch."

DeeDee grabbed Phineas's arm and shook it. "What happened to Ismene? Did she marry and have children, maybe a boy and a girl, like in the movies?"

"At the end of the play, her fate is uncertain."

Reynald seemed perplexed. "Unless I am moreen, I think zat Monsieur Creon he makes a fat stupeed meestake. N'est-ce pas?"

"Ah, that's the question," replied Phineas. "Why did Creon behave as he did, and in his circumstances would you?"

CHRISTY SURVEYS HIS DOMAIN

One oppressively hot evening, a few days before he officially took office, Christy let himself into Tinnitus House with his master key. He could hear someone rustling upstairs, probably the custodian. Opening his office, he admired the grandeur of the room, which resembled the dining hall in a medieval manor. At one end stood a large unused fireplace, at the other, floor to ceiling windows. The wood-paneled room had originally held just a handsome wooden desk, with matching credenza, conference table, and chairs. Christy had requested two additions: a well-stocked bar and a large pool table with a rack for his cues and chalk.

A small room adjacent to his office housed the secretaries (three) and the special cubicle for Laura Favoloso. Several months earlier, Laura had installed a bug inside the fireplace so that she could eavesdrop on the president. The bug, her own idea, had come from the Nocciola family. Thanks to her mother's Sunday lover, Laura could sit at her desk in the anteroom and listen on her earphones to the conversation, while the secretaries, assuming that she was listening to music, commended her thoughtfulness for keeping the sound so low.

Christy seated himself behind his desk and took stock of where he had come from and what work lay ahead: create a championship football team, raise money, subdue the faculty, settle the sexual harassment cases, improve academic standards, see that Professor Monroe Larson received tenure, and, the toughest personal job of all, amend his own grammar.

He could smell the polish that had been recently applied to his desk and noticed the ebony letter opener, the new dictionary, still in its wrappers, and the small framed photograph inscribed "The hills of County Mayo, from your staff." The drawers held stationery and envelopes, and a handsome case with a Mont Blanc fountain pen. His daily calendar rested on an

91

elegant leather desk mat, and a vase stood on the credenza. Yes, CEOs knew how to live, and he would maintain the style, at whatever cost. He turned on the CD player built into the credenza next to a computer and listened to Ella Fitzgerald. He could feel a draft from the chimney and puzzled why no one ever used the fireplace. He would have to make a note to ask about its condition. Restless, he chalked up a cue, racked the balls, and cleared the table with only a few errant shots. He liked the clicking sounds of balls caroming off each other; it brought back memories of hustling nickels and dimes at the pool hall on Surf Avenue and his titanic match with Butch Barkley, the match that proved to him for the first time that he had the guts to stay the course, to fight back, to win.

They had played for hours and it finally came down to one shot, the toughest in the game. He would have to skip the cue ball over the one in front of his to reach the ball that he needed to sink in the side pocket. Butch had said, "Double or nothing you don't make it." The place, Curly's Billiard Hall, was raucous, thick with smoke, and the hour two a.m. His eyes smarted and his head throbbed. Dozens of kibitzers were making side bets, and he could hear people mumbling that he'd choke. But he sank the shot—without a crutch—and made off with five hundred big ones, the biggest payday in his gambling life. Racking the balls a second time, he heard a key in the door, and Sophanna Houth entered pushing a wheeled aluminum frame supporting a large blue canvas bag that held a feather duster and pan, broom, mop, rags, escharotics, and a miniature Hoover. As they warmly greeted one another, Sophanna congratulated Christy on his good fortune. Inviting Sophanna to play, Christy handed him a stick.

"Only once or twice I tried. I'm no good."

"Come on, I'll show you," said Christy, who demonstrated how to rest the cue in his hand and stroke true. "School all right?"

"I way behind."

"Already?"

"No money, classes too big, teachers have no time for someone like me. My English is not so well. I can't keep up."

"If you had more dough, what would you do?"

"I'd learn good and study for a doctor and help people too much in pain. Many sick people in Cambodia."

"How much they payin' you for this job, kid?"

"One hour, I have four dollars."

"I'll give you ten. Get a tutor. I'll pay for that too."

"What's a tutor?"

"I had one as a kid . . . to help me with readin'. She was good. I learned a lot. The school paid." Christy paused, thinking about Mrs. Nolan, who had also taught him the names of the states and their capitals. Maine, New Hampshire, Vermont, Massachusetts, Rhode Island . . . He could still remember the litany—and the difficulty he had learning it. Thank god for his mother. Every morning, as soon as he woke, she would start him off with a cue: "Tennessee, Alabama, Mississippi. . . ." Christy rested a hand on Sophanna's shoulder and said, "A tutor is like your mom or dad, a private teacher."

"Ten dollars you give me for one hour and *also* a tutor? Why?"

"Because you need to catch up."

"No, why for me you do this?"

Christy, already regretting his softness, said brusquely, "Because some day you'll pay me back."

"How?"

"You'll figure it out," he muttered, wanting to escape a conversation that bordered on the maudlin, or, as Christy would have called it, the mushy.

Sophanna put away his cue and said simply, "Yes."

NIGHT SCHOOL

On the eve of his first official day at Tinnitus House, Christy dined in a steak house, alone. He barely tasted his porterhouse, thinking of the honor and homage awaiting him as he sat behind his desk in his green leather swivel chair and received the royal treatment. To discharge his restless energy, he left the restaurant and drove to his office. From the basement came voices. Quietly making his way down the steps, he stood in the darkened stairwell.

"Which: 'The letter came from John and me, or from John and I?'"

Christy recognized Laura's voice and peeked around the door. She and Sophanna were seated at the round table that staff used for coffee breaks. Except for a sink, with a small wall mirror, and a counter with a coffee machine and several badly stained cups, the room stood bare. The day after Christy had offered to subsidize Sophanna's education, the lad, not blind to a pretty girl or the value of learning, had asked Laura to tutor him. She sat with several grammar exercises and a handsome leather folder that held a writing tablet bearing four Latin words: *Res severa verum gaudia*.

Uncertain how to answer Laura's question, Sophanna digressed. "What does that mean?" he said, pointing to the Latin.

"We'll get to it . . . by the end."

Christy, given his new position, had mixed feelings about returning to school. Imagining the possible embarrassments he might encounter, he nervously bit off a fingernail.

"Well," she said, "which is it: the letter came from John and me or from John and I?"

"John and I. Don't you put the 'I' last?"

Laura wrote the sentence on the pad and put two fingers over the words "John and." Then she asked, "Would you say, 'The letter came from I'?"

"No, sounds funny."

94

"Well, think of covering up all the names that precede the 'I,' and then decide. In most cases, your ear will prove a good guide."

She then wrote, "He invited Sarah, George, and me to the party," and "He invited Sarah, George, and I to the party."

"Which is it?"

Sophanna pondered for a moment and slid a finger over the names Sarah and George. "He invited those people and *me!*" he exclaimed, "because I will never say, 'He invited I.'" Pointing to his ear, he said, "You're right. My ear told me."

If Sophanna can do it, thought Christy, so can I—and bounded into the room.

"What are you doing here?" she asked.

"Just came back to pick up some papers and heard people talkin', so I dropped in to have a look-see."

"Join us."

"Don't mind if I do," he said, as he pulled up a chair and shook hands with Sophanna. "I couldn't help but hear what yous was sayin'." To show that he could learn as quickly as the next guy, he volunteered his own example. "So, I would say Brooklyn Benny insulted the boys and me, not the boys and I."

Laura ignored the "yous," knowing that Christy would have to learn a new language, and said, "Correct."

"You shoulda—"

She interrupted. "Should have."

"Yeah."

"Yes."

"I should have had you for a teacher. I might've learned somethin', right, Sophanna?"

Sophanna, unhappy to share Laura, reluctantly agreed.

"Something. Hit that 'g.' How you speak reveals volumes about you. Remember, don't drop your g's. It makes you sound lower class."

"Right."

A bell on the coffee machine sounded. Sophanna went to the sink and poured three cups of java, putting them on the table.

"Let's continue," she said, shoving another sheet of paper in front of the two men.

"Here's a quotation from the Texas College of Propaedeutics."

Christy read it aloud. "To those to come I leave the flame! / Hold it as high as you can reach. / If a better world is your aim, all must agree, / The best should teach."

"What's wrong with the logic?"

"Sounds kind of sappy to me," said Christy.

"Forget the sentiment and tell me where the thinking goes awry."

"Well, just because some guy leaves a flame doesn't mean the next guy has to hold it up. Maybe the second mug disagrees with the first."

Sophanna shook his head. "No, no, it's something more deep." But he couldn't quite put his finger on what was wrong.

"It's a non-sequitur."

"What's that?" both men asked in unison.

"One idea doesn't follow from the other. For example, if I said, 'Although Joe loves chocolate cake, his father is out of work,' you would tell me that Joe's loving chocolate cake and his father being out of work are unrelated."

Christy had an idea. "Yeah, but what if Joe devours so many cakes that he eats his old man out of house and home? Then the two things would be related."

Laura, unamused, said impatiently, "Look, we expect that the second part of the sentence will say something like, 'he never gets fat.' Eating all that chocolate cake would lead us to that conclusion, or a similar one, but not that his father is out of work. It doesn't logically follow."

Christy conceded the point, but actual comprehension didn't dawn on him until Sophanna said, "To get a world better doesn't mean the best you must have teach. It may take a little only of something."

"Not bad, Sophanna."

"What do you think, Christy?"

Drawing a blank, he said, "I'm all ears."

"The writer moves from passing on the flame to talking about something unrelated. He says, 'If a better world is your aim, all must agree / The best should teach.' Well, I may wish for a better world and hope to realize it through medicine or law or engineering or any number of ways. I certainly don't accept the premise that just because I want a better world I must agree that the best should teach. To the contrary, I want people pursuing all kinds of endeavors, including teaching. The poem, if you can call it that, makes absolutely no sense. And the worst travesty is that Texas defaced a public building to exhibit this sentimental rubbish."

"I'll have none of that here," said Christy.

"In some ways it's perfectly fitting. Colleges of Propaedeutics produce the least educated students, although Departments of Semaphorics run them a tight race. You wouldn't want a profound statement adorning any College of Propaedeutics. There's a certain symmetry and justice to having nonsense emblematic of those colleges."

Christy could understand the gist of Laura's explanation but found some of her words daunting. He therefore decided to screw on his courage and confess that her vocabulary intimidated him. "You use a lotta fancy words, like 'premise' and 'propaedeutics' and 'causal' and 'travesty.' I gotta learn 'em, too. Whadda you suggest?"

"The SAT vocabulary study book. It's the same one kids use to get into college, and has all the fancy words you'll need to know."

"Great! How about you just teachin'—"

"Teaching!"

"Hey, nobody's perfect."

"Now you sound like school kids. That's what they say."

"Whatever."

"They say that, too."

"I got an idea. Why not teach me at least one word a day that'll make me fit in good."

"A learned vocabulary and fitting-in diction are two different things, Christy." She finished her coffee and stood up. "Fitting-in words are jargon. I'll give you some of those, like 'facilitate' and 'impact' and 'parameter,' but you'll have to teach yourself some real words, the kind that educated people use." Writing on her tablet, she tore out the page and handed it to Christy. "I think I'll have you read George Bernard Shaw's play *Pygmalion*." Christy looked blank. "I can see you never heard of it. Try *My Fair Lady*. That's what they called it on Broadway."

Smiling radiantly, Christy said with great animation, "I seen the video four times!"

"Then you'll remember what the professor said about enunciating your consonants, not dropping your g's, and using correct grammar."

"Yeah—yes."

Christy folded the paper neatly and, before following her out of the basement, stopped to check his face in the mirror.

Laura looked at him quizzically.

Seeing her expression, Christy explained, "When I was a kid, the other punks used to make fun of me and say I looked like a sap. So I got in the habit of lookin' in mirrors to check out what they said. I guess I'm still wonderin', otherwise I wouldn't be lookin', right?"

Laura patted him on the shoulder. "You needn't worry, Christy, you look just fine."

Christy beamed. "You know, Laura, you're a real dish."

"I'd rather you said that I'm a redoubtable guide to the recondite underworld of Bogus U."

Christy's eyes momentarily glazed as he followed her up the stairs and into the light, with Sophanna close behind.

CHRISTY LOOKS IN THE MIRROR

On moving into the presidential manse, Christy was awed by the profusion of marble: the ebony-tiled floors, the tan-and-white fireplace, the rust tabletops, the yellow kitchen counter space and bathroom vanities, all marble. Someone had also made a killing on the glass contract, with mirrors in every ground-level room reflecting the light of the numerous crystal chandeliers. Repairing to his bedroom, he undressed in front of an ornate mirror with a gilded frame, which gave him the full measure of his insubstantial self. He decided that he looked like a street urchin, a runt: sparse beard and skinny face, blood-shot eyes and henna–colored ratty hair, thin lips and chipped front teeth that he had been meaning to have capped. To ward off harm, he would have to develop a menacing mug. Curling his lip to one side, he imitated Jacob Shapiro and said "Gurrah."

From gangster gossip, Christy knew that Jacob Shapiro had earned his nickname "Gurrah" because of the way he snarled "Get outta here!" Having read *Chin Music*, Christy yearned for the Twenties and fast women and cars, jazz and mournful clarinets, Thompson submachine guns, speakeasies and stills, Rum Row, motorboats equipped with Liberty engines to outrun the coast guard, Harlem playing a hot beat with swells dancing left, right, kick, swing, and famous street corners home to hoods.

Although Christy nourished his youthful dreams with hyperbolical fancies, the fact remained: he wasn't much to look at. His legs, the best part of him, resembled those of a marathon runner, lean and thin. All his life he had been called names like squirt and shrimp, half-pint, peewee, and runt. His only comfort had been in knowing that he could outrun the other thieves, a talent he hoped would earn him the sobriquet "Legs," in honor of Jack "Legs" Diamond. But when he asked the gang to address him this way, they just laughed and told him that the real Legs thought nothing of burning an interloper to death. Christy, they taunted, had no stomach for the rough stuff. He was a penny-ante punk who hung around ATM machines hoping that someone would leave behind a bill or a coin, a chiseler who would ask for his money back if the pinball machine registered "tilt," a short con who rifled pop machines, a nickel-and-dimer who stole apples from carts. The biggest job he'd ever had was collecting change from parking meters, work that Brooklyn Benny gave him because Christy showed up one day at the firehouse headquarters of the Robaccia family to ask if Benny needed a numbers runner, a job that Christy had enjoyed until he shorted the boss, Goe Dung Gee, a sleazy racketeer hailing from Vandergraft, Indonesia. Presenting himself as a skilled numbers operator, who had been discriminated against just because he wasn't Asian, Christy persuaded Benny to make him one of the family, but not until Christy had proved his worth by showing the Robaccia family how to horn in on his previous employer.

Despite his physical failings, Christy, who had stored up in his ghostly heart a valorous view of himself, glimpsed in the mirror a slick operator, someone who had insinuated himself into the presidency of Bogus U. At this moment, he had a glimmering that people form personalities by copying from others, and that behavior was the sum of practiced plagiarisms. He smiled at the thought that undressed we all have the same equipment, give or take a few inches, and that the plagiarism occurs when we clothe our bodies and speech, and ape certain habits. In this guise, we convince ourselves that we have become the people we want to be.

He certainly knew, having been one of them, that the faceless imitated the behavior of those they admired. The examples were endless: the women who resorted to bleach and silicone to emulate Marilyn Monroe, the men who talked out of the sides of their mouth and smoked cigarettes à la Bogey, the crooner look-alikes, the It girls of the Twenties with heart-shaped lips, the Twiggy anorexics, the tennis-shoe clones, the haircut wannabees, the swagger and swing of the me-toos.

No less with Christy. He was fully aware of the person in the flesh, and the person he hoped to fashion at Bogus U.'s expense. If he could blend mensch and menace, he felt reasonably certain that he could handle all his constituents, who would savor the vicarious danger of association with a mobster and then return to their own safe preoccupations. Yes, he would genuinely become Christy the Chop, play the different roles, and enjoy the ride.

As he reflected on the many purloined personalities he had tried out in his youth, choosing first one, then another, he realized that his fraudulent imitations had taught him invaluable lessons, not least of which was that originality is not an essence but a choice, in fact a number of choices. What and why one chooses defines the self, from the tie that we wear to the car that we drive. Choice individualizes the person. Seeing himself in the mirror, Christy reveled in his growing powers of rumination and concluded that people who can't or don't choose are unfree.

Exhilarated by his musings, Christy undressed, climbed into bed, read for a few minutes from the *Song of Solomon*, turned out the light, and dreamed that Laura stood in a garden, with flowers and fruits. A brown-skinned man resembling Sophanna attended her. She held out her hand and beckoned to Christy, who could see that her breasts were like two young roes that are twins, which feed among the lilies.

THE FIRST DAY

Unaccustomed to rising at six, Christy arrived at his desk suffering from want of sleep. He immediately instructed his appointments secretary, who had already scheduled every hour but lunch, that he worked nights and attended early-morning Mass, blatant fabrications to ensure that in the future he did not have to awake in the mists of morn.

Although he would have preferred inaugurating his first day in office with a pleasant appointment, Christy had specifically asked to meet with the CEO of ASP Corp., Martin Stiffler. This gentleman had personally signed the contract that bound Bogus U. to ASP's computer services, and, as well, he had trustee connections.

Shaking Christy's hand, he familiarly pulled up a chair and said, "You called. I'm honored."

Christy smiled warmly. "I understand Bogus has a long-term deal with ASP, and you think we need an update. Fill me in."

Martin Stiffler stroked his gold tie clasp, which, like his cuff links, bore the initials ASP with a small serpent entwined among the initials like ivy. Here was a businessman: dark suit, blue tie, white shirt and starched collar, mottled black shoes, attaché case, cologne. Christy had once seen a book called *Dress for Success*, and assumed that Stiffler's uniform came from that source.

"It's time," said Stiffler, "for a change in systems hardware and software that will make Bogus competitive with the Big Twenty schools, maybe even the Ivies . . . time to introduce the next phase of the computer streamlining program."

Although skilled in street crime, Christy had no familiarity with university scams. His want of knowledge prompted him to play for time.

"I'm listening."

"What we gave Brummagem, we'll give you. Same percentage. But this time, since the job is bigger, the amount will be a lot more."

Christy knew enough about rigged contracts to say, "I know some guys who will give me a larger cut."

Martin stood up, exhibiting his full height of six, six. "ASP has a contract with the university. You need an S-I-S."

"I ain't got no sis."

"Of course you don't," said Martin. "A fully computerized Student Information System is the next project to come on line. Your predecessor agreed that it would be costly, but consented when I spelled out the rake-off."

"The last job . . ." Christy deliberately paused.

"It made us all a hefty sum. Brummagem walked off with ten percent of thirty-five million. Not bad, eh?"

"I want twelve percent. That's what your competitors are offering."

Martin blinked and took a deep breath. Working with trustees and academic administrators had taught him to expect the worst. Not surprisingly, then, he had a ready response. "We had to cut corners on the last job. We'll have to cut even deeper on this one to make up the difference."

Christy, still smarting from the dressing down Brooklyn Benny had given him about his family's reputation for cheapness, said, "I want only the best materials and workmanship—and twelve percent. Otherwise the job goes elsewhere."

A paroxysm of anger colored Martin's face and frayed his patience. But he tightened his lips and buttocks and said crisply, "Since when does Bogus U. care about quality?"

"From now on!"

"That'll be a change," said Martin, as he huffily excused himself and exited.

Christy, after just one interview, realized that if even where you sit is a luxurious leather chair, the trouble with sitting was that it left little time for loo breaks, put boils on the butt, deformed the spine, and made one wish for the excitement of street crime. Seeing that he had a few minutes before his next appointment, he rang for Laura. She entered sprightly, well aware of what had just taken place.

"Stiffler's got an umbrella up his ass," said Laura. "Always has and always will."

Her pungent language dispelled his earlier annoyance with her. The truth was that he wanted to like her and to discover that her attractions eclipsed her provocations.

"Your next appointment will be here shortly. Professor Narcissa Whitman Poseuse."

"What's there to know about her. Remind me. I can't keep the names straight anymore."

"She's a born schemer and has every administrator believing she's a telephone call away from millions for research. If her accounts were audited, she'd probably land in jail."

"Anything good about her?"

"I guess you could say she has a genius for self-promotion and she's generous, employing all her ex-husbands. She'll probably begin by telling you that she changed the world of research."

Laura's remarks made Christy feel ill at ease. He knew that he had risen to his current position through boasting and also knew that self-promotion made him feel good. So what was wrong with a little bravado, or even a lot? It gave him confidence, made him feel good, fostered respect in others. No, he could not fault a person for exaggerating, given his own indulgences, but when did one cross the line? Perhaps Professor Poseuse would provide the answer.

The secretary in the outer office rang to say that Professor Poseuse and her aide had arrived. Laura shrugged, as if to say "beats me," and opened the door to admit a man wearing a serape and a sombrero. As Laura exited, he approached Christy and handed him a flyer. In bold letters appeared the statement:

Narcissa Whitman Poseuse discovered the Rosetta stone for all academic inquiry. Since that time, many imitators have followed in her footsteps, but none has gone beyond her original footnote that deductions proceed from observation, which in turn proceeds from induction; hence one cannot say, like the chicken and the egg, whether induction or deduction comes first. That footnote set learning on a new course.

"Where's Professor Poseuse?" Christy asked.

"She will make her entrance in a minute, as soon as your staff spreads her red carpet."

Two secretaries unrolled a carpet that extended from the outer office to the president's desk.

Christy waited but no one appeared.

The man then announced, "You are now about to meet the most distinguished and eminent academic in our midst."

"And who the hell are you?"

"Her publicist."

"If she's that good, how come she needs you to toot her horn?"

"Fear not! She toots her own horn on every occasion. Just listen. Here she is now."

A small, rotund woman, with a face colored by the application of betel nut juice, sporting a crown of curls, confidently strode into the office. Crossing the carpet, she stopped a few steps from Christy and asked her publicist to identify "this person." Upon learning that she was in the presence of the new Bogus U. president, she remarked, "You may, if you like, sir, kiss my hand." Christy declined. "I have awards from every institution on high. I have even won acclaim from the Society for Clotted Prose." She extended her hand. "This is the hand that wrote my deathless axiom: I observe therefore there must be something to observe; otherwise I am disassembling what doesn't exist, making me a dissembler or a mad person."

"Huh?"

"Every part of the universe has its constituent parts. The question is which parts do we see? It's all in the thinking process."

Christy timidly ventured, "What's the point?"

"That's a question for priests not pedagogues."

The publicist left and Professor Poseuse, after reading a narrative form of her bibliography, tinned Christy's ear for an hour about the importance of his giving tenure to Monroe Larson. She compared Larson and his research to Galileo, Isaac Newton, Charles Darwin, Gregor Mendel, and Jonas Salk. "The only person he does not compare with is," and here she gave a little giggle, "is me." She omitted the name of Einstein only because she felt a little awkward speaking of herself in Albert's company. "My sweet poodle dog, Monroe, is . . . is . . . is, well, he just is!"

Inhaling, she seemed to indicate that she would have another run at comparing Monroe and herself to the world's worthies. But fortunately, Laura saved Christy by barging into the room and declaring that he had an urgent call.

Grateful for this patent falsehood, Christy said, "And it might take a while."

Rather huffily, Professor Poseuse said, "My carpet, please, it goes wherever I go." As Professor Poseuse departed, Laura noticed Christy's defeated look and befogged eyes. Pointing out that his next appointment would not come until after lunch, she suggested he take a break, adding that she had to run next door to fill a prescription.

"As long as you're goin', get me a large box of Alka-Seltzers. I've hardly been on the job and already I got a splittin' headache and stomach pains."

Her expression signaled her displeasure.

"Now what the hell's wrong?"

"Try the word 'please.'"

"Please," he said grudgingly, wanting to deck her with a right to the chops.

"A few manners won't hurt you."

Yes, he would either change her or dump her. No matter how good she looked, he wouldn't be pussy-whipped by any dame.

Laura cut through the parking lot to the campus health center and greeted her friend Jane who worked in the pharmacy.

"Shawn dropped in earlier."

"It seems everyone has a cold or the flu."

Jane blushed.

Laura asked, "Something wrong?"

"No, why?"

"You're red as a beet."

Jane directed Laura to the end of the counter. Out the window, Laura could see a few trees in shock from the recent drought, and on the field across the way, she espied the marching band practicing for the football season. Jane stared at the counter and whispered:

"I thought you were on the pill."

"I am."

"Are you afraid it won't work?"

"No."

"Then—"

"Yes?"

"Why did Shawn buy a box of those?" She pointed at a shelf holding condoms, twelve to a box.

"He did?"

"Yes."

"Strange. Maybe it's for some kind of field work in one of his Semaphorics classes."

"Maybe," said Jane unconvincingly.

Laura bought the Alka-Seltzer and asked Jane if she could use her phone. She called and left a message for Shawn, and then returned to

Christy's office, deeply perplexed. She tossed him the Alkies, and he handed her the amount written on the tag.

"Would you like a cup of java?" he asked. "I'll get one of the dames to bring us some."

"Get it yourself!" snapped Laura, feeling annoyed about Shawn.

"Huh?"

"The secretaries are professionals. They're not here to run your errands."

Christy sat dumbfounded. Since when didn't secretaries bring in the coffee and doughnuts? Who'd changed the rules? Miss Favoloso was beginning to get under his skin in more ways than one.

"Hey, where I come from—"

"Forget it! This isn't a restaurant with waitresses."

"Speaking of restaurants . . . how's about if I take you and I—"

"Me."

"Huh?"

"Accusative case."

"Never heard of it."

"Don't you remember our lessons? Direct object."

"Look, spare me the foreign language. I'm buyin'; you eatin'?"

"Thanks, but I have a previous engagement, a tête-à-tête with a friend."

"What's that?"

She reached across his desk and handed him the new dictionary she had bought for him. "Here, try this. But first remove the wrapper."

At that instant, he decided that for all the profit he hoped to squeeze out of Bogus U., the presidency had one major drawback: a president couldn't sock his aide.

MEETINGS, MEETINGS, ALWAYS MEETINGS

Promptly at ten, Christy's appointment of day two arrived: Gretchen Edsel, née Gretchen Narr. According to Laura's briefing notes, she had graduated from Bogus U. ten years earlier and was currently married to Trustee Frank Edsel. Her older sister, Heidi, had earned top honors from Bogus—in German—and attended graduate school at Yale. What Laura's notes failed to mention, we shall add.

Gretchen disliked her sister's plainness, which she felt unworthy of her own Teutonic good looks, accentuated by heavy blonde hair and limpid blue eyes. But most of all she disliked Heidi's moral durity and smarts: she had graduated from Bogus U. summa cum laude. At an early age, Gretchen chose a different path, associating with a fast crowd that drank the hard stuff and smoked pot. Instead of applying herself to study, she practiced twirling a baton and doing cartwheels, skills that led her to become a cheerleader, a role that supremely satisfied her desire to exhibit her curvaceous figure in a skimpy costume. She had been admitted to Bogus U. not on her grades but on her gams—and on her sister's reputation for scholarship. At Bogus, she had joined the Moo sorority, whose files of old exams and term papers got her through four years of bogus schooling. On the basis of her forwardness and her having serially been selected beauty queen of the freshman, sophomore, and junior classes, she became president of Moo Upsilon Tau, attracting the attention of Frank Edsel, president of the next-door fraternity house, Delta Epsilon Delta. In her senior year, she had easily won the election for prom queen, and had reigned over the year's festivities with Frank, a buzzcut blonde party animal who had been selected prom king. Together they made a dashing couple, always to be seen at the best fraternity parties and in Frank's BMW touring car, reputed to have been owned originally by Erwin Rommel. Gretchen, who had no mind for history, liked the white BMW, a gift from Frank's father, an upscale used-car dealer, because she felt it suited the couple's Germanic coloring. For this reason, she insisted that he drive with the black canvas top down, except during inclement weather. In their last semester the couple became engaged, and shortly after their June graduation they married in the Episcopal Church of the Holy Redeemer in her hometown of Rhinelander, Wisconsin. Her brother, Cranmore Narr, served as best man.

Owing to the generosity of Frank's father, Gretchen and Frank Edsel bought a home in the wealthiest neighborhood of a right-wing fundamentalist area within driving distance of Bogus U. Frank went to work for the family business, and the couple, wishing to make a success of their new life, quickly took on protective coloration to match the community. They joined the country club, eschewed excessive drinking, condemned dope, associated themselves with the religious-conservative wing of the Republican Party, and railed against the wild ways of university students. Like many converts, they zealously embraced their new faith, whether in penance or as a means to efface the memory of their sins. In short order, Frank joined the Rotary Club and gave a speech about the sanctity of family, even though his mother had run off with a retired Air Force major, and his father had married a woman twenty-five years his junior, a high-school dropout, whom Frank rather fancied. Business flourished. Given the many poorly paid workers in the area, Frank had no trouble introducing and selling a line of low-scale used cars. At Gretchen's urging, he ran for trustee of Bogus U. and, with the help of the religious conservatives, the military personnel, and the Republican Party, found himself elected as the standard bearer for righteousness and right thinking.

Although he found the transformation from partygoer to party hack an easy one, Gretchen did not. With each passing day she felt less comfortable in her skin. She tried to dissect what had happened to her and why she felt unsatisfied, lonely. She realized that glances, smiles, gestures—the private language of lovers—had fallen out of Frank's vocabulary. He had become formal, had become the mask that he assumed when he relinquished wastrelism and entered the worlds of worship and work. Luigi Pirandello could have explained to her the danger of masks, and of their becoming the real "we," but she had never heard of the Italian playwright and probably would not have understood him even if she had read his plays. She brooded constantly about what it would be like to take a lover. Then one day she did.

"I understand," said Gretchen, crossing her long shapely legs to provide a look above the knee, "you met my brother Cranmore."

"Yeah, a smart cookie . . . he got right with the plan."

Running her hand over her skimpy skirt, she continued, "Frank, who of course you met, he's a trustee, likes things to go smoothly. He's a great football fan, you know?"

"Really?"

"He loves the Wildebeests—travels to all their road games—but hates the Bogus U. scoreboard. So does Boaz. I mean Coach Caiaphas."

"Nothin' to worry about," said Christy, "I've already given Cranmore the go-ahead."

"You *are* an enterprising young man. To be honest, I had no idea what you'd be like. I heard so many stories . . . but I can see that you share a common vision with us."

"What's good for the trustees . . ." and here he paused, "is good for Bogus U."

"Just what I was thinking."

"Then we needn't spend any more time on scoreboards." She disengaged one leg and crossed the other, perhaps to correspond with the change in subject. "A matter related to football concerns the tenure of Monroe Larson."

"Really?"

"If Bogus U. gives him tenure, the school will be able to recruit a star high-school football player in California."

"I had no idea such things was connected."

"Normally, they're not. But in this case, Professor Larson, for reasons we needn't get into, is a drawing card for this boy. That's why we want Monroe to receive tenure."

Christy, knowing better than to contradict a trustee's wife, said, "Sounds good to me." But just to give himself breathing room, he stalled for time. "You don't mind, do you, if I study the file? You may be sure. . . ." He trailed off and smiled.

Shortly after she left, he darted across the grass to Puppet Hall for an eleven o'clock hearing with the university counsel bearing on the Grand Vizier's sexual misconduct.

Oh Babylon, oh Bogus, how costly are the wages of sin!

Cummings Dailey, a generous man, always rewarded his pliant secretaries with promotions and presents. For services rendered, secretaries in Class I went to II, II advanced to III, and so on. But with the formal announcement that he would be vacating the office of Grand Vizier, three secretaries

immediately sued Bogus U. for lost income owing to his planned depar-
ture. The university's legal office, rightly concerned that the affairs of the
school not be aired in public, asked for a private meeting with the women.
University counsel hoped that the complaints could be settled in house.
Christy attended the hearings, since it was he who, if the university found
the complaints justified, would have to agree to a settlement and pass on his
recommendations to the trustees.

The cases were heard in a windowless room with leather furniture that
smelled like a steaming steed. A coffee table exhibited a bronze model of
a Wildebeest. On the walls hung photographs of Wildebeests in the wild.
Christy reclined on a couch that swallowed him like quicksand. The first
secretary, Justine Dallas, a buxom bleached blonde, whose loud red dress,
several sizes too small, made it difficult for her to sit, slumped into a lounge
chair. She smelled as if she had been pickled in perfume. The attorney, David
Drury, a flabby fellow with a football-shaped head, cascading nose, and fat
fingers, sat facing her in a swivel chair. Although stylishly dressed in a pin-
stripe suit, he wore his clothes badly. They sagged. Even his blue tie looked
rumpled. He disliked cases of this sort and much preferred drafting contracts
for visiting artists and musicians. It was litigation that had driven him from
private practice into the university, and he knew that a confrontational
posture would just make his job harder. Holding a clipboard and legal pad,
David looked up, smiled, and began.

"You charge that you have suffered a loss of income because Grand
Vizier Dailey refused to proposition you. Is that correct?"

"Yes, he wouldn't give me a tumble," Justine said nervously, opening
her pocketbook and removing from a silver wrapper a stick of gum that she
folded in half and stuck in her mouth. "He told me he wasn't interested,
even when I told him I was."

"Do you suppose he refused your advances because he thought them
improper?"

She cracked the gum. "That's not what he told some of the other gals.
He told them I was unattractive. Now if that isn't discrimination, I don't know
what is. He was turning me down on the basis of looks. I may not have the
best face in the office, but I got the best bosom. You can measure if you don't
believe me. My hips and legs ain't bad either. So he was only going by looks."
Again she cracked the gum. "I've read the rules of the university. You can't
not promote a girl because of her face. If he had slept with me, I'd now be a
Class II secretary. I gave him every opportunity, but he refused me. Some boss!
Just 'cause he didn't think I was pretty, it has cost me plenty in lost wages. If I

don't get back pay, I'm going to court to sue for facial discrimination. I have a cousin . . . she's a lawyer. She told me I have good grounds."

Crack, crack, crack. Her gum sounded like a pop gun.

"Then as I understand your complaint, Miss Dallas, you are charging the Grand Vizier with unequal treatment. Whereas the other women got to share his bed, you did not. And that omission cost you a promotion."

"And presents . . . but I'm willing to leave that part out."

She crossed her legs.

"Were there any other women whom the Grand Vizier snubbed?"

"No. We have a staff of five women. Four of them, uh, they, you know what I mean."

"Received his favors."

"Yeah, that's it exactly. Favors. A couple of them got promoted right over me, and they couldn't even use a computer. I guess," she mused, "they could use other things."

"Apparently," Christy murmured.

She cracked her gum several times and returned to the attack. "Well, I got the same apparatus and I can do word processing!"

David Drury made a few notes. "As a matter of fact, another secretary never received a promotion. So you are not alone."

"From what I hear, that was a special case."

David made another note and asked, "Anything else?"

"Yeah. With Dailey leaving, I'll never get another chance. It really pisses me off not getting promoted. And since everyone knows the reason why, it's been, like, mental cruelty. When I spoke to my cousin, the lawyer, she said I could probably get Bogus for that, too, mental cruelty, but I'm not greedy, I just want the promotion and the lost wages."

"Dating from when?"

"From the day I first propositioned him." She fumbled in her purse and chomped her gum. "I brought along my diary so you can see the actual date." She removed a small book with a thin pen fastened to a silk string. "I put a marker at the exact page. See?" She handed the diary to the lawyer. "September third of last year. I therefore figure I'm owed for a year at the secretary II level, for services unrendered. That's the exact word my cousin used."

"You want damages?"

"Yes . . ."

"And if we cannot satisfy you?"

"I'll call the local newspapers."

Christy hated to cough up cash needlessly, but remembered Trustee Feather's advice and agreed: a private settlement would cost less in greenbacks and adverse public opinion than a public trial. So he leaned over and whispered to David, "Settle!"

David quickly calculated what they would have to reimburse Justine, including the promotion.

"If we offer you immediate advancement, without any financial recompense, we won't have to clear the deal with the trustees. I worry for your sake because the trustees do not look kindly on these kinds of cases. But promotion is an internal matter. We don't need their approval."

Christy decided to sweeten the offer, knowing that he could cover the expense from his discretionary funds. "I'll throw in a thousand dollars. We'll call it a bonus. What do you say?"

Justine hesitated, removed the silver wrapper from her purse, and dribbled the gum from her lips to the paper, which she then squeezed into a ball. "I come from a farm family and know a good mule when I see one. You've got a deal."

Christy wanted to pun on the idea of good asses but under the circumstances thought better of it. David gave Justine a paper to sign and she left. The next secretary entered carrying a briefcase and talked through clenched teeth. Beverly Burbank, a petite pretty blonde, looked as discommoded as a cornered rat. The only secretary in the Grand Vizier's office with a college degree, she both attracted Dailey and put him off his game, which worked best with women who had no more than a high-school education. Her pale-blue sweater, which for the sake of the Grand Vizier she normally wore unbuttoned to her cleavage, today hugged her neckline. A silk scarf of Indian design hung carelessly but raffishly across her shoulders.

"According to your letter of complaint, Beverly, Grand Vizier Dailey said he would promote you, but didn't, and therefore you feel that he violated a verbal or oral agreement. Is that the issue?"

"Yes, but there's more to it."

"Would you care to explain?"

She shifted nervously, looked around, as if trying to determine whether the coast was clear, and then said with considerable passion, "Is it fair? Am I not attractive? Did the Grand Vizier not say he would possess me? I finally meet him alone and what happens? He can't get it up! Despite my desire, despite his desire, he's as limp as a boiled noodle. In vain I threw my arms around his neck, in vain I twined my legs with his, in vain I put my tongue in his ear. And more! I lavished on him the sweetest names, called him lover and stud, and told him he was hung like a horse, even though he looked like a dead corn husk. He apologized and said that he had longed for this moment, but there he lay, a lifeless pod. I even did things you see only in porno films, not that I rent such movies myself, but nothing happened. Cummings even cried that this had never happened to him before. 'I am no man!' he wept. I comforted him and told him we could do it some other day, and he agreed, saying next time we would make love all afternoon and all evening. But the following week when I approached him about his promise, he said his calendar was booked up and he'd be leaving Bogus shortly. I asked, 'What about the promises you made me: the promotion, the matching turquoise necklace and bracelet?' He shrugged and explained that he gave promotions and gifts only to women he'd actually made love to, and said something about our affair being but, and I quote, 'the simulacrum of one.' I therefore want what's owing to me. Just because he couldn't raise his pecker is no excuse for the Grand Vizier breaking his word. A promise is a promise! And I intend to collect. Or else!"

The attorney rubbed his pencil eraser on the bottom of his shoe to remove a residue of carbon and then applied it vigorously to a note he had previously written. "Oral agreements are notoriously hard to prove. If the Grand Vizier denies your allegations—"

Beverly declared triumphantly, "I secretly taped some of his phone messages!"

"It's against the law in this state."

She opened her briefcase and removed a manila folder containing several letters. "Would you like to read what Cummings wrote to me over a period of six months? It's hot stuff. If the press got hold of it . . . but frankly revenge is not my motive. Money is."

Christy admired Beverly's frankness. Her motives reminded him of his own. If education were a marketable product, certainly sex was even more so. How could anyone slight her behavior in a country run on the principles of capitalism? He therefore directed David to negotiate with Beverly in order to arrive at a figure satisfactory to both Bogus U. and Ms. Burbank. Privately, he noted that to put Bogus in the black, he would have to take into account the X factor, the unknown charges that might arise against the books.

The last woman, Florence Richmond, a leggy lady in her early thirties, and a natural blonde with a long pony tail, had gray-green eyes and perfect skin. Her mouth, too large for her slender face, constituted the only flaw in her facial arsenal. She had been Dailey's regular mistress for five years, having assumed that position shortly after the Grand Vizier spotted her working in the mailroom and transferred her to his office. She wore a white turtle-neck that looked as if any moment her pointed breasts would pierce the fabric.

Although Christy and David could not see it, she sported a small tattoo of a teddy bear on the lower right side of her abdomen. The "body art," as its practitioners call it, had been applied in her teens when she and a girlfriend got drunk and decided "to make a statement." Once elevated by the Grand Vizier, she seriously contemplated adding to her teddy the name "Tuna," but decided that although it might please the Grand Vizier it could prove indiscreet.

"The note you sent me," said David, "hinted at a lawsuit for what you called 'alienation of affectionate wages.' Could you please explain."

"Well, like, if you have a steady income and it stops, then it's like no longer steady. Here I had this totally excellent relationship with Cummings, but now he intends to retire. So what happens to my income? I was like his working chick. You know, we snuggled at least twice a week. And in return for my affections, I got regular promotions and cool things, like a Turkish rug for my apartment and a new couch. Really neat stuff. Once Cummings leaves, who's going to make up the difference? My closet isn't full of dresses because of my salary. From what I hear, Bogus U. asked him to retire. Therefore it's Bogus U. that has alienated my affectionate wages. And in all honesty, I can't live on less than what I'm getting now. If Cummings and me were married, I'd be entitled to half his estate. So I suggest you pay me half of what you paid him. In return, I'll willingly give up my regular salary. What do you say?"

David shook his head from side to side. "We couldn't possibly justify such an increase in pay. We have no grounds."

"Sure you do. I just said. Alienation of affectionate wages."

"There is no such statute in law."

"Then call it palimony. Geez, I've been his regular almost since the day I started working here. Yeah, I know he sometimes played around with some of the other gals in the office, but I was his steady, and I've got a drawer full of cashmere sweaters and jewelry to prove it. He was really generous, and in my book generosity's a rare thing, especially when you consider all the other ways guys behave. It's almost religious."

David asked Florence to wait while he and the president had a private word next door. In the adjoining room, David whispered that he couldn't think of a way for Bogus to settle this particular complaint even if she sued for "detrimental reliance."

"What's that?"

"A reliance on promises or implied ones of benefit that induce the intended beneficiary to forgo other opportunities to her detriment when the promises don't, er, hold up."

"You're way above my head."

"I have no doubt that some of the Grand Vizier's discretionary funds have been lavished on Ms. Richmond. Should the legislature, well, you get my point."

"I don't think she'll take a cash settlement, unless it's damn big," Christy said.

"What should we do?"

"Let me study the file. I'll think of somethin'."

"In the meantime?" David asked.

"Tell her it will take a little time to work out the details."

Hearing in the distance the campus bells sounding the noon hour, Christy decided to take lunch at the faculty restaurant. Finding a table, he removed a small pad and wrote: "Restaurant needs renovation." When the waitress arrived, Christy ordered the "Chili Hot Plate." Several minutes later, she brought him his order, and two glasses of iced tea.

"I didn't order those."

The waitress smiled slyly. "You may need them."

Christy, who had gone without breakfast, voraciously ate the chili dish. The effect was immediate. His eyes rolled, his tongue lolled. His nose felt as if he had been snorting ammonia. His breath began to fail him, as he wheezed and coughed.

"What the hell is this?" he gasped, "paint remover?" As his face changed color, all he could taste was pain. He swallowed the two glasses of iced tea, croaking, "Keep this stuff away from kids!"

Once his heartbeat returned to normal, he made further notes on his pad, "Shoot the cook and change the menu." He then staggered back to his office.

Lavishly drinking from his carafe of water, he greeted his one o'clock appointment in a dyspeptic state. As always, Director of Athletics, Derek Hull, was dressed to the nines, this time in a gray Italian silk suit and matching tie, with an off-white shirt and soft leather black shoes. His hair, slicked straight back, made him eerily resemble a famous professional basketball coach, a resemblance that Derek cultivated. For years, the accountants at Bogus U. had tried to gain access to the Athletic Department's books. But previous presidents, all of whom used a generous portion of their slush funds to subsidize the football team, had refused to disclose the true nature of the Athletic Department's budget. Derek showed up with a smile, displaying an expensive set of capped teeth. When Derek heard that the president wanted to see him, he had assumed he'd merely be endorsing the size of the subsidy, a formality that had to be repeated with every new president.

"President Mahon," said Derek, full of bonhomie, "I was delighted to hear that you wanted to see me. The football team, as always, looks forward to receiving its annual stipend, which last year stood at one million dollars. Now this year, given our needs—"

Christy interrupted. "And ours . . ."

A note of concern crept into Derek's voice. "Yes?"

"Start tightenin' your belt, 'cause Bogus is broke."

A perplexed Derek said, "Since when has the general well-being of the U. ever affected our allocation?"

"Not a nickel till we straighten out the accounts," said Christy. "President Brummagem's financial records look like Enron's."

Ignorant of Christy's state of mind, Derek continued, "Of course, that sum doesn't include the chartered airplane, limo service to and from the airport, the hotels and meals, and, needless to say, the use of cars for the coaches, staff, and trustees."

"I see. Anything else?"

"Let's not forget Christmas gift money for the players and coaches, and the bonus I receive if we go to a bowl."

Christy began to take notes. Derek, thinking that he probably ought to include all the graft, lest the new president omit it, added, "Remember to include the football concessions. The contract is up for renewal next year, and we stand to make a lot of dough if we insist on kickbacks. The new parking structure . . . we can double the price on game days. And the endorsements, don't forget them. The equipment manufacturers want us wearing their logos."

"You left out the scoreboard advertising," said Christy, appearing to endorse the skims and scams. "And the marching band. Sure as hell we can dress those kids in uniforms that display someone's corporate colors."

"Great idea!" Derek exclaimed.

"Maybe even have the parking attendants wearing them, too."

"Geez, you're light years ahead of Brummagem. All he could think of was selling skyboxes."

For the first time, he wondered how much skyboxes made for Bogus. "What are we charging a season? The figure slipped my mind."

"Two hundred thousand."

An inveterate reader of the sports pages, Christy had recently seen an article about the United States Tennis Open in Flushing Meadows, New York. For that tournament, the authorities required all box holders to buy catered meals from the house restaurateurs at exorbitant prices. "We will insist that all our skybox renters buy food from a Bogus-approved source. The catering service we select will give us a fifty percent kickback. Understood?"

"Gladly!" Derek Hull could not believe his good luck. Finally Bogus U. had a president who grasped that the university should have an Athletic program that its student body could be proud of, to say nothing of the citizens of the state.

"Then we agree?"

"Perfectly!" Derek Hull leaned across Christy's desk and gave him a firm—very firm—handshake. But as he started for the door, Christy, who had a sense of the dramatic, asked him to wait upon one further detail.

"Shoot," said Derek.

"I intend to."

Derek laughed and stood with his hand on the doorknob, hoping to hear another money-making scheme that would guarantee the wealth of the Athletic program for decades to come.

Christy, who had bought a pair of horn-rimmed glasses to look professorial, though his eyes were perfect, removed them from his shirt pocket and studied Laura's notes. The interlude began to annoy Derek, an effect that Christy savored. Eventually, Christy pressed a button and summoned Laura. As she opened the door, Derek stepped back, slightly startled.

"You rang, President Mahon?"

"Laura, I believe you know Derek."

"Yes," she said, "we met at a football game."

It took Derek a second to remember. "Right, you were in President Brummagem's private box."

The two shook hands.

"Laura, I am puttin' you in charge of the budget for Athletics. From now on you will be the keeper of the books for salaries and benefits, for financial aid, and for all discretionary expenses, includin'—" and here he drew on the information that Laura had gotten from Shawn "—receptions, banquets, conventions, sponsorship parties, travel, recruitin', game operations, office supplies, equipment, parkin', police, concessions, community relations, and other Athletic charges. I want you to record carefully all the sources of income and all the outgoin' expenses. Nothin' gets spent unless I say so. Whatever Derek needs, he will come to you first, and you will ask me. Without my signature and yours, not a cent comes in or goes out."

Turning to Derek, he said matter-of-factly, "From now on, coaches fly economy class, and no more chartered flights for athletes. They can squeeze their big butts into the narrow seats just like everyone else. No more under-the-table payments—yeah, I know all about them—no more limos, no more first-class hotels, no more catered meals, no more tutors writin' papers for players, no more screwin' around with jock transcripts. Should I go on?"

Thunderstruck, Derek lamented bitterly, "You're tying my hands!"

"Exactly."

"Shaking me down!"

"No, just tryin' to sort out the books." Christy cracked his knuckles. "I don't believe in keepin' two sets."

"I know what your game is: you want to use the money for your own purposes."

"You can leave now, Miss Favoloso."

Unable to conceal a smile, she couldn't wait to reach the outer office to tell the other women what she'd just heard. To her knowledge, no Bogus U. Athletic Director had ever been put on a short leash. As the English would say, here was something to dine out on, for a long time to come.

Derek experienced arrhythmia. He didn't want to end up like his father, who had died in his forties from a heart attack. Breathing slowly and deeply, he said, "When the trustees hear of this, they'll fire you. Without my okay, you're a dead duck. No trustee will ever put the campus before football."

"You're forgetting one thing."

"What's that?"

"I know about your secret account that supplies the trustees with prostitutes for road games."

SHAKEDOWN (AN EXTORTION
OF MONEY BY DEVIOUS MEANS)

Out of sight of the campus, Christy took the president of the Rental Association for a ride . . . in the mountains. At a splendid overlook, Christy parked his Buick and told Mr. Gauger, a name he aptly pronounced "Gowjer," that Bogus U. planned to build enough dormitories to house the entire student population. However, for a monthly sum of six figures, the university could indefinitely delay its construction plans. Mr. Gauger, wearing an orange shirt, pale blue slacks, and Oxfords, shrugged, prepared to pass the cost onto the students by raising their rents. But when Christy said that part of the deal was rent control, Mr. Gauger knew that his three months in Arizona every winter had just become two.

At a hilltop restaurant, with Mr. Carleton Draper, the president of the Uptown/Downtown Merchants Group and a haberdasher known for his own impeccable suits, Christy's approach was old school. He demanded protection money from the tall, gaunt Mr. Draper and promised in return that any stores damaged from student riots would be paid for by Bogus U.

His third shakedown broke new ground. Bogus U.'s admission standards, though reasonably rigorous for out-of-state students, were painfully low for in-state ones. The legislature, having impoverished and ruined the public schools, realized that if the students were to overcome the burden of a second rate K-12 education, they needed a special dispensation, and therefore mandated that Bogus U.'s in-state requirements be substantially attenuated.

We shall not deign to discuss the requirements for football players. Let it merely be said that a passing grade in basic arithmetic and some familiarity with syntax enabled most of the gridiron behemoths, with a little tutoring, to gain admission to the campus. That most of them never graduated hardly mattered. Once they exhausted their competitive eligibility, their usefulness to the school ended.

Christy had directed the Office of Admissions to find out the financial worth of every in-state family that had a child applying to Bogus. He intended to interview wealthy parents to get what he could for his admitting marginal students. Out-of-state students, assessed inordinately high fees, had been squeezed as much as traffic would bear. Christy therefore reasoned that in-staters had to pay more than their current paltry tuition. Mr. Francis Doolittle, who wished to see his son admitted to Bogus, was a trial run.

Doolittle Junior, whose tests scores were dismal, had modest goals: he merely wanted to join a fraternity, drink, get laid, drink, spend Spring Break in Mazatlan, get laid, and drink. A polite, bovine lad, he accompanied his father to the interview wearing a jacket, a white shirt with a navy blue tie, dark slacks, and new shoes, all obviously selected by his father. The lad bore an expression of insipidity disturbed only by Christy's question:

"Why dya want to come to Bogus U.?"

Without thinking (his natural state), young Mr. Doolittle, whose first name was Henry, replied, "I want to join the TKD fraternity," which was Shawn's house. "My dad here used to be a TKD."

Mr. Doolittle, radiant in his Hong Kong threads, smiled appreciatively, as if his son had just disclosed that his father had been awarded the Legion of Merit. A tall, sinewy fellow with close-set eyes and a pinched nose, Mr. Doolittle strode like a man well aware of his merits.

"I graduated in seventy-four. Worked as a geologist in the Nigerian oil fields and settled on a ranch less than a hundred miles from here. Henry's a good boy, maybe too much play in him and not enough study. But he'll learn." Christy knew that Mr. Doolittle owned an oil exploration firm that covered the world, and that Henry's admission could bring Bogus U. big bucks. He therefore embellished a little on what Laura had entered in the young man's file. "Henry had some trouble with the SATs. By rights, he oughta go to a community college."

"He's a poor test taker," said Mr. Doolittle.

"His grades from private school ain . . . aren't so good either. If we admit him, it's a risk." Christy turned to Henry. "What do you wanna study?"

"Physical Ed."

"That department's now called Physical Therapy. It requires students to take Chemistry and Biology. Are you ready for that?"

"President Mahon," said Mr. Doolittle reaching inside his suit jacket and removing a checkbook, "I understand that Bogus is going through some difficult times. Perhaps I can help."

Laura had looked up the net worth of Doolittle Oil Exploration: five hundred million.

"We got a little problem with the library," said Christy.

"Oh, what's that?"

"Not enough books and journals."

"Geez," said Henry, "when my dad and me went through it, I saw tons of books. Your teachers must read fast."

Mr. Doolittle had recognized years before that his son, unlike his daughter, had few academic skills, and therefore it would take some doing to get him into Bogus U. A good businessman, he had entered into contracts with corrupt countries all over the world and knew how to strike deals. He told his son to wait in the hall and, after Henry had left, asked, "How much?" Christy decided to aim high. He could always come down, but once down you cannot go up. "Half a million."

"Sir, that is highway robbery!"

From Mr. Doolittle's tone of voice, Christy surmised that he had over-reached himself. But he decided to try again before lowering the price. "That comes with free room and board for four years, and a guarantee that he gets into the TKD fraternity."

Mr. Doolittle mulled over the offer and made a counter one. "Throw in fifty-yard-line football tickets for four years—two of them—and I'll write you a check."

"Make it out to," and here Christy paused, well aware of how easy it would be to say "Christopher Mahon." Instead, he replied "Cash." He would decide later where to deposit the money.

THE MONROE LARSON CASE

Turning up the air conditioning in his office, Christy said to Laura, "He's gonna be here in an hour. I hate these kinds of decisions: to either bury a guy or reward him. What's the deal? I can't put it off any longer. Short version."

Laura dabbed the perspiration from her forehead. When would this drought end? "Monroe claims that in his grandmother's attic—she lives in Charlottesville, Virginia—he found two letters that Thomas Jefferson wrote Sally Hemings, in which he states his affection for her and swears to look after the child of his that she is carrying."

Noting the puzzled expression on Christy's face, Laura proceeded to tell him the history of Thomas Jefferson and his slave, Sally Hemings, dwelling on the surmise, resisted by some of Jefferson's descendants, that Hemings had a baby or two with the third president of the United States.

"Those letters," Laura observed, "would be dynamite."

"So why doesn't he cough 'em up?"

"He insists that until his study is complete, he can't make them public. Once he does, he promises to give them to Bogus U."

Initially inclined to obediently follow the trustees' directive, Christy dug in his heels, remembering a particularly painful episode in his youth, in which he had saved up for a used catcher's mitt that a kid promised to sell him, only to take the money and run.

"No letters, no tenure. First I wanna see the goods."

"He won't release them. He says that if the National Endowment for the Humanities, the Ford Foundation, and the American Council of Learned Societies were willing to give him money to edit the letters, then Bogus U. should be equally trusting."

Christy could think of several ways of extracting the letters, but not wishing to incur the charge of assault with a deadly weapon, he wondered aloud, "Why don't Larson—"

"Doesn't."

"Yeah . . ."

"Yes."

Christy paused and waited for his frustration to pass. "Why doesn't Monroe just give us a glimpse, and then lock them up again?"

Laura made an unladylike gesture placing her thumb under her upper teeth—the sign of the figa—one that suggested she and Christy had the same wish in mind. "He says the paper has yellowed and in its fragile condition cannot stand the light of day."

"Hell, he can show them to us in the dark, with a flashlight."

"Christy," said Laura patiently, "you must realize that professors are some of the most skillful confidence men in the game. Even better than you. We have no way of knowing if those letters are for real unless someone tests the paper and ink and analyzes the handwriting. But Monroe won't allow the letters to be touched, lest he be exposed as a fraud."

"Can't we just read them?"

"What about forgeries?"

"Are you telling me—" said Christy indignantly, rising to his feet and raising an arm as if he intended to make a telling point. But before he could finish, she concluded the sentence, though in a manner that Christy had not intended.

"Professors are accomplished forgers."

This statement caused him no little upset: first pedophilia among priests and now paper-hanging professors. Where had all the honest people gone—and all the old verities? Thumbing through the file, he read the lapidary praise bestowed on Larson by the viziers and Professor Poseuse.

"Why the hell should they care, one way or the other, whether he gets tenure? Poseuse ain't even in his department."

Laura repeated what she had heard from the secretaries in the History and Biology and Athletic departments and Puppet Hall, the things that only aides who had read others' memos and mail and listened in on telephone conversations would know.

The case involved myriad interests. Monroe, of course, intended to trade the letters for tenure. Narcissa Whitman Poseuse, who had prominently insinuated herself into the Hemings project, was to write the introductory essay, comparing Jefferson's contributions to the country with her own—to her advantage. In fact, she intended, as a literary conceit, to cast herself as a modern-day Sally Hemings, a woman bedded by greatness. Vizier Pinchbeck, angling for a job at a Big Twenty school, claimed that his generous support of Monroe had made possible the discovery. In fact, he had split the air fare with Monroe so that the young man could attend a professional meeting at the University of Virginia. It was mere serendipity that while there Larson had rummaged through his grandmother's possessions to see if she had left behind anything of value. Pinchbeck even included the discovery of the letters in his *CV* under the category "Contributions to the Humanities," with a parenthetical note that he had played a major role in their find.

Bill A. Stine, according to Laura, wanted to see Monroe receive tenure because in large part he owed his current position to Narcissa Whitman Poseuse. In return for her help, he had promised to see that Monroe succeeded. Brigham Pyrosis knew that if Monroe failed to receive tenure, the Sally Hemings letters would leave the campus, dooming his efforts to win a diversity award from the NAACP, and diminishing his chances of ever being appointed president of Bogus U. Coach Caiaphas, who normally took no interest in matters academic, also had his motives. On a recent recruiting trip to California, he had discovered that the leading high-school running back in the state was distantly related to Sally Hemings, and understandably proud of the connection. Since Coach Caiaphas had promised the athlete and his family that if he came to play at Bogus U. he would be in close proximity to the only extant letters from Jefferson to Sally, he had to make sure that they remained at Bogus. For this reason, Trustee Frank Edsel supported Monroe's tenure bid.

Needless to say, all the self-interested parties represented their positions as serving the greater good. Narcissa Whitman Poseuse insisted that without Monroe Larson on the faculty, Bogus U. would rest on only one pillar, herself, and would therefore lose its stature in the academic world. Students, she said, would suffer from the dearth of greatness and, notwithstanding her Herculean efforts to maintain the reputation of the school almost single-handedly, the other faculty would be impoverished by his loss. Vizier Bill A. Stine, echoing Professor Poseuse, though lacking her analogical flair, feared that a No vote would remove one of the legs of Bogus's two-legged stool. Vizier Pinchbeck opined ironically that if Bogus wanted to enrich another university, Monroe's dismissal would accomplish that goal. Vizier Pyrosis clutched his chest and gasped that Monroe's absence would undermine the health of the institution. And Coach Caiaphas, the only one to tell the truth, said flatly that if Walter Hemings did not come to Bogus U., the football team had no chance of winning a national championship.

And what of Monroe Larson himself? Given Laura's limited knowledge of the young man and her dislike of his ingratiating manner, we will supply the few remaining details.

Monroe Larson, an opportunistic assistant professor of History, had taken his degree from a southern university and specialized in eighteenth-century American history. Shortly after arriving at Bogus U., he realized that Ms. Poseuse's public relations machinery could serve him equally well. So he attached himself to her, not sexually but sycophantically, and, to be doubly sure, made a point of fawning over the viziers: Pinchbeck, Stine, and Pyrosis. Monroe could well have become a first-rate scholar—he certainly had the training and the intelligence—had he not been congenitally lazy. His long-range plan was to get tenure and then ease himself out of the classroom and into administration, where he would be paid well for doing little. In his case doing a little would amount to a lot, given his profound fear of ever disagreeing with anyone. Willing to suck any hind tit for tenure, he knew that a job in the administration would require additional talents, for example false swearing and fraud, activities he felt he could perform flawlessly. His immediate problem, however, concerned his poor scholarly record.

He had written a few articles that he subsequently revised and collected in a book, which he managed to pass off as original. His colleagues in history, however, had their doubts about his honesty, his scholarly stamina, and his willingness to slurp at the slough of slavishness. If given the chance, they would have denied him tenure, despite or perhaps because of the efforts of Ms. Poseuse. Vizier Pinchbeck, however, declared that votes told him little; what mattered most were the opinions of the faculty. He therefore met with the eighteen tenured members of the Department of History to listen to their reservations and their modest praise of the candidate. During the meeting he took notes. A few days later, he e-mailed the department to tell them that the vote had been fourteen in favor of tenure and four against. To those faculty who asked how Pinchbeck had arrived at a numerical count when no ballot was held, he explained that his years in administration enabled him to discern from the discussion the mood and wishes of the tenured professors. Viziers Stine and Pyrosis saw nothing wrong with this procedure; in fact, they lauded Pinchbeck's powers of divination. The case had now become Christy's problem, given the trustees' wishes, Brummagem's inaction, and the protests of the tenured faculty in history.

Such was the state of play when Monroe Larson entered Christy's office. A tall cadaverous fellow who sported a red beard to hide the scars of childhood acne, Monroe had succeeded in academe not for his mental accomplishments but for his polished manners. He greeted Christy with a glib compliment.

"At last we have a president rooted in the culture of the people and not lost in the ivory towers of academe. I salute you, sir, for being salt of the earth."

Christy got right to business, asking Monroe about his unprepossessing academic record.

"A person has to make a choice, President Mahon, between tossing off ephemera and crafting works that last. I chose the latter course. In the humanities, it takes a great many years to acquire the experience and knowledge to write a big book, an important one. Some books are two-year books, some five-years, some take a lifetime. My book has been several years in the making. From the moment of my fabulous discovery, I knew that it would be eight or nine years before I finished the project. When I complete the editing, Bogus U. will bask in its glory. That I can promise."

Monroe went on to explain that his finding the Sally Hemings letters was the equal of a scholar discovering a new play by Shakespeare. The course of American history, he explained, would be altered quite as much as the course of English drama would be were a new Shakespeare play to come to light. Great discoveries caused reevaluations of societies and cultures. The disclosures in the letters would—with his analysis—lead to a reexamination of slavery, of the Declaration of Independence, of the Jefferson genealogy, and of American race relations in the twenty-first century. For these reasons, a number of funding agencies had subsidized his work with generous grants. How many faculty in the humanities could say the same? University, private, and national libraries, including the Library of Congress, had called him to make fabulous offers for the letters, but he had explained that they would be deposited in Bogus U.'s. rare-books room, making it one of the premiere research sources in America. The donation of the letters would cost the university nothing; all he asked in return was a positive tenure vote so that he could continue his scholarship within the comfortable confines of Bogus. Were he less devoted to the institution, if he didn't care quite as much for the mountains and skiing, he could take the letters and parlay them into tenure at Harvard, Princeton, or Yale, schools that had contacted him to ask if he would be willing to trade them for tenure and promotion to associate professor. Narcissa Whitman Poseuse, his champion and model, had already enriched Bogus with her crowning accomplishments; he would put the jewel in the crown.

"Pretty impressive stuff," said Christy, uncapping his fountain pen— only the hoi polloi used ballpoints—as if he planned to sign Monroe's tenure papers, which lay in front of him on his desk. 'I'm willing to put my John Hancock on the bottom line right now. Just hand me the letters."

"I can't do that."

"How come?"

"They're in a safe-deposit box."

"Open it."

Christy capped the pen.

"You don't understand. Because the letters are so valuable, I stored them in the Wells Fargo Bank, with the understanding that the box is not to be opened until I receive tenure."

"How do you study the letters if they ain't in front of you?"

Monroe pulled on the lapels of his brown tweed jacket and then fingered the knot in his tie before replying, "I've memorized the contents. They were too delicate to Xerox and I didn't trust anyone to photograph them. So I committed the letters to memory."

Christy returned the fountain pen to his desk drawer. "I'll tell you what, Monroe, you repeat word for word what's in the letters and I'll listen. Take your time, 'cause I'm in no hurry."

Monroe laughed nervously. "The spoken word is evanescent."

"Yeah, passing away like mist or smoke," Christy said proudly. He had already memorized the "e" words on his SAT vocabulary list, including "ephemera" and "evanescent."

"The vocal cannot be sustained. One sentence will die before the birth of another. How then can there be any continuity? The written language is one thing, the spoken quite another. Your listening to me recite the letter would be the same as if you heard a new musical piece. Unless you could study the score or hear it repeated, the phrases and movements would not cohere. It would sound like a farrago of notes. Therefore, it makes no sense for me to recount it."

"I said: I got time. You can tell me over and over, then I'll follow it nicely."

Monroe insisted that though he could hear the words in his head, they would be lost when transferred to speech. "As I tried to make clear, words, like musical notes, can be heard but not retained."

"Oh, I can sing a tune. You wanna hear the 'Rain in Spain'?"

"Uh, no thank you. I have to get back to my office."

"Not until I hear the Sally Hemings song."

"You don't seem to understand, sir. Unless you can see the cacographic errors for yourself, you cannot grasp Sally's meaning. In her spelling and handwriting reside truths that only the eye can discern, not the ear."

Although Monroe's vocabulary intimidated Christy, he remained outwardly unmoved. "As you relate the letters, you can explain what I'm missing."

Monroe again laughed, this time stridently. His hands shook. Summoning all the self-control at his command, he replied, "President Mahon, scholarship is like a lovely virgin. It should not be exposed unless the moment is ripe. To rush it would despoil it. What's needed are patience and restraint. So I ask you to wait for the right setting and time. Then I shall unveil my Galatea."

"You're no Pygmalion," Christy shot back, having read Bernard Shaw's play in Cliff Notes, which had also acquainted him with the myth. "You couldn't sculpt a turd, much less the truth. I don't believe you found any letters. You're nothing more than a prognosticator."

Monroe left Christy's office upset and confused. Had Christy called him a prevaricator, as he intended, Monroe would have understood, even if he didn't like what he heard. But to be called a prognosticator gave him pause; perhaps his remarks about the letters had led President Mahon to conclude that Monroe could predict the future of race relations in America. The president gave no hint of that drift, but shifty, unpredictable types like the prez invited special attention. Monroe would have to tell Professor Poseuse, who anxiously waited to hear about his meeting with Christy, that the papers remained unsigned, and that he by no means felt certain that the president would sign them.

DOUBTS, DISCRIMINATION,
AND DECEITS

Leaning on his elbows, hunched over his desk, Christy said, "I'm havin' second thoughts. If I give him tenure, I know what he gets, but what's in it for me, besides the goodwill of the trustees and a few other stiffs?"

Laura looked skeptical. "If I were you, I wouldn't underestimate the importance of that goodwill."

Christy cracked his knuckles. "I don't, but what's the financial payback?" Thumbing through Monroe's file, she never looked up as she replied, "None, except that you're saddled with a lame horse for the next thirty or forty years."

"Since I hear tenure's worth a million smackeroos, why don't we sell it and make a few bucks?"

"We already do."

"Then where's the dough?"

"It doesn't work that way. The university gives lifetime contracts in return for a professor devoting his-or her-life to teaching and to writing articles and books."

"Who reads the stuff?"

"Other scholars."

"Maybe I oughta read some of it."

"Spare yourself the pain. Most of it's unreadable."

"How come?"

"Jargon. I'll let you in on a little-known secret: most professors write execrably." This word, absent from his SAT book, caused Christy to frown. "Horribly," she translated.

"There's just one thing I can't figure out. How do you know who gets tenure and who doesn't?"

"Every university has a seven-year probationary period. During that time, the professors have to prove they can teach well and publish. In addition, they run errands and behave like gofers. Monroe has been sucking around since the day he arrived."

Christy scratched his head and briefly pondered Laura's analysis. "It sounds like the Mafia. You kiss the Godfather's ring, as well as his butt, and get into the gang in return."

"Monroe will never be a Don, but he would disown his dad to become a lower lieutenant."

"How did this Monroe fellow earn his bones?"

"Betraying his friends, trimming, following the money, and sucking around the people with power. For example, behind the scenes he knifed in the back the fellow who hired him and supported Pinchbeck on issues hurtful to his own department."

"Maybe I'll just out him."

"Forget it! In public when he has to make a choice, he twists and turns and makes it appear that he agrees with all sides."

Christy shrugged. "I could, you know, turn him down."

"The gang of four—Poseuse, Pinchbeck, Stine, and Pyrosis—will put up a fight, not to mention the trustees."

"I don't like bein' taken advantage of and pushed around, as Brooklyn Benny found out."

"If Larson gets a lawyer and sues, he could tie you up in the courts for years, unless you buy him out."

"No way."

Laura then proceeded to tell Christy about the case a year before of a woman in Uzbek Studies who had been denied tenure and hired a lawyer, an Uzbek himself, to charge Bogus U. with discrimination on the grounds that she was the only person west of the Mississippi who taught such a course, and that the western Uzbek population would be without a spokesperson if she were let go. The lawyer conducted a population study to determine how many Uzbeks lived in this area, and concluded that they were underrepresented in the schools of higher learning. Although the Uzbek professor smoked peyote—for religious reasons, she claimed, having come under the influence of a Native-American lover—and though she rarely met her classes, she contended that one of her lectures was worth five given by anyone else. On those rare occasions when she did come to class, she would sit on the end of the table and ask the students what they wanted to talk about, a teaching technique that requires no preparation on the part of the teacher, and makes no demands upon students. As a result, the students supported her efforts for tenure. Her scholarly publications, which had all been written in a little-used Uzbeki dialect and published in a journal printed in Bukhara, could not be refereed in the U.S. Since no one could understand what she had written, she was asked to translate her work into English, but refused on the grounds that in translation her prose would lose its piquancy and profundity.

Unable to evaluate her written work, Bogus U. looked for other grounds to dismiss her, and claimed that because so few students took her course, it didn't pay to continue her on the payroll. But the woman insisted that the fewer the students the greater the need to introduce them to ethnic studies. The university paid scant attention to this argument and countered that it already had Chicano, Black, Native-American, Asian, Latin-American, and Eskimo studies. Finally, she sued on grounds of gender discrimination. Since women on the Bogus U. faculty were outnumbered by men three-to-one, and she was the only Uzbek, she could demonstrate an institutional bias against hiring women, particularly those who came from Uzbekistan. In the end, Bogus U. gave her a million dollars, which she and her lover took back to Tashkent, where they opened a McDonald's franchise and earned enough money to build an estate adorned with peacocks.

Upon hearing this story, Christy decided it would be cheaper to pay a hit man to whack deadbeats than to cough up a million.

"Last year was a particularly bad one. We had several notorious cases."

Christy poured a glass of water and threw in two Alka-Seltzers. 'I'm listenin'."

"I keep telling you, don't drop your g's."

"It's hard to remember. Ing, ing, ing. I gotta—"

"Try: 'have to.'"

"I have to keep working on it."

"One fellow from English had friends of his from other universities send him letterhead stationery, on which he wrote letters extolling—"

"That's one of them words on the list you gave me."

"Not them words, those words. Yes, it's on your list. Do you know what it means?"

"Yeah, to praise highly."

"Good. Well, this character would write letters addressed to the chair of English and the viziers extolling the lecture that he'd presumably given at the university printed on the stationery. His friends mailed the letters for him so they bore the right postmark. He got caught when he used Yale stationery, and the chair of English called a friend of his in New Haven to ask about the lecture."

"What did he hope to gain?"

"A raise for having given a lecture at a prestigious university. But relax, there's more."

Christy finished his drink and wiped his mouth with his new red silk handkerchief.

"By the way," Laura instructed, "buy white hankies. Red ones make you look like a gangster."

"I really gotta . . . have to make notes of these things." He scribbled one note and then told her to continue.

"Professors often pad their résumés. Articles they list also show up with different titles in books they list separately."

"A kind of double dipping, you mean."

"Yes, and they even invent articles and make up journals, usually in some foreign place. One fellow listed journals, supposedly published in Shanghai, that didn't exist. And then there are the scientists. Most of their articles are coauthored and you have no way of determining a person's real contribution. Friends will often put their pals' names on their article, and expect the favor returned."

"If you can't trust professors, who can you trust?"

"Whom can you trust. We'll have to work on that one."

"Only stiffs use that word."

Laura, well aware that poorly educated people resent those who employ a vocabulary and grammar inaccessible to them, smiled and assured Christy that he would one day reach the Promised Land. "But let me continue. Another scam of professors is to appropriate the work of their students and publish it as their own. They steal ideas, they steal research data, they even steal the papers the students have written. I know one such guy in our rhetoric program, a rather portly fellow, who has never had an original idea in his life. Everything he writes comes from others."

"I need somethin' stronger." Christy went to the bar and removed a bottle of Scotch.

"A shot?"

"No, thanks."

Christy took two gulps from the bottle, capped it, reconsidered, took another swig, and put the bottle away. "How come I can get sent up for forgin' twenty-dollar bills, but these bozos don't get busted for theft?"

"You've heard of the fellow who forged Hitler's memoirs?" In fact, Christy had. "Well, I wouldn't be the least bit surprised if Monroe Larson forged the two Jefferson letters. How would we know, unless we solicited an expert opinion? By that time, Monroe will have tenure and I can assure you that the letters will either disappear, if they ever existed at all, or will somehow be lost through fire or theft. Want to bet?"

Christy grew reflective. Hadn't he been hired in part to corral the felonious faculty? Surely the trustees would understand why he didn't want to buy a lame horse. And if they insisted he do so, why shouldn't he profit from the purchase? In his youth he had read about the great con men. He knew all the scams, from pyramid schemes to off-shore real estate, and though he had never heard about university frauds, he quickly perceived that if he could catch the coneys, he could easily blackmail them. According to Laura, Bogus U. had dismissed one or two profs for fraud. Christy regarded that as a waste of good money. Why not just threaten to fire them, and then collect? In fact, as he sat there listening to his guide through the underworld, not in the least aware of Boccaccio's Laura, he envisioned a monthly check-off system for those who had been caught and wanted to hang on to their jobs. A hundred or two hundred dollars a month times ten professors, maybe twenty, would bring in nearly fifty thousand a year. Small potatoes perhaps, but fifty here and fifty there could pretty soon add up to real money. Now if he could just get tenure on a fees-paying basis, he would be putting Bogus U. on the right track. But in the back of his mind the question still lingered whether to use the money for himself or for Bogus. He was yet to have that discussion with Laura.

"You free for dinner?" he asked.

Still smarting over Shawn, Laura relented. "How about Chez Lee?"

"What's that?"

"A Vietnamese restaurant."

Never having eaten anything more exotic than artichokes, Christy harbored deep suspicions about ethnic foods. But he agreed. She did the ordering. To his vast pleasure, Christy ate Hao Nuong (grilled mussels with lemon pepper sauce), Banh Chien (dumplings), BoLa Lot (beef and shrimp rolled in grape leaves), and Mong Co (Pad Thai).

The owner of the restaurant stopped to ask how they liked their meal. A beautiful older woman, Madame Lee had turned more than a few heads in her day. Christy, slurping a mussel, wiped his mouth and exclaimed, "Best food I ever ate!" She said the fried bananas would be on the house.

CHRISTY'S RECURRING
NIGHTMARE

After a week of appointments, briefings, interviews, engagements, receptions, and gatherings, Christy never wanted to see another Vizier, Pasha, or Bey; not another professor, student, or staffer; not another contractor, vendor, or donor; not another legislator or parent. Although his doubts had begun on day one, he was now certain that he had entered an underworld more vicious and devious than any he had ever known. By week's end, he understandably wondered about the wisdom of continuing as president. For three nights running, he had had the same disquieting dream: Laura, holding his hand, was leading him downward into the lower depths of the university steam room, with its maze of passages and tunnels, its screaming generators churning out heat and boiling water and electrical power. As they descended, they passed different levels, each inhabited by another grotesquerie: a talking penis, lodged flaccidly in a light fixture, whining about having been assigned a classroom without windows and having to teach three days a week instead of two; a microcephalic Bakeless repeatedly burping; a creature in the shape of a $, saying over and over again, "Bottom Line," "Leverage," "Game Plan," and "Synergy"; a hideously bloated man growing larger and larger beseeching Christy to relieve him from the disease of grade inflation; a skeleton, with the head of Ms. Steif, clicking its jaws and chattering, "A rule is a rule, Mahon's a fool I A rule is a rule, Mahon's a fool"; a jaundiced torso confined to a chamber pot shitting constantly, because so full of it; an enormous nose with a dark stain around it genuflecting and mumbling, "Bend over, Brown Rover"; a disembodied mouth jabbering through a profusion of curls about "my incomparable contributions to the scholarly world"; a fingerless homunculus bewailing the false entries in his bibliography; a pretzel-shaped man holding a black baby clutching a transparent safe-deposit box with nothing inside.

134

LAURA INTERROGATES SHAWN

"It's Millicent Caiaphas, isn't it?" Laura snarled. "The coach has six saintly daughters. But you had to pick the seventh, the fallen angel."

"What makes you think I'm seeing her?"

Shawn and Laura were seated under the gazebo at the west end of the campus. She studied his face for signs of lying. His nostrils always flared when he did. Shawn Keogh, an athletic lad of middling height, blessed with striking good looks and straight black hair, had but one physical imperfection, a deep scar on his chin from an errant lacrosse stick. His moral imperfections came from his relish for slumming. Brought up in New York City among wealthy Eastsiders, he had accompanied his father, the Chief of Police, on some exciting busts among the demimonde, people who'd given him a taste for the down and dirty. Shawn had graduated from Bearfield Academy, in Massachusetts, where he spent a fifth year taking pre-college courses, before he accepted a scholarship from Bogus U. ostensibly to play lacrosse, only to discover that the money had come from the football coach, a Bible thumper who, in his imperfect understanding, had understood Shawn's high school coach to say "duh cross." Instead of playing either sport, Shawn, who had stayed at Bogus to complete a Master's degree, worked in the Athletic office at the public relations desk, where he was privy to the gifts and the graft underlying the Bogus U. football program, information that he readily passed on to Laura.

Putting his hand around her waist, Shawn tried to kiss her, but she brushed him aside. He adored Laura's good looks, but was slightly scared of her smarts. In her company, he felt like the guy who shows up at the prom with the homecoming queen. He knew that she gave him a certain cachet with all the young men on campus, to say nothing of the lascivious faculty.

By no means stupid, he did find abstract thought taxing and had therefore chosen to major in Semaphorics, the favorite subject of his Athletic Department pals. His admiration for Laura eclipsed whatever passion he felt for Millicent; but the former prodded him mentally, while the latter praised him profusely. Lacking the discipline to earn Laura's honor, he lived a double life. In public, Laura graced his arm; behind closed doors, he divided his time between both women, an arrangement that had brought him to his current pass.

"I already explained. If I want to keep my job in the Athletic office, I have to be on good terms with Coach Caiaphas and pretend to like his daughter."

"Since when does Millicent come with the job?"

Clearly frustrated, he sighed and repeated, "Coach often calls me to come over. That's why I'm inside the house."

"And her."

"How can you say that?"

"You bought rubbers at the pharmacy." Shawn's nostrils flared.

"Your face gives you away."

"No, I'm ashamed to admit it," he blustered, "I bought them for one of the football players who's on probation for pawing some coed."

Laura looked toward the mountains. In the afternoon sun, the trees exuded a blue glow.

"Chill out, Laura, I would never cheat on you."

She gave him the silent treatment, knowing that eventually he'd say something incriminating.

"You know Ronny Rambut, the linebacker. He took some sorority girl for a woodsy and instead of roasting marshmallows over an open fire, he got free with his hands. Now the girl and Billy have made up, except that he's on probation. So he asked me to buy him some condoms." Shawn paused. Laura failed to respond. "He probably could have bought them off campus, but he said he needed them right away. I dashed in and picked up a three pack."

Laura ran her tongue over her teeth and then bared them. "You, my dear boy, are a fucking liar, or should I say a lying fuck? You bought a box of twelve Sheiks, because that little pussy Millicent, like her jackass father, Coach Caiaphas, doesn't believe in the pill. I remember her marching with her old man outside the women's clinic protesting both the pill and abortions."

"You can say what you want about me, Laura, but—"

"Your little sweetie's going to put you in trouble. Just wait. You'll be sorry. The last guy who humped her met an untimely end."

"I swear, Laura, I'm seeing her just to get information."

Laura pondered the word "seeing." It could mean dating, viewing her parts, screwing, or even understanding, as in seeing the point.

"The question is: is she seeing you?"

Shawn, not nearly as quick as Laura, replied, "If I'm seeing her, then she's seeing me."

"In your birthday suit."

"Why don't you believe me?"

"You sound like a song title."

"How can I prove to you that I'm not cheating?"

"Ask Millicent and me to dinner. Sometime during the evening, tell her that we—you and I—are an item."

Shawn's mouth suddenly felt parched. He worked his tongue to generate saliva.

"All right, Laura, I admit it. The Sheiks I bought for myself. Just in case something came up."

"Oh, knowing you, I can definitely say it will come up."

"If I promise—"

"Spare me the lies. You're just lucky I didn't bring in some friends to cut off your dick. But frankly it no longer matters."

"You sound as if you're breaking it off."

"I should have broken *it* off a long time ago."

The emphasis gave Shawn pause. But he rallied. "Look, you've got me all wrong. I'm not doing it with her. I swear."

Laura noticed that one of her fingernails had split. She violently bit it off. "Let's not make a scene. We're both adults. A friend I'll always be, but a—"

He interrupted. "Don't say it. I beg you, just trust me. You'll see that I'm as good as my word. Millicent is a means to keep my job, which comes with free football tickets, nothing more."

WORD SPREADS:
CHRISTY'S A MARKED MAN

In no time, the street buzzed that there was a contract to polish off Christy, and that the killer would be masquerading as a professor. Christy, feeling the need of a hideaway, ordered that the first floor of the power plant be soundproofed, fortified, and fashioned into a comfortable retreat. It was here, in fact, that he occasionally met with workmen to play cards and craps. He also had Laura scrutinize all recent hires. She came up with four names of people who had been appointed to replace ailing professors.

"Which departments?" asked Christy anxiously.

"Classics, Fine Arts, Dance, and Music."

"I never met a trigger man who knew a damn thing about Latin or Greek," he said. "So the person's gotta come from one of those other departments."

"Don't slur your consonants."

"Here I'm worryin' about gettin' iced, and you're correctin' my pronunciation."

"It's never too late."

"What do you think I ought to do?"

Laura appreciated Christy's concern on more than humane grounds—she was in fact beginning to enjoy his company—and therefore replied, "Call in each one for an interview and test them."

"I get the picture. Quiz 'em. Chances are they don't know beans about their subjects."

Laura sighed. "Unfortunately that's true of a good many faculty. Ignorance of their fields is no way to judge."

"What then?"

She went to her desk and returned with a sheet of paper printed with two sentences:

1. Only the inherent metaphoricity of Renaissance realism could exalt this humblest of garments to such efflorescence and convert the *ostentatio genitalium* decently into a fanfare of cosmic truth.
2. Only Renaissance realism's tendency to symbolism could turn a breechclout into a banner.

"Ask them which sentence they prefer."

"Why?"

"It's a long shot, but the person who picks the second one may well be your man. Professors love complexity. Laypeople prefer simplicity. I suggest you make several copies. In the meantime, I'll run a police check on their backgrounds."

CHRISTY TRIES TO
DISCOVER THE HIT MAN

Laura's research turned up nothing unusual. The four people—one man, Panjang Sutra from Classics, and three women, Galena Isadora from Dance, Artemisia Gentileschi from Fine Arts, and Troxy Dollop from Music—had all received their Ph.D. degrees in the last four years, and had all worked as gypsy scholars teaching wherever and whenever they could. Christy had assumed they'd all be men, and that he could omit the classicist from his list. But upon learning that three of the new hires were women, he had to rethink his assumption. He directed Laura to tell them that he wanted to get acquainted—just a friendly how-do-you-do.

The first, Panjang Sutra, a well-built young man of forty, came from a family of scholars. He had received his first degree at the University of Singapore, had taught briefly in Texas and at a preparatory school in North Carolina, and had now found a position at Bogus U. His short hair and unlined face gave him a boyish appearance. As Christy studied his résumé, Panjang silently hoped that he had not been summoned to the president's office to explain his rigorous grades on the first test, which had prompted a number of student complaints. He shifted nervously in his chair.

"I see that your specialty is Greek."

"Particularly Greek armaments."

"Really?"

"And warfare. I wrote my thesis on the Greek way of dying."

"So I take it you know a lot about how to croak a guy."

"Classically speaking."

"How'd they do it in them days?"

"With swords, and knives, and lances, and arrows, and of course poisons."

"Yeah, of course." Christy suddenly felt uneasy.

140

Panjang reached into his pocket and removed a small brown bag. "Would you like a fig, President Mahon? I eat them all the time. They're good for the digestive system."

Somewhere in the back of Christy's mind he remembered seeing a television show about the early Romans, and someone killed by means of poisoned figs.

"No, thanks, I never touch them. By the way, what happened to your last boss, the headmaster of the school where you worked?"

"He died from ingesting arsenic."

"Ain't that unusual?"

"He apparently confused the saltcellar and the rat poison."

"In North Carolina does that sort of thing happen often?"

"In fact, it's rather common."

"I see." Christy removed from his desk the paper that Laura had given him, bearing the two sentences, one written in academic jargon and the other in straightforward English. "Mr. Sutra would you take a look at this and advise me which is the better."

Panjang reflected. "The first is publishable, the second is not."

"Yeah, but which do you like?"

"If I wanted to get into print and didn't want my colleagues to think me simple-minded, I would pick the first and nix the second, even though it has the virtue of pellucidness."

Christy, unable to interpret Dr. Sutra's remarks, sighed, "Well, thanks for coming in, Panjang; I'll be watching how you do."

"May I ask a favor, President Mahon?"

"What's that?"

"If any students call your office to complain about my grades, have them put their complaints in writing. Then you can judge whether they deserve your attention."

"I'll do that."

Panjang left and Christy hastily scribbled a note to himself to have the campus police check on Panjang's recent grocery purchases.

The next instructor, Artemisia Gentileschi, a dark-haired Italian painter and art historian, elicited a broad smile from Christy. Her folder indicated that she was single and widowed. Her yellow sweater, which accentuated her bosom, and her full red lips put a rise in Christy's pants.

"Whaddya paint?"

"Death masks."

"You're kiddin'."

"No, I take for my subjects the death masks in the Vatican galleries."

"How come?"

"I am also a historian. A number of artists died violent deaths. The subject fascinates me."

She had studied in Venice and had finished her postgraduate work in Rome, where she had met her husband at the Accademia.

"I see your husband recently died. My condolences."

"It was terrible. He died from strangulation. While painting a mural, he got caught in the ropes of the scaffolding."

"An accident?"

"I saw it happen."

"How awful. Anyone else there?"

"No, only me."

Christy found the rise in his pants receding and his interest plummeting. "Would you mind takin' a look at this paper and tellin' me which of the two sentences you prefer."

Pondering the words, she hemmed and hawed. "You see, it's a matter of taste . . . of course some would say the first has the whiff of the academic lamp while others would say that the other speaks to the person in the street. But of course the average Joe would not be interested in this subject, to begin with. So the second sentence is really speaking to a non-existent audience, if you follow my meaning."

Christy did, concluding that academics were incapable of a straight answer.

"Well, good talkin' to you. If you need anything, just call my office and ask for Laura Favoloso. She'll help you."

Artemisia exited and Christy made a note to have the police investigate the cause of her husband's death.

The next instructor, Galena Isadora, thin as a string and graceful as a swan, slipped into his office balletically, with toes pointed outward. "Do sit down and tell me about yourself."

"I studied vith Kief ballet and have performed in Moskva at Bolshoi, in London at Royal Opera House, and in New York at Carnegie Hall. Dee smaller cities shall go unnamed. You can read dem in my file. Truth is . . . outside of Moskva, London, and New York, every city is feeling like Dubuque."

"I've been to New York, but not them other places."

"You don't know vot you are missing."

Galena had a small mouth, almond eyes, a long thin nose, and skin as smooth and white as alabaster. Her gentle finger movements reminded him of water lilies stirred by a breeze. Although flat-chested, like most dancers, she intrigued Christy, who quickly perused her file.

"It says your specialty is ballet and the classical forms."

"For my purposes, I adopt from Russian ice skaters 'death spiral,' which I frequently perform. Death fascinates me. For example, I am loving to dance to *Death and the Maiden* and to a dramatization of *Murder in the Cathedral*."

"What is it about death that grabs you?"

"Its suddenness. A number of friends perfectly healthy one moment keeled over dead next."

"Did you see it happen?"

"I vitnessed each and every one."

"No one else saw it, right?"

"Yes, how you know?"

"A hunch. I've been havin' a lot of them lately."

"Me, too, strange premonitions of death in high places."

Christy showed her the two sentences, and she dramatically threw her hands in the air, exclaiming:

"Dee first must have been composed by someone with a flair for arabesques, and dee second by a Puritan. Neither has the rhythm I vould admire."

"Yeah, but what about clarity?"

"Clarity depends on your level of education and range of experience."

"Do all professors speak this way?"

"How else are vee to distinguish ourselves?"

As Galena glided out, Christy made another note to the campus police. The last instructor, Troxy Dollop, a radiant, androgynous-looking Asian with satiny brown skin, had earned a degree in paleomusicology. She studied ancient musical instruments, and her materials ranged from bones with a few holes drilled through the surface to hollowed-out gourds, presumably strung at one time with some kind of hatching to produce a sound. She preferred whistles to drums, which she regarded as less sophisticated.

"I see from your file," said Christy, detecting about her a familiar smell of sweetness, reminiscent of cloves and strawberry, "you were born in Malaya, went to Yale, and got the job at Bogus when Professor Dithyramb died suddenly."

"Yes, what you say is all true."

"His death was awfully peculiar."

"Quite. He was trying to play an ancient flute and inhaled some kind of pestilential dust."

"Let me guess. The flute came from you?"

"Actually from a friend. But you were close. How did you know?"

"I have a sort of sixth sense."

"Professor Dithyramb served as my friend's doctoral advisor. He was passing through town and stopped to say hello. Professor Dithyramb asked about his research. My friend showed him a bone flute he had unearthed in Borneo. Professor Dithyramb put his mouth to it and immediately took deathly sick."

"Just the two of them, by themselves, right?"

"You really are psychic."

For some reason, the aroma she exuded made him think of a tropical island and someplace exotic, and her shoulder-length hair invited his attention. Heavy and black, it shone and floated lightly around her face when she moved her head. He wanted to touch it but wouldn't dare. She smiled and he noticed for the first time her high cheekbones, delicately curved mouth, perfect teeth, and seductive eyes. He could see a naughtiness in them, which directed his gaze to her figure. She had great trotters and a small waist, but a flat chest, like a dancer's. Leaving his desk, he walked behind her and brushed her hair with his hand.

"I pace when I'm thinking," he said, and walked back to his desk, again touching her hair. Intoxicated by her presence, he dreamily handed her the paper with the two sentences and remarked, "Ain't that first one a pisser? At least the second one makes sense."

"You're absolutely right," said Troxy, observing that sense without grace was tantamount to salad without dressing.

"I like your taste. You wouldn't be free Saturday night? I know a good Vietnamese restaurant."

"As a matter of fact, I am."

"Ever had Pad Thai?"

"Numerous times."

"You'll love the way they make it at the Chez."

"Let me scribble my address." She opened her bag and removed a gold fountain pen and a small memo book with removable pages. "I just found an apartment."

"Say about seven? We can stop at the Cameo Hotel and have drinks first, and then go have our eats."

She handed Christy the page. "Be sure to come up. I'm on the second floor, number 204. Just ring from downstairs. I'd like you to see my place."

Christy knew enough to play it safe. "I'll wait in the lobby."

"It's a rather attractive flat."

"You got a flat of some kind?"

"I just said so."

"How come? You keep a bicycle in your pad?"

Troxy chuckled. "Flat is just an English expression that means apartment. You'll be the first to bang around in it."

Christy paused over her meaning, and decided that security came before sex. "I have a bad foot."

"Take the elevator."

"I suffer from claustrophobia."

"Well, then, perhaps some other time, when your foot has healed and you can climb the stairs."

"Yeah, I wanna be ready."

"It could prove new and exciting. You know, start slowly, work our way into things, and then—"

CREON'S DEFENSE

Phineas Ort awoke late and, without disturbing DeeDee, extricated himself from the bed. He could smell fresh croissants and strong coffee. Reynald, as always, had prepared a bracing breakfast. As Phineas dressed, he smiled to himself. Events had turned out better than one might have expected. DeeDee regularly enabled him to pop his cork and even taught him a few tricks that Phineas thought more Roman than Greek, tricks that should be kept from married couples, he felt, lest that fragile institution be undermined by the knowledge that sex is best when it's dirty.

DeeDee stirred and murmured. Phineas divined that she was asking him a question and requested she repeat it.

"I want more," he heard her say, but the rest of the sentence was lost in the blankets.

"More," he exclaimed, "we did it three times!"

"No, not that. I want more of Antigone. Jackie Brown led you on a wild goose chase when he wanted to know about the gods. After all the stories you told about Zeus and Hera and Achilles and all them others, my head's spinning. Let's get back to the play."

Phineas reflected a moment before responding. Having been trained as a professor, he felt obliged to explain how art imitates life and the importance of context. "The function of the gods in Greek literature must be understood. One must have some familiarity with the role they play in life's unfolding drama." He smiled in admiration of his own exposition.

DeeDee flounced out of bed, threw off her shift, shook her pendulous bosom for Phineas's sake, and shouted as she grabbed a stick of gum and entered the bathroom, "Wait for breakfast. I just wanna take a quick shower."

Like a great many people, she did her best thinking under the influence of hot water. It relaxed her and set her flesh tingling. In the shower

146

she plotted a romance novel, her favorite genre, which would begin with a mysterious stranger showing up in Schroon Lake during the off season, where he meets a beautiful woman strikingly similar to DeeDee Lite. Her first sentence would read, "He suddenly appeared out of nowhere, tall, very tall, blonde, and sort of handsome."

Phineas finished breakfast and turned, as he had every morning since arriving, to the large dining-room table, where the group had read Antigone out loud several times and now, given his explanation of the Greek gods, were prepared to discuss the knotty moral issues or, as Jackie Brown called them, the ball busters.

Waiting for Reynald and DeeDee to load the dishwasher, he looked over his notes for the day's lesson. Eddie and Jackie, who had been having a smoke on the deck, joined him.

"We was, if yous can believe it, talking about Creon. Me and Eddie," said Jackie proudly. "That's my part. I gotta lot of things to worry about if I'm duh king." Jackie went on to share his thoughts about the importance of not being "disrespected," while conceding that "if there ain't no honor among thieves, you're headin' for a fall." By the time he finished his musings, Reynald and DeeDee had joined the group for the discussion.

Phineas started right in. "Creon's statement to the people, after the death of the two brothers, could pass for French existentialism." Seeing the adenoidal stares around him, Phineas quickly retreated, as he often did during these sessions, to a simple diction and explanation. "During World War II, the French observed that you could never predict in advance how a person would behave under the pressure of soul-testing circumstances, like torture and fear. We are how we behave, which may or not be as we imagine ourselves. I, for example, may regard myself as brave, but I can't really know how bravely I'd behave were I subjected to electric shock or beatings or sleep deprivation. Our actions define us."

Jackie Brown shook his head in agreement. "Yeah, I never thought I could earn my bones, but whacking Little Sonny Weiss turned me into a new man."

Phineas directed the group to look at line one-six-nine. "Here Creon says that 'You can never know what a man is made of, / His character or powers of intellect, / Until you have seen him tried in rule and office.' So at this moment we have no idea how Creon will behave."

DeeDee interrupted to say that they did know because they had read the play several times, and that she disagreed with Creon's decisions. Phineas patiently explained that an audience willingly suspends its skepticism or prior knowledge and accepts the convention of the play, namely, that the story is unfolding before us for the first time.

DeeDee said she knew what he meant. "Six times I seen *The Sound of Music* and I cry every time, even though I already know the ending."

"My point exactly," said Phineas. "You come to it new each time." He then proceeded to outline Creon's dilemma. "If the king appears weak, the people will have no respect for him or the state. But untempered punishment invites the charge of ruthlessness. Creon says, 'A man who holds the reins of government / And does not follow the wisest policies / But lets something scare him from saying what he thinks, / I hold despicable, and always have done.' He then goes on to make clear how he views his responsibility to the state. 'I have no time for anyone who puts / His popularity before his country.'"

Phineas explicated. "Creon, you will note, goes on to explain that if he saw even one danger signal, he would speak up, and would never allow an enemy of his country to be a friend of his. For example, Eddie and Jackie here are good friends. They both work for Brooklyn Benny and his gang. Let's call the gang the kingdom or state. Supposing, Eddie, your buddy Jackie did something to undermine the gang; would he still be your friend?"

Eddie had been exceptionally quiet during Phineas's seminars, and even now found it hard to put into words his troubled thoughts. "I've been listening every day. These Greeks, they don't sound like the guys in the cop shows. On the TV, it all works out okay. But these guys ask some tough questions. Creon and Antigone . . . hell, they're related. She's his niece. I couldn't top my niece."

"What about Jackie?" Phineas asked. "Could you top him?"

"He's not really blood of my blood, but in some ways he is. We both took the oath when we went to work for Benny. Geez, that's a hard one."

"What if Benny asked you to execute Jackie; would you do it?"

"You're going to drive me crazy with these questions."

"Pretend that Benny said that it was for the good of the gang."

But Eddie insisted that Jackie would never betray the gang. When Phineas pointed out that he was being evasive, Eddie wisely said that he agreed with the French: you couldn't tell until the moment arrived. For him to speculate in advance was useless. Phineas found Eddie's retreat amusing and asked Jackie the same question: would he remove Eddie if Brooklyn Benny gave him that assignment.

Jackie looked at Eddie and confessed, "I couldn't do it. I'd get someone else to finger him."

"You would!" said Eddie, obviously hurt.

"Benny's the boss."

"Yeah, but we're friends!"

"Shit, I hate when we go on about these things. They ain't got nothin' to do with the real world. They're all hyperheretical. I'm strictly a meat-and-potatoes man."

While Eddie rued what he had heard, DeeDee allowed as she would not kill a relative or a friend, only an enemy.

"But what if the enemy were a relative or friend?" said Phineas.

"How could he be," she replied incredulously, "when we're related or good pals!"

Unable to make DeeDee understand how a friend might become a foe, he abandoned the field, deferring to Reynald, who said he needed to prepare the lamb chops for lunch.

"After we eat," said DeeDee, "I think we oughta rent *The Sound of Music* and have a good cry."

"With any luck," added Phineas, "we might be able to find a movie of *Antigone*. Then you can appreciate the force of Creon's crisis."

"What do you want to do," complained Eddie, "turn friends into enemies? No wonder my old man told me to stay away from college. He said it would just confuse me and ruin my mind. He wasn't kidding!"

CHRISTY WINES AND DINES TROXY

At the appointed time on Saturday night, Christy stood in the lobby of Troxy's apartment, the Crescent Arms, and read the names next to the eight buzzers: A. Rothstein, C. Luciano, L. Diamond, V. Coll, J. Masseria, F. Yale, A. Flegenheimer, D. O'Bannion. No Troxy Dollop. Apartment 204, the number she had given him, bore the name F. Yale. Christy remembered that she had received a Ph.D. from Yale. Perhaps, he reasoned, that explained the different name. He rang and waited. A few seconds later, Troxy's voice trilled over the intercom.

"Christy?"

"I'm in the lobby."

"Sure you don't want to come up?"

"I'll just wait for you here."

"Down in a minute."

The elevator opened and Troxy swished out in a gossamer red dress that faintly revealed her pink bra, her flat, firm stomach, and her bikini underwear. On her arm she carried a glossy carmine coat. Christy vaguely recalled a story told to him once about a woman in a red dress, but couldn't remember anything more definite than the color and its relation to a movie house. As she took him by the arm—Christy liked tactile gestures—he detected about her the familiar scent of cloves and plums. She led him to his car at the rear of the apartment building. How did she know where he'd parked? Christy rightly concluded that Troxy's flat, as she called it, stood at the back of the building, and that she had seen him drive up. He further deduced, correctly, that she had probably been watching for him, because the chances of her just happening to see him park seemed rather remote.

His reservation at Chez Lee gave them more than an hour's time to linger over drinks at the Cameo Hotel. Entering the large paneled lobby,

with its tiled floor and its towering ceiling topped with a skylight of Tiffany glass, he prided himself on his recent triumphs: snuffing out Brooklyn
Benny, finagling an appointment as president of Bogus U., cowing much
of the faculty, and enlisting for companions two fine women, Laura and
Troxy. Christy gently touched Troxy's elbow and led her upstairs to the
mezzanine lounge, where a waiter seated them and took their order. She
removed a cigarette from a silver case, tapped it on the lid, handed Christy
a butane lighter and leaned toward him as he ignited the flame. Inhaling
deeply, she asked:

"Have you been well?"

"Yeah, not too bad."

She relished her cigarette and admired the surroundings. He savored
the sweet smell and told her what he knew about the Cameo Hotel, information that Laura had assembled in a three-ring notebook listing all the
eateries in town. When the waiter returned, they sipped their drinks, he,
Bols gin, chilled and straight, she, a Bloody Mary. He asked how she liked
teaching at Bogus. "What I expected. Self-indulgent faculty and spoiled
kids. More important, how do you feel being a marked man?"

"How do you know?"

"Word gets around."

Laura immediately came to mind, and Christy wondered whether she
could be entirely trusted.

"I do what I can to protect myself, but it's a crap shoot."

"What precautions have you taken?"

He reviewed what he had done: reinforced his house and car, obtained
a permit and gun (he touched his coat jacket), and arranged for the police
to discreetly observe his house. She nodded sympathetically.

"You're right. After a certain point, it's just a roll of the dice."

Christy sipped his drink. Troxy silently smoked.

"The campus cops say they have some leads," said Christy.

"Oh?"

"They think it's someone from the Robaccia gang."

"If I were they, I'd check out the student body."

"What did I ever do to any of them?"

She snuffed out her cigarette.

"They know you issued an order telling the faculty to crack down on
grades and lax graduation standards. You could hardly have done anything
more provocative. They're in a state of rebellion. In all my classes they're
complaining."

"To tell you the truth, I don't see the gripe. I'm only tryin' to give the
kids a better education."

Christy speared an olive with a toothpick, as Troxy told him that students loved grade inflation.

Gnawing on the olive and putting the pit on his napkin, he said, "I can understand why the kids don't like it, but what do professors get out of givin' high grades?"

"Good evaluations, which translate into raises, student adulation, and free time. No student complains about an A."

He asked for a refill and two olives. When his drink came, he vacantly stirred it. An idea was taking shape in his mind.

Troxy told him that his attempts to curb grade inflation had led only to whining about academic freedom. He could solve the problem, she said, by telling the registrar to include on the transcript not only the student's final grade but also the class average.

"If all the students in the class received an A, then the person reading the transcript would know that A was the average grade. If that doesn't work, you can use the English system: send student essays off campus to a panel of impartial readers."

Christy hardly listened. His mind was churning. Why give away grades for nothing? Just sell them: $1,000 for an A, $500 for a B, and no charge for a C, D, or F. He would run the entire operation out of a new enterprise he envisioned. And by installing his own person and telling the students all grades were negotiable at a higher level, he could keep his faculty content and the students happy. This scheme, he felt, could be a real money-maker.

Troxy found his idea intriguing but warned, "Some faculty, though not all, will object."

"We'll give them a cut. That way they get an allowance and at the same time keep their hands clean."

Troxy pondered what she had just heard and nodded. "President Mahon, you really have a genius for working all ends."

Christy thought of an end he hadn't worked yet, but perhaps that would come later.

Leaving the Cameo Hotel, Christy and Troxy drove to Chez Lee for dinner. As a young woman led them to their table, Christy spotted Laura sitting with Shawn, who appeared to be pleading with her. He greeted them and introduced Troxy. The two women scrutinized each other and seemed to come to the same conclusion: women, beware women. At their table, Troxy questioned Christy closely about Laura. Her inordinate interest put him on guard.

"She's quite good-looking," said Troxy, "and well-spoken. Where does she come from?"

Christy had no intention of saying Brooklyn, studiously avoiding any mention of the scene of his crime. "I don't know much about her. She works in my office and does a terrific job."

"Did you see the way that young man—"

"Shawn."

"Was fawning over her? If I were you, I'd watch her. She could have something up her sleeve."

"What does that mean?"

"Be careful. That's all I'm saying."

Christy puzzled whether Troxy had privileged information, and if she did, where it came from. His thoughts tumbled in riotous confusion, flooded by questions that he dare not utter aloud. Would Laura ever do anything to hurt him? No. Impossible. Why, then, did Troxy say what she did? Could Troxy be trusted? To be unable to anticipate another's behavior rendered one vulnerable. Hell, it drove gangs, societies, and civilizations crazy. Try to stay cool.

"Where do you come from?" he said.

"Me? London."

"In England?"

"Spot on. That's right."

"So that explains your accent."

"I suppose."

"Tell me about it."

He already envisioned the two of them visiting the Tower of London and sitting in a theater enjoying a musical.

"I left Malaya for London as a child. My father distilled rum and felt that he could make more money in England. Both my parents died in a car accident outside Hull, which is a port city. I went to work for a sempstress."

"What's that?"

"A seamstress. The social worker said I would need to earn my own keep. That's what I didn't have, keep! You know what it's like being a sempstress? I worked for a Miss Simmonds, a milliner and dressmaker, who had a shop in a narrow little street leading off Covent Garden. I worked there for two years—earning a pittance. I slept on a cot in Greek Street, in Soho. A rough area. I had a room below ground level, where I could look up through the grating and see the whores walking by. Every morning I had to be at work at six. I worked till eleven at night, often later. A dress ordered in the morning and fitted in the afternoon had to be finished the same night, and sent home the first thing next day. I slaved for two years and then met a barrister who took me into his home and paid for my education. He saved my life. I'm twenty-eight now." She laughed. "If I were to die tomorrow, I'd be twenty-eight forever. At least that way I wouldn't grow old. Twenty-eight forever." She smiled at Christy enigmatically and remarked, "There are worse things than dying young."

Christy felt uneasy. Why mention dying? Was she ill? Before the food came, she removed her cosmetic bag from her purse and went to the ladies' room. Across the room, he could see Shawn leaning across the table, using his hands in an entreating manner. No more than a minute after Troxy had disappeared from sight, Laura left the table and followed her to the restroom. He wondered what they would say if they actually ran into each other. Lewd thoughts raced through his mind. Didn't all the major mobsters have several molls? If he could induce Laura and Troxy to play Jane and Jill to his Jack, he'd be one of the boys. A schedule for alternate lovemaking danced in his head when Troxy returned and gave him a come-hither smile. She had reapplied her lipstick; he could tell from a slight misdirection on her lower lip. Laura, too, had returned to her table. Christy wanted to say to Troxy, "You're a great looking broad," but given what Laura had told him about feminism, he feared that she would take such a comment amiss. Instead he told her that he loved her cocoa skin, her high cheekbones, her dark eyes and hair, and concluded by telling her that she was a "knockout."

"If I understand the meaning of that word," she replied, "someone loses consciousness. Who might that person be?"

"You mean who gets knocked out?"

"Precisely."

"Me! I'm sayin' you knock me out."

"Delighted to," she said, and smiled wantonly.

Christy threw diplomacy to the winds and proposed, "How about comin' over to my place after dinner?"

"Believe it or not, Christy, I'm an old-fashioned girl. I like to be wooed, courted. Why don't we go to dinner a few times, take in the theater, maybe even attend a few lectures."

"Can't we just skip the prelims?"

"At the moment, I'm not prepared."

Understanding her to mean birth control, Christy said, "I have stuff we can use."

But she declined. "I'm a careful person. Everything has to be just right."

SHAWN KEEPS A
CLANDESTINE DATE

For some time Shawn had feared that Laura would find out about his affair with Millicent Caiaphas, a moon-faced, Barbie-doll pretty nineteen-
year-old, who used too much eye shadow and rouge, wore tight mini-skirts,
and waddled around on stiletto heels. Reared in a new age, she believed
in the magical power of crystals and magnets. Proudly calling herself a
"homebody," she could spend half the day sunning herself or, as she called
it, connecting with nature, and the other half frolicking in bed, since she had
a mind for little else. Shawn found her insatiable sexual appetite appealing.

The Caiaphas house, a two-story rambling brick structure with a
swimming pool, stood on a small rise overlooking a large aerated pond and,
beyond that, a bird sanctuary. A sloping lawn, interrupted only by aspens,
ran to the water's edge, where an aluminum canoe bobbed at anchor. In the
evening, coyotes filled the night with their high-pitched cries, prowling for
rabbits and errant domestic cats. Shawn parked in the driveway next to an
unfamiliar car, and rang the front bell. Millicent opened the door. She told
him that Pastor Schuft, the family minister, was down at the pond with her
parents, and that shortly he would be saying a prayer for the sanctity of family and the passing of the evening light. Shawn and Millicent exited on the
west side of the house, passed the sauna and paused at the head of the lawn.

"If I had a baby girl, I'd maybe name her Rose. I like that name, don't
you?" Before Shawn could respond, Millicent continued. "One of the girls
at the office was talking about a movie star who has a daughter Rose—and
also about Elizabeth Taylor's divorces."

Shawn took her arm and led her down the slope. Next to the pond
they joined the others for the evening prayers. The pastor, a tall reedy fellow
with a chalky face, yellow hair, and equine teeth, shook hands with Shawn,
who greeted him deferentially, calling him "Sir."

"Why so formal?" said the pastor. "Just call me Pastor Schufty." Shawn rolled his eyes.

"He's such a geek," Millicent whispered, "but a sort of cute one," and giggled behind her hand.

The pastor summoned his breath and began. "Although some ministers treat ignorance of the Bible as a grievous sin, I do not. My own *modern* opinion," said Pastor Schuft, "is that the less a person knows about the Bible, the less inclined he is to be prejudiced against it." He then opened a leatherbound gospel to a page marked with a silk string. "In these difficult moral times, I think we can learn much from the story of the Good Samaritan." He adjusted his glasses and read. "A man was on his way down from Jerusalem to Jericho, when he fell into the hands of robbers, and they stripped him and beat him and went off leaving him half dead." Clearing his throat, Pastor Schufty apologized for the interruption and continued. "But a Samaritan who was traveling that way came upon him, and when he saw him he pitied him." The pastor looked benignly on his small audience, coughed, and closed the book. "Now the question is: should the Samaritan have stopped or not? Unlike our ancestors who lived in a simpler age when the answer would have been a resounding yes, we have to consider the situation in light of the law and the amount of personal liability insurance we carry. You see, if you help him and he gets hurt, he may sue you. But if you don't help him, he may also sue you. Therefore we have to understand the Bible not as a source of morality, but as a source of philosophical conundrums designed to test our legal expertise." He bowed his head and prayed, "Lord give us the courage to face each day in the full knowledge that we will be constantly tested, and the faith to be true to our natures. Amen."

The group said "Amen" and Coach Caiaphas recited the benediction. "Let us always be true to one another, always faithful, always true to our vows of friendship and marriage."

Another "Amen" followed, and then the group retreated to the house, entering through the screened porch that led to the kitchen, where the coach's wife, Miranda Caiaphas, served coffee and cookies. As soon as they could, Millicent and Shawn excused themselves and went downstairs to her bedroom, which she had decorated with billowing muslin strung from the ceiling, indirect red lighting, and vermilion linens. On her bed she had a vast assortment of stuffed animals. Shawn could hear the coach and his wife saying goodnight to the pastor and then the couple milling around upstairs. Directly below her parents' bedroom, Millicent's enabled them to hear her parents' movements but not their words.

"How come you were late?"

"I couldn't get away."

She locked her bedroom door. "You're not cheatin', are you? Because if you are, I'll tell my father."

As Shawn slipped under the covers with Millicent, his mind was assailed by a plague of worries, principally what would happen to him if found in bed with the Caiaphases' daughter. Surely, the wrath of the coach, like the sword of the Lord, would be visited upon him. Had Coach Caiaphas not just a few days before asked him whether his intentions were "honorable"? At the time, Shawn nearly choked and had said that he and Millicent, though very close, were much too young to be thinking of that. In addition, Shawn worried about the reliability of the condoms. He could not afford any accidents. Millicent would never agree to an abortion; and a marriage to her would be a life sentence of boredom. He felt certain that she would not go silently if he left her. Within an hour, she would tell Laura all. And then what? His parents were quite fond of Laura, but would never allow Millicent to set foot in their Eastside penthouse.

Lacking any interest in foreplay, perhaps because Millicent liked climaxes and not preludes, he slurped on Millicent's breasts as she bounced on the bed, causing the springs to beat a squeaking tattoo that Shawn feared would be heard overhead.

After a couple of minutes, she panted, "Let's play!"

"I have to get the rubber on."

"Forget your galoshes. Just do it!"

"I can't."

At that instant, he heard raised voices; a few minutes later, a thumping sound issued from the upstairs. Footsteps. Shawn froze, certain that they had been caught. A door slammed, and someone came down the steps. By now Shawn had lost his erection. The person paused and then exited through the basement door.

"Shit! Your father must have heard us."

"Naw, he storms out of the house and goes for a walk in the bird sanctuary whenever my mom ain't in the mood."

Shawn heard a cell phone ringing, a sound that seemed to come from the backyard. For at least half an hour, Shawn and Millicent lay side by side, but he could not rekindle the urge, even with her help. Looking out the window, he saw car lights in the distance, across the pond. Curious, he got out of bed and pulled on his clothes.

"When will I see you again?" she asked.

"I'll call you."

She handed him a crystal of some kind. "Put this in your pocket. It will keep you safe and bring you back to me."

"Right," he said unenthusiastically and ducked out.

Instead of returning to his car, he circled the pond, heading in the direction of the now vanished car lights. Stealthily passing through the field west of the pond, he reached the trees and darted through them cautiously. Out of the corner of his eye, he detected movement at the foot of a swamp willow. At this time of year the occasional bear came out of the mountains to forage for food. Fearful, Shawn knelt and waited. A minute later, he thought he saw a shadow on the hillside, to the north. Then he heard moans that sounded unmistakably like love sighs. Making a long semicircle that brought him to a distant point behind the willow, he could see in the leaf-fractured moonlight Coach Caiaphas's sweaty face as Trustee Edsel's wife peeled his banana.

Laura's father and associates had taught her a trick or two about how to shadow a mark, a useful skill now that she knew Shawn couldn't be trusted. She had originally fallen in love with his looks, but as amorists must eventually speak to one another, she soon, though reluctantly, discovered that he traded on stale ideas and second-hand observations, living vicariously through his daddy's adventures. Lacrosse and police work constituted the staple of his stories. Ideas he valued little and literature even less. His past presidency of the Tappa Kegga Day fraternity (TKD) gave him entree with the ladies, particularly sorority girls, whose envy she rather enjoyed exciting. One day in early fall, as she passed a group of them in front of their house in abbreviated skirts, kicking their legs and caterwauling,

> *We think you ought to join*
> *Alpha Beta Chi;*
> *We're the best there is,*
> *And that's the reason why.*

she had actually shouted, "Have some self-respect!" Her comment quickly made the rounds—as did the fact that the once president of TKD had eyes only for her. In large part she had been seeing Shawn for the pleasure of annoying those feckless sorority girls, who would have given up their SUVs for the chance to wear his fraternity pin. She could not, try as she might, hide her vast intelligence from herself. Recognizing that her mind was tantamount to a howitzer, she knew that she could blast holes in most arguments, a skill that she had discovered in grade school and honed in high school, in Rome, and in college. Although she could use her stunning good looks to get what she wanted, she understood that her beauty had come to her through birth but her intelligence had been refined through hard work. She therefore preferred making her way by means of the latter.

Laura wanted to give Shawn the benefit of the doubt regarding Millicent Caiaphas, so she persuaded herself she needed ocular proof. That decision led her to follow Shawn to the Caiaphases' house, where she secreted herself on a hillside that overlooked the pond. From this vantage point she saw Coach Caiaphas rush out his back door and call someone on his cell phone; she saw Shawn follow shortly thereafter; she saw a gray Saab park outside the sanctuary and a slender woman make her way to a willow bower; and she saw Shawn seeing this unknown woman playing Coach Caiaphas's skin flute.

GRETCHEN EDSEL TAKES A LOVER

One Sunday in church, Gretchen had found herself irreligiously praying for a steamy affair. The chance had presented itself at a pre-game football party when Coach Caiaphas addressed the gathering in stirring words about the need for a pact between the faithful and their Lord, concluding with the plea that those who had strayed from the Bible return.

"Husbands and wives need to resume the roles God originally intended for them. Women must do as their menfolk command. In return the males must protect and support the frail vessel that is woman."

To thunderous applause from the men and polite finger tapping from the women, Coach Caiaphas seated himself between Frank and Gretchen Edsel. A minute later, as Boaz bent over his plate to say grace for the guests, he put his hand on Gretchen's thigh. After dinner, he offered to show her the third floor of the alumni building, an apartment normally reserved for prominent out-of-town guests. Closing the door behind him, he asked Gretchen if she ever strayed. When she failed to answer, he locked the door and embraced her. She responded warmly, baring one of her ample breasts and gently cradling it for Coach Caiaphas to tongue. As he did so, she felt an involuntary discharge of lubricant that dampened her bikini panties, which she deftly removed and threw to one side, all the while observing that she had never before been unfaithful, and that she hoped not to go to hell for her infidelity.

Coach Caiaphas reassured her. "You needn't worry, because the last shall be first."

"And what," Gretchen asked, "does that mean?"

"Those who have fallen will be received first into heaven."

Gretchen couldn't remember reading that passage in her Bible, but not wishing to appear uninformed said, "Old or New Testament?"

"The Gospel of St. Thomas."

The names Matthew, Mark, Luke, and John ran through her head. Had she forgotten one, or had her Sunday school teacher and pastor neglected to mention a fifth gospel? Never mind, she admonished herself. Who was she to question an elder of the church? With the coach's assurance that the last would be first, Gretchen stretched out on the bed. One glance at her furry muff and Coach Caiaphas creamed in his pants, causing immediate detumescence. Gretchen, unwilling to lose the opportunity to have an affair *and* enter paradise first, exhorted him. "Bobo, as a religious man, you should not lose heart, even if you lost your hard on. There's always a second coming."

Comforted by these words, the coach waited until nature restored his vitality, at which time he crudely declared, "It ain't the angle or the dangle, but the heat of the meat," and without further ado asked her to join him in prayer for simultaneous orgasms. They then did the naughty and, perhaps owing to divine intervention, climaxed together. From that day forth, she lived with the constant desire to have Coach Caiaphas fill the vacuum in her life. Frank was no better than a loose-fitting screw, a man stripped of his thread, but Bobo Caiaphas . . . that was different. He would drive his bolt right up to his balls and drill away in Bushey Park until he had satisfied her ache, and then withdraw to let her haul out his ashes. Such ecstasy! Not a day passed that she didn't wish to play wind up the clock. But living far apart made it difficult for them to grease the wheel. So she took a part-time job as a counselor at Bogus U., which brought her to town three times a week. Because she commuted, they were forced to do it where they could: in the Coach's office, in the church vestry, in the bird sanctuary, on an old water-stained mattress under the stadium (below section H), in the steam tunnels. Unfortunately, the third floor of the alumni building was unavailable during the day. Had Frank not objected to her staying in town overnight, she would have rented a room and met Bobo there. As for Bobo's house, although Mrs. Caiaphas occasionally returned to Alabama to visit her mother, his daughter was still living at home.

The night that Shawn had seen Gretchen savoring Bobo's manhood, the adulterers were consummating a deal they had discussed earlier that evening. It was a deal that Gretchen's husband had reluctantly approved, and that had caused Coach Caiaphas's tardy arrival home, which in turn had led to the quarrel that drove him out of his house and into the backyard, where he called Gretchen on his cell phone. He had agreed to insist on a new million-dollar computerized scoreboard for the stadium, one that would be purchased through Cranmore Narr. In return, Gretchen would get to use her bachelor brother's house for assignations whenever he was on the road, a frequent occurrence. Lest the reader accuse him of pandering, we must point out that Cranmore, a fastidious housekeeper, had no inkling of how his sister intended to use his king-sized bed, and had agreed to let her occupy his house only after being assured that the coach would demand a scoreboard with all the bells and whistles that money could buy.

Although that night Gretchen returned home in the wee hours, Frank greeted her warmly, suggesting they snuggle. During the motions of their cold lovemaking, she told him that she would be staying over at Cranmore's house when work kept her late. Knowing the temptations of a college town—ones that he had reveled in just a few years before—he tried to dissuade her to give up thoughts of kipping at her brother's house. But she remained firm, in honor of Bobo's firmness and the sweet pleasures it brought.

"I don't like this idea one little bit," Frank remonstrated. "It's a dangerous place, with radicals and rapists."

"My dear," she replied coolly, "you were party to hiring a president known for his roughness. Who are you to talk?"

He wanted to say that at least he had prospered from the deal, but couldn't reveal his sordid bribe-taking. Had he brought up the need for a quid pro quo, she would have emphasized how much Cranmore stood to gain, never mentioning of course the multiple pleasures she herself would realize. Self-interest, alas, has a way of representing itself as a concern for others.

LAURA AND CHRISTY
DISCUSS MONEY

" **A** silk suit costs money. Tailors ain't givin' them away for free. So
why shouldn't I be sellin' tenure and promotion and grades and
everything else the faculty wants? You say I should think of the U. Well, I've
been around here long enough to spell that word Y-O-U." They were at this
moment slipping on rented shoes and preparing to bowl. Laura tested the
fingering on several Viz-a-balls and selected one bearing the characters of
Popeye and Olive Oyl. Christy, who regularly rolled over 200, eyed the racks
and picked a marbled ball with a wider grip. He invited her to throw first.
She bounced the first ball in the alley and also the second. Christy left one
pin standing, which he spared with his next throw. Laura, who ranked as an
expert marksman with both pistol and rifle, regarded bowling as a lower-
class sport. She scored a five and a seven after her next rolls. Christy picked
up two strikes. As Laura took aim again, he came up behind her and guided
her arm in the right motion. He then showed her how to use her legs for
fluency and force. Her game improved immediately.

She was using this night out to convince him that his money-making
schemes should be used for the greater good and not just for personal gain.
"Once you buy a silk suit, ten silk suits, and a fancy car, three fancy cars,
what more do you need?"

He had long wanted to have this conversation with her, but he'd be
damned if he would readily renounce his belief in the salubrious value of
looking out for himself. "Since I got here, I've acquired expensive tastes.
Monogrammed shirts and diamond cuff links. You keep sayin' I have to
look presidential."

Christy's comment gave her pause, but she didn't pursue it. Instead, she
told him the story of her father running into trouble with the mob and having to lam it. At the time, Brooklyn Benny had come to her rescue and paid

for her last year at Spence. But when he said no to supporting her in college, leaving her high and dry, she had to find the means to pay for her tuition, as well as her room and board and books. So she applied to Stanford for help and received a scholarship and also financial assistance in graduate school.

"Yeah, and if I look after others," he asked rhetorically, "who's gonna look after me?"

Christy was proving a hard nut to crack. She genuinely believed in the value of helping those who couldn't help themselves—and wanted to transmit the lesson. So she persisted.

"We once had a black maid working for us, Suzie Somerset, who used to play chess with me and always won. She had a mind for strategy. I told her she should have gone to college. 'Miss Laura,' she said, 'I grew up in the South, with separate drinking fountains and toilets and seating at the back of the bus. Your mammy got money. My mammy scrubbed floors in the Elks Club. If someone had paid my way to college, I wouldn't be here. I'd be elsewhere, still black but brilliant with learning. And you want to know what I woulda done with what I learned? Pass it on to others. That's why some day I'd like to be rich. To give most of it away.'"

Christy, feeling that Laura's story was designed to exact from him a contributory emotion, remained unmoved, believing that charity began at home.

"Sweetheart, you're barking up the wrong tree." He went to the lane and threw yet another strike. "I grew up shanty Irish, poor but proud. The church was always telling us," he beamed knowingly, "to turn the other cheek and be charitable. Give money to the needy and that sort of thing. But it quickly dawned on me, what good will that do? Just ask yourself this question: has turning the other cheek ever brought about peace? Has buying off our enemy ever got us anywhere? No! And I'll tell you why. Because when we play kissy with our enemy, we are not taking his rottenness seriously. We are not treating him as he intended. When you slug a guy, you expect to be hit in return. If you don't fight back, you're being a pushover, like the parent who pats the bratty kid on the head and says, 'It's all right, you'll know better when you grow up.' Just imagine how you would feel if you had gone out of your way to put the hurt on someone, and that person said, 'I forgive you. It doesn't matter. I always turn the other cheek.' You would feel cheated, frustrated, maybe even moved to put a bigger hurt on the guy. It seems to me that's how violence spreads. So the best way to treat money is to take it and run, and when dealing with thugs make sure that your harmful acts and intentions are never misunderstood."

Laura doggedly explained that her idea of the greater good included not just a particular college group, like students, but also the community, the society, the country. Christy's skeptical look led her to expand on her thoughts, telling him her idea that education rightly ought to come under the Department of Defense.

"Putting aside all the small fry we put in jail for smoking pot or peddling it, you know, don't you, that fifty percent of the hardcores can't read or write? People with some learning in them are less likely to mug you. And that's a fact. We don't need more prisons, we need more schools. If you want to protect yourself, educate people. It keeps the crime rate down. I had a friend in Rome who used to say that a well-educated person is like a carpenter's truth: all the parts abide."

Though Laura's last comment left Christy befogged, he quickly riposted that if she, like him, had been schooled in lawbreaking as a means of support, she'd see the world differently.

"Like the song says, I've been poor and I've been rich, and it's better to be loaded," he declared. "If I can make some jack and move to Easy Street, why not? Bogus U. won't notice. Look at all the people pulling the cow's udder now. Wherever you turn, it's every man for himself. So why not me? That's what America's built on: the idea that you take what you can. Name me one person in this dump who isn't on the take or looking out for number one. You can't. Not Pyrosis, not Stine, not Pinchbeck. So you might say I'm just following in their footsteps."

Laura realized that to make an impression on his ingrained larceny she would have to use an acid stronger than logic.

DEEDEE LITE'S NOVEL BEGINS

He suddenly appeared out of nowhere, tall, very tall, blonde, and sort of handsome. It was March and very cold. He looked mysterious. She was working in a restaurant. He came in and sat down. She asked him what he wanted and he said, "You."

Grace Pallas had come to Schroon Lake to forget a very sad thing. Her boyfriend, an out-of-work miner, had left their second-floor apartment (over a pharmacy) and moved across the street to live with an older woman (50!), who owned the Ella Kay Kandy Store. When Klip Springer left (that was her boyfriend's name), she decided it was time to take stock of her life.

She had straight blonde hair that hung to her shoulders, though secretly she wished to have short curly dark hair. Unlike some girls who had breasts that sagged, hers were lovely, not too big and not rose buds, but her feet were too small and her ankles too fat. She was tallish and thin. She knew she cried too easily at sad movies and tried not to but couldn't help herself. She'd always said she didn't want children but now she wanted them, at least two. She had dreamed of meeting a man who was tall, dark, mysterious, and sort of handsome. Her girlfriends wanted to marry gorgeous men, but she knew better. If they were just a little bit ugly, they would probably stay home and help with the house and take out the garbage and not run around with other women. That's why she was breathless when Brent Harris came into the restaurant and said what he did.

She had quit her job as a manicurist at Patty's Hair Stylists on Center Avenue and taken just two suitcases to the Greyhound bus terminal, and bought a ticket for Schroon Lake because her mother and father had spent a weekend honeymoon there. When she counted the months and the days, she figured out that she had been conceived at Schroon Lake, which was another good reason to go there. She just knew something special would happen to her there. And sure enough she met Brent Harris there, because she was there when he was there.

Getting back to the bus . . . Grace got off the bus at Schroon Lake and asked the lady in the ticket office if she knew where she could get a room. The woman, Mrs. Eggbert, said, "I rent rooms—to proper girls. But I have my rules." And boy, did she have rules; she even pinned them up on the walls. Grace Pallas assured her she would be no trouble. It was a nice old house, with a wraparound porch. The woman called it a Queen Anne, probably because some royal lady once stayed there. Grace had a walk-up, medium-sized room on the fourth floor. But she had her own bathroom and clean sheets once a week. Other roomers lived on the second floor. One of them worked at the Toe Mane Chinese Restaurant, a Mr. Toady Dim Hoh Sour, who was really an errand boy. He got her a job waiting tables. And that's how she met Brent Harris. They ran into each other there.

When she asked what he wanted and he said, "You," she blushed and said, "I bet you tell all the girls that." He said that wasn't true. He said that Grace was beautiful, like a statue. After they kidded around for a few minutes (the restaurant wasn't very busy), he ordered almond chicken and green tea. But first he had won ton soup. Grace snuck him a free egg roll. He looked at her with such loving eyes she knew there would be something between them—and very soon.

She asked him his name. "You tell me yours first," he said. So she did. His was Brent Harris, but he asked Grace not to tell anybody. She wondered if he was hiding out from the police, but was afraid to ask him, because if he was, he might think she was trying to turn him in, and that was not what she had in mind, certainly not after seeing he was sort of handsome and tall and when he took off his hat he had blonde hair, which is what she always wanted in a man, but had never found, until that day in the restaurant, where fate brought them together, for what reason Grace could only guess, but hoped it was the right guess, because she had already had many lovers, all of them turning out to be cheaters, and one of them doing it with another woman right there in her own bed in front of her, which she saw when she came home from work, a terrible experience with only one good thing about it, and that was Grace saw them doing it in a way she had never done it and decided maybe that was why her boyfriend was cheating on her, so she swore she would do what that other lady had done with her next boyfriend, and that was Brent Harris, who she hoped was not a criminal and would love her, and buy her a house, and take out the garbage, and give her two children, a boy, Billy, and a girl, Betty, and she would be the perfect mom, always taking the children to school and to dance lessons and to Little League and giving them baths, and reading them her favorite children's book, *Raven Finds the Daylight*, and turning out the light and kissing them good night, and living in the same house for years and years, and not moving around, and Brent having a good job, and she not having to pinch pennies, and they would eat out at least once a month and be able to afford a babysitter, and maybe take a one-week vacation in the summer, like go to Disney World, with the kids of course, and Brent would love her and she would love Brent, and they would both love the kids, and the family would remain all together, happy, in Schroon Lake, right there.

CHRISTY MAKES A
TENURE DECISION

As a point of honor, Christy always did his own dirty work, from stealing apples to pilfering parking meters. In the rackets, he had learned that the only people more despised than hit men were those who employed them. For this reason, Christy had Laura draft the following memorandum, which conveyed the spirit of his decision if not his actual words.

To: The Bogus U. Board of Trustees
From: Christopher Mahon, President
Subject: Monroe Larson's Tenure

Dear Gentlemen:

Well aware of your wish to see Monroe Larson receive tenure, I have studied the record, consulted the viziers, and spoken to the candidate. According to all reports, Monroe's scholarly project, if it pans out, will make him and Bogus famous. I therefore recommend that we wait until it is completed before we make the decision.

In good conscience, I cannot sign the papers until I see the letters in print. But to show him that we have the utmost confidence in his finishing this noble work, I suggest we give him a down payment on tenure by extending his contract for another year or two, with the understanding that he waive his right to a tenure decision until that period has ended. We will thereby be protecting ourselves and giving him enough time to prove worthy of our trust. In the certainty that he will do so, I am

Sincerely yours,

Christopher Mahon

Within a week, Christy had his reply.

Dear President Mahon,

The trustees of Bogus U. have met in executive session and directed me, as secretary of the board, to respond to your memorandum in which you recommend that Monroe Larson not be granted tenure at this time but rather be given a contract extension. The board refuses to accept your recommendation for the following reasons.

One, tenure is first and foremost an academic decision, not an administrative one, and should therefore come from the campus. As the president, your principal responsibility is to look after the well-being of Bogus U. In the Board's opinion, your recommendation fails to consider the numerous interests involved in this decision.

Two, a contract extension could lead to the loss of at least one enormously capable student who might not attend Bogus U., Walter Hemings. Students of this quality do not apply every day. Since it is our sacred charge to do what is best for the school, we direct you to reconsider your decision and get back to us as soon as possible.

Very truly yours,

Gertrude Steif (For the Board)

CHRISTY GOES TO THE GRIDIRON

Under a green and white tent, the alumni association hosted a season-opener cocktail party for special donors, while in the stadium the students barked like seals at feeding time and the pennants waved indolently from the top of the wall. In the parking lot thousands of tailgates supported a cornucopia of food and cartons of fog-cutter, and in the locker room the Bogus U. football team prayed that starting today they could improve on their dismal record. Scheduling the Texas Little Horns for its September opening game seemed to bode well for the team, since the previous year the Little Horns had had an even worse record than Bogus. Christy had stayed long enough at the alumni gathering to conclude that he would leave the schmoozing and glad-handing to others more talented than he at ingratiating themselves with gas bags and glitterati suffering from arrested development. One fellow dressed in plaid pants and a yellow shirt embossed with dozens of wildebeests cornered Christy to tell him about his days of autumn glory when he played tackle on a Bogus U. squad that had actually held Miami to a tie. Sadly, the alum had never left that endless fall and was still playing the game over and over in his restless mind.

"The best years of my life!" he thundered, and slapped his expansive midsection as if to indicate that he could still put on pads and take the pounding.

Christy had originally invited Laura to join him at the game, but she had flown to Las Vegas to interview for the position of Director of Public Relations, soon to become vacant at The Chimera, a hotel ostensibly owned by one group but really owned by the Nocciola Family. She would not be returning from Vegas until Sunday, the day after the game. Feeling out of sorts, he found himself seated between Frank and Gretchen Edsel. Behind him sat the chairs of Chemistry and Biology, as well as D.U.M. Bakeless and the other trustees. In a less splendid box than his own, Sejanus Pinchbeck, Bill A. Stine, and Brigham Pyrosis effusively praised the Broadway production of *Cats*.

On the field, scantily clad cheerleaders performed stunning acrobatics, while a wildebeest, firmly in harness, was led around the stadium to hysterical cheers.

Although the stadium had a no-drinking policy, in the boxes the alcohol ran so freely that by the two o'clock kickoff most of the VIPs were rendered inarticulate, especially Bill A. Stine, who always had trouble holding his liquor and was therefore mentally running on empty. Gretchen made it a point not to enter the gossamer world of inebriation—having had some humdinger hangovers in college—and thus gained advantages when everyone around her had difficulty focusing, including her husband. She was delighted to be watching Bobo pacing the sidelines. Frank, however, had arrived at the stadium already ill-humored from drink.

Gretchen, lightly resting her arm on Christy's, leaned over and whispered. "We are not happy about the Monroe Larson tenure decision."

The pronoun "we" did not escape Christy's attention. Undoubtedly it included her husband and a number of other trustees.

"I thought I explained it all to you," said Gretchen.

In short, Christy had not followed her orders or the trustees'.

Christy immediately equivocated. "I'm all for the guy. Believe me, I think the world of him. But we really gotta see the letters. After all, they may be worth thousands, maybe even millions."

Gretchen would have conceded the point—albeit reluctantly—had not Bogus U.'s tailback got stuffed for a five-yard loss on the team's first possession. Gretchen silently prayed that Bobo could persuade Walter Hemings, the North Hollywood High School running-back-of-the-year for California, to come to Bogus U. Walter could run through a wall. A recruiting coup of that magnitude would make the alums and the trustees forget last year's record and overlook the current season, which already appeared lost. The Wildebeests tried two passes—incomplete—and kicked. Immediately the boo birds began.

At an earlier date, Bogus had flown Walter to campus, and the football team had hosted a party in his honor. But Walter, a straight shooter, objected to the presence of drugs and the unseemly treatment of coeds. Subsequently, one woman even declared she was raped. He would have completely written off Bogus had it not been for his parents, who felt a sacred attachment to the person of Sally Hemings.

From behind him, Christy could hear the chair of Physics saying that in the future he'd use the lounge at the top of his building to watch the game. "It's a lot more comfortable, I can tell you, than these boxes. Besides," he added, "we have a plasma television screen that can pick up games from all over the country. Most of those other teams are better than ours."

The chair of Biology, much in his cups, mumbled, "I hope you serve better stuff than this rotgut."

"Those Little Horns," said the chair of Chemistry, "are playing like maniacs. I guess it's because of that crook who tried to bribe the coach. The papers said all of Texas was up in arms."

D.U.M. Bakeless urged patience, saying his recent research showed the motion of the stars favored Bogus U. in this game. "Before the third quarter begins, we'll be celebrating with a magnum of Piper-Heidsieck champagne." But by that time, with Bogus behind by five touchdowns, Bakeless opined that perhaps his astrological charts needed redrawing.

From the next box rose the sound of an argument.

"You heard me correctly!" said Pinchbeck. "I'll see that Monroe Larson gets tenure just as soon as I'm appointed Grand Vizier."

"The hell with Larson," babbled Stine, "what makes you think you'll be Grand Vizier? President Mahon told me I was his man. Just ask him. He's in the next box."

Pyrosis, as always, maintained a surface calm. "Gentlemen, this disagreement can be easily settled. Neither of you is destined for that office because I am. You may rest confident that the final decision on Monroe Larson will rest with me."

In no time, the men fell to fighting, pushing one another and threatening worse. Christy found the disagreement a better contest than the one on the field.

When the Edsels departed, and Gretchen cooed in Christy's ear, "If I were you, I wouldn't shoot myself in the foot again . . . time's running out on the Monroe decision," Christy saw clearly that his fate and Monroe's were linked inextricably. For him not to jeopardize his presidency, Monroe would have to receive tenure.

CHRISTY AND OTHERS
DISCUSS MONROE LARSON

The day had begun auspiciously for Sejanus Pinchbeck. He had received a telephone call from an old friend at Eagle River University, one of the Big Twenty schools to which he aspired. The friend said that Sejanus's chances for an administrative position looked good; he had made the final list of three. Although the university needed a woman in the administration for window dressing, and although the other finalists were women—one had a degree in Jurassic Studies and the other an MFA in finger painting—Sejanus's academic record, though suspect in some quarters, had indeed won him government grants and deceived the many universities for whom he had worked. Besides, Eagle River had need of an administrator trained in phrenology, one who could assay the heads of the *lumpenprofessoriat*, and wished to trumpet the appointment of a scientist who had contributed immeasurably to the humanities by fostering the discovery of the Sally Hemings letters.

Vizier Brigham Pyrosis also felt upbeat. Just the day before, he had been admitted to a four-week summer program at the University of Grimsberg, in Germany, to learn leadership qualities. Founded by a Herr Himmler, Grimsberg had an unsurpassed reputation for instilling in weaklings Prussian discipline and no-nonsense administration, which included courses in draconian downsizing and labor impressment, experience Pyrosis felt that he lacked. Had he known that the school also specialized in the art of clipped speeches, he might not have been quite so enthusiastic about spending a month in the Rhineland.

Vizier Bill A. Stine, however, was feeling unwell. He had hoped to spend this time not in a meeting but jogging. His rotundity had begun to obscure his personal parts, which lay buried beneath his ample stomach. His one fear was that he might be asked to vote, which could cost him Christy's favor; he therefore armed himself with an excuse. Upon arriving, he said that he had a case of "Delhi belly" and might have to decamp for the loo.

Professor Narcissa Whitman Poseuse, knowing that lackeys were prompt, arrived late. Christy exploited her tardiness.

"I'd like to get back to the subject of leadership and, in particular, why you guys support tenure for Professor Larson when his record is so sketchy."

The viziers could feel the chill of cowardice creeping up their backs. If President Mahon had his doubts, shouldn't they also? They would have to figure out a way of saying both yes and no.

Sejanus spoke first. "There is more here than meets the eye. Although one bump in the right place on someone's head does not make a genius, it gives us a hint of greatness to come. Now admittedly some bumps just turn out to be pimples, but on the other hand. . . ."

Pyrosis dispelled the silence with a disquisition on coprolite, which we shall spare the reader, concluding that, "Buried in the stone, treasures may or may not be present."

Stine had been agonizing over how to equivocate and decided to try a different tack. "The trustees were elected by the public. They ought to know the public taste. You come from a—er—different background. Therefore—" But here he lapsed into silence, unable to figure out how to complete the sentence.

Christy decided to discomfit the men even further. "The Grand Vizier of Bogus has to have balls. What I'm hearing is a lotta B.S."

Pyrosis patted his chest and declared, "You can always count on me, President Mahon. Although you haven't yet officially announced my appointment, I have already begun to clear my desk."

Sejanus, beside himself with rage, blurted, "Since when did you start joining Bill on his binges? I've been tapped for the job." He turned to Christy. "Right?"

Christy wisely took shelter in silence.

"You can say what you want and even indulge in personal attacks," said Stine, "but President Mahon and I—"

"Yes?" said Christy, using a well-placed interrogative.

"You said that you . . . wanted . . . that is . . . were thinking of selecting me."

"He told me the same thing!" said Pyrosis and Pinchbeck together.

Christy nodded amiably. "I am, gents, I am. I just haven't made up my mind yet. A lot depends on how things go this afternoon."

That admission cast a pall over the meeting until Narcissa Whitman Poseuse waddled into the room, holding several large notebooks that contained not only her publications and newspaper clippings, designed to awe the audience, but also every scrap of paper she could round up in defense of Monroe Larson's tenure case. A flabby woman, much out of shape, she huffed and sniffled as she tried to catch her breath from the walk across campus.

None of the men had stood when she entered, a gesture that she expected not because of her sex but because of her assiduously cultivated reputation. With the exception of Pinchbeck, whose résumé had profited from friends adding his name to their articles, no one could equal her record. Seeing that the group wished to get right down to business and would not be salaaming, she threw back her head in annoyance and flung open her notebooks, as if to say: behold the evidence! Christy felt briefly intimidated. But the others, kept afloat on the gas of their egos, could never feel anything but important, even Stine, whose record gave him the most reason to tremble. With all eyes on him, Christy spoke.

"All right, we all know why we're here. I refused to sign off on Larson's tenure and you disagree. We need to be on the same page. I'll be brief. His record has a smell to it. We can't prove his Sally Hemings letters are real. And I don't like the shenanigans that pass for voting at Bogus. The Department of History never received a ballot. Pinchbeck read some tea leaves and came up with a phony count. That's my position. Now you guys can give me your reasons."

Having decided that his promotion was not in the cards, Pinchbeck said archly, "Why we disagree with you or, um, why we think Monroe Larson deserves tenure? They are two, um, different questions." He looked around in triumph, as if he had just pissed across the Mississippi River and was daring anyone to match his performance.

"Both reasons," said Christy succinctly.

Pinchbeck unctuously proclaimed his faith in faculty governance. "I defer," he said, "to the chair of Professor Larson's promotion and tenure committee, um, Professor Poseuse. Given her, um, outstanding credentials in the science and history of Muscle Biology, how could I do otherwise?" On that rhetorical note, he fled the field.

"How many other people served on the committee?" asked Christy.

"Two from outside the university and two from the department."

Christy then posed a question that Laura had told him to ask. "Who'd you contact from outside?"

"Professors Steven Twiddle and Jennifer Dee, both learned scholars from Big Twenty schools."

"And from inside?"

"Two others," said Narcissa. "Professors Matthew Lickspittle and Roger Toady. But since I was the senior member they agreed to—" And here she paused, uncertain whether to risk undermining the credibility of the committee with a display of self-congratulations or to lie. The need to compliment herself, however, superseded all other needs; she therefore declared that the committee had, understandably, been guided by her expertise in scholarly matters and her critical assessment of Monroe Larson's chances of making a splash in American Studies. "In other words," she said, "I wrote the final report, as you can probably tell from the prose."

Christy looked at his copy. Laura, having studied it beforehand, had appended in the margins the words "slack," "attenuated," "non-sequitur," "prolix," "garrulous," "puffery," and "rubbish." Admittedly, the president had to look up some of the words, but to his credit he had committed their meanings to memory.

"The other two members of the committee . . . which part of the report depends on them?"

"Oh, you mean what did they contribute? Well, they visited Monroe's classes and read his articles—"

"I don't suppose that took much time."

"Quality, President Mahon, not quantity matters at Bogus U."

"And after your two friends did what they were told, you wrote the report."

"Are you suggesting that my colleagues lack the character to speak their own minds?"

"Yeah, you could say so."

Since all the viziers knew that they had contributed to Bogus U.'s spinelessness, an embarrassed silence fell over the room. Even the tenured faculty had been rendered invertebrate by an administration that rewarded lackeys and punished independence. Although a few fearless faculty continued to speak out, the silent majority embraced sycophantism with a fervor that could be seen in the endless procession of professors humbly shuffling to the viziers' offices, with hat in hand and words of praise dripping from their lips. So blatant had the bribery become that a particular Psychology professor had set up a cot outside Pinchbeck's office and groveled every time Sejanus entered or exited.

"Well, I have no such reluctance. In fact, I revel in being me," said Poseuse, well aware of all the deals she had cut. "Monroe is among the three of four most brilliant young historians in America, and his residence at Bogus U. can only increase our reputation, enrich the library, attract the very best students, open the purses of donors, induce the legislature to temper their faultfinding, and persuade the National Endowment for the Humanities to look kindly on Bogus, which it has not done in the past."

"Where's your proof?"

"My word!"

Having no reluctance to debase the mint of truth, she went on to point out that "Monroe Larson's presence at Bogus would serve as a magnet, attracting the best minds in American Studies to the campus." Christy, unfamiliar with the false encomia that appear regularly in tenure cases, simply repeated that he needed further proof, and would seek it from outside experts of his own choosing. At this disclosure, Vizier Pyrosis became visibly nervous. Having doctored his own reputation, he feared that he would be exposed as nothing more than an administrative cheerleader and shill, unworthy of being Grand Vizier. He therefore chose to discourse on the many meanings found in coprolites and how they reflected on the current case.

"Some people find in amber the remains of insects, seeds, pollens, parasites, and the like. But in fossilized excrement, like the petrified turtle droppings that I uncovered in Washington State—"

Christy interrupted. "What's your point, Brigham?"

"Turtles, though slow locomotive creatures, eventually arrive at their destination. My studies show that they exhibit the same determination as serious tenure seekers. Slow and steady, but focused. That sums up Monroe Larson," he said, adding the qualifier, "I think." The moment Pyrosis had waited for was now at hand. "Of course, no person can be certain, but *die Professorenschaft* at the University of Grimsberg has full confidence in my judgment." He smiled gnomically and continued. "Yes, I am happy to tell my dear colleagues that I have been invited there because of my paper on coprolites and their relation to academic behavior. No less an institution than this famous German establishment has admitted me to its leadership program, with reading privileges in its dung file."

Christy held up a hand to silence Pyrosis. "What about you, Bill, where do you stand in this matter?"

Bill A. Stine just shook his head and stared at the table.

"All right, then," Christy concluded, "we'll bring in some experts from England, Oxford and Cambridge. Whatever they decide, I'll accept."

Professor Poseuse, frothing with anger, exclaimed, "Brits! We threw them out of this country. Our history is a mystery to them. They probably never heard of Sally Hemings." Unable to restrain herself, she indulged in a tantrum of self-praise. "Why, had it not been for me, Monroe Larson would have never been introduced to the subject of Sally Hemings and Thomas Jefferson, a hobby of mine. I even suggested he look in his grandmother's attic for old letters. Had it not been for my suggestion, he'd still be study-ing the sexual appetites of the upper classes in Colonial America. You might even say his discovery is *my* discovery. Yes, *I* made it!"

Although no one could follow her logic, Sejanus Pinchbeck, never one to be eclipsed, declared, "He'd still be, um, scrounging for a topic to write about if I had not made his trip, um, to Virginia possible. I gave him the, um, grubstake."

"Yes, but I told him where to dig for the ore," replied Professor Poseuse testily.

"Juuust a minute!" said Vizier Pyrosis; "you probably don't know it, but when the legislature heard Bogus planned to finance a research trip for Monroe Larson to look for some letters that could bring discredit on one of the greatest American presidents of all time, who was it that kept them from making a public issue of it? I, I, Brigham Pyrosis!" He looked at the others with a little boy's smirk of satisfaction and trumpeted, "You didn't know that, did you? If not for me—"

Professor Poseuse interjected. "Rubbish! I took some legislators on a tour of the campus and explained what the Sally Hemings letters would mean to Bogus U's reputation. Had I not brought them on board, they would have sunk our ship."

Pyrosis, whose temperature, like his penis, rarely rose, flushed. "That tour of campus took place because I persuaded them to see for themselves that the work we do here is world class, like my own coprolitic investiga-tions." The exertion expended on this outburst caused him to experience palpitations.

Vizier Pinchbeck, seeing his opening, stroked his mustache and leaned across the table, as if to reveal a confidence. "Say what you will, but, um, without my permission for Monroe to be absent from campus, to miss class for a week, and, um, as I've said, without my providing the means for him to travel, none of what took place would have happened." Leaning back, he surveyed his audience, convinced that he had had the last word.

Christy, having frequently admired Brooklyn Benny's ability to set one person against another, turned to Bill A. Stine and asked, "I thought you didn't believe in faculty being gone from the campus. Did you know that Larson canceled classes for a week and went off to Virginia—with Sejanus's approval?"

To say that Bill A. Stine oozed sweat would be to engage in litotes. It would be far more accurate to say that in a matter of seconds his cloth-ing dripped. Every pore of his body leaked; his face cried for a towel, but lacking one he used a sleeve. Sputtering, he proclaimed, "My stomach! I have to run."

"Stay where you are," snapped Christy.

Stine removed his tie. "How could I have known?"

He would have jettisoned his sports coat, but thought better of that action when he saw the extent of his underarm stains. Wrestling back into his tasteless brown jacket, which he liked because he'd bought it at Sears for a song, whose title could well have been "cheap and low," he mumbled defensively, "Frankly, I had no idea."

"Do you ever?"

"I try not to, that is, I try not to get in the way. I am a facilitator. Tell me what you want done." But before Christy could say another word, Bill began to shake, as he defended his not knowing about Larson's absence from classes. "It's a big campus, a lot of things happen, not just among the faculty, but among the students, too. You really can't expect me to think—"

Christy interrupted. "No, that would be asking too much."

"—of everything," Bill continued, "when my mind has so little—"

"Agreed."

"—time for the tasks that a man in my position. . . ." He finally gave up. Once again, the demands of sustaining an idea and finishing a sentence had so taxed him that he lapsed into sweaty dumbness.

The wind had picked up, carrying with it leaves and grit that struck the windows, like a rapping at some chamber door. But though the group still had Monroe Larson's tenure to explore, a subject they wished they could ignore, again there came a sound, and a woman appeared wearing a pinafore.

She whispered, "I beg your pardon, don't get sore, but I'm looking for a man called Dailey, Tuna, or Albacore. My name is Leonore, and it really is a chore," she said, "to find this Romeo who now says nevermore."

The woman, who had raven hair, departed like a tale from yore, and Christy, hearing some distant rhyme his mother used when his drunken father sought entrance to the house, told the others, "You can suck your bottles and fall on the floor, but till I have the goods, my answer is: not now or ever more."

BANG, BING, BAM: A DETONATION, NOT A CHINESE DISH

The force of the explosion outside Christy's window blew a hole in the wall and catapulted him across the room. Suddenly, a man wearing army fatigues and a black woolen hood over his face, with eye slits, burst into his office and trained an Uzi on him shouting "Tyrant, tremble!" just as Christy grabbed a pool cue and brought it down on the man's gun hand, knocking the weapon to the ground. Racing out the door, Christy dashed to the basement and into the steam tunnel that connected Tinnitus House to the power plant. The would-be assassin followed, shouting "Fear and trembling shall be the fate of tyrants!" Having used these passageways before, Christy knew that they split and bifurcated every few yards, information that he used to his advantage as he finally gave his pursuer the slip and temporarily took refuge in the fortified room he'd had built.

Fortunately his staff in the outer office remained unharmed, though stunned by the sight of the president vaulting down steps to the basement trailed by a terrorist dressed like a commando.

Laura immediately telephoned home. Teresa Favoloso, who had been led to believe that some rat had croaked Brooklyn Benny, could hardly credit her daughter's suspicions. How could Brooklyn Benny still be kicking and not be flopping in the feathers with Teresa? Moreover, he hadn't shown up for Mass since the presumed murder and had not been seen in public. Laura had to be mistaken. But Teresa, awed by her brilliant daughter's accomplishments, decided that Laura's suggestion was worth pursuing.

She knew that when the Robaccia gang had to lie low, they used a well-guarded estate in Harrison, New York, a short distance from the city. She even knew its location, because occasionally she and Benny used it as a trysting place. Driving to Harrison, she left the main street and followed

181

the twisty one-lane road to a leafy redoubt on Valley Lane. She familiarly greeted the guard at the gate.

"Marco, I've got to see Benny."

"Benny?" he said queerly. "Wait here."

He left the gate and went into the reinforced booth that held a sawed-off shotgun and a telephone. When he returned, he said, "I thought you heard: Benny's dead."

Obviously, Benny was hiding out—even from her. Once Laura heard from her mother, she told Christy the scary news. He was dumbstruck and then outraged.

"How dare that guy pretend to be dead when he isn't! So now we know for sure who's behind the bombing."

"Are you absolutely certain?" said Laura.

"Well, I don't mean he lit the match. He'd use a hired gun."

Detective Crankshaw, a square-jawed fellow with broad shoulders, a thick neck, strong hands, and a smoothly shaved head, was the campus cop's finest sleuth. Christy, concerned that his office might be bugged, had suggested that they meet in Detective Crankshaw's campus building. A bank of clerks and computer operators sat behind screens in cubicles sorting, sifting, and acquiring information. Detective Crankshaw had overlooked a spot of shaving cream on his left cheek, perhaps because shaving a jowl requires some skill. He wore a western shirt with snaps and a bolo tie. His yellow suspenders and matching cowboy boots seemed incongruous. Having grown up in rural New Mexico, he made it a point of pride to continue part of the dress code. A cautious man, he took Christy to his private office. On one wall hung a ten-gallon hat, banded in yellow. Crankshaw seated himself across from Christy behind a black, metal desk.

"I'll come right to the point," said Crankshaw. "An informant has told us that someone made an attempt on the mobster Brooklyn Benny's life—and failed. Any ideas who that might be?"

Christy hemmed and hawed. "One hears rumors . . . the grapevine . . . that sort of thing."

Crankshaw leaned over his desk. "President Mahon, I don't like chasin' after stray steers. You have a checkered past, which might account for what happened. My office discovered that you once worked for Brooklyn Benny and the Robaccia family, and even though your record is clean since leavin' their employ, we have reason to believe that the mob has put out a contract on you."

"I underestimated you guys."

"After that Jon Benet fiasco out in Colorado, the FBI put our department through a rigorous course in how to track down murderers. I now have access to confidential computer searches, technical specialists who can analyze the scene of a crime for microscopic evidence, and labs in Washington to study what we turn up."

"Informers?"

"That goes without saying. Now tell me: is your past association with the Robaccia family the cause of the bombing?"

"It could be a lotta reasons, like the Larson case and the complaints about my rules and my cuttin' the football budget."

Crankshaw rubbed his bald pate and spoke as if to the world in general. "You've got the laggards and the learners. Some people do the digging, some don't. I discovered at FBI school that to land the big frsh, persistence matters more than brains. There's a lot of scut work involved in succeeding, if you see what I mean."

Crankshaw handed Christy a list and asked if he knew any of the names. Christy ran an index finger down the page.

"Every one of 'em."

"We have cause to believe they all bear you a grudge."

"What's the beef? I never did them no personal harm, except maybe for Larson." Christy laughed and waved a hand as if to indicate that the names were hardly worth his time. "Just for the record, the three viziers and Poseuse support this guy Larson. Mr. Hasty-Pasty is related to Brooklyn Benny through marriage. His wife is Benny's sister. How you got Gertrude Steif's name, I don't know. She's a secretary who's mad at me because my English ain't so good. Believe me: it's all just small potatoes."

Crankshaw pulled from his desk a manila folder that he tapped with a finger. "We know the type of bomb, plastique, and the design—European. My guess is that someone who lived abroad and had access to a terrorist group or military installation is your bomber."

"And who the hell would that be?"

"We're doing a background check on those names now."

From his vest pocket, Crankshaw removed a small pad and a stubby pencil. Licking the point, he asked, "Can you think of any reason why the mob would want you dead?"

Christy pondered the question. How could he say that his attempt to murder Brooklyn Benny had proved unsuccessful, and therefore Benny and every member of the Robaccia family qualified as his enemy? He realized now that he had only two choices: go into hiding or ice Benny first and become head of the Robaccia family.

"Nothing comes to mind," said Christy; "let me think about it."

A BREAK IN THE CASE

Apprised of the students' hostility toward Christy, Detective Crankshaw called in for questioning the most obstreperous, those who had issued a call to arms and had burned Christy in effigy. One particularly outraged student had put the following message on the campus website, as well as on his e-mail server.

Fellow Students,

My name is Austin Black. Even if you don't know me you will want to read how our new president is screwing us. He thinks Bogus U. ought to get tougher on grades. Now, everyone knows there grades are inflated, butt thats the point, thats the way things are! Everywhere! If Bogus tightens up and the other schools dont, were fucked. Maybe you want to be treated unfairly but I dont. If we lived in the real world ld have to say the A's we get are probably not worth a C, but we live in the Bogus world where C's are A's. Some students work really hard and still get C's, just because their papers were average. President Mahon is out of touch, it would be all right if our profs ignored the president, but I got one right now who graded me down for not knowing the book we got tested on. I never bought it being that I couldnt afford it and used the one in the library. But when I went back to the library to cut out the pages I needed it was checked out to someone else. So I blew the test. When I told my prof about my problem he said there was a new polacy about grades. It frys my ass their were other kids who didnt read the book on the sillabus and got a better grade than me. Anyway, like I was saying, I got a C. A C!!! Do you know what a C is? A Jewish F!!!

If we don't put a bomb under this guy and stop what hes doing, the next thing you know hell be banning bazookas from campus. Our constitutional liberty, are being threatened. All of you that hate this new polacy as much as me, sign at the botoom and forward this to ten outher students. There will be a protest meeting in Grendaine building on Wednesday night at eight. Show up!

Don't let the new president take away your right to an A and to bare arns!!!

Sincerely Yours,

Austin Black

A check on Mr. Black revealed that he belonged to the NRA and owned five pistols, a pump shotgun, a bazooka, and a hunting bow with steel-tipped serrated arrows. But Detective Crankshaw could find no history of his having worked around high explosives.

"All we have is his letter. And you can see for yourself, he's no genius with words. The sophisticated bomb detonated outside your window has the fingerprints of a pro."

"My other students?"

"Nothing promising. On the other hand," said Detective Crankshaw, "we have made a breakthrough regarding the bomb's type—Semtex—favored by terrorists and stockpiled by NATO forces in Malta."

Christy blurted, "If I'm not mistaken . . ."

"You're not," said Detective Crankshaw dryly. "Myrtle Steif grew up in Malta. Her father was a NATO officer in charge of ordnance."

A bewildered Christy exclaimed, "But I hardly know the woman!"

"That's what makes her such a good choice."

Shaking his head, Christy remarked, "Geez, around here some of the staff really take bad grammar seriously."

"Huh?"

"Never mind."

Christy looked out the north-facing window in Detective Crankshaw's office. In the distance he could see the hogback formation and the back range. Across the street, a small vortex of leaves, driven by the wind, danced across the grass and disappeared. Christy puzzled whether leaves, like people, mostly returned to the earth. He recalled that as a child, he frequently asked his mother where things went, like his father. It took his mother years to admit that Old Mahon, as she called him, had left Ireland several years before her on "half a ticket to the western world." He had promised to send for Christy, his wife, and his maternal grandmother, but was last seen in Detroit, and last heard from in Sydney, Australia, where, according to his postcard, he had found work as a hod carrier and was "saving up to reunite the family." That card, which his mother kept next to her votary light, had been mailed twenty years ago.

"What do you know about this Steif woman?" said Detective Crankshaw.

"She thinks I'm uncouth."

"I don't regard that as a motive. After all, you're not married to her."

"She don't like . . ." He paused, uncertain of which word to use: mobsters, gangsters, hoodlums, confidence men. He decided on "Chops!"

Crankshaw looked confused until he recalled Christy's sobriquet, Christy the Chop. But could you use "chops" in the plural?

"My investigative team," said Crankshaw, "has reconstructed her whereabouts for the last several weeks. During that period, she twice met with Laura Favoloso. According to an impeccable source, one time Ms. Steif left the meeting furious, and the other time Laura did."

"Do you know where she got the stuff?"

"No, but it could have been made on campus, in one of the labs."

Christy found himself having to think like a cop. Although he had never paid much heed, one of Brooklyn Benny's maxims was, "To stay outta jail, leave no trail."

"My guess is it was made by a student. This kid Austin Black, what's he studying?

"His major," said Crankshaw, as he looked through his notebook, "is . . . hm . . . undeclared."

"Have you looked at his courses?"

Detective Crankshaw excused himself and went to the computer bank. When he returned, he said soberly, "Thirty hours of Chemistry." He extended a hand to Christy. "You're one hell of a hound."

As they shook hands, it occurred to Christy that problems come in two stages: how and why. The police might discover the hit man—the agent, the how—but the why was equally if not more important. If, for example, Myrtle Steif turned out to be the bomber, her motives would very likely explain those of her accomplices, enabling the authorities to get at the root of the crime. The how required a detective, the why, a shrink. This line of thought led him to wonder whether premeditated crimes and ones of passion should be judged equally. He would have asked Crankshaw's opinion had the detective not interrupted his musing.

"Do you suppose this Steif woman works for the Robaccia family? After all, they're the ones gunning for you."

"They don't use amateurs for hits; it's against Benny's principles."

"Have you ever met Myrtle Steif in a social setting?"

"No, and frankly, Detective Crankshaw, why worry about her when we don't even know she's the iceman? What about the timer, for example? Did you check all the local stores to see if any of the suspects bought a clock?"

"As a matter of fact Myrtle Steif did, but it wasn't the one used to trigger the bomb."

Willing for the moment to consider Ms. Steif's involvement, Christy said, "She would've taken one from her house which she replaced with the new one."

"President Mahon, you really have a gift for police work. I think—" And here he hesitated to shape his thoughts. "I was going to say you're in the wrong line of business, but given the misbehavior at Bogus, you're probably right where you belong." He put away his pad and stood up. "I'll bring in Austin Black and Myrtle Steif for questioning this very afternoon. If anything turns up, I'll call."

DETECTIVE CRANKSHAW
QUESTIONS THE SUSPECTS

Although Myrtle Steif admitted to knowing Austin Black, she said that her only interaction with him occurred in Puppet Hall and bore on administrative matters. Had she read his call-to-arms on the university website? Yes. But she had merely laughed.

"Telephone records show that you made a call to him."

"About his late tuition."

"From your home."

"I'm conscientious."

Myrtle had no reluctance to describe her stay in Malta and her father's ordnance work. Nor did she shrink from saying that she knew a great deal about explosives and timing devices. An only child, she followed her father's career closely and he, proud of his daughter's interest, spent hours lavishly explaining the operating principles behind everything from land mines to guided aerial bombs.

"Could you construct an explosive device from Semtex?"

"I, no. But if the materials were available, I could show someone else."

"Like Austin Black?"

"Given his studies in Chemistry, I would guess so."

"The night of the explosion—"

"I was playing bridge with three other women. Would you like their names? I have them right here in my purse."

"No. I already checked."

Myrtle, wearing a tasteless dress, with blue and red camellias printed on a black background, began to trace the petals of one of the flowers. Unfortunately, she chose a camellia on her flat chest, so that as she ran her finger around the outline of the flower, she merely accentuated her lack of a bosom.

Detective Crankshaw tried a gambit familiar to all law-enforcement officers. He lied.

"You were seen with Austin Black."

"Where?"

"I don't wish to reveal our sources, at least not at this time."

The fact that she had asked for a location rather than utter a flat denial told Detective Crankshaw that Myrtle Steif had in fact met with Austin Black.

Myrtle breathed with some difficulty. "Asthma," she said.

"Sorry to hear."

"I'll have to leave now. My inhaler's at home."

"You're free to go, but before you do, tell me this: what's your candid opinion of the new regime in the president's office?"

She bit her lip and then said stonily, "Laura Favoloso's a slut, and if President Mahon were in the military, it would be no surprise to me if he were killed by friendly fire."

A Germanically proud Myrtle Steif left the office. Detective Crankshaw went to the window and watched as she crossed the parking lot, fumbled with her keys, jerkily backed out, and drove off.

Austin Black, a pudgy kid four or five inches below six feet, had a condition in which the skin, when pushed, retained its concavity for a second before returning to normal. He was round-faced with acne, and his looks had never won him many easy dates. In fact, while growing up, he was taunted by the boys and avoided by the girls. Called a geek and a nerd, he was quite talented in the natural and computer sciences. His insights had impressed the Chemistry Department and had led several professors to add his name to their scholarly papers. Like a great many other right-wingers, he came by his politics through resentment. Having been treated as a pariah by his peers, he got even by espousing ideas they found distasteful.

His genius for science did not carry over to the humanities. The writing of literary essays sorely taxed his mind. In fact, the class in which he received a C had required him to read dozens of plays and to write five or six papers. He could not forgive the university for making him study more than one subject, a grievance that had led him, as a strange act of protest, to resist declaring a major.

Detective Crankshaw decided to go right for the heart of the matter. "Myrtle Steif has told us about her contacts with you."

"How many?" asked Austin, trying to trap the good detective.

"Enough to plan a very nasty business."

"How come you wear string ties?"

"Because my father, a county judge, always used to."

Austin's right thumb pushed on the palm of his left hand. It took a second before the impression disappeared.

"I got a disease."

"Oh?"

"Too bad our fucking president doesn't have one, a fatal one."

"I gather you dislike him."

"Hate him! He's absolutely screwed up the grading system and made it nearly impossible for people like me to go to graduate school. It would be one thing if everyone else in the country had to live under the same system, but they don't. What we have here is a Stalinist lock-step."

"Austin, the day of the bombing, you said you went to a movie. The girl in the ticket office in fact remembered you."

"So?"

"You may have walked out."

"Get off it."

"What was the movie?"

Austin paused and then blurted out, "*The Road to Perdition.*"

"Tell me about it: the beginning, middle, and end."

The same day that Detective Crankshaw grilled Austin Black, he spoke to Laura, who readily admitted that both times she and Myrtle had met they argued.

"What about?"

Laura rearranged her skirt, pulling it down as far as she could. Having dressed conservatively for this meeting, she did not want Crankshaw to think she was baring a leg to blind him to her testimony.

"Before I came to Bogus, Myrtle kept the president's calendar and took minutes at his meetings."

Crankshaw pulled at his jowls, murmuring like a contented hound dog. "Mmmm. Let me guess. You displaced her."

"I asked another secretary to assume those tasks, and I became a personal advisor. Brummagem's idea, not mine."

"How did she take it?"

"Ask her."

"I have."

"I see. You want to compare our answers."

"Yup."

Laura opened her purse and removed a small notebook. "After you explained why you wanted to see me, I jotted down some notes."

"Feel free."

"She suggested sexual misconduct with President Brummagem on my part, implying that to get ahead I. . . . She also called me ruthless. When I told her that keeping someone's calendar and recording minutes didn't interest me, she asked if I felt above that kind of work. I said yes, and she exploded. That was our first meeting."

"And the second?"

"She talked about her many years at the U., her devotion to the trustees and viziers, her desire to see their wishes carried out—for example, in the case of Monroe Larson—and said that I was making it possible for a gangster to ruin Bogus."

Crankshaw looked nonplussed. "How did she conclude that?"

"She said that I gave the president a professional veneer."

"Well, do you?"

"Yes. But I also gave one to Brummagem. Presidents are notoriously under-educated."

Crankshaw guffawed and dismissed Laura, saying he might have to interview her again, though no subsequent meeting ever took place.

AUTUMN LEAVES AND
MOUNTAIN WALKS

Christy's hope of emulating the top mobsters, who always kept at least two women, did not materialize without a few bumps in the road. Laura and Troxy were not as easy as chorus girls. Twice when Christy called Troxy, she pleaded "fatigue" and "bad timing." Laura, too, kept putting him off, until he said:

"I know why you keep saying no. You think I'm a dead man walking."

But whether out of pity or spunk, she agreed to join him on a hike. With a map detailing a lovely walk to a mountain meadow and lake, Christy drove Laura to the Alpine Peaks parking area. Their backpacks brimming with food bought from a deli, they hiked the Blue River Trail. Unaccustomed to the altitude, they stopped frequently to catch their breath and admire the last of the wildflowers. Every now and then a deer would dart out of the woods and then disappear. The dampness underfoot gave life to rushes and reeds, and accelerated the decay of trees that had fallen from storms and from age. They slowly climbed until the trees stood leafless and the vegetation grew more sparse; eventually they reached a point above timber where the mountains that had looked so close still stood at a distance. Without the tree cover, the wind whistled, leading them to a rock outcropping behind which they took cover. They would have retreated to the timber had they not been captivated by the views above and around them, and just off to the west, resting in a depression, the glacial lake. Some birds, attracted by the sunlit water, softly landed on the surface and fluttered their wings. Laura stood up and walked out in the wind. Her lustrous black hair blew over her face, giving her the aura of a free spirit, an impression that Christy found fetching. She observed other hikers coming up the trail.

"Too bad," she remarked. "It would have been nice to have this piece of paradise to ourselves."

Christy could see in the distance three people. When they got within hailing distance, he called out. The party joined him and Laura, and identified themselves as a photographer, a poet, and a tri-athlete. Together, all five made their way to the lake, where they sat with their backs to the wind, watching the birds dive and rise in the air. The poet, a robust white-haired fellow, said this place had been sacred to native Indian tribes, and recited some lines:

> Listen for dear honor's sake,
> Goddess of the silver lake,
>   Listen and save.

Christy could have hugged the poet for introducing just the right tone for seduction.

The following weekend, Christy persuaded Troxy to accompany him to a local rodeo. Riding around the ring, followed by an equal number of men and women on prancing horses, the mayor held a billowing flag. Calf roping, the first contest, elicited appreciative applause for the ropers, who quickly brought down the young animals and applied a hooey, the half-hitch knot used by ropers to tie together three of the calf's feet. Barrel racing followed, a timed event displaying the skills of women riders who performed a cloverleaf pattern around three barrels. But the action that Christy liked most came from the bareback and saddle-bronc riders. They appealed to him sexually; they heated his loins. In each event the rider had to remain seated for at least eight seconds and start the ride with both feet over the break of the horse's shoulders to give the horse the advantage. The cowboys grasped the leather and rawhide handhold, the rigging, with one hand, the other could not touch the horse. Christy, envisioning himself in bed with Troxy, riding her hip movements and sitting firm throughout her feverish thrusts, wiped the sweat from his forehead.

"Do you like it?" he asked.

"It depends on what you mean by *it*?"

Christy's mind raced, certain he had not mistaken the message.

"Since you like the mountains, we could drive to Sun Valley and stay at the Bogus U. lodge. I've never seen it, but I hear the place is a—" he would have said "knockout" but chose "stunner"—"with great views of the mountains."

"I have too many things on my plate at the moment."

"It sounds like a great atmosphere to . . ." he paused, not wishing to say "screw" but unable to find a better word.

Troxy came to his aid. "Know each other."

"Yeah, that's it," Christy replied, certain that Troxy's phrasing corresponded to his own lustful thoughts.

"If I am free and if that's where you want to . . ."

"Come together." The moment Christy uttered the words, he realized they could be taken the wrong way—or the right way, but not the polite way—causing him to blush and his speech to become disordered as he tried to qualify his language. "You know what I mean, nothing rude, it's not what it sounds like . . . though that's what I'm hoping for. Think of it as a contract of sorts, you know, between you"—he hesitated just a second till he remembered—"and me."

"In Sun Valley we will, so to speak, consummate the contract. Is that it?"

"That's it exactly," said Christy, beginning to sweat at the thought of seeing Troxy in a state of undress. Just talking about the prospect of lovemaking with her put him in heat. A screw-and-bolt man, Christy would have liked to get his rocks off that very evening and would have pressed the matter, but for Troxy's next comment, which he felt bespoke refinement and poetry.

"The waiting makes the consummation devoutly to be wished."

SHAWN AND MILLICENT
GO SHOPPING

As Laura distanced herself from Shawn, he drew closer to Millicent, not from genuine affection but rather to show Laura that he could do very nicely without her. He defined his self-respect in terms of how often he could bed the coach's daughter. As her birthday approached, Millicent indicated that she wanted to pick out her own gift—with Shawn. "The couple that shops together," she burbled, "stays together." Chary of being led to a jeweler in search of a ring, he suggested that they look around the Bogus U. bookstore, a place of few books and a great deal of kitsch.

As they entered the store, a charmless space that had withstood the efforts of architects and artisans to improve its interior, he hoped that she wouldn't head for the computers and electrical gadgets that he couldn't afford. He needn't have worried. After stopping at the first rack to buy chocolate kisses "to honor the outing," she was immediately drawn to the rows of meretricious merchandise. At the stuffed animal display, she lingered for five or ten minutes till she settled on a wildebeest that bellowed when squeezed. "Isn't the white dot on its nose and tail cute!" she squealed.

Picking up a shopping basket, she indicated that her idea of a gift was not one, but many "small items" that she could crowd into her bedroom. Her next selection, a gold and white pennant that said "Bogus U.," elicited a comment that gave Shawn Keogh pause.

"I want everyone to know where my husband went to college."

Did she mean him? He chose not to ask.

Her last gift, pink baby socks with red crewelwork reading, "Go, Wildebeests!" prompted the question.

"Are you trying to tell me something?"

She giggled. "You never can tell."

Although she didn't lead him to a jeweler, she did stop in front of a glass case to admire the silver rings bearing the initials B.U. At the cash register, she saw a novelty item that she just had to have: a fuchsia coffee mug with a tiny hole drilled just below the lip so that anyone drinking from it would trickle the contents on his shirtfront.

"Isn't it darling?" she said. "My friends will all love it."

When the tab came to less than fifty dollars, Shawn felt that he had got off unscathed. In the student union, she suggested they have lunch. A junk-food counter stood next to one that served real Asian dishes. She meandered up to the former and ordered a cheeseburger and fries, with a cherry coke. He asked for a Hero sandwich. Carrying their food to an empty table, they found themselves seated next to a group of faculty eating fried rice and spicy tofu. She leaned over and whispered, "Don't you just hate the smell of that awful foreign food? It's so yucky!" In fact, Shawn wished that he had ordered hot and sour soup and some glazed almond chicken. He listened while she praised her favorite restaurant, a pizzeria, and explained why she hated to cook. "It's all those directions and stuff. So I just make it up and it usually tastes icky."

Never knowing what to talk about with Millicent, he always took refuge in asking about her job.

"Oh, it's all right. You know, the usual, filing and stuffing envelopes." She put her mouth to his ear, giggled, and said, "I'd rather have you stuffing me." Other than sex, they had nothing in common. He hated the moment of detumescence because then he had to talk to her. That's why he preferred meeting at her house, even given the danger. Any untoward noise provided him with a ready excuse to bolt. The few times that she had spent the night with him at his apartment or at a motel, he'd awakened the next morning in a panic. How could he escape or get rid of her? He quickly learned to feign sleepiness and roll over.

Why had he ever started up with her? His current reason—revenge— did not explain the roots of the romance. He thought at one time that he actually cared for her; but he had to admit that what he liked were her bountiful breasts and breathy urgings to "play." His father's advice that "a stiff penis has no conscience" was all too true. Whenever he felt the urge to rut, all thoughts of restraint were exiled. He concluded that not only women but also men must be subject to heat. In which case, when Millicent called, what could he do?

The prospect of his spending a life with her, however, put him not into heat but into a chill. His mother had told him often enough that you marry a family as well as a person. He would become part of Coach Caiaphas's household, with its framed gold Jesus against a black velvet background, its private altar facing the lake, its plaque on the front door with the inscription from Jeremiah, "His word was as a fire shut up in my bone," its daily prayer sessions, its sanctimonious incense mixed with the putridness of hypocrisy. Though he recognized in himself a fundamental mental laziness, he did occasionally engage an idea, and certainly had the genes to sustain one. Marriage to Millicent, no doubt about it, would be the death of thought.

Now, as he made his way to the Caiaphas house for Millicent's birthday party, he mused about the symbolism of the house having been built at the top of a hill and about the brass plaque on the front door. Coach Caiaphas felt a fire in his bones, all right. One need only consider his religious convictions, as well as Gretchen Edsel. If he brought the same energy to seeing that Shawn married Millicent, Shawn would be saddled with a flock of kids. And if those brats had her brains and not his, they would be a lifelong burden. By the time he pulled up to the Caiaphas house, he had decided to tell Millicent that he was not the marrying kind. Staring at the plaque, he knew that he could no longer use Millicent as a stick to beat Laura, an abuse of Millicent, whatever her defects. But before he could resolve this moral dilemma, the door opened and Mrs. Caiaphas warmly invited him to join the revelers in the back garden, some of whom, notwithstanding the autumn season, had taken a plunge in the heated pool.

A bar with non-alcoholic drinks adjoined a table with numerous hors d'oeuvres. A black couple served. Coach Caiaphas offered Shawn a pair of swimming trunks. In the cabana, where he retired to change, he encountered two unfamiliar young men talking about Millicent.

"I hear she's got a new guy," said one.

"If there's a kid, unless they do DNA testing, she'll never know the father."

"Who else is getting into her pants?"

"Some stiff."

"What's his name?"

"I told you," the second boy chortled. "You ain't gonna believe this but his name is Narr."

The lads left and dove into the pool. Shawn, now in Coach Caiaphas's swimming trunks, immediately removed them and put on his clothes. As he walked past the good-natured taunts of those in the water, he had one thought in mind: find a telephone directory. The name sounded vaguely familiar. Where had he heard it, from Laura perhaps, or maybe President Mahon? In the kitchen he asked Mrs. Caiaphas for the telephone book, pretending not to hear her question, "Why don't you join the others outside?"

Sure enough, the name Narr appeared, Cranmore Narr, with a number and an address. In the front of the directory was a map of the city. He looked up the street, a cul-de-sac in one of the new neighborhoods east of town. Before calling on Mr. Cranmore Narr, he would first talk to Millicent. He might not want to marry her, but he'd be damned if he was going to share her with some noodle dick.

Millicent, dressed in an off-white slacks suit, was standing on the back lawn, her hair wet from the pool. She warmly embraced Shawn and told him that she had already tried out the leaky coffee cup on friends, all of whom had found it "cool."

"Lively group, no stiffs," Shawn said.

"The only stiff I want is yours," she burbled.

"What about Cranmore's?"

Millicent gave no indication of having been caught out in some misbehavior. Quite the contrary. She sweetly smiled and said, "He sells computer systems and is training me at home on his equipment."

"How many RAMs?"

CHRISTY HOSTS A DINNER
FOR THE NEW FACULTY

To meet his social obligations and to canvass the new faculty for pro-
spective killers, Christy hosted a Thanksgiving dinner for new faculty,
held in the ballroom of the dance pavilion. Through Laura's arrangements, a
string quartet played and a catering service provided delicacies ranging from
fried won tons in plum sauce to cheese blintzes. Each table, handsomely
covered with a linen cloth and spread with plates and silverware, bore place
cards. Christy had specifically requested that he be seated with the viziers
and those instructors who had been appointed after the semester had begun:
Artemisia Gentileschi from Fine Arts, Panjang Sutra from Classics, Galena
Isadora from Dance, and Troxy Dollop from Music. La madonna favolosa
did not join Christy at the table. She wanted to range through the ballroom
and serve as hostess for the gathering; moreover, she had correctly gathered
that Troxy eyed her suspiciously.

Christy introduced the viziers, who, clearly feeling imposed upon to
spend an evening sitting in the company of instructors, said little but ate
voraciously.

Before tasting his squab, Christy turned to the instructors. "Well, guys,
how are tricks?"

Artemisia remarked that she was currently engaged in painting a large
mural for the fine arts exhibition hall, and invited Christy to join her on
the scaffolding to see what she had drawn as a border along the top of the
wall: an intricate line of death masks. "I based them on photographs I took
at the Vatican. You can see faces of young and old, men and women. One of
them even resembles you."

Saying he hated heights, Christy declined the offer.

"Oh," she said, "you can hold on to the ropes."

"I get dizzy when the ground beneath me ain't . . . er, isn't cement."

"If you'd like, I could put a harness around your waist and anchor it to a cleat."

According to the police report that Christy received, Artemisia's husband had died when his harness had inexplicably given way and he strangled in the ropes. The investigator on the scene had been quoted as saying that the knot around Mr. Gentileschi's neck was unusual: a timber hitch. At that moment, Artemisia leaned over and tied her shoe. Christy, noting the fancy knot, asked about it.

"Oh, this," she said, "it's a sheepshank."

Christy nodded in appreciation of her skills, and decided he would definitely not be viewing her mural.

Panjang Sutra observed that the Bogus museum's show on ancient armaments would be opening next month, and that he hoped Christy would launch the exhibit. As exhibit curator, Panjang had brought together breast and shin plates, shields, helmets, lances, swords, knives, slings, and numerous other implements of classical battle. Galena wanted to know if the ancients ever employed poisoned darts, and Artemisia inquired about the use of rancid foods as a kind of biological warfare. Panjang said that although he knew a great deal about poisons, particularly the large beanlike seed of the castor oil plant, his research indicated that the Greeks preferred manly combat. The Romans, of course, were another matter.

"How's the food?" Christy asked.

"You must try the stuffed grape leaves," said Galena, delicately putting a roll on her coffee saucer and sliding it over to Christy. "They are out of this world."

Artemisia insisted he try one of the puff pastries with creamed shrimp, and spooned one over to him. "I took too many."

Eating both the roll and the pastry, Christy opined, "Laura did a swell job picking a caterer. The food's really great."

Troxy casually remarked, "What do you know about this catering service? Have you used it before?"

Christy detected in her voice a note of concern. "Is there somethin' wrong?"

"If I'm not mistaken," said Troxy, "it's a franchise, owned or started by someone called Benjamin Bronzino."

"You gotta be kiddin'!"

"Just ask the manageress." Troxy pointed. "Over there."

Christy would have followed Troxy's suggestion and approached the middle-aged woman dressed in a smart linen suit had Troxy not said next, "The manageress and I got to talking, and in passing she told me that Laura

Favoloso and the owner . . ." She hesitated. Christy urged her to continue. "I suppose it's the Italian connection. You know . . . friends."

A waiter passed with a tray of steaming espressos. Panjang, noticing that Christy seemed preoccupied, removed a cup for him and asked if he wanted chocolate sprinkles on the foamy milk.

Stunned by what Troxy had said, Christy replied absently, "Sure." Panjang sprinkled some cocoa-looking powder from a saucer onto Christy's coffee, which the prez sipped, with his eyes glued on Laura. He wanted to ask Troxy if she was kidding, but that would introduce the subject of the attempt on Benny's life and perhaps even the contract on him. Besides, at that moment he was questioning Laura's trustworthiness. Given that it was she who had related that Brooklyn Benny was lamming it, and she who had volunteered to make all the arrangements for the evening's festivities, he leaped to his feet and, without excusing himself, made a beeline for Laura.

Grabbing her arm, he steered her to a corner, where she yanked free of his grasp, annoyed that he should treat her so discourteously.

"What's this I hear," he said, "that the caterin' service is owned by Brooklyn Benny?"

"It was," she answered, "at least until he went into hiding. And I must say, however many his faults, he always demanded that Hillside Caterers give value for money."

Although a fatalist, Christy was determined, especially after the bombing, not to let his guard down. But then it dawned on him that if she were working for the Robaccia family, she would never have told him about the contract. "Sorry, Laura, I lost my head for a minute."

"Why should you care if Brooklyn Benny owned Hillside Caterers? Are you thinking of taking over the operation yourself?"

"Yeah, there's an idea."

Laura's schooling in suspicion equaled Christy's. Coming from a mob family, she knew that you can never be too careful or have too much information. So she inquired, "How come you didn't know Benny owned Hillside Caterers?"

"He kept a lot of his investments to himself."

"Then how do you know now?"

"Troxy mentioned it. She was talkin' to the lady who manages the local franchise."

"Joyce Botulinus. I've used her numerous times. President Brummagem had me arrange all catered events."

Christy apologized and returned to his table. Troxy, who had watched the little spat in the corner, was pleased to note that matters had not gone well between the two. She wanted no other woman doting on Christy. He swallowed his coffee and grimaced.

"Anything wrong?" Galena asked.

He requested she sample it, but Galena declined. "Tastes funny. Maybe somethin' got into it."

Panjang remarked that the chocolate sprinkles he put in his own coffee tasted all right.

Suddenly, Christy grabbed his gut, gasped, and fell to the floor, writhing and foaming at the mouth.

Christy had no memory of Laura calling 911 and of two stretcher bearers putting him into an ambulance. Although he heard the siren's eerie wa-wa-wawa, he couldn't see the flashing lights as the vehicle darted through traffic streaking for the hospital. One of the male attendants tried to induce vomiting, but though Christy clenched his teeth and tightened his neck muscles, regarding a reflux as a sign of weakness, the medics forced him to puke.

Several days later, the hospital lab telephoned to say that the forensic tests on the remains of the food dredged from Christy's stomach had disclosed a combination of arsenic and castor bean poisoning—a mixture strong enough to kill a bull elephant.

"Luckily," remarked the technician, "the lining of your gut was like shoe leather. All that scar tissue, which undoubtedly came from some previous experience, saved your life."

Christy remembered the chile hot plate and silently gave thanks to the cook.

LAURA REPORTS ON HER FINDINGS

On Christy's return to his office, Laura told him that through friends in high places she had received the privileged FBI information that he had requested on the four new instructors. Inviting her into his office, he took from her a sealed manila envelope stamped:

PRIVATE AND CONFIDENTIAL

He immediately opened the envelope and read the reports, all formatted in the same way and printed alphabetically.

NAME: Troxyperine Dollopina (legally shortened to Troxy Dollop in Camden Town, London, England).

BIRTHPLACE: Malaya. Passport reads: Issued in Amsterdam, Netherlands.

EDUCATION: Universities of London and Yale. Degree in Musicology.

DISSERTATION TITLE: "Polyphonic Sound in Primitive Musical Instruments"

TEACHING EXPERIENCE: Universities of Oslo and Uppsala.

HOBBIES AND SPORTS: Wood carving and horticulture; archery, darts, field hockey, tennis, kayaking, swimming.

POLICE RECORD: Questioned about the misdirection of an arrow that seriously wounded a young man said to have broken off an affair with her. (Case dismissed)

M.O. Frequently attends concerts, particularly ones of early music; plays ancient/primitive instruments; takes long solitary walks; spends time in open markets, particularly in the company of those who sell legumes, seeds, incense, and oils; smokes imported cigarettes; prefers a vegetarian diet.

REASONS FOR CONCERN: Spent time in Baghdad and Kandahar.

NAME: Panjang Sutra
BIRTHPLACE: Kuala Lumpur

EDUCATION: Universities of Singapore, Columbia, and Texas. Degrees in History and Classics. One year of law school, Georgetown.

DISSERTATION TITLE: "Evisceration: The Ultimate Insult in Classical Warfare"

TEACHING EXPERIENCE: University of Texas, University of Sam Houston, of the Alamo, Trafford Preparatory school (NC).

HOBBIES AND SPORTS: Numismatics, skiing, chariot racing, ancient shields and swords, fig trees, and hemlock.

POLICE RECORD: Jaywalking, dog off leash, trespassing (found in library after hours: case dismissed), fermenting and distilling figs without a license.

M.O.: Frequently attends movies and rents videos; reads upscale books and magazines; spends a good part of each day on the computer; regularly walks his two dogs; eats ethnic foods; travels to foreign countries, especially in Asia (he's a devotee of Buddhism); maintains a correspondence with the famous California art appraiser Scot Marco; opposes literary theorists and rhetors.

REASONS FOR CONCERN: On two different occasions found on the premises when a colleague died, both classicists, one presumably from falling on his sword (immolation could not be proved), the other from suffocation owing to some ingested toxin. See article: Sutra, Panjang. "The Roman Penchant for Poisons," *Classical Studies*; 9:4 (January, 1999), 18-33.

NAME: Artemisia Gentileschi

BIRTHPLACE: Rome, Italy

EDUCATION: Venice, Rome, Pisa, Naples

DISSERTATION TITLE: "Women's Wrath: A Major Biblical Theme in Renaissance Art"

TEACHING EXPERIENCE: University of Bologna, University of Florence, L'Accademia, Venice; tutor in Art History and Painting to numerous well-placed Roman children.

HOBBIES AND SPORTS: Knot tying, lassoing, rope making, gardening. She mixes her own oil paints and dyes from rare herbs.

POLICE RECORD: None. She did, however, bring a charge of rape against one Agostino Tassi, her father's colleague and her art teacher. The trial caused a scandal in Italy.

M.O. Perhaps owing to her experience with Tassi, she has threatened to emasculate numerous men who courted her, leaving a trail of unrequited lovers from Indonesia to Italy to England to America. Her dislike of wealthy and privileged men resulted in her marrying a poor one, who tragically died while working on a mural.

REASONS FOR CONCERN: Her most prominent paintings are *Judith Decapitating Holofernes* and *David with the Head of Goliath*. She exhibits an obsession with themes of violent death, and to judge from her oils, seems to especially savor the deaths of men.

NAME: Galena Isadora

BIRTHPLACE: Brovari, Ukraine

EDUCATION: University of Moscow, Kiev School of Ballet, Berlitz Language School of Toronto, Canada.

DISSERTATION TITLE: "The Kinetics and Chemistry of Balletic Movement"

TEACHING EXPERIENCE: Ballet schools in Dnepropetrovsk, Bukhara, Odessa, Kuala Lumpur, and New York City (Fieldston).

HOBBIES AND SPORTS: Cooking, chemistry, embalming, ice skating, stage acting.

POLICE RECORD: Shoplifting (dismissed). Charged with pocketing a pair of expensive ballet shoes from a theatrical outfitter in NYC, she pleaded mental confusion.

M.O. A predilection for dancing in requiems and in plays bearing on death, for example, *The Dance of Death, The Ghost Sonata, Death and the Fool, Death of a Salesman, The Death of Satan, The Death of Ugolino, Deathwatch*. Dabbles in white magic, concocting potions made of mushrooms and ossified snails from which she distills an incense that she inhales for its salubrious effect. See article: Isadora, Galena. "Twelfth Century Monastery Thurificates," *The Journal of Medieval Baneful Brews*, 6:2 (Fall 1997), 78-93.

REASONS FOR CONCERN: Married three times, she buried all three husbands, each of whom died under mysterious circumstances. The first drowned in a well. The second fell on an ice skate and split his head. The third inhaled a deadly anthrax strain developed in the old Soviet Union and now found only in the United States in high-security laboratories. For two years, she worked as a glass blower (a skill learned in Kiev) at Lawrence-Livermore labs outside San Francisco.

After putting the reports back in his filing cabinet, Christy noticed a limo pulling up in front of Puppet Hall and a chauffeur opening the back door to assist Professor Narcissa Whitman Poseuse. The driver bowed as she swept into the building, leading Christy to wonder whether all professors in America had records as peculiar as the four he had just read, and whether they all suffered from eccentricities and royalty complexes. Heretofore he had believed that his life in the rackets and his exposure to the hurly-burly of hucksterism set him apart; now his old life seemed sheltered, compared with such sapient shenanigans. It struck him as well that he could make money from this menagerie by inviting scientists of all stripes to come study the unique Bogus U. genus, a word that he had initially confused with genius, but soon sorted out when he reflected on the mental accomplishments of his viziers and pashas and beys.

His ruminations about exotica gave way to the fearful reminder that he had a killer in his midst, one who had set his—or her—sights on Christy. His allowance for gender issued not from any recognition that language privileged men, but from the recognition that this killer might indeed be a woman. The question of how to proceed now accompanied him as a constant, haunting worry. He must radically change his comportment. Routine was the enemy. He would have to change his place of residence frequently, take other routes to work, open his mail carefully, eat at home, look under the hood and chassis of his car for bombs, stay away from windows and crowds, have bodyguards, arm himself, trust no one. A helluva way to live, thought Christy; it ain't even living. If he could be sure of just one person, someone he could count on, then he could manage. Yes, that's what he needed: an incorruptible, faithful friend. But who in all of Bogus U. could he trust? Sophanna Houth, he decided, that's who!

A HOME AWAY FROM HOME

Although the trustees suggested that he hire a bodyguard and employ a private detective agency to police the grounds of his home, which might prove especially vulnerable during the Christmas season, Christy thought it best to leave the presidential manse. When he broached the subject with Sophanna, the latter agreed that until the hit man was apprehended, Christy had to change his house and his habits. Having been raised on parental stories about the killing fields of Cambodia, Sophanna knew the importance of retreat. His family had rarely slept in the same place two nights in a row, hiding in the jungles of Cambodia and Vietnam, where they subsisted on a watery rice soup, supplemented with field crabs, rats, lizards, and snakes. On good days, they managed to catch fish or rabbits and foraged fruit. They had been driven into hiding because Sophanna's father, who could read and write, had opposed Pol Pot's insane plan to depopulate the Cambodian cities and transform the country into a completely self-sufficient agrarian communist state. Constantly on the run dodging Khmer Rouge soldiers and landmines, the Houths never trod the same paths twice, never spoke above a whisper, never sought food from the same source, never trusted a report that they couldn't themselves confirm, never ignored an unfamiliar sound. The family counted the price of their flight not only in lost years, but also in lost schooling for their one surviving child, Sophanna. His uncle, a college student, had been executed by a government that treated learning as a threat.

The family had come to the United States through the good offices of the United Nations and now lived within walking distance of the campus in a converted two-car garage, with four small rooms and a loft. Except for the occasional student riots, when neighbors summoned the police, the middle-class university area looked and sounded like any other.

Young people jogged and biked; the elderly walked their dogs on leashes; cars crowded the curb; the occasional drunken belch or mating call pierced the evening sky; and students, unburdened with books or much clothing, occasionally skateboarded to school to make a perfunctory appearance in class. Some of them came to campus only to pick up assignment directions for their ghost writers, to go to the sports center to "work out" (the word exercise having become passé), and to meet their friends in order to plan their four-day weekends.

Sophanna continued to work at Bogus, while attending classes and meeting regularly with Laura for tutoring. When Christy first moved in with the Houths, gladly accepting a mattress in the loft, he found himself in a world of strange cooking smells, of long silences, of Buddhist prayer, and of an unaccustomed seriousness. The family had no television or radio, and occupied themselves with newspapers and magazines written in an unfamiliar script. Unlike his parents, Sophanna read books in English—voraciously. Before long, out of either boredom or embarrassment, Christy began to read the same ones that claimed Sophanna's attention. Each day on the way to his office, Christy changed his route, sometimes deliberately extending the walk so that he could engage Sophanna in some issue he had found in their common reading matter.

"School . . . I love. My teachers . . . except maybe one. Students have a good life, but many, how should I say, not use it."

Reflecting, Christy asked, "Don't you mean appreciate?"

"No, use. It no matter if one appreciate school," said Sophanna with firm resolve. "If you use education, like weight lifts, it makes strong the mind."

Christy thought about the kids who pump iron to improve their bodies. If the brain was tantamount to a muscle, it, too, could be beefed up. Yes, he liked that comparison. His mind drifted to Sophanna's family.

"Your uncle . . ." Christy ventured.

"Yes?"

"He's the one whose picture's on your desk, right?"

"Taken at his college."

"I was readin' your book on capital punishment. If it was my uncle, I'd want to get the guys who killed him."

"Did you see the chapter 'An Eye for an Eye?'"

"That's me to a T," Christy said proudly, well aware that the author took a dim view of this behavior.

A car slowed down and Christy put a tree between it and himself. Sophanna noticed, likewise taking shelter. The car moved on innocently.

"I don't believe that way."

"Why not? I can tell you from personal experience, nothin' makes a guy feel so good as gettin' even."

They turned a corner.

"Where ends it? First, we fight the other, then his brothers, then his relatives, then his friends, then the village, then the tribe. The same of countries is true. Mr. Christy, tell me: how much death will make a man content?"

Christy had always personalized his disagreements. Having no experience with analogy or extrapolation, he found himself unable to answer Sophanna, except to point out that if you didn't give the local bully a good crack on the nose, even if it cost you personally, he would constantly torment you.

"How come you're readin' a book on somethin' like capital punishment?"

"Miss Laura. She gave it to me."

Instead of entering the president's building through one of the many doors, they followed a careful routine. In the parking lot, they slid aside the metal tunnel plate—fenced off by a canvas tent bearing a sign: Danger!!! Hard Hat Area Only—and descended into a passage that terminated in the basement of Christy's building. Sophanna always went first, checking for booby traps and inspecting Christy's office before the president entered; then he would disappear to attend to his custodial duties. Whenever he left, Christy felt guilty that this selfless young man worked at a menial job while he, a street punk, enjoyed the fruits of Bogus's many corruptions.

More out of respect for Sophanna than a love of learning, Christy had made a point of joining Sophanna and Laura in the basement for their regular tutoring sessions. Saying little but observing much, Christy soon realized that Laura had a gift for teaching and genuinely cared about advancing Sophanna's education. This experience led him ineluctably to conclude that besides Sophanna, he could absolutely trust Laura.

THE HEART'S A STATE OF MIND

Until he became a part of the evening tutoring sessions, Christy had wholeheartedly embraced the view that marriage was the slow, life-long acquittal of a debt contracted in ignorance or in heat. (He had never stopped to consider their likeness.) The women he'd previously wined and dined served only one purpose: to bank his fires. He regarded the opposite sex as an investment in money and time that never paid dividends. Married men had to account for coming home late, spending money, drinking too much, and taking out their secretaries instead of the garbage, to say nothing of having to change diapers, chauffeur kids to school and extra-curricular activities, join a church, and pretend to maintain a morality that few exercised. He remembered overhearing a conversation between Blowtorch Maxie and Danny Darter, both married men.

> Blowtorch: I never take my troubles home with me from the job. I don't have to.

> Danny: My wife's so irritable, the least thing starts her off. A real self-starter, that one.

What could have passed for a vaudeville routine was all too real for Christy. He wanted no part of the chain and ball—unless, and here he found himself in a quandary, the person was extraordinary.

Although he did not will it, with each succeeding day, his fondness for Laura grew. It came like an uninvited guest whose presence proves entirely welcome. Her education, of course, eclipsed his, but Christy was street smart and had a nose for survival. He also had a good sense of humor and learned to take her admonitions without pouting. At her urging, his tastes graduated from the Ice Capades to foreign films to serious stage plays to chamber concerts and even to opera, which made Christy, for some inexplicable reason, dream of the Ireland he had always wanted to visit. With the expansion of his cultural horizons, he experienced a growing subtlety of thought. His language, held up by a frail scaffold of tutoring, stood him in good stead unless he felt challenged, at which time he reverted to street talk. But his audience regarded that form of discourse as an affectation, not the real President Mahon, enabling him to live easily in two different worlds.

Imperceptibly a genuine fondness developed on her part as well, one that admitted of hugs and the occasional chaste kiss. But the sexual engagement that Christy yearned for she resisted, increasing not only his desire, as one would expect, but also his affection for La madonna favolosa. Convinced that she had sold herself cheaply to Shawn, she would not make the same error again, with any man. The converted, understandably, go to extremes. To justify our break with the old, we embrace the new with unmitigated fervor. Her next lover would have to earn her respect and exhibit real mettle before she again gave herself freely. Whenever she rebuffed his sexual advances, Christy replied the same way, "I'll wait."

They had gone for a hike on a clear cold day in late February. The dead field stalks, coated with ice crystals, exhibited an austere beauty, as the sun low in the sky made them appear like a blaze of diamonds. A golden retriever bounded across the field and nuzzled up to them. He had no collar and thus no name. To their delight he heeled beautifully. When they stopped, he did as well, licking their hands when they gave him a rub on the rump or a caress on the head. A few yards to the west of the path lay a stream, and here on the bank they sat a few feet apart on a fallen tree, petting the nameless dog and talking animatedly.

"You don't really believe what you said at the bowling alley, do you: all that nonsense about self-interest?"

"Sometimes by lookin' after number one, you look after a whole lot of other people, people who depend on you. If a man is happy, he treats his family good."

"Well!"

"Well what?"

"Remember what I told you about using 'well' with verbs?"

The dog, seated at Christy's feet, nudged his leg.

"I don't see his owner. What if no one comes?"

"Take him home and treat him well," said Laura. "I'm sure he'll repay you many times over. Faculty are like well-treated pets."

"Some comparison."

"I've mentioned it before. Pamper them and they'll stay around. Scratch their backs and they'll purr. Kick them . . . they become surly."

"Like I was sayin'."

"*As* I was *saying!*"

"Well, anyway, if I can raise some big dough, I'll try to see that it goes to the right programs and people. But this much I can tell you: if the trustees let the Puppet-Hall administrators have any say, the viziers and pashas and beys will take their skim and then channel the rest to those profs who kiss their asses."

The creek had patches of lacework ice, in some places spidery thin, cut by the slow-moving current. Christy picked up a stick and tossed it on the ice. The dog rose and raced across to retrieve it, breaking through the surface and landing in the water. He came out panting, with the stick in his mouth, and gave himself a good shake. With Christy's body blocking Laura from the dog, the spray hit her only partially and him full front, causing Christy to throw up his hands to ward off the water.

"Is this what I get for being nice to the mutt?"

"He brought you back the stick, didn't he?"

They both laughed in the gentle unselfconscious way that friends enjoy, and he moved next to her. But when he tried to put his hand on hers, she stopped him.

"Something wrong?"

"Friendship and fondness are two different things," she said.

"And you," he responded, "don't feel the second."

"It takes time, Christy, and requires a commitment I don't think suits you or me at the moment."

A silence followed. Then slowly they began to speak easily, traversing subjects bearing on the university and reminiscing about their childhoods. Christy put the dog through his paces, ordering him to sit and stay and lie down. His owner had either taken him to pet school or spent a good deal of time in his training. Christy had a cheese cracker in his pocket that he had purchased from a vending machine before leaving his office. He used it to tempt the dog to roll over, a trick the retriever quickly learned. Pleased, Christy smiled at Laura and said:

"Just like the faculty, right?"

"If you train them, you could win a wealth of prizes."

Looking at her plaintively, he murmured, "The crownin' prize would be to win you."

"That's a rather daring thing to say, in light of what I just told you about commitments. Besides, you know I've just broken up with Shawn and," at this juncture she deliberately paused for effect, "you're seeing Troxy."

"I am not!" Christy exclaimed mendaciously, lapsing into the Irish idiom his mother used when waxing lyrical over a dazzling day and remembering to hit his g's. "By the time the warmth of spring is gentling the air, I'll still be thinking how you're the rising moon, and how I'd like to bide my hours on the hillside basking in your silver light."

Laura, who knew the idiom, immediately mimicked Christy's playful language. "So that's the kind of lover you'd make, poaching kisses in the tall grass at night. Is that what you do with Troxy?"

"Never heard the name before. But with a woman like you in my arms I'd never again know the feel of loneliness, which has destroyed more souls than Satan, including those of a raft of saints."

"You make it sound like fun, with your fine Irish palaver, but how do I know it's not just talk, the sort of thing you tell Troxy?"

Ignoring Laura's third reference to Troxy, Christy interrupted the rhythm of the patter to ask, "What's palaver?"

"Idle flattery."

"Idle, is it? You just give me the chance and I'll show you what I can do with my wetted mouth and you—" he stopped to figure out the grammar— "lying on a brae, surrounded by the flowers of the earth."

Laura said teasingly, "And what makes you so sure that a girl would prefer a brae of flowers to a bedroom?"

Christy rose to rapture. "The priests in paradise would envy me if I could have your love."

"And what is it I have that makes me alluring to you, when Troxy or any of a dozen girls would be glad to have you calling?"

"They might gladden my heart for a spell. But none of them could move me to talk words of wonder, as you've now done, and make me feel as if I could steal under the stars of night and coax gold out of misers. Under your spell, who knows, maybe I could even turn a bogus place into one of bliss, and silver the U. with my brass. Just tell me: what miracle would it take for you to be drawing nearer to me?"

"That you not be thinking only of yourself but of others."

For a minute, Christy pondered Laura's words, and then a great smile lit up his face. "Who would believe it?" he exclaimed, clasping Laura's now willing hands in his own. "For the first time in my life, I'll be putting all the money I steal in some other guy's pocket. Well, the heart's a wonder."

DEEDEE LITE'S NOVEL TAKES SHAPE

Before writing the next chapter, DeeDee studied the notes she had taken when Phineas, one evening in front of the fireplace, with a glass of mulled wine in his hand, had talked to his captive audience about what he called the creative process. "All stories," he had said, "must have a beginning, middle, and end." She had written the beginning and now had to write the middle. Phineas had also quoted from some writer that "without a historical context for their work what most writers produce is isolated psychology, poetic music." DeeDee took down these observations in shorthand, a useful skill that she had learned in high school, where she followed not the academic track—though her teacher had once complimented her writing—but the business one, with a minor in Cosmetology. From observing Brooklyn Benny's Schroon Lake cabin and from having watched, on afternoon walks hand-in-hand with Phineas, the construction of vacation cabins in the area, she now felt ready to describe the locale. She faced one problem; the word "historical" in the phrase "historical context" made no sense to her. So she simply decided to ignore it and create a context by situating her novel in a cabin that Grace and Brent would share before they eventually married. DeeDee had always wanted her own place, even if only a modest lodging, that she and the man she loved could call home. After all, didn't her romance novels say that a home is where two people love, a place of simple pleasures? She chuckled, thinking that some of the pleasures she and Phineas enjoyed weren't so simple. In one of her more racy books, about a defrocked priest who falls in love with an ex-nun, the profligate padre induced the nun to enter the orbit of his arms by convincing her that God would be their home; but DeeDee decided that God could stay put in church, and Grace Pallas and Brent Harris would occupy the cabin that Grace with her many charms would turn into a home. She put a new sheet of paper in her typewriter, having not yet been introduced to word processing, and began her description of context.

JACKIE BROWN TELEPHONES
HIS GIRLFRIEND

Because Brooklyn Benny had told his gang to say nothing about Phineas Ort, Jackie Brown had to whisper into the phone. On the other end, Wilma Allydew, a woman learned about the streets but little else, was reproaching him for his inattention. Jackie Brown had not seen her for months, though he had made the occasional call to tell her that he had been sent out of town on a "big job." She knew better than to ask the nature of the work, but did want to know why he had failed for the last month to be in touch.

"I'm bein' driven crazy," he pleaded, "you gotta understand." He could hear her chewing a piece of gum and popping it.

"Yuh can't expect me to wait forever. It's been a year. I'm horny."

"Me, too, but there ain't nothin' I can do till this job is over."

"You ain't two-timin' me, are you?"

"Wid who, the trees and the dogs?"

"So dere are udder ladies wid you."

"Whatta you mean?"

"Dogs. You said dogs!"

"I mean Siberian huskies. The place is overrun wid 'em. Every house, on the porch, you see 'em. My favorite's one called Molly. She belongs to a forest ranger."

"So you're somewhere in a forest."

"Yuh never heard me say that."

"I heard what I heard."

"Well, I ain't tellin' you which forest."

"Jackie, if you ain't makin' it wid someone else, what are you doin'?"

"Spendin' hours with *Antigone*."

"Ah ha! So you admit you're havin' it off with someone else!"

Jackie sighed. What could you do when people were not on the same plane as you? He began to wonder what he and Wilma had in common.

"She's a classical broad."

"Oh, I see, better than me! I suppose I ain't classical! And since when did you start usin' such words?"

"Wilma," he whispered exasperatedly, "she lived twenty-five hundred years ago. Don't you understand nothin'?"

Wilma, a woman of elemental values, comprehended the verities: a hug, a kiss, a fur coat, a diamond ring, a firm penis. She also grasped the meaning of two-timing. Whatever the appellation—fling, musical beds, affair, hankypanky, cheating, playing around—she would have none of it. A one-man woman, she wanted Jackie to quit trying to cover his ass with these transparent excuses about a chick called Antigone. Twenty-five hundred years ago! Who was he trying to kid?

"Come clean or else you can find someone else," she said.

A thought crossed Jackie's mind. The more education people had, the less likely they were to find companions who would understand what they were talking about. A good reason, he thought, to keep the mind uncluttered. He would have to break off his participation in Phineas Ort's daily seminars. If he didn't, before long he would distance himself from old friends, especially Wilma. But on the other hand, he liked the brain teasers that Phineas threw at the group.

"I'm in a quandary," he said.

"What the hell does that mean? I never heard of duh word."

Jackie sighed. He would have to start from the beginning, but not here in the house. "I'll call you in thirty minutes. I have to go to the village and use the pay phone."

"What village?"

"Thirty minutes."

He hung up and shook his head. Did she really think her question would catch him off guard? Maybe she really was, as Eddie Doyle said, a dumb cluck. Well, she could just wait. It would keep her on her toes . . . make her worry that maybe she didn't have Jackie wrapped around her wedding finger. An hour later he called her.

"Here's the scoop, Wilma. So listen good—and don't interrupt. We nabbed a guy, see. It don't matter who. He decides to teach us a thing or two about ancient history and literature and philosophy, words that are Greek to you. Me, too, until the last few months. I really go for some of that stuff, 'specially what he has to say about heroism and honor and courage. Really cool stuff. I wished I woulda lived back then. I woulda been like Achilles, a tough nut to crack. But never mind about Achilles. It would take me too long to fill you in. Well, there's this girl, Antigone, and she feels she's gotta do the right thing, no matter what. Her uncle tries to stop her, but there ain't no stoppin' her. So she does it and dies. Now what I gotta figure out is whether it's more important to stick up for my family or my country. Eddie says he ain't never goin' to be put in that position. But I can see how a guy can end up havin' to choose between the gang and a girl, for example. Now don't get me wrong. I ain't talkin' about you. I'm talkin' about Antigone. She's really some dame. Never met one like her, even though she's been dead for hundreds of years.

"I can see why people like readin' books. You get to meet some really fascinatin' characters, many of 'em walkin' the earth before anyone invented a car or a cigarette. But they wasn't dumb, by no means. No sirree! They discovered a lot of things we're just rediscoverin' now. And their ethics—that's a fancy word for clear thinking—is as modern today as it was then. Which brings me back to my point. I am learnin' all about ethics and logic. What would I do, for example, if Brooklyn Benny or my old ma said, 'No more Wilma Allydew. You haveta choose between me and she.' I'd have a hard time of it. Just figure what you gotta take into account. Benny took me off the streets, gave me a job, paid the bondsman to get me outta jail, pays me good wages. He's like my father. But you . . . you are my heart's delight. Like that phrase? Our pigeon likes to use it with DeeDee. DeeDee? Forget it! She works for Brooklyn Benny and has eyes only for the guy we nabbed. And don't interrupt! I'm losin' the thread. Where was I? Yeah, you. You, I owe a different kind of loyalty. We grew up on Goldsmith Avenue together; I used to call your bro Butchy, and we started doin' it when yous was only fourteen. So you can see my root goes back a long way and I'm like really deep into you. My problem then is how do I compare loyalty to my boss, Benny, with loyalty to my doll? It ain't easy. We're goin' to be discussin' that problem in a day or two, and I can't wait to hear how it all turns out. You'd really be surprised at some of the ideas we've been chewin' over like the one I been tellin' you about, where people have to choose between one person or another, or between faith and fact. And when that happens, fact always seems to lose. Go figure."

PHINEAS LEARNS A FEW SCAMS

The numerous moral questions *Antigone* raised had turned Eddie Doyle into a poor sleeper and compulsive pacer. He had no intention of schooling Phineas in scams; that forbidden knowledge was transmitted by accident. Late one night in the kitchen, Eddie ran into the prof. They sat in the Naugahyde nook noshing on Eskimo pies.

"I've been thinking a lot lately about public and private responsibility," said Eddie. "In my world, those categories, as you call them, aren't so clear."

Phineas asked Eddie to give him an example.

"You're always saying that our actions, like a pebble thrown in a pond, make ripples, and that our decisions affect others. Well," said Eddie, reaching for another ice cream sandwich, "supposing Jackie and I pull off the following con. He withdraws cash from an ATM machine and, as he walks away, 'accidentally' drops some of the money in full view of a sucker. Jackie then takes a powder. Before the pigeon can pick up the dough, I come along, grab it, and stuff it into a small paper bag. Then I ask the pigeon if he wants a share of the cash."

"You are playing the role of the tempter."

"Just hold your horses. I see Jackie coming back, and I ask the mark to hold the dough for safekeeping, and also—just to show he's on the up-and-up—to give me his watch or some jewelry for collateral. Then I give him my business card—which, of course, is fake—so we can reconnect later. As Jackie approaches, he yells that I stole his wad. I tell the pigeon to scram. Later, when he opens the bag, he sees that it's just stashed with play money. Meantime Jackie and I get away with his collateral. Now if that guy we screwed goes to the cops, how can he claim he was had? His greed got the better of him."

"You rooked him," said Phineas, resorting to language that he knew would resonate with Eddie.

"Yeah, but I don't think the bulls would show him much sympathy."

Phineas nodded. "By agreeing to share in the money, he was lending himself to theft, because if I'm not mistaken, we all have a moral duty to report illegal activities, lest we be accused of aiding and abetting in the crime."

"All right, we rooked him, but we also taught him a lesson. In fact, I would argue that we did him—and the public—a favor by wising him up. Creon had to learn the hard way, also Oedipus, you said. Well, our scam taught the pigeon a simple but important lesson: don't buy a pig in a poke."

"Whether this experience will teach him to avoid scams and behave ethically in the future is impossible to know, but we can say with certainty that you and Jackie, by tempting the pigeon to break the law, were guilty of not only your crime but also his."

"Hey, aren't we all con men to some degree? You cozy up to your bosses one day, the next you hold your tongue when you know you ought to speak up, and the third you spiel out a lotta crap. And why? Just to lull the pigeons into seeing things your way."

"Yes, but I'm not breaking the law."

"No, but what about our decisions and actions affecting others? Isn't that what you've been talking about all along—the personal and the public good?"

Phineas had to admit that we all commit petty sins daily, and that self-interest often trumps truth to one's self. "Unless," he said, "one way of being true to ourselves is through self-interest."

"That brings us back to what you were saying the first day. How we act defines who we are. And if being true to ourselves makes us crooks, then you certainly can't say we're guilty of bad faith."

Studying Eddie's face, Phineas thought that this man, had he been soundly schooled, would have made a first-rate professor. Hell, he was already making distinctions that stumped most pedagogues.

"Let me hear what you'd say about this example of wising someone up," said Eddie.

"Another scam?"

"It depends on your point of view."

"You should have been a criminal lawyer."

Eddie wolfed down another pie. "I work with a broad who spots lonely, rich, older women. She gets to know them and introduces me. I pose as a handsome suitor."

"You mean a gigolo?"

"Say, a professor. I rent a swanky house and car and make the old broad believe that I'm brainy and rich."

"Don't tell me: you lead her down the garden path."

"I wine and dine her and tell her she's gorgeous and great company. In return, she gives me her bed, gifts, and, best of all, dough to invest for her. When I skip out, I leave the house and car unpaid for, and she's—"

"Stuck with the losses."

"Now you can't tell me that she broke the law because she doled out money to a con man."

"No, you did. Your actions are plainly larcenous."

"But, tell me, did I really commit a crime against her? I gave the woman pleasure, didn't I?"

"Which she paid for."

"And I wised her up."

"You misled her."

"So what else is new in love and war?"

Phineas sliced a piece of chocolate cake, feeling the need for a sugar surge to stoke his intellectual engine. "You also involved a third party, the woman who located the pigeon."

Eddie wiped his mouth, as if to signify that the conversation was coming to an end. "It was a private crime. She gave the money freely. I don't see the repercussions."

"But you do admit, um," said Phineas savoring Reynald's cake, "that it was a crime?"

"I'd call it self-preservation."

"On what grounds?"

"Aha, here's the moral kicker. Let's say I'm broke, my kids are hungry, my wife's sick. And that was the reason for the scam. Doesn't the responsibility I owe my family excuse my crime?"

"That's what we call a mitigating circumstance, but it doesn't get you off the hook."

Eddie lit a cigarette and ruminated a moment. "What kind of circumstances get a guy off? I mean, what makes for an excuse that will let me break the law but keep me out of jail? When can I plead conscience, like Antigone, or hunger, like a million people in the world, or principle, like the partisans who strung up Mussolini?"

Phineas reached for a second slice of cake. "To stay clear of punishment, you must be able to lay claim to some kind of goodness. There are two kinds of law, moral and statutory. Think of them as principles and rules.

Although it's a constant struggle to keep them in balance, if you have to err, err on the side of the moral."

"In other words, the law depends on morality. Right?"

"What else could it rest on?"

Eddie mulled over that idea before responding, "Money, power, greed, revenge, prejudice, and a lot of other nasty things."

"Then it would be a flawed law."

"What about practicality, plain and simple?"

Although Phineas seemed keen to answer this question, he frankly admitted he would need time to consider "the constituent parts of practicality."

Eddie, having whetted Phineas's appetite for crime and punishment, agreed to continue this conversation later, and so it was that, in what became a regular series of nocturnal meetings, Phineas turned into a scholar of scams: the bank examiner, the good neighbor, the lotto, the melon drop, the ketchup, the bumper car. But let us leave this scene lest we grow particular and instruct the reader in the ways of crime, which, alas, Phineas found all too fascinating.

THE BEST LAID PLANS

Unbeknownst to Christy, the word-processing typist in his office had long enjoyed gratuities and gifts from Narcissa Whitman Poseuse, who early in her career discovered the value of cooperative staff. From the typist, who prepared Laura's letter, Narcissa learned the names of the British professors from whom Christy was seeking advice. They taught at St. Bart's, the very university where her old chum Lars Gooly headed the Biology Department. Narcissa smiled, knowing the old-boyism among British academics.

On hearing that Professors Jonathan Sommers and Graham Arnold would be scrutinizing Larson's record, Narcissa immediately telephoned Lars, who promised to help. To her credit, she showed no favoritism, offering both Sommers and Arnold the same arrangement: a generous travel allowance and honorarium to speak at Bogus U. When each, out of politeness, asked her about the case, she repeated, "I am chairing the tenure and promotion committee of a young man whom I think the world of. His discovery will revolutionize American Studies. His name is Monroe Larson. You will want to remember it, so that when he makes a splash, as he will, you'll know that I told you first."

Narcissa worried that both men, though they had keenly accepted her offer, would find it difficult to swallow Monroe's record and his refusal to reveal the letters. Having made their way in the world not by slumming but by producing first-rate scholarship, Sommers and Arnold, she feared, might easily balk. A fortnight later, Professor Poseuse received a telephone call from Cambridge, England. It reached her at 8 a.m., as she sat down to breakfast.

"Professor Sommers," she enthused, "how good of you to call. What time is it there? Three p.m., of course, you're seven hours ahead of us. No, I've been up for ages. I try to spend two hours each morning at the computer." The toaster popped and she removed a piece of raisin bread. Juggling the phone on her shoulder, she buttered the bread and took a bite carefully so as not to sound as if she were eating. "Ah, the material reached you yesterday and you've already looked at it." She listened and then replied coldly, "Yes, as you say, a thin file makes a quick read. But what of the promise buried in those few pages?" Driven by frustration or hunger—some medical experts regard them as synonymous—she folded the bread and took a big bite, no longer caring if her caller could hear her chewing. "I can't foretell the future either, but I know promise when I see it." Chomp. Chomp. She finished off the bread and reached for the second slice. Before she buttered it, she said indignantly, "What do you mean 'A gallimaufry of insignificant notes?' Why, my own work. . . ." She stopped, thinking of the scholars she had cribbed from. "Frankly, I am disappointed that you cannot see the implications of his work and take my word for the authenticity of the letters. But if you won't, I'll of course respect your decision. Angry? No, just disappointed. Terribly. What's that?" A smile brightened her face. "But only if you mean it. A tepid letter can be worse than a negative one. Oh, you are a gentleman, Mr. Sommers, and I promise that Bogus will roll out the red carpet for your visit. Thank you for calling." She hung up and murmured, "One down and one to go."

Christy, knowing that you can never have too many sources of information, had directed Laura to bring to campus a Canadian whom a professor at Harvard had recommended. "Keep him under wraps," said Christy. "I don't want Poseuse and the viziers finding out about his being here. Get him a room in one of the visiting faculty suites and tell him that this operation has to be hush-hush. Maybe he should use a disguise. If the viziers find out, they'll try to undermine him."

Laura met Professor Georges Gautier, dressed as a Bedouin, at the airport and brought him by way of back roads to his living quarters. Stressing the importance of secrecy, she explained how the process had become personal and controversial. Studiously avoiding all mention of names, except the candidate's, she showed him to his digs. To be on the safe side, she had told Christy to direct the switchboard operator at university housing to keep a record of Professor Gautier's calls, and to have the building manager contact her immediately if Gautier left the complex. In the small world of academe, one couldn't be too careful. Fortunately, Professor Gautier thought it beneath his dignity to make more than two trips a year south of the Canadian border. Americans, to his mind, were provincial and pastor-ridden. A Deist himself, he regarded American history as a wonderful experiment gone wrong once theistic beliefs supplanted a reverence for nature. Short in height and heft—he couldn't have weighed much over one hundred pounds—Georges taught courses in eighteenth-century North American studies at the University of Toronto. Although his father was French, his mother came from sturdy British stock. Her influence had prevailed, particularly in his preference for understatement and British idioms.

"It's been donkey's years since I visited this part of the country. Quite a nice flat you found for me. I'm awfully knackered. If you don't mind, I'll just rest a bit before looking at this chap Larson's file."

For the next twenty-four hours, Professor Gautier neither left his apartment nor made any compromising calls. He had rung his university four times, twice the day he arrived and twice the next day, and had called his wife once. Since Laura had arranged with an off-campus food service to bring him his meals, he had no need to leave the premises. A man of serious intent, he assiduously read and reread the scant material with a critical eye. The next afternoon, when he met with Christy and Laura, his frown bespoke reservations.

Christy, an acute observer, a defensive skill he had acquired in the rackets, said, "You look worried, Mr. Gautier. Something wrong?"

"I've been at sixes and sevens about this man's record. Really, it's quite confounding."

"How so?"

"When I tried to separate the claims from the achievements, I saw they were of a piece: codswallop."

Puzzled by the word, Christy asked, "Is that good or bad?"

"Unmitigated rubbish."

Laura, having little faith in Christy's command of vocabulary, requested a translation. "What in particular do you object to?"

"The few articles and scraps that he's written show a command of style and a competence in research, but no imagination. His work plods. It wants liveliness. It also lacks courage. Given all the things he could say about his material, he ducks the hard issues and takes cover under a cloak of civility. Then, of course, there's the matter of paucity. It weighs nothing. At Toronto, Professor Larson would be lucky just to earn a part-time position."

"What about the letters of Jefferson's girlfriend?" In truth, Christy had forgotten her name, though not the saucy details.

"Sally Hemings? What about her? I don't see the letters. We have only Larson's word for their existence. You theists take entirely too much on faith." Christy looked blank; as far as he was concerned, Professor Gautier had just spoken a foreign language. "Where's the proof? While it is true that I love reading fiction, I govern my life on the basis of fact. I advise you to do the same."

"I wannabe absolutely clear about what you're saying."

"The man's academic record is a *scandale*."

"If that word means what I think it does. . . ."

"It does!"

The day after Professor Sommers telephoned, Narcissa received a call from Professor Graham Arnold. She was sitting at her desk scheming, fittingly under a portrait of Trofim Denisovich Lysenko. "Yes, this is she. I'll wait." She opened her window a few inches to enjoy the chinook breezes that had pleasantly warmed the air. "Ah, Professor Arnold! Thank you for telephoning. To what do I owe this pleasure? Uh, huh. I couldn't agree more. If we have to choose between some abstract principle and the person, always pick the person. Yes, I know him very well and can assure you that he will deliver on all his promises. You are a mensch, sir. I certainly appreciate your faith in me. What's that? A trustee of the St. Bart's Archives. No, I didn't know. Quite an honor." Pause. "I'm sure he would look favorably upon selling the letters—or even donating them—to the Archives." Pause. "Then we're agreed."

PHINEAS AND DEEDEE HAVE A TALK

The men and DeeDee were lounging in white Adirondack chairs on the lodge porch, enjoying an unusual softness for April. Thirteen months had passed, and Phineas was now well ensconced in Schroon Lake, where Brooklyn Benny continued to subsidize his writing. As the men sipped German beers and watched an eagle hover over the lake, DeeDee sighed. Like most discussions theirs moved as aimlessly as air—until it settled on Antigone. When Phineas pointed out that some scholars, a minority, contended that Creon had no choice but to stand up for his country's laws, and was therefore truly caught on the horns of a dilemma, the others agreed that the stamp of great leadership was the willingness to put the individual before the state. With the group in complete agreement, Creon bit the dust. Jackie Brown delivered the last rites when he announced that even though he had played Creon, "Duh guy was way off base dissing the chick and her brother."

"I could not more agree," said Reynald.

"Otherwise," Jackie Brown proudly announced, "you got communism, not democracy."

Having discovered his reflective powers, Eddie Doyle had put his sleepless nights to good advantage, schooling himself in other plays that Phineas had suggested and even reading some philosophy. "Let's say the godfather and nine of the boys," Eddie analogized, "vote to go to war, but one votes against." He directed his question to Jackie. "Are you saying that the godfather ought to listen to the one?"

"The one goes wid the others. That's democracy," replied Jackie.

"But then you're putting the many before the one. I thought we agreed that a great leader doesn't let the state force its citizens to act against their consciences."

Jackie Brown rubbed his furrowed brow. "You know, Eddie, lately you been actin' kind of strange. If you got a beef, let's hear it."

"I'm just pointing out the contradictions in your statement."

"Who's contradictin' himself?"

"You."

Jackie squared off in a boxing stance, and raised his dukes. "I had enough of you bein' Mr. Brains. Let's settle it like men."

"Fighting means a failure of mind."

"Since when did you lose your nerve? You're yellow!"

Eddie pondered that statement for a long moment, considering whether to engage Jackie in a physical tussle. Instead, he replied, "Make an argument, Jackie, not a fist. Don't you remember any of the lessons the prof taught us?"

Jackie's simple mind raced. He wanted to show the others that Phineas's seminars had indeed improved his ability to think. So he lowered his hands and declared, "If you let the minority tell the majority what to do, then what good is a majority?"

Eddie had recently been trying to make sense of Baruch Spinoza's *Social Contract*. In response to Jackie's question, he said, "Did you ever hear of the tyranny of the majority? Just because one group gets more votes than another doesn't make that group right. We should be concerned with what's right, not with numbers and rules. That's what *Antigone* was all about."

A crestfallen Jackie knew in his gut that things would never be the same between him and Eddie.

Phineas observed that democratic societies can become totalitarian ones when they vote to suppress voices of dissent. "Then they are no better than a communist society."

Jackie fought with his limited mental capacities and arrived at a conclusion. "Yous guys are right. I'm contradictin' myself." Although he found this a difficult concession to make, he took pride in his having seen the conundrum.

Phineas reminded him that months before, the group had talked about categories and how one mustn't confuse them. "A vote is a political act. Behavior based on conscience is a moral decision. What was *Antigone* about if not the problem of the political and the moral clashing?"

"Shit, Doc, I ain't been happy since the day you talked about them categories," said Jackie. "Any mug who don't like the rules can cry foul and say it's his conscience talkin'. How can you tell the difference?"

"You can't."

That simple declaration left the group speechless, as each person in his—and her—own way weighed the implications of how a government, for and by the people, can function when some or many of those people vote out of self-interest.

As the earth turned away from the sun and the light waned in the west, an orange streak burnished the lake. Phineas and DeeDee sat, hand in hand, admiring the sunset. The boys, who now had the utmost trust in Phineas, had gone into town to carouse at one of the local bars. As they had hopped into the car, Jackie could be heard telling Eddie, "Just don't get philosophical with those lumberjacks in town or we'll have a fight on our hands. They ain't as refined as us."

The months had flown by quickly. Phineas wrestled with how to tell DeeDee that when he finished his book, he'd be leaving. After all, in America how does one speak of class differences? Although money and birth matter, education trumps them both. Wealthy, high-born, well-educated men will more readily marry a poor woman with a college degree than they will a rich woman without one. In fact, education is the great divider, a fact not lost on politicians, who often go out of their way to dumb down their speeches lest they be accused of being elitists. It would not do for Phineas Ort to return to campus with a buxom, gum-chewing floozy on his arm whose command of the English language would invite his colleagues to wonder if he was thinking with his head or his dick. Given the nature of his job, he couldn't hover over her, prepared to correct every ill-advised word or thought. Seeking for a way to explain their unsuitability, he decided to say that the fault lay entirely with him, and that it would be unfair to bring her into a university setting because, sadly, their respective educations set them apart. Outside of the bedroom they had nothing in common. Further reflection, though, led him to realize that such a statement would sound cruel. But no matter how he tried to formulate a way of saying that they were culturally and educationally incompatible, he could not get the phrases to ring true. She would never understand such an argument. Her appalling sentimentality would lead her to say "love conquers all," or something equally bromidic.

Again, he felt a pang of remorse, as he remembered her generous intimacies and her willingness to limit her gum chewing, and now and then read a book. But it would take another lifetime for her to catch up, though he admired her for trying. Anyone would. Wasn't America built on Horatio Alger stories and the belief that in the end pluck wins the day? Unfortunately, those stories had never been true and would never become so in the future. He decided that the only way to spare her the hurt of rejection was to enlist her maudlin feelings. He therefore shamelessly told her that his blind mother, a missionary in Madagascar, had written imploring him to care for her in her final throes of terminal cancer.

Had DeeDee stopped to think a minute, she would have realized that no mail had arrived at the lodge or left it, except for the two letters Eddie Doyle vetted, the one Phineas wrote resigning from his university and the other to Bogus U. withdrawing his application for president. In short, he had been almost completely incommunicado the entire time he and DeeDee had been sporting. But the heart has a way of clouding the mind. Such was the case with DeeDee, now overcome with respect and pride for her professor lover who would be returning to his mother.

Lest our fair readers think poorly of Phineas for inventing this story, we would remind them that truth rarely consoles. Every day people are spared pain and often immeasurable grief owing to the kindly lies of physicians, priests, coaches, teachers, husbands, wives, and myriad others, all of whom create fictions and anodynes to mitigate life, including stories about the astral canopy, which we invest with a metaphoric meaning that gives our lives a destination and purpose.

CHRISTY AND LAURA
WATCH A VIDEO

Upon Laura's receiving a job offer from the Chimera Hotel in Las Vegas, Christy entreated her to remain at Bogus, saying that he would match the salary and improve on the perks. To celebrate her accepting his offer, he invited her to have dinner—catered—and see a video at the president's house, which in his absence had been maintained by a skeleton crew. He arranged for a squad car to cruise the area and check the house every thirty minutes. Sophanna politely declined Christy's offer to join them, even though Christy told him that they would be watching *Godfather I*.

With the final credits on the screen, Laura began to talk about the book. "It's a ripping good story, but Puzo also has some telling things to say about America."

"I didn't pick that up from the flick."

She then expanded on her comment, pointing out that the novel begins with the name Amerigo Bonasera, a play on "Goodnight, America." She explained that when America failed to protect its immigrants, they had to band together to survive, forming a country within a country, where justice could be sought and found for crimes against one's person or family. To become part of that secure world one had only to swear loyalty and to promise the Don a favor in return, if asked.

"The Mafia," she said, "is no different from big business. Same rules, same Old Boys club."

"They're just protecting their interests—and their dames."

Also the double standard, she mused. Friend Shawn thought nothing of diddling Millicent Caiaphas while expecting her to remain true. Turning to Christy, she asked, "Are you still dating Troxy?"

At that moment, Barney, the Labrador retriever, bounded into the room and sniffed them both before settling at Christy's feet.

"This dog needs a bath. He smells."

"Don't change the subject."

"No . . . and yes."

"What the hell does that mean?"

"We've never done it if that's what—"

Laura cut him off. "I should hope not, when you're dating me!"

"She's a good source of information about some of the faculty. I gotta protect myself, don't I?"

"I thought you believed in fate and, like Don Corleone, in destiny," she said sarcastically.

"Yeah, but why tempt the bastards? That's why I go around armed." He patted his jacket. "A thirty-eight special."

"Packing a rod isn't enough. You have to tap phones and read mail, even hers. Maybe even mine!"

Christy dismissed the idea with a wave of his hand.

"You may not have read *The Godfather*, but you just saw the film, so you know that when Michael shoots Sollozzo in the restaurant, the hit is made possible only because of the planning. You can be sure Benny's boys have done their homework."

He laughed sardonically. "They've already failed twice."

"It's not like them."

Christy poured her a glass of white wine, while he sipped from a bottle of Pilsner ale. "Well, anyway, so far, so good."

Laura replied skeptically. "From what I remember about those guys, the longer nothing happens, the more likely it will."

Barney growled and perked up his ears. Laura's expression exuded concern. Christy edged to the window and opened the metal shutters. On the distant highway, lights flashed. Apparently the police had caught a speeder. Barney perched next to him, growling repeatedly. In the open fields behind the house, nothing looked amiss. Perhaps Barney had smelled a prairie dog or a family of raccoons. The town and countryside were especially overrun with the latter, and Christy wondered why the City Council didn't order the wholesale trapping of these pests, with their constant breaking into trash cans and perching under porches. His dentist, Christopher Brauchli, had got it right, "When the human race has run its course, the world will be occupied by cockroaches and raccoons."

Christy reached down, petted Barney, and returned to the couch.

"I've made numerous calls," she said, stroking the stem of the glass. "My mother says no one's talking."

Barney again sat up and growled.

"It's probably a coyote," Christy said.

"Animal or human?"

"I have on the floodlights and the cops are in the neighborhood."

Barney left the couch. Padding back and forth, he refused to respond to Christy's order to sit. Christy grabbed his collar and petted his head, but Barney kept glancing toward the window.

"My dad used to say dying and wiving go by destiny," said Christy.

"I don't believe in preordination."

As Christy tipped back his bottle for a swig of the cool beer, a shot shattered the window.

BROOKLYN BENNY HUDDLES
WITH THE HIT PERSON

When the newspapers reported that for the third time someone had made an attempt on the life of the Bogus U. president, Brooklyn Benny called his hit person back to New York. The venue, his elegant house in Harrison, seemed out of place for plotting a murder: handsome furniture, a hutch holding Waterford crystal, views of sweeping lawns and majestic trees, a pond with two facing fountains at either end spouting long arcs of water. An irate Benny puffed on his cigar.

Seated in the living room, the two principals eyed each other warily.

"I thought we had a plan? Yes or no?"

"You wouldn't let me explain on the phone, so it cost you a bundle to bring me out to tell you in person."

"I wanted to hear it from the horse's mouth."

"Just like the first two times, I didn't do it."

"If yous wasn't the shooter, who was?"

"Some student, pissed off about grades."

"What's the world comin' to?" With some relief he blew a cloud of smoke in the air, but his concerns about his assassin were not yet completely allayed. "How do you know?"

"I had gone for a walk along the footpath behind the president's house to give the place a once-over, in case I had a chance to pop him at home. But as I'm sitting in the tall grass, enjoying a cigarette, I spotted someone crawling toward the house with a violin case. Yes, I swear, a violin case! I guess he'd been watching too many old movies. So I followed at a distance. The kid opens the case and assembles a rifle, with a telescopic lens. He really had to be stupid, because a cop car, with its lights flashing, stood on the highway, a few yards away, and another one was cruising the area. At first,

I thought it was some kind of joke and he really wouldn't shoot. But the kid takes aim and pulls the trigger. That's when I got the hell out of there."

"These kids nowadays can't get anything right. I oughta know. My own sons wanna go into a straight business. Can you imagine?"

"If I'd done it, he'd be dead. I don't approve of these long-range jobs with high-powered rifles. Maybe we ought to forget the plan. Just say the word and I'll go up to the front door, ring the bell, and when he answers it, blow off his head. That kind of job, though, will cost you more, because of the risks."

"Just stick with the plan."

"Can I have a drink?"

Benny went to the small bar that tastefully fitted into a corner of the room and poured two drinks. "You still like sherry? Good. I got some imported stuff." He handed the hit person the drink and threw back a shot of rye. He shuddered, thereby validating the authenticity of the booze, and continued. "How far was the kid from the house?"

"At least fifty yards away. It would've taken a sharpshooter to plug him. He had to put the bullet between the piano and a parlor chair. Instead his shot hit a vase of flowers on a bookcase, punched a hole in the wall, and ended up in the downstairs bathroom shower. That's what the papers say."

"Did they nab the guy?"

"No."

"Then how the hell did you figure out it was a student?"

"I followed him. Two blocks away he jumped in a Beemer and drove off. I got the license number and checked with our man in the Transportation Department in D.C. and found out the kid's name, Austin Black. One night I paid him a visit. When I told him what I'd seen, he said if I remained mum, he'd tell me his motive: bad grades."

"You oughta work for the cops."

Smiling, the rub-out artist lit a cigarette. "I never leave anything to chance, Benny. That's for believers, not killers."

"Huh?"

"Never mind."

"Just make sure you got a clear head when you wax 'im. I don't want no slip-ups."

Benny then reviewed the plan. "We send a letter about givin' the U. money. We say the guy sendin' the letter wants to meet wid 'im. You get Christy to come to Sun Valley, to the Bogus lodge there, up on a mountain, away from neighbors. Right?"

"You couldn't be righter."

"Harry and you whack 'im—."

The hit person interrupted. "No, Benny, remember your promise to your sister, Agnes. I shoot him and Harry's there just in case."

"If I was Harry, I'd want to be in on the fun."

"You promised Agnes to keep Harry out of this sordid business."

"I don't know what that means."

"Dirty."

"Then why didn't you say so?"

"I did, but in other language."

"Look, I'm just a simple guy who runs a racket. Sometimes I have to put out a contract on someone. But nobody can miss my meaning. You know why? Because I talk straight."

"So do I, Benny."

A long interval followed, in which Benny reviewed his dislike of "smart guys" and wondered why English had different words to say the same thing. He felt good that his reflections took him into what he would have called the field of philosophy. After all, how many mugs thought about the lexical richness of English?

"You know," he said, "something just occurred to me. We got a lotta words for the word crap and all of them fit that shit Christy the Chump Mahon."

"My point exactly," said the executioner. "We have a vocabulary. Why not use it?"

"Yeah, you gotta point. Maybe I oughta learn some more words that mean fucking. I can't spend the rest of my life sayin' to broads, 'You wanna fuck?'"

DEEDEE RELATES
BRENT'S SAD TALE

After college, Brent wanted to go to Greece to study archaeology, but the Vietnam war was going on and he got drafted, even though he told his draft board he suffered from some mental illness, which he really didn't have, but said he did. In Vietnam, he worked in a Saigon military hospital as an orderly. One day a beautiful young girl was brought there from the countryside. She had lost three toes because she stepped on a land mine. (There are millions of them still unexploded in that poor country, land mines not toes.) Her name was Em Butterfly. Never in his life had Brent seen such beauty. She looked like one of those Greek statues of young boys, with perfectly shaped arms and legs and round lips and big eyes. Her cinnamon-colored skin felt like satin and glowed, maybe because she rubbed coconut oil on her body, which gave it a wonderful scent. Brent visited her room every day, and even combed her shoulder-length hair a few times. (She could do it herself, but he wanted an excuse to touch her.) Em Butterfly cried a lot because of her injury, not from the pain but from the loss of three toes. She thought the wound made her unfit for work (so the translator said), but Brent knew she'd be okay. Every day, he came to her room and pretty soon they were holding hands. She spoke only a few words of English, but her smile said plenty. The only thing that surprised him was she wouldn't let any of the nurses bathe her. She seemed very shy about exposing her body. Brent knew some cultures are just that way. One afternoon, while he was holding her hand, she fell asleep. He unbuttoned her shirt. No breasts! He gently lifted her thong. A penis!

He wanted to waken her to say, how come you never told me, but realized that they had said very little to each other in English. How could he have been so misled? He refused to believe he was like all those Greeks who preferred young boys to girls. He knew it was all a mistake, but how could he tell her/him he Brent was NOT that way. His mind raced. He stuffed all his cash under her bed sheet, which was his way of saying I've made a terrible boo-boo, which he had, when he fell in love with a woman/man who reminded him of Greek statues, which should have tipped him off there might be something phony about Em, but which didn't because he was so taken with her/his beauty, and now realized boys could be as beautiful as girls and maybe this was why so many Greek men were peculiar that way, you know, wanting boys instead of girls, though Brent knew for sure (thank God!!!) he was not that way, never having done it with a boy in his whole life, and never wanting to—ever, ever, ever!!!

THE POLICE ISSUE A REPORT

Detective Crankshaw came to the president's house, which the campus police now patrolled twenty-four hours a day, to tell Christy in person the results of his investigation into the shooting. Christy led Crankshaw into the living room and offered him a drink.

"Not while on duty."

"A soda?"

"Sure, whadda you got?"

"Name it."

"How about a Pepper?"

"It's yours."

Christy removed a can from the small refrigerator under the bar. "A glass?"

"No, the can will do."

Christy poured himself a combination of orange and cranberry. Just to be safe, he made sure the metal shutters were closed. The two men sat facing each other on parlor chairs. Detective Crankshaw removed a manila folder that held several computer printouts. Wetting his forefinger and thumb, he picked through the papers.

"Here's what we got. There were two of 'em. We could tell from the trampled grass. We identified the type of firearm, a rifle, and the caliber of bullet. Just so you know who you're dealing with, the killers meant business. It was a soft-headed bullet, which would have blown you apart."

"Nice guys."

"When we interviewed you after the first attempt on your life, you said that you had made a lot of enemies. We're checking out that list now. So far nothing's turned up."

"The viziers?"

"Except for what you already know, nothing new."

"Any of them own high-powered rifles?"

"No."

"How many faculty do?"

"Six staff members, that's it. We visited all of them and tested their weapons, but none of them had been recently fired. We're also checking on other people in this and adjoining counties. But because a lot of westerners love hunting, hundreds of folks have the kind of weapon we're looking for."

Detective Crankshaw sipped his drink and carefully read through his papers. Looking up, he remarked casually, "One of the killers was a smoker."

"You must have found a cigarette butt in the field."

"Hundreds of them, in fact. But when we tested the content of the tobacco, we learned that only one of those butts had been recently smoked. And the evidence from the ash confirmed our findings."

"Well, since sixty million Americans smoke cigarettes, you've got this thing pretty well narrowed down."

Detective Crankshaw closed his file and looked gravely at Christy. "We are not bumblers," he said coolly, piqued by Christy's irony. "We know the brand of cigarette. Now if we can match the brand with someone in the Robaccia family who smokes these particular cigarettes, we will indeed have narrowed the search." He leaned back and smiled smugly.

"Maybe I can help you."

"That's why I'm here." He held up the Pepper. "Would you mind?"

Christy gave him another. Then removing a bottle of Stolichnaya, he poured some into his drink, carried the vodka back to his seat, and put the bottle down at his elbow.

"What's the brand?"

"That's where the mystery comes in."

Christy took a long draught. "I'm listenin'."

"They're foreign."

"So what?"

"Not from Europe or Turkey or Russia, places you might expect."

"Where then?"

"Indonesia. They're called Kreteks."

IN FLAGRANTE DELICTO

Although Bogus U.'s faculty and past presidents had been known to turn tricks in labs, offices, steam tunnels, closets, lavatories, and the library stacks, Christy preferred a bedroom. Unfortunately, the evening that he had set aside in hopes of tasting a liquor never brewed, Laura could not get away, having agreed to a "Platonic" date with Shawn. Christy decided manfully to use the time to good advantage: he threw a dinner party for a few malcontents whom he wished to win over, including Trustee Frank Edsel and Dailey's secretary, Florence Richmond. As chance would have it, that very same evening, Gretchen Edsel and Boaz Caiaphas were meeting at Cranmore Narr's house, and Millicent Caiaphas was waiting near the phone in the hope that Cranmore would cut short his trip to Boise, so that in the comforts of his king-size bed the two of them could really "celebrate" his birthday, as she had promised.

Shawn, whose parents had given him two box seats, asked Laura to join him at a baseball game. Wanting to draw Laura back into his romantic orbit now that he suspected Millicent of double-dealing, he said, "I want to make amends." Reminding Laura of good times past, he asphyxiated her with platitudes and whined that "there were things between them that no one could sever," a line that he bungled from *The Great Gatsby*. He pleaded, "let bygones be bygones," and immediately quoted another inanity, "life is too short to quarrel."

Needless to say, Laura did not find his arguments compelling. "Shawn, I like you, but you are a fucking two-timer."

She made this comment in the car on the way to the game. Although the brusqueness of it took him aback, he rallied to say, "You've always been regular. No beating around the bush. Straight-to-the-point Laura."

She thought of the unintended naughty nuances in his words, but remarked only that baseball, for all its critics, didn't suffer from the endless parade of fouls that one saw in basketball, and the start-and-stop rhythms of football, both of which impeded the flow of play. She readily admitted that she had agreed to accompany him to the game not for his wit but for the love of the game.

"Just give me a second chance," he bleated.

She told him to keep his eyes on the road.

"I'm sure we could be happy again."

But she dashed his hopes with the curt comment, "As friends, but nothing more."

He told her to look in the glove compartment. The box of chocolate candy she found had been bought for her, he claimed. She smiled gnomishly and said:

"Is Millicent getting too fat, or did her doctor tell her that pregnant young women should stay away from sweets?"

"Neither!" he grumbled, though Laura's speculations were not far from the truth. Millicent had developed acne, which, according to her doctor, had resulted from some kind of hormonal change. Fortunately, the box was well sealed, so it could be recycled as a gift for Laura.

The baseball game proceeded as one might have expected, with the home team losing in extra innings. Shawn bought hot dogs and peanuts and cotton candy and, since Laura had no taste for beer, a lemonade. He even gave her a pennant. But she remained immune to his blandishments, repeating her wish for them to continue as friends—but not lovers. When he asked if she had found another beau, she replied, "You know how I dislike indiscreetness."

They spoke little on the ride home. When they arrived at Laura's apartment, he asked if he could come in for a few minutes. As they entered, he helped her out of her coat, and put his left arm around her shoulder and his right hand on her breast. Driving her elbow into his stomach, she spun around and seethed:

"Don't you dare!"

"In the old days, you used to melt."

"Used to . . . past tense . . . no more."

"You're seeing someone else, aren't you?"

"My life is my own."

"You know about Millicent and me. Why shouldn't I know who you're seeing? Don't tell me it's that hoodlum president of ours!"

She lied. "I never mix business and pleasure. He's my boss. That's all."

"The guy still stinks of the streets."

Laura, who could normally hide her feelings behind an impassive stare, shot back, "Yes, of dew and rain, and bread and butter. He's not full of pretentious bullshit."

Shawn smiled liked the Cheshire cat. "So he *is* the one!"

"What makes you think it's one? Maybe there are others."

They were still standing.

"Aren't you going to ask me to sit?"

"Only if we can talk as friends, and not like rivals or divorced couples who go to shrinks to learn sincere pretenses."

Shawn wanted to arrest her tongue. He always felt at a disadvantage when she rolled out her heavy artillery of metaphors and similes. Although those particular terms would never have crossed his mind, he had often felt the sting of her language. At such times, he would suppress his urge to retaliate and would embrace her instead; but that alternative had been taken from him. In the company of his father, he had more than once seen the police resort to violence when words could not persuade, an admission of the failure of language. Not wishing to behave like some enforcer, he said amiably, "All right, I agree. Let's be friends."

They shook hands. "Can I ask a favor?"

"And if say no?"

"I won't be mad."

"Then ask."

"Help me break into someone's house."

Given her background, she didn't flinch at the idea, but she did wonder why a police chief's son would be willing to take the risk.

"Whose?"

"Cranmore Narr's."

"The computer fellow who has a contract with the U.?"

"Yes."

"What's so special about his house?"

"He's having it off with Millicent, and I want to catch her in the act."

Although tempted to make an ironic comment about Millicent's predilection for athletes having matured into a taste for businessmen, she answered, "How do you intend to break in?"

"I've cased the place. A garden door has window panes. I have a glass cutter. If you'll just stand lookout . . ."

Without a word, Laura went into her bedroom to change into Levi's and a navy blue sweat shirt. She couldn't resist a challenge, as well as the opportunity to observe a bust. If the job looked dangerous, she could always disappear into the night.

As they drove to the Narr house, Shawn wondered what he'd actually say if he caught Millicent red-handed or, to be more precise, with her pants down.

Inside the house, Gretchen and Bobo were engaged in energetic foreplay, working themselves up to what they sensed would be a particularly passionate evening of lovemaking. They bit and blew; they pawed and fingered; they tongued and twined. He felt as if his member had been rubbed with steaming jalapeno pepper, and she in high heat would need no lubricant. The bed covers landed on the floor, so, too, the pillows. The sheets grew damp from desire, the air hung heavy with moans. Oblivious to their surroundings, they heard and saw nothing but each other, their minds besotted with the consummation and climax to come.

No wonder then that they failed to detect Millicent and Cranmore entering the house. Cranmore had driven directly from Boise to the Caiaphas home to collect his little butterball, she who had put a fire in his pants with her sexual innuendoes and her wish "to celebrate." She, like no other, had taught him the meaning of arousal. He could see stretching before him a lifetime of pulchritudinous pleasures.

Approaching his house, Cranmore failed to notice Boaz's SUV at the curb but saw Gretchen's car in the driveway. He knew that he and Millicent couldn't return to her digs because her mother was at home; and he didn't want to pay for a motel. So he told Millicent to wait at the garden door. He would enter through the front, greet his sister, excuse himself to finish some paperwork in the basement study, and meet Millicent for their lovemaking.

Upon entering the living room, he could hear thumping upstairs, and concluded that his sister was engaged in vacuuming and moving furniture. A fastidious housekeeper, she had even rearranged his quarters, converting the dining area into a living room and the latter into a den. She's at it again, he thought, and swept quickly into the basement study, remembering to lock the door behind him. He then admitted Millicent, but before he could secure the latch, she threw herself into his arms and led him directly to the divan that made up into a bed. As she tore off her clothes and his, they sucked at each other's ears, nose, and throat, like parched sexual pilgrims.

"It's been so long," he gasped.

"A week," she groaned.

"Have you got your diaphragm?"

"I can't wait."

Cranmore, ever careful, took from his wallet a packet of condoms. "Give me a second."

"Since when do you carry them with you?"

"Since I met you."

"But you didn't need them in Boise. You ain't foolin' around on the side?"

"I'd never be unfaithful to you."

The sock in place, Cranmore nosed her navel and mounted her, as Shawn tried the garden door. Finding it open, he walked into the scene unobserved. It took only a second for him to discover Millicent's infidelity, and also Cranmore Narr's inadequacies as a lover. Shawn stood for a minute until Millicent, on her back, looked over Cranmore's shoulder and saw him across the room. She turned so sharply to rise from the divan that Cranmore's weenie took a U-turn and, since he suffered from premature ejaculation, shot himself with his load. She flew into the basement bathroom, slamming the door. Cranmore, finally noticing the cause of the *coitus interruptus*, sheepishly pulled on his pants and marched upstairs, with Shawn at his heels.

"Listen needle dick," said Shawn in a fury, "that's my girl you're screwing!"

He would have said more, considerably more, had he not heard a crash from upstairs. The box springs had broken the bed boards and hit the floor.

"Geez, what the hell was *that*?"

The two of them scrambled up the stairs to the master bedroom and discovered Boaz on his back in full penile flight as Gretchen, perched on his pecker, with her back to him, repeatedly lifted and fell on his rod, like a feverish piston. A furious engine of love, she neither stopped for the broken bed nor noticed the two intruders, who stood in awe of the RPMs and the horsepower. When Gretchen saw in the mirror her brother and a stranger, she leapt off Bobo's manhood and bolted for the dressing room. Boaz, uncomprehending, sprang from the bed, his toy still in top form; but upon seeing Cranmore and Shawn, he suffered a detumescence that, had it been timed, would have entered the annals of medical miracles. Without dressing, he grabbed his clothes and ran down the stairs and out the door. To Laura's astonishment, a naked Boaz Caiaphas, caught clearly in the glow of the street light, raced across the lawn and drove off. A few seconds later, Shawn emerged from the house with a half-dressed Cranmore Narr at his back expostulating wildly. "It's not what you think . . . I was closing a deal on computers. A practical joke . . . for my birthday. I'm thirty-three today."

Shawn, quivering with anger, grabbed Laura by the arm and the two of them drove silently back to his apartment, where he described what he'd just seen.

"I warned you about that tramp," said Laura triumphantly, "but the rest of the story is just too delicious!"

As soon as she could, she extricated herself from Shawn's company and telephoned Christy. With his party just at its height, he asked her to join them, but she demurred, saying that he would want to speak to Frank Edsel privately once he heard what she had to say.

"I'm all ears."

When she finished her story, Christy commented, "You've just handed me the key to success."

After he hung up, he hovered around Frank Edsel until they had a chance to be alone. Pointing to Florence Richmond, Christy said, "Pretty girl. Dailey had good taste in women. Apparently she's some hot number."

"I don't approve," said Edsel.

Christy told the bartender to freshen Frank's drink "with a healthy refill."

"Depends on the circumstances," said Christy.

"What do you mean?"

"Bottoms up," said Christy, as he and Edsel knocked back their booze. "Good stuff. Glenlivet." He smacked his lips. "What I mean is . . . some affairs are good for a marriage."

Edsel looked at him blankly.

"Think about it this way," Christy explained, "if you're bored with your broad, I mean wife, you take a mistress. And that brings enough spice into your life to keep your marriage going. See?"

"What are you, a Mormon?"

For a second, Christy thought that Edsel had said "a more man," but decided that Frank would never joke about sex. "No, just a practical guy. Frankly, a lotta wives don't like it, or not with the guy they're married to. What's a husband to do then, beat the meat?"

"There's entirely too much promiscuity now."

"Better a little on the side than a divorce, which really hurts the family."

Christy, who made it a point never to have more than two drinks, directed the bartender to keep Frank's glass full. The result: Christy remained sober while Frank, with his low threshold for alcohol, became glassy-eyed.

"Take Boaz Caiaphas, for example," said Christy. "He's a good man, a good coach, but thinks nothing of having a little on the side."

"You're kidding," Edsel slurred.

"Not at all. In fact, she's a real looker, like your wife."

"Gretch thinks the world of him."

"I'll bet she does."

"Wait till she hears . . ."

"Maybe she knows."

"How could she?"

Christy let the dastardly thought seep in before he remarked, "What I like about Florence Richmond is she can keep a secret, unless of course someone betrays her, like Dailey."

Edsel said nothing.

How the word got out is beyond our authority to say, but it quickly made the rounds that Coach Caiaphas had taken up streaking. He had been seen dashing across a lawn in his birthday suit. Some of his straitlaced fans interpreted his behavior as an endorsement of apostolic poverty, but Frank Edsel and the other trustees, shocked by the disclosure, inquired into the details and soon learned the location of the said offense and the fact that somehow the coach's daughter was involved, as well as the attractive young woman who often stayed at her brother's house.

What passed between Frank Edsel and Gretchen would have made good material for kitchen realism. It had tension, tears, and travail. He insisted that she tell the truth. She said the rumors were false and base. He told her that she was no longer to stay overnight in town. Gretchen declared that she would not be bullied. He reminded her of her marital obligations. She replied that she wanted her own space—and bank account. The following day, they went to see a marriage counselor who put them both on Prozac and then excused himself to keep a lunch date with his secretary.

Their domestic strife would have remained unresolved had not Christy asked Frank Edsel to chair Bogus U.'s centennial committee, ably assisted by Florence Richmond. In that capacity, Frank learned, like Gimpel the Fool, that blindness is a boon and that an experienced secretary is better than an indifferent wife.

BRENT'S ESCAPE FROM HANOI

Stranded in Saigon, when the North Vietnamese entered, Brent figured that to escape he would have to bribe someone. But he had given all his money to Em Butterfly. It was then a beautiful and lucky thing happened. He met Missy Saigon, a girl like Em Butterfly (who of course was not really a girl) and she helped him. According to Brent, Missy had a little boy by an American G.I.—but not Brent!!! And then the G.I. left her in the lurch. She wanted to get to America to find the man who got her in trouble, whether to make him marry her or just to get even Brent didn't know. She had been working in a bar. But when she found out she was having a baby, she moved in with her parents. She had saved up some money, most of which she gave to her family. But for an emergency, she kept about fifty American dollars in an old shoe. With that money, she bought a used motorcycle with a sidecar, and headed with Brent for the border. (Brent drove and Missy sat next to him holding her son, Dew Drop Bi.) They rode until they came to a banana grove; when they spread their blanket on the ground to spend the night, they discovered three American airmen hiding there. When they (the pilots) heard Brent speaking English they thought at first he might be a North Vietnamese agent, so they asked him some questions. "Identify DiMaggio, Mantle, and Whitey Ford." Brent did, and guessed they were New York Yankee fans, and they said "Right!"

They (the pilots) told him and Missy Saigon they were in radio contact with a helicopter rescue team, and the men would be coming soon to save them. Brent felt like crying because he was so glad to be going home. But the chopper had to wait for a break in the weather. Then one day it cleared up, and they got a radio call the whirlybird (Brent called the helicopter both a chopper and a whirlybird) would be coming to get them. But because they couldn't land in the banana grove, they would have to hover overhead and lower a rope with a harness. Pretty soon Brent could hear the chopper approach. And sure enough there it was and there was the rope with the harness. The pilots wanted Missy Saigon to climb up first with her son, but she insisted the pilots go first because they were more important than she was. Brent tried to forcibly put her in the harness, promising that he would follow with Dew Drop Bi. But she scratched him with her nails and kicked him with her feet (she had on rubber sandals so it didn't hurt) and said Vietnamese women were not that kind. Brent guessed she meant pushy. The pilots said they would draw straws, but Missy, to the surprise of everyone, made a speech. (She had learned a lot of English working in South Vietnam among American G.I.s.) Brent said the upshot of the speech was the Americans had to live to fight another day. They represented the greater purpose and she was only two people (counting her son), and therefore the larger good had to be served. Brent realized if they kept on arguing, everyone would be lost, so he told the pilots to go ahead. They did, and then because Missy wouldn't have it any other way, Brent went next. But just as Missy was strapping herself into the harness, with her son in her arms, a Vietnamese patrol spotted the helicopter and started shooting. The whirlybird therefore had to make an escape and lifted off, leaving Missy Saigon standing in the banana grove with her son in her arms. And that was the last time Brent ever saw Missy or Vietnam, though he says he will go back someday to see if he can find that wonderful lady, Miss Saigon, and even Em Butterfly, who he says really was beautiful, even though Brent is not that way!!!

ONE HAPPY FAMILY

Once the furor ended, the Narr house became a love nest for Caiaphas and Gretchen, as well as Millicent and Cranmore. Frank Edsel and Florence Richmond used her apartment. After a date, Christy took Laura back to the president's pad, though not for erotic pleasures. The two people left out in the cold, Mrs. Miranda Caiaphas and Shawn Keogh, had on occasion conversed warmly. It would never have crossed his mind even to consider a romance had he not been feeling horny and beating the bishop to the accompaniment of Simon and Garfunkel's record *Mrs. Robinson*.

"Why not?" he asked himself. He would come to the house when Millicent and Coach Caiaphas were gone. He would apologize for the interruption. She would, as always, invite him to have a cup of coffee. They would sit across from each other at the kitchen table looking out on the lake. Miranda would probably say how sorry she was that "things hadn't worked out." He would say lightheartedly that, in all honesty, he had come not to see Millicent but to have the opportunity to see her. She would laugh and probably blush. And before she could make some comment about the great bond between her and Boaz, he would move his chair closer to hers, brush an imaginary speck of dust from her shoulder, and say how sorry he was to have heard about the streaking incident. He would then add a fact that rumor had omitted, for example, that Coach Caiaphas, instead of dressing immediately in the car, had dumped his clothes on the seat and driven off. She would look at him with alarm and ask how he knew such a thing; and he would appear uncomfortable and say he had already said too much. She would press him, and he would reluctantly admit that he was in the neighborhood of the incident. "What does that mean?" she would ask, and he would explain haltingly that he had gone to a certain house to see Millicent and had found her enjoying the company of another, when suddenly two streakers burst out of another room, raced across the rug and out the front door. "Two," she would say incredulously. "Two," he would answer, "Coach Caiaphas and a pretty young woman." Then he would stroke her hand.

If she cried, he would offer her a handkerchief, a monogrammed one from a set of three that he had received for his birthday from his Aunt Anne. If she bit her lip and looked angry, he would put his arm around her and tell her not to fret. In either case, he would say that such things happen. "It's the way of the world." In the following days, he would bring her candy and maybe some flowers that weren't too showy. Slowly, he would convince her that a certain young man found her beautiful, even though the difference in age between them was twenty-five years. He might even say, "Have you ever heard the song *Mrs. Robinson?*" Events would then take their natural course. Millicent would be jealous; Miranda, with her years of experience, would be wonderful; and he would have the advantage of two women fighting over him.

This plan, though, got shoved to the back burner when Millicent discovered that she had a bun in the oven, a disclosure that ostensibly cooked Shawn's goose when she named him as the chef, or should we say cock, of the *chef-d'oeuvre.* This turn of events had come about when Cranmore, fearful that Coach Caiaphas would cancel the contract with ASP for a new scoreboard, had pleaded with Millicent to name some previous lover. Grudgingly, she had fingered Shawn, leading him to demand that both he and Cranmore submit to a DNA test.

At this announcement, Millicent whined, "You're not facing up to what you did, Shawn. Believe me, you're the Dad."

"I just want proof positive."

"That's so nasty," she raged. "I'm not even sure I want you."

The Keoghs, no strangers to life's vicissitudes, given the father's police work, immediately demanded that the tests be conducted by a New York City lab that worked closely with his own department. Cranmore, tested first, had cause to celebrate when his results came back negative. Cheerily, Millicent insisted that Shawn had to accept responsibility for his child and marry her. But Mr. Keogh had other plans for his son. When the lab technician, a friend of the police chief and his wife, found that Shawn tested positive, he immediately doctored the results and reported Shawn free of fatherhood.

Intimations of the virgin birth came to Coach Caiaphas's mind. The mystery might have gone unsolved had Millicent not admitted to her mother that she had known others, including, *mirabile dictu,* Pastor Schuft! Although Coach Caiaphas did not want to believe that his beloved minister could have stooped to such base behavior, he told the good pastor that he would have to return from Waco to marry his daughter. Pastor Schuft, a proponent of creationism, had no faith in science and therefore declined to have his own DNA tested. Declaring that a man had "to own up to his sins," he admitted his "shameful" conduct and readily agreed to the marriage.

Although Cranmore and Shawn had been left off the guest list, it did include, among others, members of the faith and the Bogus U. president, who briefly fell into conversation with Coach Caiaphas in the vestibule of the church.

"I regret," said Christy, "that we really haven't had a chance to chew over the fat, you and me. Thanks for the invite. The church really looks good with all the flowers and the bulletin board and photos of your daughter."

Fingering his corsage, the Coach replied, "Marriage is a sacrament. One has to honor it properly."

"Outside on the lawn, I got to talking to some of your church friends. They sure have some definite ideas about the ladies."

Caiaphas nodded emphatically. "We have to restore biblical customs with respect to handmaids. Women have become entirely too independent. The Lord put them on this good earth for the pleasure and purpose of man."

Christy, who had often entertained the idea of giving Laura a knuckle sandwich, hazarded that "maybe times had changed."

"That's exactly why we have such need of the Brotherhood of Men, the organization I belong to. Women need to be governed. Just look at all the illegitimate births and diseases spread by promiscuity. Thank goodness for the biblical injunction that men shall lead. Take my wife, for example. She follows faithfully my every instruction, and my daughter, ah, well, at least she did as she was told. Believe me, having a man in control is the only way for America to survive."

With the balcony organ trilling overhead, Christy had an epiphany: that Coach Caiaphas's view on the place of women undermined love. Moments later, Millicent became Mrs. Gottfried Schuft, promising to honor and obey him until death, presumably at which point she could strike out on her own.

THE SPRING IS SPRUNG

Art and high crime happen by design. For Spring Recess, which came in mid-April, Troxy had gone off to Sun Valley, but not without asking Christy to join her on the slopes and leaving a number where she could be reached. Deep in his plans for changing the U., he begged off politely. Laura, too, was out of town, having told Christy that she and her mother planned to spend the time together in New York. Her absence would give Christy a not wholly unwanted respite. Like a guardian angel, Laura had been hovering over him and investing his life with rituals that made him more efficient and kept him safe. Before leaving town, Laura had sorted Christy's mail. When he returned from a morning spent in the power plant playing poker with some of the plumbers and fitters, he found a note from her directing him to read the following letter.

Dear President Mahon,

As a graduate of Bogus U., I want to do something nice for the school before I grow feeble and am stolen blind. My wife has already persuaded me to leave a hundred million to Harvard, where she got her education. I want to leave Bogus the same amount. My money comes from boats and hauling cargo.

Since I don't like go-betweens, I'm writing to you in person. I figure that between the two of us we can work out some plan so as I can give you the money, deduct the tax, and keep my name incognito. Here's what I suggest. I have to make a business trip to Sun Valley. Usually I get a room at some ritzy hotel, but truthfully I'd rather stay at the Bogus chalet. It seems that's the least you could do for me, seeing as I'm planning to give the school so much money.

I'm a man who always does his homework. That's how I know about the chalet and the couple who run it, Mr. and Mrs. Harry Hasty-Pasty.

My sources tell me she's a fine cook and the house is better than a splashy hotel. So let's meet there to do our business. On Easter Sunday, we can go to church, to pray for a successful conclusion to this contract.

Sincerely yours,

Jasper Sandalwood

P.S. If you need to reach me, my number is: (617) 007-7734.

Telephoning the number in the postscript, he spoke to a woman who identified herself as Mr. Sandalwood's private secretary.

"Tell Mr. Sandalwood I'll meet him at the Bogus U. chalet Easter morning. If he's of the Roman faith—"

"He certainly is."

"Good, we can go to eleven o'clock Mass together at the Holy Cross Church. It comes recommended."

Christy smiled to himself. Wouldn't Laura be proud of him, managing this killing on his own? Yes, he was glad to have her gone so that he could, for once, fly solo. But the next day, feeling bereft of her company, he went in search of some talisman that would remind him of her presence. On the top of her desk, he found one earring and remembered that she had complained about losing the other. He pocketed it and would have returned to his office had his eye not alighted on her writing tablet and some notes she had scribbled: Sun Valley Airways, followed by times of flights. Below, she had written down the initials B and B and three names with telephone numbers: The Eaglecrest, The Marigold House, and Walton Rooms.

If Laura had gone to Sun Valley instead of New York, why? A perplexed Christy worried that the presence of Laura and Troxy in the same town was no accident. Thoughts of collusion danced in his head. He attempted to reach the other instructors—Artemisia, Galena, and Panjang—who had been present at the dinner when he had been poisoned. Artemisia's answering machine said that she was vacationing in Sun Valley, and that those attending the May conference she was sponsoring at Bogus could receive from the Fine Arts secretary an advance copy of her paper: "The Cutting Edge: The Myriad Uses of Palette Knives." Galena's landlady had been instructed to tell callers that Galena could be reached at the Crook Lodge and rehearsals would begin on Monday for *Death and the Dwarf*, her new ballet based on the demise of a recent American president. Panjang Sutra's answering machine merely stated that he would be in Sun Valley for several days, returning the following Friday. Wishing to contact Laura, Christy called the B and B's on her list, but none of them had a Laura Favoloso registered there. Next he tried the Crook Lodge and spoke to the owner, James Crook, who told him that the three people he asked about had all checked in. Dialing the number that Troxy had given him, he reached the manageress, Ms. Metz, who indiscreetly said that though Troxy had booked a room she never occupied it.

"But she does periodically call in to check on her messages."

Christy found this information disquieting and, not knowing what else to do, requested that Ms. Metz leave a message for Troxy to call him. That evening Troxy rang Christy at home.

"I understand," she said, "you've been trying to reach me."

Christy spoke in the street language that surfaced whenever he felt anxious. "Yeah, your landlady said you ain't been around."

Silence.

"Are you still there?" asked Christy.

"Why, yes, I was . . . just removing my ski boot. It pinches."

"What's going on?"

"I thought you had no interest in skiing."

"Where you stayin'?"

"At a B and B."

"But they said you're never there."

"Christy, did you ever hear of après-ski? I met some friends I haven't seen in ages and we ate dinner late. Rather than disturb the people at the B and B, I put up with my friends, on a sofa."

"Listen, we can go to the Bogus U. chalet. You don't have to stay on anyone's couch. You can shack up . . . I mean sleep with me. From what I understand, there's plenty of room. Whaddya say?"

"Where is this place?"

"I'll give you the directions and meet you there tomorrow night for dinner. The guy that looks after the place . . . his wife's a gourmet cook and will have somethin' special waitin'. We can have a good time. You know, all tucked away. It'll be cozy. Like you said: a consommé devoutly to be wished."

The next morning, he prepared a small overnight bag, wrapping his pistol in a sweater. On the drive to Sun Valley, he stopped for lunch at a big hotel with an enormous outdoor swimming pool heated by underground springs. Sorely tempted to don his trunks, which he had brought along in anticipation of a dip in the chalet's heated pool, he decided to wait, so that Troxy could join him. As he sped toward the resort, he remembered hearing his staff say that the Sun Valley old-timers had all moved elsewhere because the rich had made it impossible for anyone but the wealthy to live in the valley. He remembered when his mother could no longer afford Brooklyn rents and moved him to the Bronx, several blocks from Bathgate Avenue. Here he had met a kid named Billy—he couldn't recall the last name—who had grown fabulously wealthy in the rackets. Billy had a friend called Arnold Garbage. Yes, he fondly remembered those kids and their story. There was a beauty to it, a mythic quality that made Christy believe in the fathomless depths of the American dream.

After some inquiries, Christy found the forest road that led to the Bogus chalet, twinkling in the winter night. A modern stone and shingle structure, with steeply pitched roofs, the lodge had not, like so many other wealthy homes, been built on a shelf carved out of the mountain. The architect had fashioned the house to the hill, including the four-car garage, with its own side entrance to the house. The front door, which sported a large porpoise knocker, opened on the third level. From here, the chalet cascaded down the hill, until it reached a basement that held a billiards table, a sauna, and dressing rooms that faced the pool. Floor-to-ceiling insulated windows offered spectacular views of the valley and the surrounding mountains. A decorator who favored the Swedish style had given the place a cool look, with sling chairs, white couches supported on stainless steel frames, glass-topped tables, and white rugs. The wall paintings, all abstractions and mostly original, included a small canvas with a green background displaying a gold orrery and pencil-thin black lines at oblique angles, signed Paul Klee. White curtains, edged with a blue thread, ran on tracks electrically controlled. At the press of a button, they slowly closed or opened. Speakers discreetly embedded in the wall were serviced from a small room off the bar, where hundreds of CDs stood neatly racked next to shelves of bourbon and Scotch and vodka and gin and sherry and even slivovitz, a favorite of Nell Gwyn, Trustee Feather's mistress. The musical tastes of the trustees we shall not comment on, though their choice of liquor showed discrimination and a willingness to invest public funds in the best that money could buy. The bar itself, equipped with the means to serve beer on tap, had been crafted of a single oak plank with fine grain that glowed from the wax that the Hasty-Pastys lovingly applied.

Christy entered through the main door and not the garage, met by Harry, who took his overnight bag, and disappeared. Mrs. Hasty-Pasty, known to her friends as Ags, ushered Christy into the living room and immediately took him on a tour of the house, all the while puffing on a cigarette. When Christy saw what riches lay before him, he knew that all the pains he'd suffered as a poor boy and all the ones he'd taken to become president of Bogus U. were worth the cost. His Bogus house counted for nothing in comparison to this one. Wasn't he the fool not to have come to Sun Valley in the months gone by?

Ags, who seemed ill at ease, said nothing, lighting one cigarette after another. Harry returned and poured Christy a drink. They sat looking out the window at the skiers darting through the moguls and tucking to increase their speed as they neared the bottom. The flashy ski outfits reminded Christy of the clothes he'd dreamed about as a kid, spiffy sneakers and brightly-colored rugby shirts. He could see from the chalet and the scene out the window that Sun Valley and money were harmoniously related.

"So Harry, whaddya been up to?"

"Just working on the place . . . you know, the plumbing and sound-proofing. I even installed a sauna. You ought to try it."

"Maybe I will when my lady friend gets here."

"I heard she was coming," said Agnes. "Is she your steady?"

"Just a friend. The one I'm really crazy about—" Christy paused as he realized that Harry knew her from the search committee and from the tour through the power plant. "Laura Favoloso."

"Great boobs, a hard bod, and movie-star looks. What a broad! You should see this chick, Ags."

Agnes, feeling that Harry had described Laura with undue enthusiasm, told him so. "Easy, Harry, easy boy."

"Listen Ags, once you see her you'll see what I'm talking about."

"How come," said Ags, "you didn't bring her here, instead of the other one?" Christy struggled to answer. "She's . . . travelin' with her mom. So to keep my mind off her I arranged with another chick . . . well, you understand."

"You guys are all the same."

Christy leaned back in his chair and savored his drink. Outwardly relaxed, he looked to all the world like a man free of trouble, even though he worried about the meaning of Laura's and Troxy's presence in Sun Valley, as well as their possible connection to the other instructors. Harry, on the other hand, appeared anxious. He paced and frequently glanced at his watch. Christy couldn't help but notice. "You expecting someone?"

"No, it's just that . . . that Ags needs some things at the store and I want her to get there before it closes."

Agnes took her cue, snuffed out a cigarette, and said, "Yeah, I got to buy a few things." She had learned over the years not to question the need for her absence, though her imagination could fill in the spaces. "I'll be back in a couple of hours," she said, and smiled at Harry, who shook his head knowingly.

Ten minutes later, Troxy drove up to the chalet. Her car, a red Saab, had a rack on top that held both a pair of downhill skis and a snowboard. Dressed in an expensive matching silver ski outfit, she warmly greeted Christy, who introduced her to Mr. Hasty-Pasty, the caretaker of the chalet.

They shook hands and Harry asked, "Can I get you a drink?"

"Thanks, but what I'd love most is to change my clothes. I planned on skiing today, but spent the time shopping instead. I'll model my new strapless dress."

"Christy, your room is next level up, last door on the left."

Troxy turned to him. "My bags are in the car. Would you mind getting them? I'd be honored."

While he went to the Saab, Troxy and Harry made small talk. "Nice place, eh?" said Mr. Hasty-Pasty.

"Lovely. Not a bad situation being caretaker here."

"Yeah, whatever needs looking after, I take care of."

"You must have all sorts of tools."

"I got what I need."

"My daddy used to say that in an unguarded moment anything can happen. So be prepared. Of course, he was talking about sex; but I've always made it a point to err on the safe side."

Christy entered on Troxy's last sentence and laughed. "You're so damn careful, a guy could die waitin'."

"It all depends on what you mean by die."

"Huh?"

"Never mind. Just lead the way."

Christy, with a bag in each hand, took her upstairs to a room paneled on three walls with mirrors. In one corner a small fireplace glowed from a low gas fire. On the mantel stood two hand-carved wooden candlesticks. The king size bed left no doubt that they'd be sleeping together. Troxy said nothing about the arrangements. She put her handbag and a perfume bottle on the nightstand and took both her suitcases into the enormous walk-in closet/dressing room to unpack and disrobe. Leaving the door partially open, she asked:

"How are things on campus?"

Admiring the effect of seeing himself in the array of mirrors, he said distractedly, "Now that I know the ropes, I've been workin' on some schemes. When I told the viziers what I had in mind, you'll never believe what they said."

"From that bunch of cowards? I can imagine."

From the closet came sounds of undressing.

"I'm sure they went runnin' to the trustees to complain."

"We live in a traitorous age. You can't trust a soul," she advised. "I some-times wonder what has become of our educational system. There was a time when well-educated people lent themselves to school improvement and cul-ture. It showed class consciousness and good upbringing. But nowadays one can hardly get a person to lend his name to even the most inoffensive reform."

Reaching an arm out of the closet, Troxy asked Christy to hand her the perfume bottle on the nightstand.

"I knew from the first you were different, not like the others. They're all trying to cover their asses."

"Unfortunately, I've dealt with them all," replied Troxy.

Christy paced back and forth.

"First, I called in Bill A. Stine. He agreed to do what I said, but nearly had a stroke when he heard the details."

Troxy extended a hand and reached around the closet door to return the perfume bottle to Christy.

"That trimmer! As you know, his brain is addled from drink. Most people ascend a few steps to reach their level of incompetence. In his case, he arrived at the first step suffering from an advanced case of arrested de-velopment."

"Yeah, I suppose that's why he comes to all the wrong conclusions even when his aides give him all the right numbers."

"No self-respecting university ought to have a man like that in his position."

"Then I called in Brigham Pyrosis. I was afraid he'd have another heart attack when I outlined my reorganization plans. He immediately started to ramble."

"He's what I call a motor mouth. If you asked him about his family, he'd start with Adam and Eve and arrive at the subject an hour later. Some tellers of tales have a gift for storytelling. He's a monstrous bore. His ideal job would be the Chamber of Commerce."

"That's why I don't let him out in public to give speeches."

"His wife deserves combat pay."

Christy chuckled. "Then I spoke to Sejanus Pinchbeck . . . or tried to."

"That preening peacock! Whatever you say, he'll interrupt and tell you it's not the issue. That's because the only issue he cares about is himself. And talk about a poor public speaker! I heard him give a talk on campus and nearly died from the number of 'ums' he introduced into each sentence."

"Yeah, I sure got stuck with a lotta creeps. Except for their wantin' to keep their jobs, I can't figure them."

"It's just as well you can't. There are no end of personal reasons to explain why a person does one thing and not another. We're told this one came from a poor family and that one had an abusive father. Who cares, since there's no way of our ever really knowing the truth. Hell, the person himself doesn't know, self-deception being what it is. The secrets of the heart are what you find in people's diaries. Motives? That's for a novel and for those who like simple answers to difficult questions. What people do and say to one another—for whatever reasons—that's all we have to go on. So don't be trying to understand people's behavior. What finally matters is a Yes or a No."

"Hey, I thought you wanted to change. What's keepin' you?"

"I'll be only a sec."

From the front of the house, Christy heard a commotion, which quickly died away. "What was that?"

"Anybody's guess."

Eyeing her handbag on the nightstand, Christy gently unzipped it. Instantly, he got a strong whiff of clove, the same smell he had noticed at Chez Lee. He withdrew a package of cigarettes: Kreteks, stamped Sampoerna, Indonesia. He gently tried the handle of the bedroom door. It had been locked from the outside. Opening his overnight bag, he discovered his pistol was gone. Mr. Hasty-Pasty must have locked the door and removed the thirty-eight. Suddenly, the plot lay before him like a map, with the major arteries highlighted in red.

"Turn down the lights and get undressed," said Troxy. "I'll meet you between the sheets."

Christy immediately shoved his overnight bag under the covers to make it look as if he were lying in fond expectation. He then took one of the wooden candleholders and positioned himself so that when Troxy opened the closet door, he would be behind it. "Good idea. You know, Trox, you're one of the few people on the faculty I can count on."

"There's far too much talk these days about counting on others. I'm not my brother's keeper. No man keeps me, and I keep no man."

"How about all the dinners and private talks between us?"

"I never mix business and pleasure."

"What kind of broad are you?"

"Has it ever struck you, Christy, that I might—"

"Might what?"

"Be the one Brooklyn Benny paid to hit you?"

He tensed.

A padded bra, thrown from the closet, preceded her stark-naked entrance. Troxy had changed into a very man with testicles and penis. She (or should we say "he") trained a Beretta on the bed. A second later he fired. The blasting bullets sounded like a chain saw, and the air reeked from sulfur. He approached the bed and ripped back the blankets, discovering Christy's riddled leather overnight bag, just as Christy came up behind him and brought the candleholder down on his wrist. The automatic weapon fell to the floor. Grabbing the Beretta, Christy pointed it at Troxy and said:

"Your real name, please?"

ON EASTER DAY. THE EXPOSÉ

Brooklyn Benny arrived late, having flown from Salt Lake to Sun Valley in a prop plane badly buffeted by stormy weather. Out of sorts that Mr. Hasty-Pasty was not there to meet him, and in no mood to wait, he tried to telephone Harry. But the phone rang through to an answering machine, on which Benny left a sour message that he would be taking a cab. Unfamiliar with Sun Valley and the whereabouts of the Bogus U. chalet, Benny asked a taxi driver, who said that he would need an address for a private residence. Annoyed with himself for depending on Harry and for not getting the number and street, Benny directed the driver to take him to "a high-class hotel." On the drive from the airport to the hotel, the cabby said he had the distinct impression that a car was following them, "with a broad at the wheel." But when they pulled up in front of the hotel, the car continued on and disappeared around the next corner.

Once in his room, he again tried to reach Harry, but to no avail. Taking a shower, he dressed and went to the bar for a double Scotch on the rocks. Afterwards, he dined alone. A red-meat man, he could see the people at other tables eating foreign food: vegetables in colors he had never seen, different kinds of lettuce, none of them iceberg, and entrees without beef, pork, or lamb. He felt out of place in this strange culinary world, but decided that when in Rome . . . and took a chance on a safe dish, fresh Sun Valley trout. He had been brought up to believe that the poor ate pasta, until he saw the prices on the menu. The astronomical figures, as much as anything else, led him to order the trout. He found the meal satisfying but not filling, so later that evening he stopped at a small bistro and had a cheeseburger with fries. The counterman, whom he asked about nightlife, directed him to a loud club, where the après-ski crowd skinned off their inhibitions and danced in their bones. He liked the nubile young women he saw, and the

261

slangy language he heard, which was a cut above the Robaccia gang. But most of all, he thrilled to the sums of money tossed around. People dropped it on liquor, on dope, on nicotine, on any essence that would induce a high. He lit up a cigar.

A drum roll cleared the floor of dancers and an aggressive young woman sailed out in a costume trailing feathers and ribbons. Although Benny and the patrons didn't know it, they were watching an Eva Tanguay imitation. She took the stage with a loud chattering voice, high-pitched and strident. All vitality and vivacity, she had blonde hair in a wild, stiff mop, a saucy, broad, good-humored face, with large smiling mouth and pertly turned-up nose. The eyes, small and impudent, snapped and sparkled. Her colorful dress bounced with her quick, fluttering steps, as she sang three naughty songs: "I Don't Care," "It's Been Done Before but Never the Way I Do It," and "Go as Far as You Like." She left the stage to thunderous applause. A trio of horns then played an oozy melody that put the party-goers in a mood to ply themselves with more chemicals to enhance the effect.

Benny felt horny, but he could see that his style hardly fit in with this crowd. He lingered over a drink, paid the bill, and slowly made his way down the street to his hotel. The cabby's remark about their being followed lingered. At this very moment, he had the feeling that someone was tailing him, but when he looked, he saw nothing suspicious. As he walked, his mind wandered to what Christy must have thought when Troxy pulled the trigger. Nothing like a surprise. Did he gasp, plead, whine, cry, declare his innocence? The two-timing, murderous runt. That he should even suppose he could whack Benny and get away with it! He now regretted he hadn't been there for the hit. How he would have enjoyed seeing that murderous weasel go down for the count.

Maybe tomorrow, on Easter Sunday, he would attend Holy Cross and pray for the soul of that fink. Or maybe he would pray for his parents instead. Yes, that seemed the better course. When he arrived at his hotel, he inquired about the location of the church, and requested the desk wake him for Mass. Back in his room, he tried the chalet number again, even though it was midnight. As before, he reached the answering machine and angrily hung up. He could only hope that since Harry missed him at the airport, he would show up at the church.

The next morning at Mass, kneeling in a row near the back, Benny heard a familiar voice whisper in his ear.

"So how are you, Mr. Sandalwood?"

Benny swiveled so quickly he lost his balance and fell off the polished rail onto his butt. "You! What the hell. . . !"

A chorus of hissing voices rose in the incensed air. "Shh," "Quiet," "You're in church."

Behind Benny sat Christy and another row back, Laura. Christy put his hand inside his jacket and said, "Outside."

Benny went first, with Christy and Laura right behind him.

"Walk straight ahead to the parkin' lot. You'll see a red Saab. Get in the front."

At the car, Benny nearly dropped dead. Sitting at the wheel was a smiling Troxy Dollop, with a bandaged wrist.

Let us now resume our narrative from the point at which Christy asked for Troxy's real name. With Laura training a twenty-two caliber pistol on Harry, she ordered him to open the bedroom door. The sight that greeted them looked like a picture out of the *Police Gazette*. Troxy was confessing to his real name, Tuah Bahar. Grasping his injured wrist, Tuah kneeled before Christy, who had a gun trained on him. Smoke still hung in the air as Christy marched Tuah and Harry down to the living room and told them to sit on the couch. Laura stood guard at their backs and Christy, with the Beretta in hand, sat opposite the plotters.

"If the phone rings, don't answer it—under any circumstances."

As though on cue, the phone rang and Brooklyn Benny left a message that made any talk of his death a fiction and his presence in Sun Valley abundantly clear.

"Well, I guess you know whom we're working for," said Tuah and, resigned to having been caught with his hand in the till, proceeded to outline the nefarious details of the plot against Christy.

Harry stared at his feet.

When Tuah had finished, Christy, still not clear about certain details, asked, "Tuah, he got you on the faculty, and you tried to do me in with that poison, right?"

He shook his head yes.

"Were you involved in the bombing?"

"No."

"I didn't think so."

"Harry, is Ags in on this deal?"

"Absolutely not, Christy. I swear—"

"Save it. I believe you. Next question: Mr. Sandalwood is Brooklyn Benny?"

"That letter business was all his doing, not mine," said Harry.

"Was it you, Tuah, who took a potshot at me from the field behind my house?"

"No, some student effed off about grades."

"Christ, they'll go to any lengths for an A."

He paused to digest what he'd heard. Then he turned his peepers on Laura.

"I owe you for keeping Harry at bay. How did you get here?"

The pistol still in her hand, Laura used it to orchestrate her explanation, punctuating one point and then another.

"The Sandalwood con is a favorite of Benny's. When his boys used to buy me a soda so Benny and my mother could be alone, they often talked about the gangs' different scams. Apparently the Sandalwood letter, as they called it, never failed to smoke out some mark. The moment it arrived at Bogus, addressed to you, I knew that Brooklyn Benny was heading for Sun Valley. So I changed my travel plans. Arriving in town before Benny, I shadowed him. Luckily, I lost him and concluded that he had beat a path to the chalet. When I came to the door, Harry tried to prevent me from entering. I drew. He protested. We heard shots. Harry ran to the door and unlocked it."

Christy, unable to conceal a smile of admiration, told her, "You really are one hell of a dame!"

On this occasion, Laura did not gainsay or correct him. She let the macho diction remain.

"A couple of other questions. The Bogus instructors at the Crook Lodge . . . what's the story?"

"It was my idea," said Tuah. "I paid for them."

"Why?"

"I reasoned that after I got out of town, suspicion would fall on one of them, because they had all been present at the dinner when I tried to poison you."

Looking at Harry and Tuah, Christy asked, "I want to know how much you're both bein' paid, *and* I want to find out if you're willin' to work for me."

Upon hearing Christy's proposal, they both warmly agreed.

"We can even find a place in my operation for Ags. But for now, since Benny's message says he has no idea where this place is, he'll have to show up at the church. We'll be waitin'."

CHRISTY AND LAURA
FORGE AN AGREEMENT

At a four-star mountain restaurant, not far from campus, Christy proposed marriage to Laura. She smiled in appreciation, but coyly looked around and said, "Don't ask me here."

They drove to the president's house. All the staff had been given the evening off.

"Is this intimate enough?" he asked.

Without answering, she walked into the living room and sat in a chair with a reclining back. Christy repaired to the couch and invited her to join him. But she demurred.

"What was that all about in the restaurant?"

She replied, "Public displays of affection don't invite sincere replies, just obligatory ones."

As Christy tried to fathom her meaning, Laura knew that the time of trial had arrived. She had a genuine affection for this unlettered fellow— a fondness that bordered on love—but she would never commit to a life with him until she had determined the nature of his mettle and how much freedom she could enjoy.

He leaned forward resting his arms on his knees. "Are you playing hard to get for a reason, like makin' the chase all the more fun? Or are you tellin' me that my feelings are not returned?"

She struck a playful tone. "I'm not to be caught, like a fish."

Christy smiled. "What if I have the right hook?"

"Don't be naughty."

"Come on, Laura," he coaxed, "you know how much I care about you."

"But do you know how much I care?"

Christy panicked, losing the comic thread. "I thought I did, but maybe I don't. Tell me."

Laura divined that his feelings ran too deeply for him to be teased, so she said candidly, "Since high school, I've been my own person, and I intend to remain so after marriage."

"I wouldn't want you to change."

"If you think I'll be a trophy wife gladly adorning your home and your parties, you're wrong. I want a husband who doesn't assume I'll be at his beck and call."

"But I suppose I'm to be there for you?"

"I admit: I'm spoiled and must have my way and my pleasures."

"Before we're married, you're free to go and spoil yourself. But afterwards, you'll have pleasures aplenty—with me. That I promise."

"Christy, never undervalue liberty. I will not give up being single without conditions."

He walked to the bar and poured two liqueurs. He handed her one and sipped the other.

"For example?" he said.

"If I leave for work early, you'll prepare your own breakfast without complaint."

"Fine, you can cook my dinner."

Her arched brow nearly touched her hairline. Christy got the point.

"Also, I absolutely refuse to be called names."

"Names?"

"Like Sweetheart, Dearest, Honey, Love, and the rest of that nauseous stuff. And I won't stand for public displays of affection, kissing in restaurants or at parties or in the park. In the company of others, I want us always to behave like good friends, like cultured people who can save their passions for their private moments."

"No problem," he said, tossing off the drink. "I can't stand mugs and molls moonin' over each other."

"I'm no moll. And what I've mentioned are mere trifles."

"Let me hear the worst."

"I'll select my own wardrobe and won't have you chiding my taste."

"What if it ain't becomin'?"

"You'll tell me how wonderful I look and not question the cost."

"Even if it breaks the bank?"

"I'll keep the checkbook."

"For your account, not mine."

She sipped her drink and puckered her lips, as if savoring not only the liqueur but also her next line of attack. "I will have my own friends. You will not read my mail. I will subscribe to whatever magazines I please.

You will not insist that I make your friends mine. I will speak like an educated woman and not a chirping coed. You will not pressure me when I'm not in an amorous mood. I will have my own dressing room and you shall always knock at the door before entering. If you agree, I will consent to an engagement."

"Do I get a chance to tell you what my conditions are before I start buyin' a ring?"

"Certainly. I believe that what's sauce for the goose is sauce for the gander."

A stray cat yawped in the dark.

"You can forget about prowlin' around at night. No lovers or fluttterin' your eyelashes at other men. No gossipin' with girlfriends about me nor lettin' them tell their husbands they're at our house when they're out screwin' around. And if you want to do somethin' highfalutin, and I want to stay home to watch a football game, you don't start bawlin' me out for bein' Joe Sixpack."

"I thought you enjoyed entertainment a cut above the gridiron?"

"Hey, haven't I been a good student?"

"You still drop your g's and continue to say ain't."

"Give me time, I'll get there."

"Do you remember me telling you about a friend who said, 'a well-educated person is like a carpenter's truth: all the parts abide'?"

"I admit it, I'm rough and need smoothin' . . . smoothing out."

She smiled at his correction and ran a hand through her black curls. "Thursdays I see the hairdresser."

"Just so long as you don't frost, frizzle, and fry your hair. I like it natural."

"And if I want *être à la mode*?"

Christy mistook the French for something sexy and therefore, without any forethought—or should we say foreplay?—ejaculated, "You mean you wanna have kids, right?"

She smiled indulgently. "So long as I'm not confined to the house while pregnant."

"Since liquor ain't—isn't—good for women with something cooking in the stove, I insist you not drink till the kid shows his head."

"And if it's a girl?"

"Fine with me, but I won't stand for some snooty name like Tiffany or Chandra or India or Phaedra."

"And if it's a boy?"

"Stay away from the fancy D names."

"For instance?"

"Dakota, Dalton, Drew, Drake, Denison, Dorsey, and Doyle."

"I accept your conditions."

"Good. Then we can marry as soon as the baseball season ends."

"'Fraid not."

"What? I thought we were all but married!"

"My mother will decide the wedding day."

"Already I'm henpecked."

CHRISTY INKS HIS
NAME TO A CONTRACT

With Sun Valley now but a bitter-sweet memory, Christy turned his attention to the Monroe Larson case. Myrtle Steif ill-humoredly reminded him that the trustees wanted a decision and that the June meeting of the board would take place in two weeks on a Saturday. On a Thursday, nine days before the meeting Christy approved Monroe Larson's tenure. Signing the contract in the presence of Myrtle and Monroe, he put it on the agenda as a late item and told Monroe to produce the Sally Hemings letters by noon the next day. When Monroe failed to appear at the appointed time, Christy sent Laura to find him. He knew that she would not be deterred by Monroe's sham civility. After all, it was she who had warned Christy to make Monroe's tenure contingent on the receipt of the letters, and had grown furious when he failed to follow her advice. Monroe's office, however, was locked. After making several inquiries, she found him carousing in mid-afternoon at one of the local watering holes, where a number of graduate students had taken him to celebrate his forthcoming tenure. Barging in on the boozy blowout, she unceremoniously ordered Monroe "to get your ass down to the bank now and open the safe deposit box. We want the letters."

Reluctantly, he left the graduate students, and the two of them drove in her car to the bank. She stood outside the vault while he went in. A few minutes later, he returned carrying a flat case that resembled a child's paint box, only wider.

"The key?" she said, finding it locked.

"You don't want to expose the contents to the light. Not here."

They drove back to school and parked behind Tinnitus House. Inside, Laura and Monroe picked up Christy, retreated to the basement, and turned off the lights. Training a pocket flashlight on the box, the prez directed Larson to open it.

Monroe reached into his pocket and, smiling uneasily, withdrew a large ring holding numerous keys. "I got dozens of them . . . for my office, for my filing cabinet, for the humanities building, for the History Department, for my gym locker, for my apartment, for my car, for the bank box, for the case, you name it." He tried each key but none worked. "I must have left this one at home." He then slapped his head as if he remembered. "It's in the safe-deposit box. How stupid of me!"

Laura turned on the lights and glanced at her watch: five minutes to five. The bank would close before they could get there, and the vault closed on weekends. She looked at Monroe contemptuously. For some reason Christy seemed unruffled.

"I'll get the key first thing Monday morning," said Monroe. "You can have the case, if you like. But keep it in a secure place."

"No," said Christy, "I'd rather you hung on to it."

After Monroe had gone, Laura asked, "What was that all about?"

"If he left it with me and the letters weren't inside, he'd accuse us of taking them."

In Christy's office, behind closed doors, Laura said tersely, "You don't really think we'll find any letters!"

"No."

"Well, then, you've just given tenure to Monroe without any conditions. I warned you."

"Yeah, you did."

Monday morning, Larson, in a state of high anxiety, showed up with the key. Laura, running an errand, missed the dramatic unveiling. Monroe and Christy retreated to the basement, where the pocket flashlight again provided the only light. Inserting the key, Monroe opened the box to disclose several yellowed, folded papers in an advanced state of decay. He delicately parted the top one, and gasped.

"The ink must have faded! The words are gone! My God, what can I do?"

Christy put an arm around the young man's shoulder and told him to buck up.

"Acts of nature," he said, "can't be helped."

Monroe's whole body visibly relaxed. He then took Christy's hand and pumped it, exclaiming, "You're a real gentleman," and then added without thinking, "who would've guessed?"

When Laura saw the contents of the case, she upbraided Christy for his carelessness and told him in scabrous terms that she couldn't understand his mellow attitude. Threatening to quit on the spot and break off their engagement, she restrained herself only because Christy asked her to wait until the end of the week.

On the Friday before the meeting, the university attorney telephoned Christy to tell him that the tenure papers for Monroe Larson, forwarded to him by the trustees with their official imprimatur, had arrived on his desk without the president's signature. Would Christy please come to his office to sign the contract. Declining, Christy explained that he had in the presence of two witnesses signed the contract and, as far as he was concerned, the laws of the trustees did not require him to sign twice.

Upon hearing that the omission of the president's signature made his tenure contract null and void, Monroe marched into Christy's office and demanded an explanation.

"No letters, no tenure. It's as simple as that."

"I'll take you to court and sue the university for millions."

"For what?"

"For your refusing to sign my tenure contract after you signed it before."

"I met my contractual obligation, now what about you?"

"I'll bring in a chemist to test the paper to prove that you signed it."

"Good idea. I'll do the same with the letters." Larson looked distinctly ill. "*And* once I start talking about the Sally Hemings letters to the press, I think the trustees will want to duck and cover, even if they do lose the best running back in California."

"You really are a gangster!"

"Monroe, don't blame me. The ink must have faded! The words are gone! My god, what can I do?"

DEEDEE CONCLUDES HER NOVEL

Although Grace Pallas and Brent Harris had their differences, love united them. Every evening, while Brent read books written by Greeks and Romans, Grace thumbed through her fashion and movie magazines. Just the fact she and Brent sat side by side in front of the fireplace, feeling the warmth of each other, made her feel good. (Of course the fireplace gave off heat, too, but emotional warmth can't be compared to logs.) Brent's company erased all the bad things that had ever happened to her. Now all she wanted was to have his baby. So she asked him if he would mind her going off the pill. He said why would you want to do that? And she said because I want a child, two in fact. Twins, he said. No, she said. One now and one later. He said, how can we afford kids; and she said when two people are in love they find a way. He looked at her strange, but maybe that was because he had never considered what she said might be true. She could often say smart things—really smart things—and he would compliment her. Like the time she said his boss looked awfully sick and it might be a good idea if he volunteered to do some of the boss's work. That way he could get in good with the boss. Well, guess what happened? The boss gave him a bonus and swore one day he would do a very nice thing for Brent. But more about that in a minute.

After months of excuses, Brent finally agreed to let her go off the pill. At first Grace didn't get pregnant. The reason wasn't because they didn't do it, or do it like they did before; it had something to do with her state of mind. So she went to see a doctor who told her to relax and enjoy it and not worry about the sperm and the egg. The next few nights she just had a good time, like before. And guess what? She got pregnant. And guess again! She was pregnant with twins, a boy and a girl!!! It was then she knew there was a higher force in the world and He had heard her prayers. To show her appreciation, she decided to go to church. The trouble was she didn't know which one to go to. So she went to them all, just in case that special person in the sky was present in only one. But she kept it a secret from the Man Upstairs she wasn't married. Brent didn't believe in such things.

After the birth of the twins, she of course named the children Billy and Betty. She couldn't have been happier, except for one thing: Brent did have to be asked to take out the garbage. But maybe she was expecting too much. He did, after all, help with the children's feeding and did change diapers. A lot of men would never do those things. And he did bring his check home and not drink it up at the local tavern. The children kept her so busy that she never even thought about her stage career, although when the babies were napping, she did kick her feet in the air and do a few song routines, just to stay in shape in the event some impresario called. Grace remembered the story of Helen Litwak, who always practiced her routines. One day the hotel where she worked as a maid in the Catskills had a flu epidemic and she was the only one left standing. So they asked her to perform for all the sick guests, which she did, going on to a famous career in South Orange, New Jersey.

Then the wonderful thing happened. Brent's boss died. (His dying was sad not wonderful but it led to a wonderful thing.) In the boss's will it said because he had no heirs, and because Brent had always been kind and honest, he was leaving him his cross-country skiing business. Grace thought it was like a miracle, but you shouldn't talk about miracles out loud, and Grace did, which led to a bad thing.

Brent announced he could not sleep or eat (that was bad but not so bad) because he was worrying about Miss Saigon and her son. I'll bring back Miss Saigon as a maid, he said. You can't do that, she said, not under the same roof with me. After making a number of calls to Saigon and the Vietnamese embassy in Washington, he drew up a will, packed his bags, withdrew cash from the bank, and left for Asia.

A month later, Brent telephoned from Kuala Lumpur. He said he would not be returning to America because he and Miss Saigon had moved to Malaysia with her eight brothers and six sisters. Her mother had T.B., he said, and her father was being treated for opium addiction. They were all desperate and needed him to support them. So he planned to open a fruit stand, because he knew Grace would not want him to return to Schroon Lake with twenty-three people. He was right!!!

At first, Grace was lonely a lot, then a little, then hardly at all. This is the reason why. She had her children, who kept her busy. She had inherited the ski business, which took up even more time than the children. Also, she had been subscribing to a women's magazine that printed articles written by feminists. Though she had no idea what they meant by self-realization, it slowly dawned on her that with Brent gone she could do as she pleased. In one issue, the magazine ran a naughty article saying women could even live without *that*: They could buy a d___o and have a good time. She tried it and liked it, though she had to admit the real thing was better than the fake. But best of all, she didn't have to nag a man about taking out the garbage because she just took it out herself.

THE END

CHRISTY REFORMS BOGUS U.

Like alluvial silt, Christy's impressions of Bogus U.'s seaminess had been coalescing into an incomparable richness. In late June, he told Laura to set aside two days for appointments with the pigeons he intended to pluck. She dutifully arranged his schedule so that he could devote himself uninterruptedly to the fleecing at hand.

He met first with the chairs of the science departments: Astrology (D.U.M. Bakeless's home department), Astronomy, Biology (animal, plant, and molecular), Chemistry, Geology, Physics, and Meteorology. The department chairmen—yes, all men—had decided among themselves that they had been summoned to receive the president's praise for their successful grant-raising activities. For a school so small, Bogus U. had an enviable record in the sciences for winning lucrative awards from government and industry.

"Gentlemen," Christy began, prepared to hit all his g's, "the money Bogus U. charges you for overhead costs has been far too little. In the future, I'm increasing it by ten percent. Before you start complaining, I can tell you that heating and maintenance have gone up twenty percent. So you're getting a good deal."

The objections came loud and fast. Christy listened and then gave them, in his own lingo, the old one, two. "In the future forget about matching outside faculty offers. We're not gonna screw the many to enrich the few. The same goes for teaching. You guys will have to assume your fair share." The clamor collapsed as quickly as a spent penis. "No more of this teaching one course, maybe two a year." Electrified, the group collectively gasped. Christy seemed prepared to gore the sacred cow. "For all I care, you can teach nothing, year in and year out." A collective sigh swept the room. "But here's the deal. Everyone at Bogus U. teaches two courses a semester, four a year. Each course you duck out of will cost ten grand. You don't wanna teach, fine; fork up forty thou." The palpable anger that issued from the chairmen raised the room temperature. Sweat broke out on brows. Ties were loosened and shirtsleeves rolled up. The chair from Molecular Biology audibly gulped.

"Teaching or tin," Christy declared, "take your choice."

"Unheard of!" exclaimed one. "Who do you think we are, History or English professors? We are scientists!"

"Highway robbery," another huffed.

"Extortion, pure and simple!" the meteorologist howled.

"Write it off to research," said Christy, "you write off everything else."

The science chairmen, not expecting this frontal assault, found themselves unprepared. They exhorted Christy, shredding the air with their lamentations; but they had no real argument to buttress their privileged positions.

"Do you have any idea how long it takes to write a grant proposal?" asked the chair of Astrology. "The competition is fierce, particularly from creationists."

"Your graduate students grade your papers and run your experiments. They even hold office hours."

The geologist replied indignantly, "Why single out scientists? Every department has its . . ." Here he paused trying to select a word that would strike home and, at the same time, sound diplomatic.

Christy filled the silence. "Slackers."

"I would have said deadwood."

Christy, knowing from Sophanna that a great deal of good teaching actually took place, said candidly, "I'm picking on you guys because you have the jack. I always follow the money."

"Our best professors will leave," said the chair of Physics.

"If best means money makers, that's one thing. If best means teachers, that's another. And don't tell me they're one and the same. I know better. So which is it?"

The biologist replied, "The less grant money one has, the less he or she can—"

Christy interrupted. "Skim."

Had the biologist not been cut off, he would have said, "devote to research." But instead he groused, "The government has strict rules. We have to account for every penny."

"I approve. Tell the feds that the money is buying time, and that, my friends, as the aged will tell you, is the most precious quantity in the world."

On that philosophical note, the science chairmen left, agitated and needing to regroup. But in fact the damage had been done. Christy had revealed that he knew their tricks. They had no recourse but to whine, and some of them, to their credit, regarded that kind of behavior as unbecoming. So although they left swearing to return, they did not. Instead, they quietly prepared to buy themselves out of teaching and went on with their work.

As soon as the science chairs had left, Christy called Laura into his office and asked her to distribute the following notice to faculty, staff, and current students.

STARTING JULY 1, THE SCHOOL OF BUSINESS WILL BECOME THE HEAD-QUARTERS OF BOGUS U.'S NEW ENTERPRISE ZONE, CALLED "COMMERCIAL VENTURES INC." AT THE END OF THE SEMESTER ALL BUSINESS COURSES AND DEGREES WILL BE DISCONTINUED, REPLACED WITH PROACTIVE, SYNERGISTIC, RESULT-DRIVEN ACTIVITIES.

Laura's initial amazement gave way to wonderment, as she asked, "Did you write it?"

"By myself," he replied proudly.

"Not bad, but I thought you hated business jargon."

"If you're gonna ruin a guy, you wanna use his own tactics. By shutting down the School of Business in their own words, I'm telling those bozos I know the score. It's poetic justice."

"For a minute," she chuckled, "I was afraid you'd lost your own way of talking and become infected with the academic disease."

COMMERCIAL VENTURES, INC.

Even the trustees approved of the money generated by Commercial Ventures, Inc. Hundreds attended the grand opening on June 1. The few conspicuous absences were owing to Christy's having made Tuah Bahar the Chief Administrative Enforcer. At Christy's direction he had fired a number of incompetents, and reassigned all the viziers. Sejanus Pinchbeck would have gone to the motor pool, in charge of selling Bogus U.'s worn-out vehicles, had not Eagle River University, to his great relief, offered him a position as senior bookkeeper. After he left, his delighted neighbors held an "Ice Man Goeth" party. Brigham Pyrosis, reassigned to manage the museum's fossilized rock collection, retired to Arizona in search of coprolitic treasures, certain that a rare breed of turtle had once nested and defecated near Tucson. Bill A. Stine, also given a new position, seemed perfectly content as director of the new Bogus U. microbrewery to be constructed adjacent to the faculty restaurant, where he declared it would make handsome profits from a ready clientele. The restaurant, already undergoing refurbishment and staffed with a new cook, Reynald Eclaire, and manager, DeeDee Lite, would keep the cash register ringing from the sales of French cuisine and pastries.

Myrtle Steif and Austin Black, when told separately that the other had confessed, admitted their participation in the bombing. Myrtle, as Christy had suspected, had provided the blueprint, which came from friends in Malta, and Austin the lab work. Their motives, however, were different. Myrtle had hoped that the bomb would find Laura in Christy's office, where she spent much of each day, and thereby kill two birds with one blast. Austin just wanted to "waste" the president "for messing up the grading system." With Christy's approval, the court allowed them to escape hard time, in exchange for agreeing to work for two years at a non-union minimum wage in the Bogus U. power plant servicing the inside of the refrigeration unit.

In the foyer of the old School of Business now stood an information booth, run by Agnes Hasty-Pasty, with a large overhead electronic board indicating in flashing multicolored lights the names of the newly-staffed divisions. In alphabetical order, the ten divisions read:

Fines
Gifts, Gratuities, and Subsidies
Grades
Lottery
Pharmacognosy
Promotion and Tenure
Protection
Sports
University Press
Visitors' Bureau

Given the revolutionary nature of Christy's reforms, we should explain the function of each so that other universities contemplating the corporate path may know how to proceed.

"Fines" covered innumerable sins, from blatant fraud, like forgery, to poor teaching. Christy put in charge of this office Sophanna Houth, who exhibited discriminating taste in the matter of instruction. He observed different classes, and if he could comprehend what was being said, the profs passed the litmus test for clarity. Owing to his sensitive nature, he was particularly hard on soul murder. Professors who had profoundly bored their classes and thereby contributed to an increase in student drinking received major fines. But those professors who missed or excused classes, arrived late or unprepared, taught classes by asking students what they wanted to talk about, or failed to shape a thoughtful lecture received especially heavy fines. Other sins included grade inflation (see "Grades"), failure to read student papers carefully or to return them promptly, assignments lacking any analytical point, self-esteem exercises, pandering, slumming, posturing, excessive use of jargon (Christy had considered a complete ban, but Laura explained that the habit was too ingrained to break), mistreating and patronizing staff, and numerous other offenses.

"Gifts, Gratuities, and Subsidies," one of the wealthiest organs of the new corporation, raised money from alumni; sold naming rights to all the campus possessions; accepted graft for choice seating at sporting events, and particularly large amounts for football games; set aside places (at five thousand apiece) on the bench of the football team during game day for gridiron groupies; auctioned off parking spaces, which brought in untold sums; took bribes for touting an industry's product (for example, "Semaphorics 101: The Cereal Box as Cultural Icon" and "Semaphorics 212: The Gustatory Rhetoric of Peanut Butter"); garnered mind-boggling payoffs for turning Bogus U's labs into industrial research engines; skimmed fifteen percent from all contracts, such as the new million-dollar computerized scoreboard; pocketed an additional million for conducting business only with ASP; hit up Cranmore Narr for a yearly donation of ten thousand clams; contracted to include industry logos on everything from athletic equipment and uniforms to personal tattoos; offered "sweetheart contracts" to vendors and builders of every stripe with the understanding that Bogus receive half of the profits; reserved one hundred admission spaces for semiliterate students at five hundred thousand a pop; collected fifty percent on all patents; conferred honorary degrees for a staggering price or a pricey piece of real estate; allowed the immensely wealthy to teach on a lark in return for valuable equipment, like a recording studio; printed family names on the bricks in the walkways for a grand. But lest we exhaust the readers' patience, we will end, since the work of this office cannot possibly be captured by means of a list. Christy had only one regret: that Noodles Moran wasn't running this office.

"Grades," which Eddie Doyle, a reflective fellow, managed expertly, took for its domain the delicate task of easing Bogus U. out of the business of altering transcripts, so that it could sell grades openly. To increase the demand for good grades, he first eliminated the faculty-course evaluations, which had been hijacked by students years before for purposes of blackmail: good evaluations in return for good grades. Eddie figured that if students were already receiving astronomical marks, they would have no need to buy them. He therefore discontinued the evaluations and amended Christy's previous order to read that if faculty gave more than fifteen percent A's and B's, they would be fined for reducing demand through oversupply. In return for faculty cooperation, he gave generous bonuses.

The delicate problem of selling grades, Eddie solved humanely and brilliantly. He represented grades as having a salubrious effect and changed them upwards, charging outrageous prices, but only for the following official reasons.

1. Lack of self-esteem
2. Threats from parents
3. Thoughts of self-immolation
4. Failure to get into graduate school

5. Expulsion from Bogus U.
6. Impotence
7. Frigidity
8. Insomnia
9. Anorexia
10. Alcoholism
11. Drug addiction
12. Stupidity (which required a psychiatrist's letter)

Eddie omitted from his list laziness and immaturity. At first, Christy feared that this enterprise was the one likeliest to invite the wrath of the trustees. But he needn't have worried, given income flow and strong endorsement from the parents, normally the greatest obstacle to education in America.

"Lottery," run by business professor Bingo Donnie, sounded like a simple affair, but it actually comprised numerous lotteries, the winners receiving free admission to Bogus U. (from one to four years, depending on the price of the ticket), or to football games, or to a private audience with President Mahon or a famous professor, or to a week at the Sun Valley chalet, or to a parking space, or to concerts or films or theater performances, or to the ice rink, or swimming pools, or squash courts, or to the holy of holies: an executive session of the Board of Trustees. Bingo Donnie, an experienced administrator, was the only person allowed the use of excessive jargon, since he could speak in nothing else.

"Pharmacognosy," eclipsed in riches only by "Gifts, Gratuities and Subsidies," normally would have been entrusted to a chemist or pharmacist, or even a biologist. But Christy had put those people to work in the campus greenhouses growing and processing the very products sold by this division. Instead, he selected Jackie Brown to oversee harvesting and distribution; this last required firmness with the drug-loving population, on and off campus. Jackie's product list, as one might expect of him, was simple. Every sale bore a seal stamped: "For Medicinal Purposes Only."

Hair Restorer (pills and liquid)
Penile Hardener (pills only)
Bunion Remover (liquid only)
Pain Dissipater (pills and liquid)
Cannabis: aka herb, weed, headie, doobie, jive stick
Poppies: aka smack, junk H, Heron, dooley, Rambo
Cocaine: aka yay or yay-o, nose candy, party, blow, yoda, gold dust

Methamphetamine with mescaline: aka Ecstasy, E, Molly, roll, doctor, chocolate chips

PCP: aka jet fuel, amoeba, angel dust/hair/mist/poke, krystal, lethal weapon, green tea, soma

Pharmies: aka over the counter meds, like ephedrine and pseudo-ephedrine

Etc.: aka other drugs

The prices, of course, depended on the dosage and quantity; and since we have no way of determining the habits of the myriad customers, some of whom, for example, restricted their buys to Moroccan hashish, we will refrain from hazarding a guess about sales, observing only that the profits ran into seven figures.

"Promotion and Tenure," second to salary as a cause of faculty complaint, was put in the able hands of Won Hong Low, Brooklyn Benny's intelligent and sensitive lieutenant, who believed in the virtue and value of vulpine ambitions. Some faculty, we hasten to add, had no need of this office because their records unquestionably qualified or disqualified them for both promotion and tenure. The marginal profs, left up to Won, could pay either up front or over a decade of monthly deductions. Those faculty who came from wealthy families chose the former, discharging their debt immediately; the latter frequently moonlighted in the greenhouses to cover expenses until the ten-year period had expired.

"Protection" was run by the Robaccia gang. In this capacity, they sold their services to the Rental Association and the Uptown/Downtown Merchants Group. They also leased bodyguards to profs who exceeded the grading standards and, through a contact that Christy had made with the notorious munitions dealer Andrew Undershaft, sold explosives and firearms not only to the campus NRA, but also to other students, a practice that earned the wrath of local gunsmiths who would have taken their complaints to the state legislature had they not received a personal call from Bobby Solomon, Three fingered Tony Pazzia, and Paddy I.R.A. Murphy.

The gang also oversaw the secret research, conducted by the Department of Physics and the College of Engineering, into a super laser that would reshape the face of modern warfare. Needless to say, this research received munificent funding from the feds.

"Sports," the single greatest reason for the state legislature's support, niggardly as it was, found in the director's chair none other than Shawn Keogh. Christy, a generous man, had decided to be a good winner—Laura and he were to marry shortly—and to recognize Shawn's thorough sleuthing in the Athletic office, where he had culled from the files priceless information. Warned that the football team had no choice but to win, and privy to the Sally Hemings fiasco, which had cost Bogus Walter Hemings, Shawn recruited professional players from around the world. He merely gave them new names and erased any record of their having been paid. In this manner he could recruit athletes from Europe and Canada, as well as from the American semipro circuits. The result: smash-mouth football that took the Wildebeests to successive championship seasons, an appreciative alumni and legislature, and a modest increase in state support.

"University Press," a small operation that previously had little to show for its well-intentioned efforts, thrived under the inventive leadership of Laura Favoloso, who intended to live as a working wife. Although Christy gave her a real budget that enabled her to publish books on subjects other than local ones, she supplemented it with a simple but effective plan. She instructed each department in the natural and social sciences to produce a textbook for its own introductory courses, with the understanding that students would have to buy the book, revised every year to prevent the used-book market from undercutting her profits. In no time, textbooks made the press rich, enabling it to publish books of real merit: poetry and fiction, scholarly studies of ancient and medieval history, marine archaeology, the Baroque cantata, and of arcane subjects befitting an academic press. With the exception of Ms. Lite's *Schroon Lake Fantasy*, which sold exceedingly well, the press dedicated itself to the advancement of learning. The books, handsomely printed and liberally adorned with color plates, soon became the envy of academic publishing.

"Visitors' Bureau," an innocuous-sounding division, actually had an important function, and also turned a pretty profit under the direction of a familiar face, Mr. Harry Hasty-Pasty. Besides the usual guests that any campus hosts, Bogus U. invited worldwide dignitaries to see how to commercialize a university. In no time, Bogus acquired so great a reputation that Harry Hasty-Pasty, an enterprising fellow, entered into a contract with the local hostelries to feed and house the thousands of visiting administrators, trustees, legislators, educators, congressmen, and senators who flocked to see the free-enterprise system and American capitalism at its best. A special booth, set aside for Narcissa Whitman Poseuse, enabled her to promote her reputation and works directly to the public. The energy she expended on behalf of herself convinced thousands that she belonged in the pantheon of feminine greats, seated between Sappho and Joan of Arc. So effective was her self-praise that she eventually left teaching to develop new forms of public relations, opening her own publicity firm and hiring Monroe Larson as a shill.

Harry personally led the campus tours, assisted by some statuesque coeds, who caused Ags to frown. But Harry and his aides did a bang-up job—no pun intended—showing the visitors the greenhouses and the labs, the lottery and the press, the protection business and the division of Gifts, Gratuities, and Subsidies, and all the other ways of turning a licit or illicit buck. At the end of the tour, Harry, a lively speaker, would hold forth on the virtues of living in a country in which money talked, always concluding his address with the observation that "making a buck by any means was an American tradition" and that "healthy universities avoided the disease called lack of money." His talks inevitably received tumultuous applause and, on occasion, elicited generous tips that he reported neither to Christy nor to the IRS.

The last division, which could not be publicized and had to be kept off the books, was Banking. All the illegal money that flowed into Bogus U. eventually reached Brooklyn Benny, housed in the fortified room of the power house. This location reinforced Bogus's gangster ethic that money is power, generates energy, and makes enterprises run. Benny laundered a good deal of it by investing in legal gambling establishments from Las Vegas to Atlantic City. He also ran a productive loan-sharking operation, lending money at usurious rates, taking as his model credit-card companies. A healthy percentage of the profits Christy invested in capital construction, the rest in faculty perks and student aid.

Four-flushers and two-timers, as well as campus seducers and liars, found themselves removed to rooms a floor or two below Benny's and subjected to punishments administered by the Robaccia gang: bee stings, dog bites, excrement dipping. . . . As a result, perjury, penile pride, and other sins abated.

Lest our patient readers wonder what transpired when Brooklyn Benny climbed into the front seat of the car unaware of what had happened at the Sun Valley chalet, let us return to that moment. During the brief drive, Benny assumed his best minatory snarl, but his captors never flinched. Tuah parked at the front door and Christy, Beretta in hand, rudely shoved Benny into the house and told him to sit. His ex-boss had blood in his eye and wanted to flense this fink who had conked him. But the gun was a persuasive pacifier. Ags brought drinks for the party and, before exiting, told her brother, Benny, "to listen and listen good." Laura sat to one side, casting a wary eye over the scene—just in case. Christy, cradling the weapon in the crook of his arm, stood with his back to the picture window that showed to exquisite effect the mountains outside. In his mind, he had imagined this setting; it corresponded to the grandeur of the speech he'd rehearsed.

"Brooklyn Benny," he began, "you have a choice. You can make a pile working with me or you can be killed a second time."

"Work with you!" Benny scorned. "Why you murderin' chiseler—"

Christy pointed the gun. "Not another word. I'm master of all fights from now. on"

Benny looked sourly at Tuah and Harry, but received no succor from them. The second he'd climbed into the car, he knew that Christy's explanation of the new dynamic—and its rationale—suited him and the Robaccia gang, though Benny at first was loath to admit it. A practical man, he listened carefully and then asked, "What's in it for me?"

Christy explained the percentages and the cuts.

"I usually get more," Benny grumbled.

"For once, you'll be doing something for the greater good."

"You sound like a preacher."

"That's why you go to church, Benny, to be told how to behave."

"Yeah, but that don't mean I have to like it."

"What don't you like?"

"I listened to your spiel and accordin' to my calculations there are still millions unaccounted for. Where are they goin'?"

Every good speech requires the proper occasion. In some debating societies they would call it an opening. Christy now had his.

"Benny, when you and I were growing up in Brooklyn, times were tough." He smiled, glad that he had said "I" instead of "me." "Our families never knew where the rent money and the next meal were coming from. For Chrissake, you once told the boys that when you were a kid you passed out from hunger, and a strange lady came out of one of the tenements and fed you a bowl of soup, right there on the street. You said you'd never forget it."

Brooklyn Benny nodded his head in sincere remembrance of that unforgettable day.

"Well, what I propose to do with the dough is like what that lady did for you. Feed kids. Get them on their feet again. Make it possible for them to attend Bogus U., which I hope to transform into what Laura calls Benign U. That means kindly and good. What I've learned is that education makes a difference. Look at me. I'm no longer Christy the Chump or Christy the

Chop, but Christopher Mahon, and I can understand words and ideas that I never knew existed."

Benny was incredulous. "You intend to give money away for nothin'!"

"Yeah, to deserving students for scholarships and books and free eats and no-cost trips to concerts and plays. For beefing up the library and helping the arts. For staff and faculty perks, like paying for their kids to attend the college of their choice. Those sorts of things."

"When did you lose your mind?"

"When I looked around and realized that education is more than beer and butts." And here he paused, inwardly smiling at the line to come next. "When I discovered that a well-educated person is like a carpenter's truth: all the parts abide."

"Huh?"

"You heard me. One more thing, by smarting up these kids, we all benefit. They don't mug you and they give back: to the school, to their children, to their neighborhood. Right?"

Benny nodded.

"Well, then, are you in?"

"Yeah, but I worry: where's the fun?"

Christy put the Beretta on safety and replied proudly, "*Res severa verum gaudia*: to be serious is the greatest joy."

EPILOGUE

After two years in office, Christy resigned to become president of Sham State, a southern school under the influence of a religious and political fundamentalism. But before leaving Bogus U., he recommended that Phineas Ort succeed him, and the trustees concurred. Phineas, having exhausted his fictive powers, realized that his real genius lay in refining Eddie Doyle's scams and devising a few of his own. At his formal inauguration, his black silk suit and silver tie, his vaselined hair combed straight back, and his pregnant pinky ring seemed fitting. His speech was inspirational:

"In the past, professors have acted like anarchists. But those days are over. We must behave like a family, and protect ourselves against outsiders. As President Mahon has shown, competition is wasteful, monopoly efficient. For Commercial Ventures to succeed, just remember that the name of the game is crony capitalism."

He concluded his speech in the old Phineasean fashion, with a formal, elegant plea "that we remain constant in our endeavors, for this country that lies before us as a land of easy pickings, so various, so beautiful, so rich, hath need of thoughtful leaders."

DeeDee sat in the audience smiling radiantly, pleased to have worked out an arrangement with Phineas in which they rendezvoused once a week, dined privately, watched a blue movie, and then frolicked.

And what of Jimbo Brummagem and Cummings Dailey? The first pleaded temporary insanity and got off with probation; the second retreated to India, where a swami was teaching him how to delay ejaculation indefinitely.

FINI

287